Embers an

Ronald G. Munro

Copyright

Acknowledgment

As the eye is drawn to a path,
so too is the heart drawn to a journey,
and though the journey's end may be destined,
the path to get there is discovered
only as it is stepped.

In fiction and nonfiction, family and friends form the reality on which our perceptions and beliefs and the tenets of our lives depend. They frame the path we travel.

I am thankful, first and foremost, for my wife, Carolyn, who has made all the steps of my literary journey with me, from original compositions to updated editions like the present one. Her attention to detail is invaluable.

I am privileged, too, to have encountered special friends on my path, and among them, I owe a particular gratitude to Linda and Richard Eichhorn and to Betty and Wes Batten who have been constant in their encouragement and support.

The Southjoy Mission Series

Book 1: *Southjoy Mission 1808-1809*

Book 2: *Lingering Missives*
(Set in 2008)

Book3: *Embers and Echoes*
(Set in 2009)

Table of Contents

Prolog

Among the living, there is only one hell. It is called fear. So, too, the living may find only one heaven. It is called love. These we find in only one here-and-now. It is called life. The quest of life is love; its nemesis is fear.

It is said that each quest has a destiny. Each and every destiny, we are told, is written in the Book of Life. If you listen carefully, you may even hear the whisper of the pen as it glides upon the pages of your Book. Like the crackle of an ember, it is vibrant with its livid certainty. Like the flush of echoes in an empty shell, it is delicate in its subtlety. Always, but always, it speaks to your quest.

Why, then, do we seek to immerse ourselves in the raucous din of catastrophe? Are we afraid to hear the whisper?

Consider a life smoldering in agony, a manifestation of fear. Might it be an ember waiting to become a searing flame? To ignite into a burning rage? Or merely to die, extinguished into the bleakness of ashes?

Can it be that flames and ashes of this nature are a staple of life, like a necessary evil? A discriminant between fear and love?

We do seem to feed our fears more actively than our loves. Every day, cataclysmic events burst without warning onto a world scene that is desperate for news to feed its fears. These are celebrated in the eruption of headlines that echo repeatedly around the globe. Their echoes resonate, growing in fervency until they gasp in a crescendo of astonishment. As befits the event, their calls for attention claim all the purity of righteous concern or the ire of indignant outrage. Hour by hour, even minute by minute, the headlines rivet the attention of the uninvolved and feed their insatiable hunger for drama and bedlam and mayhem.

A meager discovery of a dead body, however, is less riveting, warranting a front page story only in local news. A young American inherits a wealthy British estate? Home & Garden section. The wealthy heiress abducted, kidnapped? That goes viral.

For the uninvolved, you see, one catastrophic disturbance succeeds another. Heinous acts are countered. Murders solved. Victims rescued. Then on to another story. Such is society's determined muffle of destiny's whisper.

Not so for the fully involved. For them, the greater cataclysm may be what follows. The intensely personal struggle, the memory that won't stop taunting, the life that just can't move on. Because fear rallies in the ashes of love, and the internal voice of the mind cannot be so easily muffled.

And if sorrow engages in fierce combat with guilt, what of their battles? For certain, their clashes echo in the mind with all the fury of a blazing rage. Never doubt it. The embers of such echoes can sear the mind as surely and as deeply as any flaming ember can sear the flesh.

Yet, we are nearly intolerant of apathy or depression. These do not fill headlines. Courage without catastrophe? Lifestyle maybe, if there's no real attention getter.

Catlyn Stacey knew what it was to be fully involved. Kidnapped, tormented, and betrayed, she knew about courage in the midst of terror. Surrounded by murder and death, she knew about persevering when there seemed to be no next moment, when survival was a matter of unrelenting exertion pushing beyond the limits of her depleted strength.

And what then? What becomes of those who've survived such cataclysms? Are they simply forgotten, left to resume a normal life? Such would be a good and proper end to their ordeal, yes?

Maybe. But in the aftermath of the cataclysm, the righteous cacophony of the headline news distorts to mere noise, a clamor of whispered innuendo rendered in an echo a little less pure, a little less aggressive, and probably much less sympathetic.

So we are left to ask – When the riveting headlines have been un-riveted, is anything ever normal again? For them, the fortunate survivors of the cataclysms?

We like to believe that life is orderly, that when the quake that causes our lives to tremble and shake is finished, all is once again calm. Normal. But, is it even conceivable? A disrupted life re-normalized? That is the true test of survival, and it often requires inordinate courage.

Sometimes, too, we like to think we have the power to choose what we believe. We like to believe Sebastian risked his life for the woman he loved, but could it have been that he risked his life to salve his guilt? Catlyn's devotion to his care flowed naturally from her love for him, or was it, perhaps, that she felt guilty because his risk, and therefore his death, was her fault? Could a kinder, more honest thought on either side have spared them such personal agony? Had Catlyn not engaged her friend Courtney in the confrontation with the developer, Alister Knipsyk, might Courtney still be alive? Good questions all.

In the end, a mind chooses what best accommodates life. When it can. But minds are funny things. They're not arbitrary. Sometimes the choice isn't ours to make. The only dependable in all of this is the inescapable admission that life is complicated.

Long is the journey, Catlyn's distant ancestor, Lady Ariana Stacey, wrote in her diary in 1825, *faraway the end of trail, and many a step remains for me to tread.*

For the fully involved, those victims whose shattered lives must be pieced together, the wounded who must heal, the betrayed who must learn to trust again, there is no counting of the steps.

Yet, they step on. They step on.

I am in awe of such courage.

Chapter 1: Tilly

That morning, sunlight was knifing through the trees. It came in quick flashes flickering right across Miss Stacey's eyes, but she didn't look away. She didn't even blink. She just stood on the second story portico at Southjoy Mission, the legendary estate near Bath England, standing rigid as a statue, staring straight into the glare of the sun as it rose up through the trees. I think she was daring it to be proud.

As biting as the gusting cold wind had to be, she simply stared into the morning sky without even flinching. It was like her face was a mask that you might wear for All Hallows Night, all pose and no true emotion. Her eyes had no focus. I should have expected that, I suppose. The lack of focus, I mean, not the standing in the cold. She was just empty. At least that's how I thought of it, because I could scarcely imagine how she truly felt. Every sense of focus was gone from her life.

Grannie Effie, dead.

Father, dead.

Grandfather, who never spoke to her, dead.

Lenny, erstwhile boyfriend/tormentor, dead.

Courtney, as close as a new friend could be, dead.

Gaston, trusted chauffeur/betrayer, dead.

And Sebastian.

Sebastian, who loved her; Sebastian, whom she loved; Sebastian, who offered his life for her; dead.

I remember that morning vividly, like a stark, haunting, minimalist painting. If I could paint it, I'd call it "Humanity Lost." Sweeping across the canvas in broad stokes, a vast onslaught of tragic forces converge on one small, cowering entity barely discernible in an obscure, off-center location. But the eyes, the eyes of that entity radiate defiance.

Rose says I see these things in vivid contrasts because I'm too young to see the nuances of color. Maybe it was so then; maybe before that morning; but not after. For me, even as a teenager, that morning was the beginning of new life; for Miss Stacey, it was the beginning of new torment. For me, that beginning was a hope. For her, it was another take-one-step-at-a-time situation she had to endure.

Watching through the window, I could see shadows reaching out from the neighboring trees. Their limbs were already naked because of the early arrival of frigid air pushed into the region by a shifting polar jet stream. Their shadows seemed to be stretching out to embrace the portico with their sharp silhouettes. The portico had already been dressed for winter, so the tables and chairs were covered and set back against the house where they'd be protected from the elements. That left the main stage empty like a barren plateau where the shadows of the limbs could sway to and fro in a secret dance of furtive bows and sudden sweeps. On the periphery, the broader shadows of the rhododendrons splayed out to give the dancing silhouettes a border of diffuse ambiguity.

Miss Stacey stood motionless in her vigil, awaiting the début of her next dawn, while the silhouettes swirled around her, awaiting the finale of the gusting wind. The ambivalence this created was eerie, like Miss Stacey was waiting for the universe to progress, while the universe itself had shifted into idle, waiting for Miss Stacey to pay attention to it.

What she was actually thinking out there, I don't know. I just presume she was thinking about something. This much I can guess though. Her thoughts must have been skewed and warped in some terrible way. Imagine a dark, dank, rat infested alley. You're walking all alone. You sense someone is nearby. Noises and foul smells loom all about you. There's nowhere to turn, nowhere to run. You're lost. Suspended in darkness. Unable to escape. That was Miss Stacey.

It hurt me to see her like that, and it made me think of crazy stuff, like if I cried for her, maybe she'd feel better.

But then I thought, maybe it wasn't the loneliness. Think positive; that's what Dr. Ulma told us. So maybe it was just some little thing she'd noticed. She'd gotten like that lately, you know, being aware of little things to the point of being fixated on them. I saw her not long ago watching a spider for maybe ten minutes; she seemed to be totally engrossed by it. The spider raised its leg to take a step, only to stop midway, holding its leg suspended. It was like a comedy. It stopped. Miss Stacey stopped. It waited. She waited.

I asked her what was so fascinating. I mean, the spider wasn't even moving. She said she was just curious. Was the spider reading the vibrations in the air? Was it trying to get a sense of what was around her or maybe just trying to figure out what had become of its web? That morning on the portico, I had to wonder if Miss Stacey was reading the vibrations in the polar wind, trying to sense what had become of the fabric of her life.

I'm not saying there was anything strange about her watching a spider. It really wasn't unusual for Miss Stacey to be fascinated with all kinds of things. That was part of her charm. And it still is, like when Miss Stacey first came here from the US. She was fascinated by the rhododendrons. They were in full bloom, and she could see them at their best from the portico. Unfortunately, they were gone now too, and that probably didn't help Miss Stacey's mood. It's hard to think of how beautiful they're going to be again in the spring when you can't even imagine tomorrow.

That morning as I watched her through the window, Miss Stacey suddenly snapped her eyes shut tight, tight enough to cause her forehead to wrinkle. It startled me because it was done with such anger. It looked like she was shouting, only not out loud. She was shouting at something in her own mind. Dr. Ulma told me that's probably exactly what she was doing. People sometimes talk about being stricken with grief just as though their grief was actually trying to strike them down. In her mind, Miss Stacey was striking back, trying to beat off the grief that wouldn't leave her alone. That made sense to me at the time. I knew it for a fact; in her mind, there was no peace.

After a moment, though, she took in a deep breath of air. She held onto it, like she was waiting for its icy coldness to expand over her lungs. Watching her, I imagined I could feel it myself, how the cold was spreading all the way into her spirit. I'm sure she was hoping that, this time, it would stir her mind and wake her spirit enough to protect her from the demons left over from her sleep, as little as that was.

I'd have to say it was nearly a passion now, the way she welcomed the sunlight in the morning and the way she immersed herself in the open air. After weeks of being held captive in a cave, uncertain whether she'd ever behold a sunrise or bask in the warmth of sunlight or feel the freshness of the open air, she had acquired a mania for open spaces and all the light that sun or moon could pour into it. In this, she disagreed with Dr. Ulma. It wasn't a matter of avoidance, a fear of confinement, not at all. It was a discovery of how wonderful the openness of the natural world is. That's what she said, and I believed her.

She'd been waiting on the portico that morning since

long before dawn, standing there in her flannel nightgown and fuzzy slippers and bare ankles, her petite frame braced against the wind, paying no attention at all to the biting chill. She'd have gotten a severe scolding if Sweetgrove had seen her like that. But Miss Stacey was content to stand there, allowing herself to grow numb in the cold, like maybe that could make her numb to the circumstances of her life.

This had become her mission. In the early hours of the here-and-now, she awaited the arrival of the morning sun, awaited the glorious resuscitation of life celebrated daily by nature. That's how she described it to me, the glorious resuscitation of life. I liked that a lot because it proved to me she hadn't given up on hope, the hope that, today, she could participate in that celebration. Perhaps today with the rising sun would come something more than just light. Maybe today enlightenment would come with it.

Okay, so maybe that was just my own hope and my own imagination wanting everything to be right for her. I remember thinking about it and deciding it was actually a ritual for her; you couldn't call a habit or a custom; it was just something she'd invented for herself, a kind of mini quest. And now, she repeated it every day because she didn't know yet what she was supposed to do with this quest, how it would end, or if it would.

That worried me because she used to be so together about everything. At first, I tried to keep my worrying to myself. She didn't need to be upset by my silliness on top of everything else. But I kept thinking about it, and it kept bothering me, and then I just had to know. So I asked, was it like a sacred ritual? She didn't get angry with me, but she didn't answer me either, not right away. She just looked away and quietly wandered off in her thoughts. I waited while she roamed around in her mind looking for answers, and finally, when she remembered I was still there, she offered me a sad, lost smile. "That must be what it is," she told me like we'd been talking all along, "my personal Ritual of Inheritance."

That whole inheritance thing was dropped on her without any warning. She'd never even imagined the possibility. Suddenly alone, in a foreign country, without anyone's good wishes, there she was, heiress to a great estate, but not even granted the privilege of imagining what a grand future it could mean for her. Instead, inheritance for her was a steady stream of schemes and scandals and death, all of it hitting like a storm raging over her life and flooding it with sorrow and sadness and grief. And she hadn't asked for any of it.

She tried to resist it, of course. She tried to make sense of it all. We could all see that, I think. But the kidnapping, and most especially Lord Silverworth dying, just seemed to rob her of any sense of purpose to her life. Someone, probably Dr. Ulma, said she was disengaged from life.

But Miss Stacey was a fighter, as we all learned sooner or later. If anyone even hinted that she should give up, she'd reply, "That's not the Stacey way." And if you've met her, you know she's a Stacey through and through. But truth be told, she was beyond listening to reasoning right then. It wasn't that she was irrational or anything like that. She just couldn't be distracted from her grief.

§§§

I think I'm being too negative, giving you a poor picture of what she was like right then. It wasn't all darkness in her thoughts. There was way more than a glimmer of light in the words written in the diary of her greatly great grandmother, Lady Ariana Stacey. She was Lady Stacey because she married Cedric Stacey who later was knighted for his service to the Crown. Lady Stacey was dead too, of course, dead for about a hundred and fifty years. But the words she left in her diary were alive with inspiration. I fully believe with Miss Stacey that those words were written so faithfully and passionately in that diary just so Miss Stacey could discover them. Clinging to Lady Stacey's diary was as close to focus as Miss Stacey could manage on any given day right then. That, and well, me.

She called me her beacon to the future, a connection to life, a reason to marshal on. She got that idea, that every life needs a quest, from Lady Stacey's diary. With me, she called it a quest in search of a quest. This, I learned much later, was a great irony; Rose called it "an ingenious perversity of life." Before Miss Stacey came, you see, I had no direction. Now, I was the direction.

I was orphaned early in my childhood. I have no recollection of my parents at all, and I really don't think about my life before Southjoy Mission which, from all I've been told, wasn't worth remembering anyway. I suppose I was simply disconnected from the world until happenstance fabricated a family for me amongst the staff at Southjoy Mission. That was a critical stage in my life. Cook had become my legal guardian when my last foster mother, Cook's sister, passed away. Cook persuaded old Mr. Stacey, Miss Stacey's grandfather, to allow me to have my own room in the staff quarters of the mansion. For me, it was like I suddenly had a solid foundation, a real point of reference with a firm fix on the world, a place I could hold onto like it was my own identity. That lasted six years, long enough for me to think it would last forever. Then, just a month before my thirteenth birthday, old Mr. Stacey passed away.

Suddenly my place in life was all confused and jumbled.

I was afraid, and I was bewildered. But mostly I was scared. Everyone was sure the American heiress would just sell the estate, and we'd all be cast out with nowhere to go.

I imagined myself disappearing like all the other displaced people of the world. I was sure I was going to be one of the disremembered, you know, those people not even worth being noticed long enough to be forgotten. From time to time, I still wonder about things like that, you know, like, if you died and nobody missed you, were you ever really there? If you've no proof of it, you probably weren't. If it hadn't been for Miss Stacey, I'm sure that's how it would've been for me. Now I thank God every day that she wasn't anything like what we expected.

When Miss Stacey talks about her earliest days here, she takes a much more romantic view of that time. She likes to say, Ariana was the pilot charting the course of her ship of life, but I was the rudder steering it.

On that morning with the cold blustery winds, I was about to get my first inkling of that fact.

§§§

The first thing that I remember clearly is that there was an ornery gust of wind that startled Miss Stacey from her reverie. I could see her shivering, so I quickly brought her a warm wrap to place over her shoulders. She didn't seem to be surprised at that. She just smiled like you do when you say "Thanks" to somebody without actually speaking. I think, though, she was more grateful to me for joining her in her vigil than for bringing her a quilted comforter. For my part, it wasn't anything I had to think about. I knew she'd refuse to come back into the house until the sun completed its task of rising up. The sun, you see, was revolting against the darkness and chasing it away. Miss

Stacey was there to be sure the sun had succeeded in its mission, that it had routed the darkness. Only then could she be sure there'd once again be a visible definition to the living. There'd be no rest for her until she'd confirmed it with her own eyes.

We stood side by side, a minute or so, I think. Then she asked me about Cook. "Has there been an update on Cook's health?" Somehow, in spite of everything that's happened to her, she still had a part of herself to spare for the care of her staff. Maybe that's why it was so easy to dismiss any big worries about the way she'd changed. I thought she was sad, but not different. I mean, that's what's supposed to happen with grief. You're just sad, that's all.

"Nothing yet," I reported. "There's been no improvement, but she's not any worse either. I'm just up because I couldn't sleep."

Of course not. Not when I knew Miss Stacey would be distraught with her recurrent nightmares. She would never tell me anything about them, but I knew they were awful. They became less awful for a little while after Lord Silverworth's funeral, and we all thought Miss Stacey had conquered her fears. But, she hadn't. The nightmares returned worse than ever after the trial of Rupert Errique. The anguish from that seemed almost unbearable for her.

I always seemed to sense when the nightmares were nearby. There was an imminence to them, a change of attitude, or maybe a certain mannerism. I can't be sure, but I like to think it was because I'd become sensitive to her moods and feelings. That was just the kind of bond we had. If one of us didn't feel well, the other knew it without asking.

It might seem a little self-centered, but I'm convinced I was sensitive to her because she made me believe in myself and gave me a sense of belonging, especially after Miss Stacey moved me upstairs, so my quarters were next to hers. Anyway, an approaching nightmare for her invariably meant my own sleep was going to be restless too. I'd twist and turn in bed. I'd listen to the night sounds. And I'd wait for the one cry that'd be a little sharper than the others, the one that would be more piercing. That one would come from Miss Stacey, and nothing could stop me from hearing it. Nothing could stop me from understanding how it tormented her. And nothing could stop me from crying when I heard her cry. Not even Biscuit, the beautiful little sheltie Miss Stacey got for me. Biscuit would jump on my bed and nuzzle me and comfort me. And she did comfort me, but I still cried.

I never felt that I was being disloyal to Cook in any of that, you know, for being more concerned about Miss Stacey than about Cook. If anything, Cook's recent health issues served to accent the closeness that I'd come to feel towards Miss Stacey. In point of fact, Cook had been a good guardian. I had no complaints, and I will be forever grateful that she brought me to Southjoy Mission. There just was no closeness between us like in a real family. I was a responsibility shared by all the staff. The arrangement worked well as far as it went, and I was fine with it. Then Miss Stacey arrived, and my world changed. For the first time in my life, I wasn't just a responsibility. I wasn't just someone to look after. I was a valued, wanted person. Not just here, but wanted here.

That said, it was, nevertheless, a closeness that had yet to be challenged. I mean, sure, I was crazy out of my mind when Miss Stacey disappeared, but so was everyone. What I meant was, I hadn't really been personally challenged, you know? On a person-to-person basis, how far would I go to stay true to everything Miss Stacey taught me? That was the real issue for me, a critical one, as it turned out.

Miss Stacey was in a fragile place, and she was much in need of solid truths to shore up the structure of her life. I'm truly astounded every time I realize how she took control of her own destiny and how carefully she considered how to go about it, building a life, seeking it, rather than waiting for it to come to her. And how much she thought about what it'd mean not only to herself, but most especially to me.

In that sober morning vigil, peering into the still dawning sky, Miss Stacey chose to ask me one of those questions so loaded with ambiguity and ill-defined portents that it stuns you right to the core of your being. She started speaking softly in a voice that sounded as wistful as a hush in the twilight. She was looking into the distance, someplace far away, not even seeing me, when she asked me, "Do you ever wish I hadn't come here?"

I was stunned. Maybe stupefied would be more like it. If she'd accused me of some horrible deed, I couldn't have been more unsettled. My pulse started racing along my neck, and I know my face was flaring. The sudden panic of it made me feel like I was going to be sick, but somehow I whirled around and tried to shout back at her "Never!" But it's hard to shout when you've got practically no breath left in you. Because I couldn't seem to breathe. And I know my voice was straining. But I couldn't help it and I didn't care. The question horrified me. All I could do was gasp, "I could never wish that."

I couldn't tell if she heard me because I was suddenly fighting back a sea of tears that were filling up my eyes, and I couldn't quite see straight. I was certain the only reason she'd ask a question like that was that she was going to go away, far away, and I was never going to see her again. "Please," I tried to say, "please don't ever go away."

That was *my* nightmare, and I was trying for all I was worth to wake up and find she hadn't said any such thing. I was trembling and shaking and couldn't stop. I was desperate. There had to be some other reason she'd ask a question like that. Yet, she just stared into the distance.

Maybe because I was desperate, it suddenly sprang into my mind that I'd probably just misunderstood what she meant. That had to be what it was. Yes, of course, she must've heard about what I'd been saying to the kids at school. "It was wrong of me, I know," I tried to explain myself to her, "but I just wanted to be like one of them. They're always talking about how mummy and I did this, and mummy and I did that. So sometimes I talk about you. I told them you're like a mother to me. I meant no harm by it. It's just that if I'd had a mother, I'd've wanted her to be like you. Please, Miss Stacey, you've got to believe me. I could never wish that away, never."

I can still see her. She turned ever so slowly to look at me; it was like Time had taken her by the shoulders and was trying to stop her from turning, to stop her from speaking. That's what I was wishing anyway. My mind was just so bent, I knew with complete certainty what she was going to say, and I didn't want to hear it. But she was unstoppable.

"Tilly." Her voice had that kind of firmness I absolutely dreaded. "I don't want to be like a mother to you."

My mind went blank. I cringed as nausea surged, and I thought I'd never breathe again. Then I was babbling. "I didn't mean anything by that Miss Stacey really I didn't. It's just that I love you as much as I could love my own mother if I had one. I didn't mean to upset you, honestly, I didn't..."

"Tilly," she commanded my attention. "I don't want to

be *like* a mother to you, because I want to *be* your mother. Or at least I want to be your mom."

That *did* take my breath away. "You want to be..."

Miss Stacey was nodding. Her eyes suddenly were brighter than I'd seen them in a long while, probably not since she discovered Lady Stacey's diary. It seemed to me, if hope has a look, that's how her eyes appeared.

"We made a pact once; do you remember?" She said, "We agreed that it would be you and me, together, heeding whatever it was we were supposed to be heeding. Maybe it was all silliness on my part, but that thought has been with me ever since. So, I'm proposing another bargain. Me, a mom to you, and you, a daughter to me."

I could only stare at her. I stopped breathing for real.

When I didn't say anything, she hesitated, her eyes pinned on me. The truth was I couldn't speak. I think I was afraid that if I tried to say anything, I'd wake up from a dream, and if *this* was a dream, I didn't want to wake up from it.

In my state of shock, I hadn't even moved. I was utterly stunned that she'd remembered the pact at all. For me, it had been a constant force, always in my thoughts. I fantasized about it all the time.

I couldn't speak, and that must have spoken volumes, none of it good. Suddenly, Miss Stacey seemed to be doubting herself. I heard her saying, "I know it may be selfish of me to ask this of you, especially now, and if you don't want it..." Then she was having difficulty getting the words out. She managed to say, "I'll understand," and then she fell silent. Time stopped. My heart stopped. The fire drained from her eyes; they dimmed as though shutters were closing on the windows to her world. Everything was turning to shadow and darkness.

When she could speak again, it was all she could do to

say, "I'm sorry. That was stupid of me. Of course you don't want to be brought into all this." Her voice quivered like her words were riddled with static discharges. I'm pretty sure that's what panic sounds like. Then, all of a sudden, she was speaking very fast. "How could I even think it? How could I? All this misery, wherever I go; wherever I look; wherever I stop? It was a foolish, stupid thought. Please, forgive me; forget I even..."

For one horrible instant, I thought she was going to turn and run away before I could manage to speak for myself. To this day, it seems to me that Panic, in person, grabbed me by the seat of the pants and hurled me forward. All I remember clearly is clutching my arms around Miss Stacey before those awful, horrible, unspeakable words could leave her lips. It was an all-out life-sustaining clasp. "Mom," I bellowed and exclaimed and chided, all at one time, "weren't you listening to me? Honestly," I tried to tease, "you moms are all alike."

I think it took a second, and then another, before Miss Stacey could comprehend what I said. It took that extra second so she could peel back the dark shutters she'd closed against the offensive world around her, but when they were thrown back, her eyes filled with the light shining from my face. No more was there a frigid wind to batter her. No cold chill stifled her will. Nor did autumnal darkness enshroud her eyes. Nothing clung to her now but purpose and future.

"Grannie Effie was right," Miss Stacey whispered. But she had to swallow hard and inhale a deep, deep breath before she could say, "Grannie Effie used to tell me, simple deeds beget great glories. I think this is one of them. I believe it is."

To me, there was nothing simple about it. It was monumental. In one brief instant, my whole life changed.

Suddenly I dared to think things that were totally inconceivable before that moment. And it wasn't pretending anymore; it was better. Never had I pretended anything so extraordinary as this, or even dared to wish for it.

It absolutely changed me. Even the way I look at the world is different. Since that morning, I find myself looking for the little glories, trying to discover the simple deeds that make up people's lives. And I find them, that's the amazing thing, I find them all around me.

Lady Stacey wrote, *True glory carries its own torch. No darkness can quench it.* I don't recall what tribulation prompted her to write that, but I do know Miss Stacey agreed with it. We talked about it later, not that day, but later when we could just sit and ponder what it all meant. What I most remember is spending an afternoon tea toying with what an unquenchable glory might actually mean in real life. We tried to spin it in different ways. I decided she meant, when misery is all you can see, then everything looks dark; so even the smallest good deed, by contrast, seems to stand out; it's like seeing a beacon of light in the darkness.

Miss Stacey gave me a hug for that. It inspired her to say, "I think one of those old-world philosophers might have put it this way. True glory's the only harbinger of humanity that has no need of invitation, and is always welcome."

It was certainly never more welcome than it was to me in that moment, and that's how I remember that morning. We heeded what was needed in our lives, and there was glory in it. I prayed the rest of the world would see it that way too.

§§§

Rose says that last thought might make me sound selfish to you, but I wasn't praying for me; well, not just for me. I was praying for Miss Stacey because I was desperate for her. I think that's what people do. They pray for real only when they're desperate and they're begging God to help them. Rose is upset that I think that, and she's adamant that I'm wrong about it. Well, maybe she's right; she usually is. But if that's selfish, then I *am* selfish, because that's what I did. I begged. That day, I just begged. And I'm not ashamed of it.

Chapter 2: Rose

Before her ordeal, Catlyn had a way of making everything seem personal. Above all else, she valued the closeness of the people around her; life was about trust. Even after Courtney was murdered, she reached out to us. Catlyn's abduction, though, changed something in her; it made her more fearful, more withdrawn, harder. Where once she told us about everything, now she confided nothing. I think Tilly had it right. Sebastian's death just left Catlyn vacant inside.

If I sound more like an older sister than a contractor hired to do an environmental study, it's because that's how she made me feel and how she treated me. We talked about our personal lives, past and present, shared good and bad days, and even dared to imagine what our futures might be like.

It pained me to see how all that changed, how she was becoming more remote, less trusting, less willing to share her thoughts. When she asked me to stay on permanently at Southjoy Mission, I was ecstatic because it meant she hadn't given up; she was going to carry on despite everything. The position she created for me, Estate Naturalist for Southjoy Mission, was proof of her determination. The deed was the proof, even if you couldn't hear it in her voice.

I had no hesitation in accepting her offer. After too many unfulfilling years in forestry, wildlife preservation, and environmental studies, too many boyfriends who'd "moved on," I'd finally found a niche for my life. The position was ideal for me. But even if it hadn't been, nothing could've forced me to leave. I would've stayed because any fool could see Catlyn needed the closeness of her family more than ever, and we were all the family she had.

When Catlyn confided to me that she intended to adopt Tilly, I was filled with relief. I know it should have been joy, but relief is what I felt. It meant she was moving past her loss and beginning the reconstruction of her life. In a way, she reminded me of a beautiful forest I saw devastated by wildfire. As time went by, new shoots grew naturally from a few root systems apparently deep enough and hardy enough to survive the fire zone. Other plants required new seedlings. It was a slow process, but eventually natural regeneration and deliberate reforestation created a new thriving balance.

It seemed to me, Catlyn's decision to adopt Tilly was evidence that her emotional roots ran very deep. So it was up to those closest to her to provide the deliberate reforestation of the rest of her life, and I counted myself as one of those making up her ad hoc family.

Not everyone thought it was such a good idea, though. Lady Wythiry didn't approve of Catlyn's intentions, nor did Dr. Ulma, though their reasons were quite different. Dr. Ulma didn't disapprove; he just didn't think it was a good idea at that moment. Lady Wythiry declared it a bad idea at any moment. Her Ladyship, though, was prejudiced in the matter beyond Catlyn and Tilly, and we all knew why. She was envious of the estate. It was too grand for a commoner. It should belong to someone in the aristocracy; to her.

Lady Wythiry was unequivocal about matters of station. She categorically disapproved of advancing a person of questionable birth into the higher ranks of society. She pointedly reminded everyone that no one really knew anything about Tilly's parentage, as though that in itself should be considered a crime. Tilly's parents, Lady Wythiry was quick to suggest, could have been deranged for all anyone knew, or worse, anarchists. And then there was the fact that Catlyn herself was a commoner, which was bad enough, but she was a foreigner, and an American. Commoner, foreigner, and American; what is it the Americans say? Three strikes and you're out? According to Lady Wythiry, Catlyn had no business meddling with British lives. It didn't matter that Catlyn's father was British; he renounced any claim to relevance when he emigrated from here to live in the States.

However, Her Ladyship couldn't quite reject the idea out of hand. Amelia saw to that. I don't think any of us will ever forget it. Catlyn had invited a few friends to Southjoy Mission for a small, let's-keep-in-touch social evening. It was mostly just us, but Catlyn had included Lady Wythiry in an attempt to smooth her ruffled feathers. While Catlyn was out of the room, Lady Wythiry made the mistake of saying something about Catlyn's "silly notions" within earshot of Amelia. Her face turned beet red as she stormed across the room and lit into Lady Wythiry with a tongue lashing that nobody, but nobody, ever administered to Her Ladyship ever in her life. Pushing her little nose right into Lady Wythiry's face, Amelia flat-out accused Her Ladyship of being a vile toad (or words to that effect, which we were shocked to learn she even knew); she accused Lady Wythiry of reneging on the obligation she'd earned "in spades." I think she might have slugged Her Ladyship if Rip hadn't pulled her back.

Lady Wythiry sputtered and huffed, but didn't deny the accusation, which would have been hard for her to do because it was Lady Wythiry who had embroiled Amelia in the scam being run by Rupert Errique, the same scam that led to the kidnapping of Catlyn Stacey. If Lady Wythiry hadn't been so absorbed with her own greed, she might have realized her chauffeur, a man named Rimwell, was in on the scam too, and maybe the whole affair could have been prevented. Rimwell was one of many "moles" used by Errique; he was the one who fed Errique the very information that was used to ensnare Her Ladyship in his bizarre scheme.

Anyway, the rest of that evening was quietly reserved, and no one ever told Catlyn what had happened. The incident did have the positive effect of revising Lady Wythiry's thinking. She never actually embraced the idea of Catlyn adopting Tilly, but after thoughtful consideration, she did reconcile herself to a distasteful, but workable, acceptance of it. She decided it really wasn't necessary for her to actually *say* anything in support of Catlyn's proposal. Her visible presence alone, on suitable occasions, would be sufficient to fulfill any obligation she might be owing to Catlyn. It would suggest nothing less than non-committal support. That much she thought she could live with. But her resolve lasted only until her next social event at which she ungraciously disparaged the idea and dissociated herself from Catlyn.

Amelia Endbrook, as you might guess, staunchly supported Catlyn in whatever she wanted. Amelia, more than anyone else, understood Catlyn's need, not only to get a good grasp on the future, but also to hold onto it for dear life. She understood that need because she'd been part of Catlyn's trauma, shared in it, even if she unwittingly contributed to it.

Part of that contribution resulted from the discovery of the very cave where Catlyn would eventually be held captive. Rupert Errique had become convinced that old Mr. Stacey had hidden a fortune in stolen artworks in a cave that was located somewhere on the estate, and

Errique was determined to find it. To do that, he had to have a reason to be searching around on the estate's property. We learned later that Errique had a penchant for bizarre schemes, and the one he devised for this purpose was his most bizarre ever.

Using information gleaned from a recent discovery in the Somerset Lesser Archives, Errique invented a saint, Saint Sanaa. Errique claimed Saint Sanaa had actually been on the estate in the person of Edmund Plagyts, a Lollard who was in fact killed on the property in 1503. To give his scheme an appearance of legitimacy, Errique involved Lady Wythiry in the scam. Lady Wythiry, however, thought to exploit the situation herself as a means to harass Catlyn Stacey. Conned by Errique into believing that the remains of Edmund Plagyts, aka Saint Sanaa, might still be on the estate, it occurred to Her Ladyship that the services of an archeologist would be exceedingly valuable to their discovery. That led Lady Wythiry to involve Amelia Endbrook who, at that time, was still in need of a thesis project for her archeology degree.

Subsequently, to everyone's surprise, Amelia did find a cave. Errique insisted on keeping the discovery a secret to protect it from poachers and vandalism, which was a normal and customary practice. There was, however, no trove of artworks in the cave. When Catlyn was abducted, a cave so well concealed seemed to be the ideal place to hold her captive.

Dr. Ulma told us that Errique is a sociopath and has no sense of shame or guilt. Catlyn being captive was just another opportunity for him. He decided Catlyn must know where her grandfather hid the artworks, and he was going to force her to tell him where they were.

At that point, Errique's scheming took a bizarre twist too many. It involved exposing Amelia to the kidnapping of

Catlyn and forcing her to participate in it under the guise of service to Saint Sanaa.

Amelia, though, is no dummy. Eventually, she deciphered the scam and attempted to help Catlyn, with the result that she too was held prisoner. By that time, as I understand it, Catlyn had already been thoroughly traumatized. So Amelia was spared much of the terror that Catlyn had to endure. But, because of the role Amelia played in the whole thing, Amelia bore the guilt of it, and guilt has a way of being its own burden. It's just my opinion, but I think it was that guilt that made Amelia fiercely loyal to Catlyn. In her mind, the burden of that guilt was a debt so great it could never be expunged, not when she couldn't even forgive herself for it.

All things considered, though, Amelia was a fortunate person, guilt and all. She had family to support her, particularly her grandfather, Ethan Endbrook. A retired professor of history, her grandfather had been her role model. It was his influence that had inspired her to pursue a degree in archaeology. Even now, he was an important part of her life, a guide channeling her thoughts to a useful end.

Although her program of study had taken an unfortunate turn under the devious misguidance of Lady Wythiry, Catlyn offered Amelia a way to salvage her program by redirecting her study to the archaeological history of Southjoy Mission which extended back about five centuries. Amelia embraced the idea, accepting it as a further debt to Catlyn.

Amelia's new study complemented the existing effort of Rip Seimor, himself a research scientist who'd been working of late on a collection of ancient documents discovered by Professor Endbrook and his associate, Willy Hartsdell, at the Somerset Lesser Archives. The documents pertained to the estate's history and brought Amelia and Rip into frequent contact. It didn't take long before they were more than colleagues. We should have seen it coming, of course. Put two intense individuals together, both with personal vacuums to fill, mix in some common passion, and presto, two fulfilled lives. Nature does abhor a vacuum, you know.

It wasn't that Amelia and Rip went looking for each other, not with Amelia's guilt and Rip's former infatuation with Catlyn. In fact, when Amelia discovered her feelings for Rip, she was distraught about it. How dare she accept such happiness when it derived even indirectly from Catlyn's grief? She regarded it as an act of betrayal. Eventually, the conflict of desire and loyalty became too much for her, and she asked my advice. It wasn't hard to give – Talk to Catlyn.

It was good advice. "When I was a teen," Catlyn told us, "I was shy with guys. I turned down dates because I didn't think I'd measure up to the popular girls. I was afraid what they'd say about me. My father would shake his head and scold me, 'You've got to engage life if you want to be part of it.' That's my advice to you." She smiled. "He's intense. You're dedicated. Who knows what wonders will come of that?"

How ironic that was. Engaging life is what we all wanted for Catlyn. She could find the words to say to someone else, but she couldn't think of them for herself, except for her decision to adopt Tilly. That was a big step towards engaging life, and it raised our expectations for her. We were all agreed, the bold, fearless Catlyn we knew and loved was still with us. She was fighting back, taking charge of her life, refusing to stay a victim. So, yes, we cheered for her. It's what friends and allies are supposed to do, not dissect and analyze you, but support you.

Whinehardt and Sweetgrove, of course, Catlyn's butler and housekeeper, didn't budge one iota in their loyalty to Southjoy Mission. Sweetgrove is Catlyn's closest ally amongst the staff, now that Tilly's no longer regarded as staff. I believe that's why Sweetgrove was able to broach the delicate issue of Cook one morning as coffee was being served. Cook had again taken to bed with a chill, leaving Catlyn's coffee to be brewed by a kitchen aid. "I hope it's not too strong," Sweetgrove apologized. "Cook usually makes it for you herself. I don't know if you knew that. She says, the little pleasures is what makes a good start to a day."

"The coffee's fine," Catlyn allowed, "but it's lacking the finesse Cook gives it. I'll be sure to tell her so later."

"Does Cook know about your plans for Tilly?"

At that, we all kind of held our breaths thinking Catlyn might take offense at the question, but she just nodded her head comfortably like all was right in the world. "I think she knew before I did," Catlyn remarked. Then she told us how Cook planted the idea in Catlyn's thoughts in the first place.

"Cook was baking bread," Catlyn told us, "and I said something about how luscious the aroma was. I remember that because she was so pleased that I even noticed."

Not only pleased, but eager to explain it all. "The secret's in the dough," she told Catlyn. "Course, the dough's gotta rise and bake b'fore it turns to a fine loaf. It all starts with the risin', I'm sure ya know, and the dough can't rise without the yeast, and it won't bake without the right proper warmth of a good oven. Mercy me, ain't that just how people are too? Jus' look at Tilly. She's gonna make a fine loaf now you're here to bake her proper."

Catlyn seemed to be pleased about that herself. She told us, "Cook's such a dear person. I do hope she'll get well soon. Tilly and I've talked it over, and we're agreed. We don't want to do anything formally without Cook there with us. It just wouldn't be right." Then, as an afterthought, Catlyn noted, "As Tilly's legal guardian, I'm sure the assessment panel will be very interested in what she has to say about it. It might even be the most important thing they hear when they review the application." I believe she meant that as a compliment to Cook. Regrettably, I conveyed that remark to Dr. Ulma, and he immediately twisted it around as evidence that Catlyn was just being conniving and self-serving. He didn't use those words, but that's what it sounded like to me.

Up 'til then, Catlyn had every reason to believe she'd have the support of everyone on the estate. But that wasn't quite the case. The first hint of discord came, much to everyone's surprise, from Heinrich, the gamekeeper. Never one to be comfortable with social issues, he'd always enjoyed an easy interaction with Tilly. But Tilly's ascension into the family changed all that, at least in his mind. How could he ever again tease her or laugh with her about some silly foible? Tilly was family; he was staff; and that was the end of it.

Heinrich could still talk to me of course. I had interacted frequently with both Heinrich and Catlyn because of the environmental assessment I was doing for the estate. That interaction would continue in my new capacity as Estate Naturalist. In the long run, I think it's been helpful for me to be Heinrich's liaison to the mansion. In the short run, though, it allowed Catlyn to let her connection to Heinrich lapse. That wasn't like Catlyn, and it should have alerted me that Catlyn's inner struggles were worse than I'd suspected. Maybe I just didn't want to believe they could be.

Maybe, too, it was just that I had my own distraction in

the person of Ned Malbec. Following Catlyn's rescue, I became flat-out in love with Ned, and he reciprocated. That wasn't the problem. The problem was that Ned is Detective Inspector Nestor Malbec. DI Malbec, you see, was in charge of the investigation of Catlyn's abduction. It tortured me that my romantic involvement with Ned might aggravate Catlyn's distress because it would remind her of events best forgotten. It bothered me enough to talk about it with Dr. Ulma. He told me basically what I told Amelia – Talk to Catlyn. His position was that this issue could actually be good for Catlyn because it would give her a way to recall those events without feeling threatened. Malbec, he contended, was a force for good, a rescuer, a defender. I had to smile at that, because that's exactly how I've thought about Ned for quite some time now.

Chapter 3: Dr. Ulma

The death of Lord Sebastian Silverworth had a devastating effect on Catlyn. As victims sometimes do, Catlyn blamed herself for it, because he died in an effort to rescue her. But it was more than just a tragic event for Catlyn. It was that tragedy that crystallized the love Catlyn and Sebastian had for one another, and therein lies part of the complexity of the unresolved issue in Catlyn's mind.

Sebastian lived for six months after being shot in the head trying to rescue Catlyn. For those six months, Catlyn's devotion to Sebastian was extraordinary, and already then, I admired her courage and self-discipline. I have yet to discover whether it was love or guilt that drove Catlyn and caused her to commit herself to such extreme devotion.

One clue, albeit an enigmatic one, has come from her recurrent nightmares. In them, she hears the voice of Lord Silverworth reciting a verse from the Rubáiyát of Omar Khayyam. It's Quatrain XXXII in Edward J. FitzGerald's first translation, published in 1859.

> *There was a Door to which I found no Key:*
> *There was a Veil past which I could not see:*
> *Some little Talk awhile of Me and Thee*
> *There seemed – and then no more of Thee and Me.*

The compositions of her nightmares vary somewhat from night to night, but all the nightmares invariably end with this same recitation. Catlyn is certain that Sebastian never read or recited this verse to her when he was alive. When she began hearing it repeatedly in her nightmares, she searched the web to discover what it was. Before then, she denies any recollection of its identity.

If I may speculate, I'd have to suppose that Catlyn read that verse herself, possibly in grade school, but had since forgotten it. I suspect Catlyn was beset by both a feeling of longing and a sense of guilt. Those feelings resonated with the mood of that verse so perfectly that her subconscious mind pulled it out of her long latent memory and subsequently applied it to Lord Silverworth.

The other symbolic parts of her nightmares were less clear, except for the presence of vultures. Her friend Courtney Haversmith had talked about the "vulture effect" when people were pressing Catlyn to sell her inheritance, so we could relate that part of the nightmares to Courtney's murder, which Catlyn had mistakenly thought was her fault. In Catlyn's mind, if she hadn't argued with developer Alister Knipsyk, who had designs on Southjoy Mission, her friend would still be alive. It was irrational, of course; Knipsyk didn't really have anything to do with Courtney's death as DI Malbec's investigation eventually showed. The argument with Knipsyk merely provided an opportunity that was exploited by a man named Rimwell. You might recall, Rimwell was one of the men involved in the kidnapping. It was Rimwell who murdered Courtney, but his reasons were unrelated to Knipsyk. Grief, though, doesn't respect rational thought. By the time Knipsyk was exonerated, the emotional damage was already done. And then, Sebastian dying to rescue Catlyn from the kidnappers compounded the guilt.

Initially, I was standing by to assess Lord Silverworth's cognitive functions in the event that he regained consciousness after the coma caused by his head wound. When Lady Wythiry learned that I was an American, as is Catlyn, Her Ladyship encouraged me to speak to Catlyn. In her practical way of thinking, Lady Wythiry presumed Catlyn would find it more reassuring to be talking to a fellow countryman. However, after Inspector Malbec apprised me of the circumstances of Catlyn's captivity, I knew she'd soon be facing deeper, harsher, and more delicate issues. And she did. Her nightmares became further steeped in anguish when Lord Silverworth died. Yet after his funeral, we thought she'd come to grips with her grief, as evidenced by how courageously she held together during Rupert Errique's trial. We soon discovered, though, she paid dearly for her effort.

So began our doctor-patient relationship. Since then, I've interviewed numerous people who knew Catlyn before her abduction, and by means of those discussions, I was able to deduce a pre-captivity profile of Catlyn's personality. That gave me a good sense of what she valued in her life. I was still in the process of discovering how her perceptions had changed as a result of her emotional trauma when she broached the idea of adopting Tilly. That seemed like a radical way to reconnect with life at this particular point. I tried to reason with her.

"I can understand your sense of responsibility for Tilly. In a way, everyone on the estate is obligated to you. They're all your responsibility."

"It isn't about responsibility. It's deeper than that. It's like we're an extension of each other, like in a family."

"There are other ways to provide for Tilly."

"Financial, yes. I could provide for her, but that's not caring about who she is. When I say she's an extension of me, don't you see, caring for who she is, is like caring for who I am. I suppose if there weren't any laws or national borders, we'd be a natural family. But, as there are laws and borders, we have to conform to them. That's why I need to adopt her."

She was being very rational, which was good as far as it went. But frankly, I was concerned that she wasn't seeing the potential for disaster that'd be lurking in every step of the process. That's what I had to make her understand, and I couldn't offer any pretension about it. If she thought for one minute that I wasn't being forthright in my attention to her care, my credibility would be shot, and I'd be useless to her.

So, when she asked if I'd support her application, I couldn't say yes. Instead, I reminded her that, as her psychiatrist, my obligation is, first and always, to safeguard her mental welfare. In that capacity, I counseled Catlyn rather bluntly. "An emotional disorder from traumatic stress isn't just about bad dreams and sleepless nights. It's a serious illness. You need to address that first."

She'd heard that before, of course, but in my experience, patients often take a selective memory approach to such matters. So, repeat the advice; repeat the warning.

"It's not something you can ignore. Major life-changing decisions at this stage could ultimately be harmful." There was no way to sugar coat it. "At this moment, the odds are good that you're less rational than you want to believe."

That didn't set well with Catlyn, not at all. She was visibly displeased. "I'm very rational. I've faced Sebastian's death, and I honor his memory." She insisted, "That should be proof enough for anyone that I'm well adjusted."

Remaining objective at times such as this can be difficult. You want to be sympathetic; that's natural. She's distressed, so you want to comfort her. But if you yield to that inclination, your objectivity is lost, and you fail her. So, you've really only one choice, push her painful buttons.

"You've talked of his death, yes, but you've avoided talking about your captivity."

"Nonsense. My love for Sebastian is all that mattered.

The rest is unimportant. That's all there is to it."

"Of course," I allowed. Be agreeable; that's what the manual says, because it's a delicate process. Catlyn did have a lot going for her, so, cutting her a little slack was reasonable, just not too much. She was young, strong, and resilient, which was good. Yet, she was more emotionally frail than she was ready to admit; that wasn't good. It seemed to me, her strength was unwittingly the very facility keeping her resistant to the dialog she most desperately needed. That dialog was going to be the best and maybe the only way she'd learn to trust herself again. Unfortunately, Catlyn wasn't even ready to acknowledge that issue.

So, how do you lower her defenses, tap into those strengths, and use them to draw her into a dialog? The answer was something I learned at a magic show. "It's all smoke and mirrors, doc." Practically speaking, when the patient is leery, the magician's art of misdirection isn't a bad idea. The mandate is clear. You've got to get the patient's attention before you can help her.

"There's a fascinating connection between love and the human psyche, don't you think?" Nearly everyone agrees with that, partly because it's nebulous, and partly because it can be frightening. It doesn't matter which. It captures their attention, and they listen. That was its purpose.

"It's still such a vast frontier. For example, you may well contend that Sebastian survived as long as he did out of the sheer will of his love for you. I certainly wouldn't want to dispute that. His survival gave you time to readjust to normal life. He gave you time to counter the terror of your kidnapping with the intensity of his love. He did what he could so that you could do the rest. He loved you that much."

Her chin lifted a bit on that. But it wasn't enough to lean

35

on Catlyn's sense of obligation to Sebastian. I had to be unrelenting so eventually she'd move forward on her own.

"Tell me again what happened to you."

"You know what happened to me. We've been over that again and again. I don't see why I have to keep repeating it."

"You were kidnapped?"

"You know I was." She was trying to sound indignant, but there's no hiding the fact she couldn't say the word herself.

"You know you were; that's good, very good in fact. Can you tell me, where were you held during that time?"

Catlyn's breathing was becoming labored. Her hands were twitching. She was looking away from me. She swallowed hard, then tuned me out with a cloak of silence.

"Take your time," I offered. "There's no rush."

"Don't patronize me!" Catlyn snapped at me. "I was in a cave, okay?" She shouted, "I was in a cave!"

She was struggling, but she was fighting a good fight. I only wished I had some tangible way to reach out to her, to touch her, encourage her, to cheer for her. But that wasn't how it worked. To help her, I had to abandon all expressions of compassion so I could push and probe and coax her mind until she could cheer for herself.

Part of that struggle was driven by the image of a dimly lit cave that was now impaled in her memory. It was a private agony that flashed repeatedly and without mercy into her thoughts. The harder she fought to shut it out, the more it refused to go away. That's why she was so resistant to this dialog, and why it was imperative that we pursue it. Indeed, I was convinced, necessity required it.

"Yes, you were held captive in a cave, and it was a terrifying experience."

Catlyn cringed, and I knew that image had flashed

again. Her head was lowered, shoulders hunched forward, her posture submissive. Images of prisoners in a POW camp came to mind. She pleaded, "Please don't do this."

How I wished I could've stopped right there, to be an emotional cushion for her, rather than an analyst. But I couldn't. The full force of her nightmare was nearby. I could feel it. We were so close to confronting it. If I could only...

Too late I saw the panic flaring in her eyes. She lashed out at me, "I didn't come here to talk about my past, not today. I'm looking ahead now. I came to talk about my future, about adopting Tilly. Are you going to support me or not? That's all I want to know."

Her clever, resourceful mind was in full tactical retreat.

"Of course I'm going to support you, Catlyn."

I meant that sincerely, but curiously, I felt anxious in saying it. Usually I have no difficulty believing my work supports the patient unconditionally. I couldn't say why, but it felt different in this case. Maybe it was because she was trying so hard, and the odds were so wrongfully stacked against her. Or maybe I just wanted *her* to believe in *me* regardless of the odds, one American to another, us standing together against them, whoever "they" were supposed to be. I'd never had that particular impression before with a patient, and I didn't understand the dynamics of it here. Whatever it was, it didn't really matter because I didn't have time for it. The patient was waiting and needed soothing.

"I'll always support you the best way I know how, and the best way is to make sure what happened to you in the past doesn't disrupt your future. You want that too, don't you?"

"Of course I do." Her tone was meek, not Catlyn-like at all.

"Okay, let's work with that. So, what's our next step?"

"I don't know. You're the shrink; you tell me."

"Ah, but you do know, Catlyn; you know very well what you need to do. It's obvious, don't you think? You simply need to recognize how extremely traumatic your kidnapping was. That shouldn't be so hard to do. Tell you what, let's just look at it academically. There's no harm in doing that, is there? Humor me; let's just try it, okay?"

Catlyn cautiously nodded. I could tell she wanted to be irritable, to lash out at me again, to be impatient. But she knew that wouldn't work; she knew me well enough by then to know she had to be more calculating then that; so she merely nodded. She was going to wait me out.

I didn't mind that so much, so long as that hesitation wasn't her edging towards a shutdown, blocking me out. Trying to wait me out was okay, but blocking me out? No, I couldn't have that. I countered with a comforting smile. That's part of the job, you know, making them feel more confident. I softened my voice and tried my best to sound reassuring and non-threatening.

"The fear, the anxiety, the anger, and even your intense resolve to fight back against your captors were extraordinary adaptations of your mind. Those weren't just transient thoughts. They were agile adaptations of your mind, all made possible because you have a strong and resilient spirit."

So far, so good. She accepted that. She was focused.

"You have to wonder, don't you, where does that kind of strength come from? What happens when you place that kind of demand on your mind?"

I could see her tensing. I was up to something, and she wasn't at all sure that she wanted to hear what it was.

"The physio-chemical processes are really quite amazing."

She canted her head and narrowed her eyes to cast a look of suspicion at me as though she was trying to discern some sleight of hand. I liked that. She was still with me.

"It seems when you place an extreme demand on your mind, it causes your body to respond by producing an excessive amount of stress hormones, particularly adrenaline and cortisol. Do you know how it is when the adrenaline gets flowing? You feel all keyed up, your heart beats faster, your muscles tense ready for action? That's your brain busy at work. In extreme cases, all those flowing hormones cause new neurological patterns to be formed in your brain to bolster the old patterns and to accommodate the extra demand. That's also more or less what makes the memory of what happened so hard to remove. You see, those are physical changes. It might be helpful to think of them as being new circuits hardwired into your brain."

Catlyn was squinting at me and becoming decidedly leery of me. She was still in synch with me, but I feared she was leaping ahead to a conclusion that would pit her more against me than with me. I had to get there first, so I said a bit hastily, "What that means is, those new circuits don't just drain away when the extreme condition stops."

It was the wrong thing to say. Catlyn was incensed. "Are you saying I'll never be normal again? That's ridiculous. I'm perfectly normal."

I had to admit to myself, that was, in fact, a rather normal reaction, but it had to be qualified. "Yes, you are, in a certain sense, but it's an adjusted normality."

She was listening, conditionally, even as tension lines were drawing tighter around her eyes. Try though might, there's just no hiding the fear when you think something may have reached into your brain and distorted your thoughts. But Catlyn still had enough trust in me, at that moment, to be intrigued by the idea, enough to wonder how a physical change, once done, might be undone. How do you stop it from being something that haunts you?

I tried to explain, "Those new neurological patterns in your brain, are not necessarily bad. You might consider them a natural defense mechanism with repercussions. In your case, it's a safe assumption that they're responsible for your nightmares. But they've also made you quicker to respond to threats. Put in a different way, they've sensitized you to emotional triggers."

Case in point, Catlyn was instantly irate. "Adopting Tilly isn't an emotional decision," she fired at me. "It makes sense, to me, to Tilly, to everyone but you."

"You're very possibly right about that. Adopting Tilly could indeed be a very sensible decision for you, but let's make sure we've covered all the emotional bases. Then it would make sense even to me."

She wasn't much reassured by that, but her anger subsided a little, and she wasn't pouting. Good enough; I could work with that.

"Adopting Tilly might just give you a strong enough positive trigger to re-train your new neurological connections or even override them. That would be a good thing indeed. But here's my concern. In an overly sensitized frame of mind, minor rough patches in your path might seem like major disasters. That would be the equivalent of inciting a major negative trigger. That could be devastating."

"So you're saying it's a question of risk?"

"Risk? I wouldn't have put it that way, but you do make an interesting point. Tell me, what do you think of when you talk about risk?"

Catlyn shrugged. "I don't know. Risk is risk. Is this really getting us anywhere?" It must have been, because

Catlyn was suddenly gripping the armrest of her chair. Her posture had become rigid. She protested, "There's risk in everything. Nothing's safe anymore."

I think at that moment I was beginning to feel my own adrenaline flowing. We're in a race; the finish line's just up ahead; neck and neck, running full tilt, it was going to be a tooth grinding finish, and we were both dead set on winning. The finish line, in this case, was drawn by the emergence of Catlyn's fear. It was coming out of hiding, surfacing where it could be observed, examined, and assessed. That was both goal and prize, and it was worth the running.

Moments like that are clinically exciting, but in practice, they can be doubly risky in consequence. That's when you have to remind yourself, a frail psyche is easily damaged; you have to remember, in the surfacing of fear, it's true, nothing is safe. Maybe more pacing and less running would be wise.

"You're absolutely right, of course. There's risk in everything." I tried not to accentuate my words; I tried to be soothing. "Perhaps we could just try to see how all this fits in with your future. You say you want to adopt Tilly. That's highly commendable, which is another way of saying it's a very serious commitment. That's why we have to think about what you said, that every commitment carries a risk. The good news in this risk business is that not every commitment is an urgent necessity. If it isn't a necessity, then it's usually wise to be extra patient. For example, I know that adopting Tilly is very important to you."

"Very," Catlyn stiffly interrupted me. There was that strong will again, sticking her chin out in defiance of any contrary view.

"Yes, very," I readily agreed, "and more than that, you

want it to be perfect, and I want it to be perfect for you."

Her expression didn't soften in the least. Obviously she wasn't going to extend any more credit to me in the trust department, so I tried a different tact.

"You've mentioned your father many times in these sessions."

The warning flags went up. I was treading on sacred ground by bringing Catlyn's father into the discussion. That tense scowl tightening across her face was broadcasting her displeasure loud and clear. But I had dared to mention him, and we were so close. I had to push for one more step.

"What was it your father told you, something about there being no shortcuts to perfection?"

An oblique nod. Her suspicion of me was running high.

"Yes, that was it exactly. Well, the same thing applies here. The more progress we make, the more perfect your perceptions of life will be. There's no shortcut to that. That's why we don't want to put time limits on ourselves. It's very important for you, and for everyone who loves you, that we use as much time as needed to fully assess the effects of your personal trauma."

Catlyn was quiet in a pensive way. I could just imagine her thinking, *Yes, Dr. Ulma, that's all very sensible. I'll grant you that much. Sensible judgment is in the province of the mind, and that's your department.* Alas, what she actually thought was more like, *But is that the proper context for Tilly?*

She recalled, "Ariana once wrote, 'As to the home, give heed only to your spirit, for it alone speaks to you truly.' Tilly is a matter of the home."

By this time in our sessions, I had unambiguously understood that the word of Ariana was not to be disputed. That left me no persuasive argument to make and opened the way for Catlyn to pointedly rebuff my argument.

"I'm handling my nightmares better now. You've been very helpful in that, and I'm grateful for all you've done. But I have no doubt in this. There's no lack of clarity in what I feel or in what I understand. My father also said that life doesn't progress in arrears. He told me, never be indebted to your fears. Maybe it's true I have no future, and maybe I'll never be able to do anything about that. But Tilly has a future, and I can help her realize it. That's future enough for me."

She meant to be obstinate, but I knew she was just being pigheaded. Sorry. That was crude, even if fitting. But, obstinate or pigheaded, she was opening new avenues to explore.

"There's no maybe about it, Catlyn; you do have a future. That very sincere sentiment you just expressed is what tells me you have a substantial future ahead of you."

That drew a hint of a smile. She relaxed ever so slightly.

"That's a bit of a breakthrough in itself. You've made me think you have a future. Now all we have to do is convince you yourself. Consider what a future means for you. You've just told me you have no future and, in the same breath, you say you want to modify somebody else's future. That's almost you seeing a future for yourself, but not quite. What that is, actually, is your sensitized emotion taking control, and that's the point we've got to get you past in your thinking. There's no shortcut to that either."

She was suddenly petulant and demanding. "Are you going to support my application or not? Just tell me!"

That strong will of hers was exerting itself again, and it was pushing to end our session. I didn't want to end on a negative note, but she was forcing the issue.

She badgered me, "I don't need your approval, you know. I just thought you, of all people, would want to support me."

"I am supporting you, Catlyn, and I will continue to do so. It's true, the adoption panel can overrule my opinion, but it's unlikely at this stage. If asked, I will say this much. I think you're a remarkable individual. You have great strength of character, and you've made great strides in overcoming your trauma. If you continue on this path with your recovery, I'll be first in line to champion your cause. Right now, I'd have to say we're facing a tough sell. An inter-country adoption? A confusion of loyalties? Unresolved personal issues? That doesn't inspire confidence. But we can get to that point. We can, and we will. I'll work with you as long as it takes."

Chapter 4: Streetside

I should've known better, Catlyn thought as she made her way from Dr. Ulma's office to the exit. Dear God, why does he have to psychoanalyze everything I do?

Petulant and disappointed, Catlyn pushed through the exit. A blast of cold air channeling straight up the walkway slammed full force into her face. She shook her head and plunged angrily into the wind.

Distracted as she left Dr. Ulma's office, she hadn't alerted Jason, her new driver, that she was ready. Scanning the lot, she spotted the limo parked farther up the street, only about a block away. She took a step to walk the short distance, then stopped abruptly.

There were two men standing on the far side of the street about halfway to the car. They were huddled against the wind, and neither one was looking happy. It struck her as odd. Why'd they be standing out in the cold if they didn't have to? Could they be waiting for a ride? They didn't give that impression at all, and there wasn't even an entrance to anything right there. Not a chance meeting then. One of them gestured with his hand. Was that in her direction? It seemed to be. That glance towards her. Was it her they were waiting for? Were they watching her?

She looked towards the limo. She couldn't see Jason. He ought to be there. She raised a hand over her head, waved it to get his attention. The two men turned to stare at her.

One pointed at her.

No response from the limo.

Catlyn whirled and ran back to the door. She tore it open and ducked inside. The lobby was warm, but her hands were trembling. She found her mobile. It seemed to jump from her fingers; she nearly dropped it; caught it; punched the number to summon Jason.

"C'mon," she exhorted when he didn't answer on the first ring. She looked frantically back out the window.

"Jason here."

"Where are you?" she snapped at him. "You're supposed to be with the limo."

"Sorry. Call of nature, you know? Be there in a sec."

"Bring the limo around to the door. I'll watch for you from the lobby."

"It's just a block up from you. You could be there as quick as me."

"Don't argue with me. I'm in no mood for it. Bring the car to the door."

"Yes-s ma'am!"

His tone seemed a little snide. He was supposed to be experienced, but if so, it didn't show. He was no chauffeur, that's for sure, not like Gaston.

"Is there a problem, Catlyn?"

She jumped; swung around in a startled turn; her eyes flared in a quick flash of fear. She caught her breath. "Dr. Ulma," she heaved. "You startled me."

"Sorry. I didn't mean to. I saw you running back to the building. I thought maybe there was a problem. Did you miss your ride? Do you need a lift somewhere?"

"No. No, that won't be necessary. Jason's bringing the limo around just now." She was rushing her words, sputtering them; too startled, her relief too exaggerated; she was trying too hard to sound in control. "It was too cold to stand out there, that's all."

She glanced quickly out the window. The two men were gone. She leaned closer to the window; used her hands to shield her eyes from the reflections off the glass. She couldn't see them in either direction. The limo too had moved. Jason must be back.

A nervous glance. Dr. Ulma was still there, standing beside her, arms folded, silently focused, intently peering out the window. Had he seen the two men?

"That's a nasty wind out there," he noted. "You're quite right to wait inside."

She looked sideways at him, suddenly wary. Why didn't he say anything about the men? Was he testing her? Was he waiting for her to bring them up? She gave her hair a toss; stonewalled. "Not too irrational of me?"

Too casual, too petulant, too much the tease.

Dr. Ulma smiled pleasantly. "A very sensible response," he allowed. "I'd have worried if you didn't feel the cold."

A horn blared out front. She tensed and flinched at it. "There's the limo." She sounded relieved. "I think I'll have to speak to him about his driving manners. Goodbye again, Dr. Ulma. Thanks for coming to my rescue."

It was a bad choice of words, and she knew it a soon as they were spoken. She scurried out the door before he could say anything about them.

§§§

"Did they follow you or try to make contact with you in any way?" Rose was watching her closely. Catlyn was almost used to that now, everyone watching her, studying her, analyzing her every twitch. If it weren't so annoying, so degrading, she might have been amused by it. *If they're all watching me, which of us is the more paranoid?*

"No, it wasn't anything like that," she tried to explain. "I was just surprised they were standing there like that; it seemed unnatural." She tried to laugh it off. "After Dr. Ulma works you over, everything seems unnatural." She signed heavily. "Chalk it up to being annoyed and disappointed, I guess. What was it Grannie Effie used to say?" She frowned. "I don't remember anymore what she said exactly, something about not expecting the worst of people."

She tried; she tried very hard not to think the worst. "A woman alone, standing in the cold. I suppose they could've been concerned for me. I mean, I was the one coming out from the shrink's office, after all. I was the one waving wildly and running away like a lunatic."

"It never hurts to be cautious," Rose encouraged her.

"I know, but being overly cautious is a different matter, and that wasn't it anyway. I wasn't cautious." She looked straight at Rose. She pushed past her hesitation.

"I was afraid."

It wasn't an easy admission. She instantly regretted it and retreated, "I shouldn't even have mentioned any of this really. I just thought it would help to talk about it." She hastened to add, "And it did." Remembering to be thankful, to be grateful; that was a good sign. That's what they wanted.

"Do me a favor? Forget I said anything about this. Please? I don't want everyone thinking I've turned into a wimp." She tried to make a joke of it. "Can't you just see those two men trying to figure out what that crazy woman was doing out there?" But there was no amusement in her face; the laughter wouldn't come. Instead she fell quiet, stiffened, gritted her teeth. Rose seemed absorbed with her changing expressions. In the growing silence, Catlyn blinked and her attention focused on Rose. She noted how Rose was studying her like she'd said something peculiar. It made her angry.

"I hate this," Catlyn decried in a sudden outburst. "I hate being afraid of everything. It's got to stop." She clasped her hands behind her head. "It's got to. I can't live my life this way." Suddenly exhausted, she sighed heavily, "I just can't."

Rose looked to the doorway. Tilly couldn't wait any longer. Catlyn quickly suppressed the tears forming in her eyes.

Full of anticipation and excitement, Tilly had been waiting patiently to be summoned by Miss Stacey, but when no summons came, she couldn't contain herself another minute. Now she stopped a few paces into the room. Something was wrong. Their faces. Dismay flared from both of them. Tilly's excitement morphed into strain.

"He said no, didn't he," she interpreted.

Catlyn could only nod.

"Why?" demanded Tilly. "He hasn't even talked to me."

"It's not you," Catlyn was quick to say. "It's me. He thinks I'm not..."

"Not what? He's the one who's crazy if he thinks there's anything wrong with you."

Their eyes locked together in a long, pleading silence. Uncomprehending eyes. Eyes peering through a steel fence. A young girl on one side questioning, "Why?" On the other side, a woman frantically searching for a way to scale the barrier, to break through it; to tear it down. She starts to climb; slips; tumbles, falls; disappears beyond...

"Dr. Ulma thinks I'm just not myself yet; that's all." Stay firm. Be positive. Rationalize. It'll be easier that way.

Tilly edged closer. She looked between Rose and Catlyn, trying to read their expressions. "You'd tell me if it was something more than that, wouldn't you? If it's something I've done or something I could do, you'd tell me?"

Catlyn promised, "It's nothing you've done. It's just me. As soon as I understand it myself, I'll tell you."

"Is it the nightmares?" Bold, demanding, no running

away. No avoiding the issue.

"Partly, I suppose, but I'm doing better with them. He said so himself." Stay firm. Don't turn away.

"Then he must think there's something else." She blurted, "There is! I can see it in your face."

Please, lord! Catlyn begged, *Don't let her be afraid of me!*

She swallowed against the bile rising in her throat; the tension was nearly unbearable. She forced herself to nod.

Yes; that's it; acknowledge your deficiency; you'll be stronger. It's what they say. But it was hard to say.

"There is, and that's the problem. It's everything else. Little things, things I've never even noticed before."

Hold strong. Speak. Don't be vulnerable yet again.

"I hear a noise, a footstep maybe, and I think, is that somebody behind me? Why's he following me? Or I catch a glimpse of someone looking my way. Why's he watching me?" She turned to look out the window. "It all just makes me want to run away. I want to run away and keep running and never stop. Just run, until I'm so far away nobody can touch me ever again."

Catlyn stopped. Her pulse was racing. She could feel her nerves pulling into a taut readiness. Her muscles were urging her, *Run! Break away now*, they said, *and don't look back!*

Suddenly, Rose sat up. "Why don't you do that?"

"Do what?"

"Go away."

"Rose!" Tilly cried. Alarm creased her voice.

"Not forever," Rose clarified, "just a get-away, you know, give yourself a holiday."

"You mean like go to London?" asked Tilly.

"No," said Rose excitedly. "Go abroad. Take a real vacation."

Catlyn squinted in thought. "What you mean is, go home." She hadn't meant for it to sound like it did, like over there in the States is home; here is someplace else.

"I was really thinking more of Paris or Rome, but I suppose the States would do too. I mean," she teased, "you already speak the language. You wouldn't have any problem asking where the water closet is."

Catlyn tried to laugh. "They wouldn't know where the water closet is. Most of us wouldn't even know *what* it is." Catlyn blinked. Us, not them.

Tilly didn't laugh. It wasn't funny. Dismay was cutting through her thoughts. Go home? If she "goes home," she won't ever come back. That wasn't funny. She wanted to blurt out loud, she wanted to plead, D*on't go.*

But Catlyn knew that. She offered sympathy in the slow, small oscillation of her head and in the sadness of the smile easing the silent longing in her countenance. No, not now. She couldn't go away right now. "Maybe in the spring," she allowed.

Spring, a point in the future. There was comfort in that thought. A future beyond today. A comfort to know.

Her gaze on Tilly was held in place by the struggle being waged behind her weary eyes, beneath her straining fatigue. Yes, she wanted to retreat, to run away. But to go away was to abandon Tilly. She couldn't have that. Tilly was her point in the future, the only point she could perceive just now.

When you've nothing else but the truth, the truth will have to do. Soberly, calmly, Catlyn noted, "I've got issues."

There, she'd said it. Issues. That much would do for now. A simple admission, a simple cleansing truth, no explanation necessary. Yes, that was it exactly. Cast aside the pretension. Air the imperfection. Acknowledge the frailty. And step boldly, towards acceptance and trust.

"I've got issues," she repeated, "and I can't avoid them, and I can't hide from them. I know that. I admit that. But I won't run from them. And I won't be a victim to them, not again."

A stern and determined silence stretched over them. Eyes locked; breathing turned shallow. Tilly eased forward. She reached out her hand to Miss Stacey. Catlyn raised her hand, accepted the grasp of Tilly's fingers.

Voiceless in their understanding, Tilly's eyes seemed to be peering and searching and gleaning, trying to discern what might be hidden in Catlyn's soul. Intently she probed. Surely, some secret essence of Catlyn Stacey must be harbored there, sheltered and protected. Tilly would touch it, say to it, I'm here too; you're not alone; you can count on me.

Fiercely, Tilly gripped Catlyn's hand. She offered a slow, tenuous nod, a penetrating gaze, a sign of acceptance. *It's my burden too. I won't be put aside.*

"I'll help."

Chapter 5: Sweetgrove

When Mr. Stacey, Miss Stacey's grandfather – some people call him old Mr. Stacey. They mean it affectionately, most of them, but there's some as do so out of meanness. It's not proper either way. He was Mr. Stacey to me then, and now, and always. I began service with Mr. Stacey while he was yet young enough to be someone you had to reckon with, and old enough to be looked up to. He always treated me with respect, and I owe him mine. It's as simple as that.

It's funny how people see things different as time passes. I read once about a barn someone found in a backwoods area. The barn had long been deserted and left to decay, but it must've been a fine barn in its day. Feed troughs for the milk cows and a loft filled with hay. Now it sat dilapidated. Wild animals lived in it by night. It was described as "an asylum of muted sounds." That's how Southjoy Mission seemed to me after Mr. Stacey passed away, an asylum of muted sounds.

We were all fretting about our future right then. Each day brought new rumors, each one worse than the one before. The more we heard, the less muted we became. Everybody turned cranky, and we'd sooner snap and snarl at each other than pass the time of day. The more we turned sour, the more we dreaded the arrival of the granddaughter.

Nobody knew anything about her, except that Mr. Stacey would never talk to her. We didn't know why, but we knew Mr. Stacey was a fair man, and if he wasn't talking to her, he had his reasons. That was enough to put us all against her before she even got here.

It shames me now to think of it. The day she arrived, she

spoke to us openly with a natural warmth. We said nothing in reply. No one smiled. We extended no welcome to her.

She certainly wasn't like any Stacey we'd ever known, and we condemned her for it. What was worse, she looked scarcely more than a child, and that just made us fret all the more. How was she going to be mistress of the house? She knew nothing of life on the estate. We did our proper jobs, but to her, I suppose that made us seem standoffish. So we resented her for that, too.

Without even trying, though, she proved us wrong; about her and us both, I think. Miss Stacey brought a freshness to Southjoy Mission that we sorely needed. Easy going, unspoiled, resourceful, we very soon adored her. That's why her disappearance was such a terrible drain on all of us. We felt so helpless, and now we've all tried to block that whole business out of our memories. I get so mad at people when they condemn Miss Stacey for wanting to do the same.

Anyways, now we measure life from the time of her rescue. Most of us, that is. But it's complicated. Isn't that what they always say?

And it is complicated, but you can see for yourself there's more life in the mansion now than there's been in years. Professor Endbrook, Amelia, Rip... I suppose I should be calling him Dr. Seimor now. He's an American like Miss Stacey, such a nice boy, and he's got that same bent towards being down to earth that Miss Stacey prefers. It just seems natural to call him Rip.

And of course, Rose is here, and I don't know what we'd do without her. Sometimes I think she's the glue holding everybody together. Rose is older than Miss Stacey, and she has a lot more experience in the ways of the world. Outside of Tilly, Rose is the closest friend Miss Stacey has. People say Courtney Haversmith was Miss Stacey's best friend, but I disagree. I think it's always been Rose.

It's been so long since we've had people coming and going here all the time like we do now. There's chatter in all parts of the house, none of which would have been possible without Miss Stacey. Even so, I fear there's a great loneliness clinging to Miss Stacey herself. I think that's why we were all so relieved when Tilly was moved upstairs to family quarters. It was like a spring breeze airing out the winter staleness.

Right from the very beginning, back when Miss Stacey got here fresh from the States, Tilly and Miss Stacey seemed to have a natural closeness. At first, we were all amused to see how Tilly tagged along after Miss Stacey like a kid sister, but they soon became more like mother and daughter. I say like mother and daughter because there was an important difference, I mean, beyond the fact that they weren't related. Miss Stacey took charge of Tilly. She was the authority figure Tilly obeyed. She determined Tilly's allowances, what she could and couldn't do, and instructed Tilly on what was acceptable and unacceptable behavior. In short, all the things a good mother would do. But there was more to it than that. Miss Stacey was inspiring.

Tilly was always a good kid, more or less, at least she was after she settled in and accepted the staff here as her family. But that was the extent of her life. She was just here. She didn't seem to warm to other kids at all, and they didn't warm to her. Cook told me she'd sometimes find Tilly crying because the kids at school made fun of her.

But, Miss Stacey changed all that. In fairness, I guess we've all changed since then, but Tilly most of all. It seemed like Miss Stacey breathed a spark of life straight into Tilly, and lord, don't you know, Tilly came alive. Her eyes opened, and she could see the blue of the sky. If Miss

Stacey said a thing, Tilly wanted to know all about it – Why was it important? What did Miss Stacey think of it? And quick to learn! None of us had any idea how quick Tilly could pick up just about anything, and I don't just mean chores and such. Really, most anything. There wasn't a gadget or a widget or any gizmo she couldn't handle soon enough.

I can tell you, though, nobody teases her anymore about tagging after Miss Stacey, certainly not since, well, not since everything that's happened to Miss Stacey. Most of us are grateful now for Tilly. I think Tilly's the only person Miss Stacey truly trusts. She's different with me, too, I think. She has confidence in me. That's not the same as trust, I know, but it almost is.

We don't like to talk about it amongst ourselves because of Gaston. I suspect the experience with Gaston has made Miss Stacey cautious towards us. She used to take all of us at face value, but now there's a hesitation when she talks to us. It's nothing you can point to and say, you did such and so and it wasn't nice. We just feel it when she speaks to us.

You must be thinking there's some resentment in us to think like that. Well, I suppose there is. And it's selfish. I mean, to want Miss Stacey back to the way she used to be, not for her sake, but for ours. That's plain selfish, I know. But it's not really so bad, is it? If the ending's right? A right ending; that's what we all want for Miss Stacey.

Chapter 6: Ethan

In this, my seventh decade, I wasn't sure I'd see the turn of the millennium, but now that I have, I'm glad to be part of it. It's a troubling era for sure, but then, most eras are. Humanity is no less fractured now than it was ages ago, but it seems to me that the present era has a more determined attitude towards living than most eras have possessed. We, as a world-wide population, think more about it. We demand more and take less for granted. We've come to our senses, almost, about global warming and conserving natural resources, and even as more militant groups crop up to stain the world with their vicious hatred, there's a growing tide of protest against violence and abuse.

Much of this forthright attitude is being propelled, I think, by the wonders of science and technology, which are appearing at an ever accelerating rate. In some factions, of course, it's still an open debate as to whether we are racing to a new future or to a new doom. Yet, by and large, for better or worse, there's an unambiguous confidence in technology that cannot be claimed in any other sector of humanity or any other era. It's a confidence that's not just about achieving prosperity. It's a raw confidence in our ability to achieve.

You only have to look at the marvels wrought by medical research to see the profound changes already made in many aspects of our lives. Diseases that have long harassed humanity are being banished, and even though new ones appear, they no longer instill us with the hopeless fear we had in the past. Perhaps they should, but our confidence is now unbounded. A new disease? No problem. If there's a disease, there's a cure, and medical research will find it, sooner or later. "Seventy's the new fifty." That's not just a fad. It's what people believe. It used to be that living to a hundred was big news. Not anymore. If you're not at least a hundred and ten, it's not news.

Ironically, aging itself is rather neglected as a medical condition. Aging is so common, so natural, so inevitable, it's just taken for granted. Everybody ages. There's nothing exceptional in that. But that's unfortunate. If it were seen more as a symptom of a disease, maybe it would be accepted less readily and countered more deliberately by research.

Dementia, of course, is one of the most fearsome aspects of aging. To date, I've been spared the fate of being an historian who can't remember yesterday. The fact that I retired voluntarily from my university chair wasn't because I'd lost my memory. What I'd lost was my purpose, my relevance, and with that, I'd lost my focus. Catlyn would say I lost sight of my quest, and she'd be right. It was Catlyn who helped me find it again, gave me purpose and relevance, a reason to get up in the morning, to begin each new day filled with anticipation. Because of the future she opened to me, I am brimming with expectations of many tomorrows.

So, you'll understand, there is no length I won't go, no effort I won't make, to help Catlyn rediscover her own focus.

In a way, Catlyn's always been an enigma to me. She's compassionate, spirited to the point of being feisty and combative; she's certainly strong willed – ask Rip about that! Yet, she came here trusting in the good will of people, trusting to the point of innocence. Maybe that was her disease. Such things are beyond me, except to say I've no doubt her unguarded openness to life made her vulnerable.

Dr. Ulma has confided that what made Catlyn so strong before, is what's inhibiting her recovery. The mental shield she created to protect herself in the midst of her trauma is still in place. So, effectively, she's using her strengths against herself. That's what she doesn't realize.

I suppose that's made my decision to continue my work with Catlyn even more determined than it would have been. I firmly believe that history is important, and so I think the more we discover about the people who restored life to Southjoy Mission, the more we just might restore life to Catlyn. That's not so farfetched as it might sound because, early on, Catlyn formed an exceptionally strong bond to her greatly great grandmother, Lady Ariana Stacey. From the day she discovered Lady Stacey's diary, she's read it like a daily devotional. Catlyn once told me that she so admired what Lady Stacey wrote, the way she expressed her deepest thoughts and feelings so unguardedly, that Catlyn rather thought of Lady Stacey as her friend, Ariana, rather than her ancient ancestor. At the time, I thought it was just a romantic notion; now, I think she was right about that.

Catlyn found the diary in an attic where it had been gathering dust for almost two centuries. After only a cursory reading of the diary, Catlyn began to talk about "Ariana's vision" and how Ariana wanted people to regard Southjoy Mission as "a monument to all humanity." Catlyn embraced that idea and made it her vision too. That was before she was kidnapped, of course. In my humble opinion, her abduction caused her to misplace that vision. I'm quite convinced that if she recovers that vision, she'll recover her life as well.

That seems to be consistent with what Dr. Ulma advised. He did caution, however, that we shouldn't think of Catlyn's recovery as getting her back to her former life.

Rather, we should think of it this way. Her life was derailed, and what we need to do now is get it back on track so her life can move forward from wherever it is. I'm sure there was something lost in the translation from Dr. Ulma to me, but that's the gist of what he said.

All of which brings me to Prunella. Shortly after I began working with Catlyn, an associate of mine, Willy Hartsdell who is the director emeritus of the Somerset Lesser Archives, discovered a collection of documents at the SLA relating to Southjoy Mission. Included in that collection was a set of letters from a young woman by the name of Prunella.

Willy had provided us with pdf copies of the handwritten letters early on, but we'd since decided it'd be better for our purposes to work with fully vetted digital epub files. Amelia intends to use them for her thesis as well, and so she's working with Willy on verifying the transcriptions. As they're vetted, either Willy or Amelia send them to us.

Originally, my interest in the letters was mostly academic, but in view of what Dr. Ulma said, I now had an ulterior motive. Prunella was Ariana's friend, so her letters may very well stimulate Catlyn's mind enough that she'll unleash her considerable strengths to apply them in a constructive way. Once unleashed, you see, she'll be back in command of her mind and back on track.

I know, that's easier said than done, but a promising future is always worth the effort, don't you think, when the alternative is anything but?

Chapter 7: Voyage

Afternoon tea had been cleared away, and a lull had settled over the household. Amelia and Ethan were both on-site today, and Amelia had been eager to show her grandfather a peculiar discovery she'd made at the little chapel beside the estate graveyard. It was one of those finds that send archaeologists into raptures, while the rest of us stand around saying, "Oh," by which we mean "Oh?" Bundled into their down-filled coats, tall boot wellies, and their arctic hats with the moisture wicking microfiber liners, they had ventured out to take advantage of the last rays of sunlight. Tilly went part way with them to give Biscuit a chance to romp through the trees, but she decided to veer off towards the meadow to explore the creek that runs along one portion of it. Catlyn had declined the outings, saying she felt like doing a bit of reading instead. Tilly gave her a studied look and would have objected, but Ethan intervened with a reminder that the first Prunella letter should be waiting for Catlyn, and it was time for her to read it.

An email from Willy Hartsdell had promised that the first letter would be fully digitized, verified, and ready today at the latest. Ethan, of course, had already poured over the original at the SLA and had more than once encouraged Catlyn to do so as well. To date, though, Catlyn hadn't been back to the SLA since the tragic death of Lord Silverworth. Not above using enticements, Ethan's most persuasive argument had more to do with Dr. Ulma than with Prunella. "Engage life," Dr. Ulma had commanded her. "Real life always trumps nightmare, if you engage it."

The stroll from the tea room brought Catlyn to the foyer

which had remained her favorite place in the mansion. In the spaciousness of the vaulted foyer, Catlyn felt most at peace with the universe. Here, she could lift her eyes to Ariana's portrait, confirm that Ariana was still there, regarding her, watching over her. It was the only safe haven left to her in the world. Here, she could smile and mean it.

The grand staircase was part of that impression too. Built by old-world craftsmen to stand securely for a thousand years easily, it suggested a strength capable of bearing the weightiest burdens that man or woman could set upon it. That's an uncommonly important perception in a world where the sense of security is underrated as a human emotion, or not considered as such at all. Knowingly or unknowingly, Catlyn imbibed it with each step she took in ascending those stalwart stairs to her private quarters.

Her e-tablet was waiting in its cradle, fully charged, as she knew it would be. Sweetgrove had become attuned to the necessity of nourishing these devices as though they were house guests with voracious appetites. It was part of her routine now to ensure that these unruly little urchins were always at the ready for Miss Stacey to discipline and tame. This she did during her periodic rounds of the family quarters and sitting areas. Any device she happened upon, if not in use, was instantly apprehended and incarcerated in a suitable charging unit.

Sitting in her private lounge, Catlyn pushed the power button to awaken her favorite tablet. Quickly entering her password, she paused to wait for the background image to fill the screen. It was a picture of Carlton Garrick's painting, *The Renaissance of Southjoy Mission*, which now hung in the gallery room at the Somerset Lesser Archives. Garrick was the artist engaged by Ariana to depict the history of the mansion before and after it had been restored in accordance with Ariana's perception of it. Using that image on her tablet was hardly a profound accomplishment, but each time it appeared on the screen, it served as a reminder of purpose and commitment. A little thing, yes, but not insignificant.

A quick update of her email showed that Willy had been true to his word. Just before tea time, he'd sent the epub version of Prunella's first letter as an attachment.

According to Ethan, Prunella wrote many letters during the forty-two day crossing of the Atlantic Ocean that she and her husband, Gerald Treavor, made on a packet boat in search of a new life. During the crossing, Prunella carefully bundled the letters together, preserving them and keeping them dry, until such time as they could be dispatched back to England by means of a return ship. The first letter, that is, the one that came first in the chronological ordering of the letters in the collection, was composed shortly after their departure from Falmouth.

Dear Ariana

Today I was well enough to cry.

Gerald says I must not burden you, but how could I tell aught but the truth to you? Am I to repay your kindness with deception? No. Whatever I may not say to anyone else, I know that I may say it to you.

It is three days now that we have been at sea. I was sick for two whole days, but I am better now. One of the officers, Mr. Joshua, says I have earned my "sea legs" and should now find the voyage more agreeable. I do believe he was teasing me, but Gerald was not amused by it. Mr. Joshua has paid particular attention to me, and that has quite displeased Gerald. I congratulate myself, Ariana, that you would have been proud of me. I did not fall prey to the officer's tease, nor did I pout when Gerald was disagreeable with him. It all ended pleasantly enough.

The blur of a passing shadow attracted Catlyn's attention. She looked up in time to see Sweetgrove entering the lounge. Sweetgrove returned her glance with a quick, apologetic smile. "Just wanted to tidy up a tad," she excused.

Catlyn canted her head with suspicion. "You're sure it wasn't just to check up on me?"

Caught, Sweetgrove objected, "Most certainly not."

That elicited a small smile. "The eyes give you away, you know. That's what they say about people who play poker. Yours tell a whole story. But," she sighed, "go ahead; examine me, if that's what you want. I'm getting used to it."

Dignified, but acquiescent, Sweetgrove contented herself with a ceremonial fluffing of a pillow, then retreated with the observation, "As you wish, Miss Stacey."

There was a hint of triumph in Catlyn's raised chin as she turned her attention back to Prunella.

Departure from Falmouth was without distinction. Accommodations are sparse and brutal, but I must not complain. They are among the better quarters allotted to passengers. Our room in its entirety is but three paces in width by nearly five paces in length, but it is to be occupied by us alone and must be seen as luxury aboard a packet boat. Gerald said Cedric must have paid a handsome premium to secure it for us, as there is one gentleman who has been obliged to quarter in steerage along with the domestics and diverse other common passengers, including two felons who, I am told, were pardoned for their crimes. The gentleman is much put out about his situation.

"Privilege," Catlyn humphed to herself. "Everybody wants to be privileged." Her thoughts diverted unpleasantly to Lady Wythiry for whom privilege was the be-all and end-all of life. Her Ladyship, as was widely known, was more than a little envious of Catlyn's wealth and especially of her possession of Southjoy Mission. Part of that situation derived from the fact that Catlyn had not always been wealthy. Prior to her inheritance, Catlyn had rarely been exposed to anything approaching luxury. The whole one-bedroom apartment she occupied at the time of her inheritance was smaller than the bed chamber of her private suite in the mansion, and the efficiency before that was little more than double the size of Prunella's quarters on the ship, there being only an open area that served collectively as kitchenette, bedroom, dining room, and living room, along with an area that was discreetly partitioned as a water closet. Still, an efficiency with all its built-in features would have seemed luxurious to Prunella.

That thought stirred a momentary pang of guilt. Sometimes she wondered if it was fair for her to have so much wealth when so many people had to work so hard to garner so little. She hadn't earned her wealth, and where others might rejoice at their good fortune, Catlyn felt guilty about it. She once commented to Ethan, "I don't even feel that it's really mine. I'm just its caretaker." Ethan had tried to be agreeable. "Whether you take it in ownership or as caretaker, it's an equally weighty responsibility. You can be pardoned for wishing it otherwise, but the responsibility is still yours." As was the guilt for being privileged. Sighing again, she tried to refocus.

I daily give thanks for the shrewd bargain Cedric struck with Mrs. Mimms. In exchange for her passage, she is to be our domestic during the voyage. As such, she enjoys our protection, which is a comfort to her, I am sure, and she is to be set to liberty upon making port in Halifax. She is a widow of middling age, but of good constitution, and should fare well in the new world where adventurous men greatly outnumber robust women.

I pray mightily that the prospects ahead of us are as fortunate as promised, but I must confess, I am stricken with great trepidation when I think of all that we have left behind. Gerald says I am not to worry. He himself has not wavered in his expectations, and that gives me great hope in their certainty. You need have no doubt for me on this issue. I am resolved to whatever that hope shall yield.

Catlyn looked up from her tablet. Trees visible in the distance swayed slowly back and forth in the light wind. Her mind drifted with them, synchronizing the sway of her meditation to the sway of the trees. *Resolved*, she thought, *to be resolved despite the uncertainty. It couldn't've been easy, exchanging the gentility of Bath for the rigors of a ship at sea. Surely there must've been an extraordinary adjustment to her life. What kind of person can do that? Resolved never to yield. Was it necessity or just human nature?*

"I wish I knew," Catlyn lamented aloud. "I wish I knew."

She looked down again at her tablet. *What I wouldn't give for that kind of resolve, not just the hope that it's all going to work out, but some sense of certainty that I can make it happen.*

66

The screen had gone into sleep mode. Catlyn stared at it. It was so easy to imagine sailing away on a packet boat, sailing away from cares and woes. *I could do that, be one of the nameless faces. There'd be room for me in steerage. I'd be that one over there, the one cowering in the corner where darkness would hang over me like a dark blank screen.*

She sighed again, forcing herself to focus. It was a thought to consider later, perhaps, all that darkness. It had its own appeal. Darkness as shield and shelter. A place to be hidden and undiscovered. She tapped her screen.

> *I think of you often. Still, I must not long for the gracious company of yourself and Lady Sylvia, the warmth of the sitting room, the gaiety of flowers, or even the sound of carriages rolling along the busy roads of Bath. You must remember it all for me, and when all is settled for us in our new home, wherever that should prove to be, you must write to me, long, long letters.*
> *– Prunella, Letter No. A1, 1810*

Letters from home, yet another thought to envy.

She thought of her colleagues back at King's Dream Memorial School where she'd been a teacher for two years. Colleagues, not friends. They hadn't even wished her well. They told her, "If you leave, your position will be filled immediately. We won't be keeping it open." Not for you, is what they meant. It seemed like such a better time ago. Lesson plans, teaching, reaching out to children, helping them to shape their lives. But it was a long time ago.

The high back of her padded chair coaxed Catlyn to lay her head back and rest it against the soft pillow that draped the top of the chair. Quickly adrift in unguarded thought, that envious desire for a sense of belonging stealthily launched an invasion of subtle yearnings. Leaving one's home to travel as a stranger, to have no sense of welcome ahead of you, that Catlyn understood. But, to have a tie to what's been abandoned, a closeness to people who kept you in their thoughts; that she had yet to discover and experience; that she envied.

Eyes heavy in reverie, Catlyn drifted into an exhausted half-wakeful, half-slumbering anxious nap. She was roused from a taunting dream somewhat later by the sensation of a warm body pressing against her leg. She smiled sleepily as she noted Biscuit standing patiently beside her, leaning against her for attention. Tilly must be back from her walk. Running her fingers over Biscuit's coat, there was a sense of fidelity in Biscuit's presence. Tilly must have given her a bath recently because the sable and white fur parted in luxuriant waves between Catlyn's fingers.

Serene in her task, Biscuit merely panted contentedly, accepting Catlyn's attention as her reward. She'd done her job, shared her loving, patient, forgiving presence with Catlyn. Counting it a good job done, Biscuit settled herself at Catlyn's feet, allowing Catlyn to close her eyes again, allowing her to surrender to the quiet rarity of solace accorded her, if only for a moment, under the attentive care of her faithful guardian. In the creeping quietude, furtive tears cleansed the weariness of her eyes.

Chapter 8: Lady Wythiry

You would think that admiration and gratitude should go hand in hand with one's station in life. I regret to say, it is not so. It seems Alexander Pope was quite correct; he insisted that fools may look on something with admiration, but it takes good sense to approve of it. Obviously, admiring fools can never be sensible enough to be grateful for the good station that I occupy in our community.

I suppose, in a way, I've been a little foolish myself, in spite of my good sense. Indeed, I've too long been pacing and sitting and tapping my desk, like I'm going to get anyone's attention with that.

I blame you, Sebastian. If you can hear me now, you're a foolish, foolish man to get yourself killed. How I do miss you. You were so pleasantly ingenuous and so easily coerced. Where am I to find another such as you? At least you got yourself killed before you did anything irreparably foolish like marrying that common American woman, not that getting killed wasn't irreparably foolish, you understand. It's so like you not to have any consideration for how inconvenient all this is for me.

And because of you, I've been deprived of Rimwell as well. He too was a foolish man, but at least he's still alive, even if he's behind bars for the rest of his life. A thoughtless, inconsiderate man. No one needs to tell you how excessively lucrative I was with rewards and favors to him, and look what it got me. Now I'm not only without a driver, I've also lost my most proficient social spy. Who'll do my reconnaissance for me now that he's gone? He was so perfectly positioned, you know, down in the lower classes. They're so much better than we are at spying and eavesdropping. They have nothing resembling discretion, and they relish telling everyone the most intimate details about their employers.

Now, of course, all anybody talks about is how I was ensnared in Rupert Errique's web of deceit. I've heard at least a dozen versions of how I was manipulated by Errique and embroiled in his preposterous scheme. I suppose if I weren't such a force to reckon with, they wouldn't care a whit about me. I take some comfort in that. So, let them laugh and have their little amusements at my expense. Let them blame me all they want for duping Amelia Endbrook. Why they should think that's my fault, I surely don't know. She's supposed to be the clever one, Professor Endbrook's darling little granddaughter. Why am I to blame that she couldn't fend for herself? Ridiculous.

And of course, let's not forget Catlyn Stacey, not that anybody will let me. She came here so righteous, so plucky, she even had me fooled. But look at her now. What a wretched milksop she's turned into. And now everyone feels so terribly sorry for her. They shower her with sympathy, like that's going to do her any good. So she proved her love for Sebastian. So she was, what did the newspaper call her, an icon of caring? So what? What about me? It was my influence that procured Sebastian's medical care. Does anybody remember that? And did anybody notice how I went to visit Catlyn while she mourned? No, of course not.

Let me tell you, all this coddling is doing her no good at all. Just look at all that utter nonsense about adopting a worthless child. That alone should tell you she's not in her right mind. At least Dr. Ulma has put his foot down. All that coddling, indeed. It just begs her to wallow all the more in self-pity. That's what comes from a lack of breeding.

So there it is. When all's said and done, what it boils down to is this. Catlyn Stacey needs to toughen up. That's the plain and simple truth of it, and no amount of coddling is going to do that for her. As usual, that leaves it all up to me, if only I weren't considered *persona non grata*.

That's the way of the lower classes, you know, never face up to a problem if you can run away from it. Well, that doesn't solve the problem. It's the problem that needs to go away, and it won't go away on its own. You have to seize it and make it go away. There's the rub, as they say. To seize it, you have to be in a position to take hold of it. In my current state of disfavor, a good grasp on the situation seems out of the question. If only there were two of me to work it out.

Two of me. Now there's an amusing thought. Could it be, I wonder, can two *non grata*s make a *grata*?

§§§

I had an idea. It was simple and dramatic and guaranteed to garner lots of attention. The tabloids were going to love it.

There were certain problematic hurdles, of course, the first being the absolute necessity of avoiding humiliation. Visiting an inmate in the care of Her Majesty's government would raise a furor if not cast in the proper light. Fortunately, my presence makes any occasion proper.

It really was scarcely any different from being gracious to a social pariah, and I had ample experience with that task. The trick is merely to maintain the appearance of superiority.

The only delicate matter was that I shouldn't appear to have any self-interest in speaking to a prisoner. That would ruin the effect. Fortunately, that's what solicitors are for. One solicitor has "a word" with another solicitor over cocktails, and quietly, discretely, it becomes known that Her Ladyship would respond favorably if perchance Rupert Errique were to submit a Visiting Order request for Her Ladyship to speak with him on a matter of public service. That accomplished, it was child's play to make a big public event of it.

The headlines reveled in it. "Magnanimous gesture," one proclaimed, while another lauded, "Her Ladyship is to be praised for stepping forward in an admirable display of civic duty to rehabilitate a convict who had wronged her personally." My favorite, though, was the headline, "Notable vs. Notorious – Tea or Ten Rounds?"

Once the stage had been set, so to speak, I selected the Visitors' Centre outside the prison proper as the showcase for my project. Cameras, reporters, and newscasters of every breed were carefully stationed to record my arrival, including of course, that vulgar tabloid mongrel, Durke Ormy. He offered me a little mocking salute when I took note of his presence, but on this occasion, I disregarded the offense, if such was its intent, and nothing untoward was made of it. Ormy himself seemed much more interested in what this stiff upper lip Punch and Judy show was going to reveal.

I had made it perfectly clear that I wanted no favoritism extended to me. The protocol for visitors, I made certain everyone understood, was established for good and proper reason, and I fully intended to comply with it. I mean, how else was I to engage the sympathies of the public? After all, they are, by and large, little more than simpering fools, and following orders is what they do. On this occasion, I had to be seen as one of them.

The process began with me surrendering my personal

items to my solicitor who had accompanied me and who, by prearrangement, would wait outside in the limo. I posed for a suitable picture or two, and then quite humbly it seemed to me, I insisted on taking my place in the waiting line where my VO, as it's known, would be verified and the visitation booking confirmed. The reporters loved it all. It gave them ample time to fire away with their barrage of pointless questions, all of which I rather patiently deflected with pointless platitudes. Durke Ormy's question, however, had a sharper point to it.

"Your Ladyship, tell the truth. Aren't you just here to gloat?"

That man is so transparent.

"Not at all, Mr. Ormy. I come only in a spirit of forgiveness. If I can, in this small way, inspire Mr. Errique to reform, I shall be glad of it and for the privilege of my public service to our community."

The barrage of procedural requirements inside the prison, however, could not be deflected in any manner, not even by the wife of a baronet. The photograph was painless enough, but the fingerprinting was a bit demeaning and the pat down, absolutely degrading. Gratefully, the dogs sniffing for drugs showed no interest in me, and I was allowed to proceed through the metal detectors, after which I was escorted to my assigned seat in the visits hall.

Naturally, I didn't have to wait long. A subtle stirring that seemed to move through those prisoners already seated was the first indication that Errique was approaching. Add to that the silent flickering of eyes forming a wave of surreptitious glances, and you have the Prisoners' Fanfare for the King of Villains, Rupert Errique.

I sat patiently, hands folded and resting lightly on the small table in front of me. Upon reaching my table, Errique tilted his head at me and promptly sat.

"Pardon me, Your Ladyship, it's outrageous, simply outrageous, but I cannot wait for your permission to sit. The Royal Innkeepers here have their own rather strict rules of conduct. I'm afraid I'm not permitted to stand either on ceremony or on my feet during your visit."

"There's nothing to pardon, Mr. Errique. I was forewarned about those rules, and I accept them without reservation. Indeed, Mr. Errique, I hope we may dispense with formality all together here and speak plainly and openly to one another."

"How very kind of you, Your Ladyship. I must admit I'm most grateful you've accepted my invitation – and more than a little anxious to discover why it is that I invited you."

"Exactly so, Mr. Errique. They're treating you well here? You've no ambition for early release from your period of detention?"

Errique cocked his head to one side. As opening salvos go, I rather thought he must have found this one quite unexpected. Revenge or verbal payback, maybe, but this wasn't either of those, not at all. To a man as perceptive as Rupert Errique, I couldn't have said "let's make a deal" with any greater clarity. All he had to wonder about was, what kind of deal could I offer and what would it cost? And should he fear a Lady bearing gifts?

My solicitor had advised me that words like "early release" were like sonic booms in the mind of a prisoner, but they'd never speak them out loud. Superstition had it that to say such words out loud would jinx the possibility; reality had it that they revealed, to one and all, a weakness to be exploited. Prison reality, you understand, can be unspeakably ugly. A dark corner. So many sins...

"I'm treated tolerably well for a prisoner, as well as any other," Errique allowed, "but I seek no special privilege, of coursc." His modesty rather suggested he didn't need to. "Beyond that, life is, well, inhibited, I guess you would say."

"Yes, I rather thought it might be. That's precisely why I'm here. It's such a pity, you know, that a person of your talent should be so limited by your circumstances. Has it occurred to you, Mr. Errique, that if you were to find a way to use your talent for public service, it would demonstrate to your prison officials that your penance is indisputably sincere?"

I contented myself to smile pleasantly while he processed the question behind the question. It was a blatant suggestion of collusion, and I could see the wheels turning in his mind as he tried to calculate what the nature of that collusion might be. Such moments are a joy to me.

"An intriguing thought, Your Ladyship, but what could possibly be done from here? There's not a prisoner here who'd admit to having any ability whatsoever to reach out to the public outside these walls."

"Plainly, Mr. Errique. I thought we were going to speak plainly. Do you deny having two men stalk Catlyn Stacey?"

That brought Errique straight up in his chair. When he pointed his finger at me, I truly thought he was going to break protocol. He demanded, "What're you up to? Who put you up to that?" He scowled at me as though trying to read my mind. His eyes closed to mere slits, then he sniffed in disgust, "Such rubbish. I've nothing to gain from her." This he stated as though it should be obvious to everyone.

"Perhaps," I chose to acknowledge, "yet, somehow I see it rather differently from that."

Squinting now, I think he was calling my bluff, as the saying goes; he invited, "By all means, tell me how you see it."

"You've nothing to gain from her? Is that because Miss

Stacey was such a worthy adversary? Could it be that she proved herself to be too much for you?"

He sat back, crossed his arms, and looked almost disdainful in his smugness. "If you're going to tell me she bested me, save your breath. The shrinks have already told me that. It's part of my rehabilitation. She bested me. There, I've said it. Satisfied?" His tone was a little testy.

"Yes, she bested you," I said harshly, "and now you resent her for it."

Errique glared at me. "The shrinks have tried that one on me too, but" – he smiled, uncrossed his arms to make an expansive gesture with both hands – "I resent no one." Alas for him, I am more astute than he. I could see clearly he spoke too calmly; it was artificial, like he was forcing himself to be calm. Still, he wasn't going to be goaded into a faux pas quite so easily.

"Perhaps not," I said, "but such is what the outside world expects of you." It was my turn to do a little play acting, so I tried to sound sympathetic. "But I suppose they could all be mistaken. Maybe they just don't see how you admire a worthy adversary?"

He was squinting again, and that caused me to smile inwardly. *Not bad*, I had to think to myself. He couldn't see yet where I was headed, but he seemed to be deciding that it just might be in his own interest to follow my lead.

"Yes, of course," he said. "That's exactly the situation. I do admire Catlyn Stacey. Her spunk and resourcefulness gave me much to appreciate."

"Why Mr. Errique. I do believe you're rather sincere about that. Was there a hint of something more than appreciation in your face just now?"

His eyes flickered in a quick scan of the room. That was as great a compliment as ever I could expect from Rupert Errique. That look said, "Are we being watched?" I had hooked the King of Villains. It was time to reel him in.

"An expression of appreciation is always viewed favorably by society, don't you think Mr. Errique? But, of course, it would really require a direct dialog to make anyone believe it."

"Direct with...?"

I ignored his question. Instead, I mused out loud, "I suspect, if I were to tell the reporters waiting outside that you've expressed good wishes towards Catlyn Stacey, that might create an opening for you." I engaged him eye to eye. "Did I tell you Durke Ormy is among them? I believe you know him."

Errique canted his head to one side; he was reading my expression with appreciable interest. I was thrilled. That meant only one thing. The great Rupert Errique was conceding like any cowed commoner. *Shrewd, M'Lady, shrewd.*

"I read the papers," he admitted, "and I'm sure Ormy would relish any scoop you might choose to share with him."

He leaned forward, pressing his elbows onto the table. "You perplex me, Your Ladyship, plainly speaking. This surely exceeds any scheme you've ever concocted before. And, oh yes, I know you're scheming. Reporters? Durke Ormy? You? I'd never have thought it. Who'd have guessed you and I speak the same language?"

"That's the beauty of it, don't you think? Because it's me, it's all indisputably proper."

"I see that, certainly. But still, it boggles the mind. What you're suggesting is that we shouldn't be working to cross purposes when we want the same thing. Catlyn Stacey and Southjoy Mission. Lesser people would've quit by now, you know. But not you or me. My dear Lady Wythiry, what missed opportunities loom in my mind."

I nodded that he'd finally understood me. In point of fact, he'd been baited and trapped, and didn't even know it yet.

I stood then to leave. I'd done what I set out to do, and whether or not he agreed, I'd won. I was already adored once again by the press and the public, and all achieved at his expense. So far, so good.

Prospects, indeed, loomed in my mind, and I couldn't resist offering a parting shot. "Opportunities, Mr. Errique. Just see to it that none more are missed. Compensation really does go hand in hand with influence, in the right hands."

Chapter 9: Tilly

If you're not in limbo, and you're not on a mission, where are you? Wherever that puts you, that's where I was.

Miss Stacey has me reading a classic novel, *Two Years Before the Mast* by Richard Henry Dana, Jr. In the beginning, he writes, "There is not so helpless and pitiable an object in the world as a landsman beginning a sailor's life." Well, there is, and that would be me, because that's exactly how I felt, like a helpless and pitiable object trying to begin a new life that wasn't yet mine to begin.

When Miss Stacey said she wanted to adopt me, it was like we were setting sail on a great quest. Our ship was readied. The sails were hoisted. And then Dr. Ulma took the wind out of our sails. But that didn't mean we couldn't put our oars in the water and try to paddle ahead. It just made everything seem to go a lot slower, you know, not becalmed like being in limbo, but not making waves either.

As it was, I had three things to occupy my time. Anything Miss Stacey wanted me to do came first. Most of the time, anyway, because there was Biscuit. Miss Stacey got Biscuit for me, and it was my job to take care of her. I guess you can't really call it a job because she's my best friend. Even when everybody's away, I can always find something to do with her, even if it's doing nothing; that still counts as something. When not doing either of those things, I was working with Miss Stacey and Professor Endbrook on the Prunella letters.

We were growing very fond of Prunella. Her letters had Professor Endbrook very excited, but he gets excited at the strangest things and often forgets to tell us why. It didn't really matter, though, because those letters meant something to Miss Stacey, and that's what was important. Even Dr. Ulma said this was "very encouraging."

Miss Stacey had invited him out to the estate to have a casual lunch with all of us on one of those rare occasions when we were all here at the same time. It was supposed to be strictly casual, no business, but you know Dr. Ulma; he never stops analyzing everybody. Sometimes he can be a little creepy that way. I haven't quite forgiven him for not supporting my adoption, but I think he means well.

Sometimes I think about it all day long until it gets to be too much. I really do want to call Miss Stacey "mom," but I'm determined not to do that until I can say it for real, you know, just in case something should happen, something unthinkable, which I won't think, ever.

I suppose saying something nice about the Prunella letters was as close to an apology as Dr. Ulma could get. I mean, he is her doctor, after all, and he's not supposed to apologize for doing his job. His point was that Prunella was somebody outside Miss Stacey's known universe which, to his way of thinking, suggested that Miss Stacey was ready to come out of her protective shell.

At one point, Professor Endbrook got into a conversation with Dr. Ulma, and I heard them talking about "transference of feelings." For the most part, I didn't understand what they were saying, but I did understand that Prunella had a connection to Lady Stacey. That's all any of us really needed to know. After that, it was just common sense that Prunella was good for Miss Stacey.

Privately, I liked Prunella for herself. I suppose that was because, in some ways, she was a bit like me, not a lot, but a little. When she first came to Southjoy Mission, everyone said she was very pretty, but beyond that, they otherwise thought she was pretty much useless. That was a little bit like me. I mean, I wasn't pretty, but I was useless.

Carlton Garrick, the Southjoy Mission artist, wrote in his journal, "My worst suspicion of Prunella is confirmed. Her manner is shallow of aspect, and her only true passion is self-indulgence." The kids at school have said things a lot meaner than that about me. I mean, being called Weasel the Measle wasn't exactly flattering, and it didn't help when it came to making friends. But in the 1800s, Garrick's low opinion of Prunella must have seemed totally gross to her.

Lady Stacey was kinder. She wrote, "It is a rarity to have a conversation with Prunella that is not about Prunella, which makes her proposal of charity all the more remarkable. I am hopeful that her sincerity is genuine." At that particular time, Lady Stacey was still Miss Atwood, and she had plenty of issues of her own, not the least of which was her love for Cedric Stacey who was off risking his life for the honor of the Crown of England.

Nevertheless, whatever view you took of it, nobody thought Prunella was worth anything, and so, of course, she wasn't. Not until Gerald Treavor came along and gave her a quest. *That's* what I really had in common with her. I had no quest until Miss Stacey came along.

I don't think Prunella ever really thought about quests at all, certainly not the way Miss Stacey does or even like Lady Stacey did. It just came naturally to her. You can see that in what she wrote to her friend, Elly Howshim.

The sailors, except for the officers, are all very crude, and they speak in the harshest manner. They frighten me, and I have been caused to blush in the reddest aspect imaginable. Gerald says it is just their way, and I should make nothing of it. They use the foulest curses as casually as you might bid me a pleasant morrow. I am resolved to think of them as speaking in a foreign

language. In time, I shall be adept at translating their discourse into my native tongue. I am sure when I have done so, their discourse will be seen to be of the kindest, most genteel nature.
  – Prunella, Letter No. E1, 1810

Prunella could have been very "disagreeable" about it all. She could have spent all day pouting and complaining about her misfortune. A lesser person might've said, "My life is over," but Prunella just wasn't like that. She tried to put a positive spin on everything and make the best of it.

Miss Stacey's a lot like that too. That's why she insisted on bringing us all together whenever she could. It wouldn't surprise me if that's how she was thinking when she put together that casual lunch for all of us. Just listen to this.

The menu consisted of English bangers, Italian pasta, and American cold cuts, including Virginia ham of course, and it was concluded with German chocolate cake topped with a French silk ice cream. Don't you see, we, as a group of people, had a consistency much like our lunch. By that I mean, we were all completely unrelated, but together we formed one very satisfying family. How's that for a positive spin? Maybe we weren't as savory as lunch, but we were certainly every bit as nourishing, you know, in Miss Stacey's romantic way of thinking.

That included Dr. Ulma, by the way. As the arabica coffee from Brazil was being served, I couldn't help noticing how Dr. Ulma's eyes seemed to follow Miss Stacey's every move. At first I was miffed with him, thinking that he was analyzing her. Then I noticed *how* he was looking at her. It was not a doctorly look.

I mentioned it to Rose later and got a scolding for even thinking such a thing. "For shame, Tilly," she chided me. "He's her doctor. Doctors don't have romantic notions about patients." I wasn't convinced, then or now, and the whole thing just made me more annoyed. If he likes her, why isn't he supporting her?

He got a chance to redeem himself, at least in my eyes, after lunch. Miss Stacey and I had planned to visit Lady Stacey's grave site, and she asked Dr. Ulma if he'd like to come with us. He was hesitant at first, and I could see him cringing at the thought of it. His forehead got wrinkled with a deep furrow like he was debating the question, and I thought he was going to say something like "bad idea" or "it's too soon." But, much to my surprise, he suddenly smiled like he'd just had a wonderful idea himself and said "I'd like that very much." I don't care what Rose or anyone else says, there were romantic thoughts in that smile.

We walked to the cemetery side by side, Miss Stacey in the middle, me on her left, and Dr. Ulma on her right. Miss Stacey is usually quiet on these walks, not sad or anything like that, just deep in thought, and I do most of the talking. Not this time. Miss Stacey gave Dr. Ulma a running commentary about the estate, the way nature is thriving here thanks to Rose and Heinrich, and how the vista was changing through the fall and what it might be like this winter.

At one point, at the top of one of the knolls along the way, she suddenly stopped and said, "Wait. Look back this way." She was pointing back to the house. "This is my favorite view of the estate. From here, you can see how it all blends together. There's a harmony to it, don't you think? Look at the way the Spanish arches stream right into the gardens where they open into a whole sea of plants and greenery, and then the gardens themselves flow out into those trees, the ones standing so high they're like mountain islands that rise up out of the ocean and reach right into the clouds, almost all the way to heaven."

83

At that moment, the expression on Miss Stacey's face was pure unblemished contentment. She was in a place free of nightmares and demons, and there was no threat of any flashback that could touch her. I can't describe the thrill I felt seeing her like that. I think it qualified as one of Lady Stacey's moments of unquenchable glory. I would've done anything to make it last forever. I would have. I would've stopped living right then if dying would've preserved that moment, that unblemished contentment, for Miss Stacey.

Then I noticed Dr. Ulma.

I think he wanted something like that too; something like that. With one difference. It wasn't just her. It was him. He was so absorbed with looking at Miss Stacey, it was like he was hypnotized. He wasn't seeing anything but Miss Stacey. He didn't even look at the house, unless he was seeing it as a reflection in Miss Stacey's eyes. I remember his face in that moment because it seemed to me, he was finally seeing the real Miss Stacey, the one the rest of us already loved.

They spoke together for a couple of minutes. Their voices turned very soft, almost to the point of being murmurs, so I couldn't actually hear what they were saying. I suppose I was miffed by that because it was like they'd forgotten I was there. I wanted to believe Dr. Ulma was just being encouraging in a supportive way. But it was hard to believe.

Then, just as quickly, Miss Stacey took a deep breath and whirled about with the announcement that "It's not much farther from here," and off we went at a brisk pace. Miss Stacey was actually skipping as we went down the other side of the knoll. She turned and laughed as we caught up to her.

There was no gaiety at the cemetery though. Dr. Ulma

seemed uncomfortable and hardly spoke at all. I didn't say
much either because I didn't yet feel like I'd earned the
right to say anything in a place of such reverence, which is
how Miss Stacey regarded it.

Miss Stacey herself spoke in quiet tones, almost at a
hush sometimes. She pointed out her grandfather's
headstone and a few of the others leading up to the largest
one that marked the graves of Lady Sylvia, Sir Cedric, and
Lady Stacey. Dr. Ulma didn't seem to know who Lady
Sylvia was, so Miss Stacey explained how she was the one
who actually started the renovation of the estate before it
had become Lady Stacey's passion. Cedric was Lady
Sylvia's nephew.

"According to Ethan," Miss Stacey told him, "the estate
was about three hundred years old when Lady Sylvia's
husband, Sir Waverly Sylvia, bought it. It had been abused
– that seems to be the only word that really describes it –
abused for most of those three centuries."

I couldn't help noticing the look on Dr. Ulma's face
when she said the estate had been abused. He looked
worried. He tilted his head, and his eyes seemed to be
searching her face like he was looking for something. Miss
Stacey didn't seem to notice any of that. She was speaking
with great fondness.

"Every attempt to make a go of the estate before then
had failed. When Lady Sylvia decided to try her hand at it,
she enlisted a young girl by the name of Ariana Atwood
who became passionately devoted to the estate. The
painting of Ariana in the foyer is actually entitled, *In
Homage of Miss Ariana Atwood*. It was Ariana's idea to
make the estate into a monument for all the abused people
of the world. A monument for all humanity is what she
actually called it."

Miss Stacey paused at that point, then after a second or

two said, "I wonder if she was already thinking of me even then."

Talk about wet blankets.

We all went dead silent at that. What could we say? Besides, if Dr. Ulma had tried to say anything at all, I'm sure I would've kicked him in the shins. I knew what he was thinking – he had that squinty look again – and I wasn't about to let him say anything mean, not out loud, not in that place. Miss Stacey's a romantic; she's not crazy. It was just one of her romantic notions.

As it turned out, nobody said anything. After a second, I took Miss Stacey's hand, and she smiled at me like she understood what I was thinking. Then Dr. Ulma mumbled something about really needing to get back, and we left. It was a very quiet walk home.

Chapter 10: Dr. Ulma

There were many indications that Catlyn was improving. Her general attitude in particular was more upbeat. I counted the luncheon at Southjoy Mission as a good example of that. She was also becoming more cautious in a sensible way, cautious rather than fearful.

A case in point was a message she received from Rupert Errique. Yes, I know; that's the very same Rupert Errique who caused all her problems in the first place. The message was delivered by way of Mr. Galler, Catlyn's solicitor. It irritated me to no end that Galler didn't talk to me first; he could've warned me, at least. But he's rather punctilious about the tenets of law, and he insisted that it was his obligation to give Catlyn the message regardless of my concerns as her doctor, and give it he did without delay. To his credit, he did advise her against accepting it. "Ignore it. Leave it be, and him too. Stay away from him; don't speak to him; don't even speak about him. Let him stew in his own pot."

In a perfectly normal exhibit of sensible human behavior, Catlyn wanted to know, "But what's the message?" It's just human nature to want to know. A more devious nature would have been more leery.

Galler's advice wasn't given lightly. With the certified IQ of a genius and the certifiable attributes of a sociopath, Rupert Errique knows how to get into a person's mind, and he was certainly well acquainted with Catlyn's mind. Errique held her captive in a cave for more than enough time to observe her and get a sense of her thought patterns. I'm certain he deliberately probed her psyche to see what she valued and what she'd fight against. That, after all, was part of his success, knowing how to exploit people, and it didn't matter whether they were strong or weak; he was that good at it. In Catlyn's case, all he really needed to know was how passionate her reverence for Ariana Stacey was.

His message was inoffensive, and fiendish. "While you were my guest, I had the privilege of perusing Lady Stacey's diary. She was a compassionate individual and wonderfully forgiving. I am inspired by her to seek your forgiveness."

Catlyn was furious. It was foul enough that he'd taken the diary away from her, but to read it too? Her reaction suggested a strong sense of humiliation, exactly as Errique intended. In her mind, Errique had desecrated Ariana's memory; he violated her privacy. Forgiveness? Was she supposed to believe he even knew the meaning of it?

It didn't seem possible. I counselled her, "In Errique's twisted view of the world, forgiveness is merely a tool for manipulating people. Whether he's speaking the truth or not, it rarely matters. He uses both at his convenience. You must never forget that Errique schemes without conscience. Never think otherwise. He has no sense of guilt for what he's done to you or to anyone else. That's why it makes no sense that he would ask for your forgiveness. You have to feel guilt before you can feel a need to be forgiven."

"He might not feel the guilt," Catlyn objected, "but surely he sees the irony of it. He's now the prisoner, and I'm now the one free to come and go at will. That puts me in the position of strength. I control the situation."

It was arguably a sensible response, but I had to caution her, "That might be what he wants you to believe."

"What do you mean?"

"You're offended by his admission, not by his

suggestion. He's attacking you by misdirection. While you're busy being angry that he violated the sanctity of the diary, you've not noticed how he's planted a suggestion in your mind. If you feel like you're in control, you might very well respond to his suggestion. Why? Because of human vanity. It's not enough to know you're in control; you've got to prove it. And by proving it, he has manipulated you. That gives him direct access to you."

"I'm not afraid of him."

"Not at the moment, because you're here and he's there. Distance creates a buffer between you and him, and that's what makes you feel safe. He knows that. Don't think for a moment that he doesn't. He's depending on it. Don't you see? By seeking your forgiveness, he's imposing on you. The first concession is the hardest one. Open that door, and you might as well ask him to command of you what he will."

"That may be his plan, but what if it isn't mine? What if I'm not looking to forgive him, but to confront him?"

That required a deep breath. The idea in itself had some merit, but it wasn't without its danger and pitfalls. "I understand what you're thinking. Some people believe that confronting your demons is one of the best ways to exorcise them. But that only works if you're ready for it. As a therapy, it's commonly done through role playing. It's intense, but it's done on neutral ground, so you know up front it's not threatening. Confronting a real individual who's seen as the root cause of your anxieties is a whole different matter. The risk of triggers and flashbacks is huge. I'm not trying to frighten you, but if you're not strong enough, not secure enough in yourself, it could destroy all your progress in one blowup. It could reinforce your demons and allow them to rule your emotions for a very long time."

Catlyn nodded her understanding. "That's why I wanted to talk to you first. What if you came with me? You'd be like a safety net. You could observe me and Errique at the same time. You'd be assessing him in real time, seeing firsthand how he operates. If you can understand how he works his influence on me, wouldn't that help you discover how to counter it?"

I just wanted to hug her. She was trying so hard; she had it all together; she was strong; her thoughts were clear. And yet, she still couldn't see the whole picture.

"It could work that way, yes. But the problem is this. When you deal with a sociopath, there really aren't any rules. To succeed against him, you might need to become ruthless yourself. That's the trap he's set for you. To succeed *against* him, you might have to be more *like* him, and less like Ariana."

Chapter 11: Rose

I watched her stirring her coffee. The sugar bowl sat covered, the creamer was untouched, and the coffee still black. Whatever had happened with Dr. Ulma yesterday had left her thoroughly preoccupied with matters that took her far away in her thoughts, and I mean that in a worrisome way. It's the way you might look when you're forced to choose between two necessary evils and no matter which one you choose, somebody you care about is going to get hurt.

"What's this, then?" asked Cook who was back on her feet and making sure everyone knew she was once again in command of the kitchen. That included making sure Catlyn had everything she needed or wanted. "Something wrong with them eggs?"

"No, they're fine," Catlyn tried to protest as she glanced down to discover there was a plate in front of her.

"You ain't took a bite."

"They're fine, really. I'm just a bit distracted this morning, that's all." She picked up a fork and offered Cook a quick smile that wasn't the least bit convincing.

"Ya gotta eat, Miss Stacey. Body'n soul, ya know, body'n soul." With that, she trundled on back to the kitchen, muttering and shaking her head all the way.

Finding a fork in her hand, Catlyn rather absently took a bite of her eggs and washed it down with a sip of strong coffee. She made a face. The coffee was bitter. She glanced towards the door. The coffee was forgotten. She asked, "Where's Tilly?" Her tone was off-handed, but her gaze was intent.

"She took Biscuit out for a romp. Would you like me to

track her down?"

"No, I was just curious."

She lifted the cup to her lips again, took several sips; she didn't seem to notice now its bitter edge.

"Did you read in the paper that Lady Wythiry went to visit Rupert Errique in prison?" There was tension in her voice.

She hadn't been looking at me when she asked that, but I could see her face in profile. It was rigid in outline and bore the flinty patina of hard concentration, as much lacking in warmth as was her voice. She was speaking, but not making conversation. I doubted she was waiting for a reply.

"She's up to something." It was another flat statement devoid of emotional inflection. It lacked feeling, yet I felt it like a chilling accusation.

Even so, there was something fragile in her attitude. Her countenance was rigid, but not strong. She was holding something back, and I coaxed her to let it out.

"The paper said something about civic duty. You don't think that's all there is to it?"

"Durke Ormy saying something good about anyone, let alone Lady Wythiry? No. I don't believe it. And hot on the heels of that, I get a message from Rupert Errique asking for my forgiveness? No. I don't believe it. Ormy and Wythiry and Errique. Separately I don't trust any of them. Put their names together, and it makes my skin crawl."

A petulance was building; you could see it in her breathing. "You could just ignore him," I encouraged her, or tried to. "That's what I'd do. I wouldn't go anywhere near him, no matter what anyone said."

"I've got to."

"But why?"

"Because I'm afraid of him." She was staring at me now,

her gaze stiff and uncertain. "I told Dr. Ulma I wasn't afraid, but I am, Rose. I am. I'm so afraid I feel nausea when I think of going there, seeing him face to face."

She looked away. Sighed heavily. She looked back at me, determined, I think, to win the debate raging in her mind.

"If I don't go, I'll always be afraid of him, of every shadow, of two men standing on a sidewalk. I'm not going to let him do that to me."

She gave her head an angry shake.

"He once bragged that he was very good at finding flaws in people. He said, find the flaw, and you can break anybody. He's trying to break me; he's trying to ruin who I am."

Her expression was turning heated with anger.

"I've got to stop him. That's why I've got to face him. I'm going to face him, and I'm going to walk away stronger."

Objections of every nature were flooding my thoughts, but I couldn't seem to find one that she'd listen to. She'd already made up her mind. She was going to face him, and there wasn't anything I or anyone else could do about it.

I asked, "What did Dr. Ulma say? Will he go with you?"

"He will."

"Because he can't stop you from going."

"Basically, yes. He said it was a decision of last resort. He's admitted it's not entirely irrational, and he understands my intent. Errique is my root cause. So my plan is simple. Eradicate the root, eradicate the cause."

"Errique, Wythiry, and Ormy aren't known for playing fair."

"That's what Dr. Ulma said too. He told me I'd have to be ruthless." When she looked at me, her eyes seemed plaintive and strained with pleading. "I don't want that to be me, Rose. I don't want to be ruthless."

I reached out to touch her arm. "What *do* you want?"

She clasped her hand over mine. "I want to be whole. That's all I want." She pressed my hand harder. "I want to be whole, and I can't be if I'm weak and afraid. I need to be strong, strong enough to hold myself together no matter how much I'm afraid." She let go of my hand; looked away. "Run away from Errique now, and I'll never be strong enough. I'll always be afraid. Of him and everyone else."

"You know I'll do whatever I can to help you. Anything. I'll go there with you if you want. There's safety in numbers."

Her head turned back to me. "Would you?"

"Yes, and Tilly will too."

"No. Just you. I don't want Tilly involved."

"She'll insist."

"Only if you tell her. First things first. She'll be helping me in ways she doesn't even know."

"Is that fair to her? She'll be hurt that you didn't tell her."

"It's as fair as I can be for now. She'll understand. Sometimes she understands things way better than me."

She sighed again, and I could sense her frustration. She tried to explain. "I need one piece of my life that's entirely normal. That's Tilly, and I want to keep it that way. I've got to, Rose. I've got to hold onto that one piece if I can. Someday, when this is all behind us, I'll tell her everything. If I need to."

Chapter 12: Dr. Ulma

The prisoner was already seated at the table in the visits hall. That was one of my conditions. The prison officials had agreed we could wait until he'd been brought in and seated. It was a minor point, no doubt, but if Errique came looming out of the void to descend on Catlyn like one of the vultures in her nightmares, she'd be lost before the battle even began. There'd be no stopping the flashback, nor Errique. I wasn't going to let that happen. It was going to be hard enough on Catlyn without that.

Walking beside me, Catlyn didn't seem to share my concern. Her stride was firm and purposeful, matching me step for step. Rose walked behind her, guarding her back. Catlyn's face appeared neutral, but I could see that her eyes were locked straight onto Errique. He was posing for her, giving her an attitude of insolence and trying very hard to disregard our approach. At the table, though, Catlyn stopped and just stood there, hovering over him. It was an aggressive move on her part, compelling Errique to look up at her.

He complied, but he tried to look vaguely baffled that she was still standing. Obviously, it was going to be a contest of wills. He gestured to the chair across from himself. "Please," he invited, "be my guest." The nonchalance of the gesture was itself vaguely insolent and challenging.

Catlyn handled it well enough. Defiant and vaguely arrogant herself, she turned her back to him, a gesture of disdain. Sharing a quick glance with me, she maneuvered behind me to sit somewhat on a diagonal away from the prisoner. It's what we'd agreed to beforehand, so I could position myself directly across from Errique. That allowed Rose to take the seat to Catlyn's left so that the two of us were flanking her.

Errique parried with a raised eyebrow, disturbing the nonchalance of his face with a carefully pained expression. It was clearly disingenuous, but it was effective. He protested, "You don't trust me?"

He looked only at Catlyn. He frowned at her, then he shrugged his shoulders and conceded, "Quite right, I suppose. I'd be suspicious too if I were you." He added a tired smile to his face to say, "Actually, I *was* suspicious, come to think of it. This whole idea of meeting with you seemed utterly ludicrous."

That drew a slightly indignant look from Catlyn.

"It's true," Errique declared, "I swear it." He sat straight up as though that would make every word of his revelation indisputable. Leaning forward to rest the lengths of his forearms on the table, he confided, "It wasn't even my idea."

To see him, you'd think it was a bewildering possibility. He revealed, "As you may know, Lady Wythiry took it upon herself to visit me in this very hall. She came with her own agenda, which is neither here nor there, but part of it had to do with urging me to look deeply and honestly at myself. I haven't a clue what put such a bee in her bonnet or why she thought such an appeal would have any sway with me, but once she got wound up, there was no holding her back."

He shook his head as though rebuffing the suggestion. "Well, I made no bones about it. I just wasn't keen on all that soul-searching fervor she was spouting. But, Her Ladyship has her ways of persuasion. She rather forced me into it."

Catlyn canted her head with skepticism.

"I see that look, Miss Stacey," he started to chastise her, but hesitated with a dismissive gesture. "But, of course, you're right. I could've declined her interest. But to what end? The way things look from here, any visit from somebody as distinguished as Her Ladyship must be worth something, so I humored her."

Errique was clearly enjoying himself. He could have been sitting on a stage performing for a large audience. Putting on a display of bemused wonder, he declared, "Well, no one was more astonished than me at what I discovered. In forcing me to think about you, I found myself admitting that you, of all people, someone scarcely more than a child, had thoroughly trounced me in a game of my own making."

He paused to see, I think, if she was buying the flattery. That was a mistake.

"It wasn't a game. I'm not a child. And it's not over." Catlyn's tone was flat and uninflected. I took my eyes off Errique long enough to glance at Catlyn, and I could see Rose beside her was visibly tense in her seat. She wasn't alone in that reaction. The coldness in Catlyn's manner chilled all of us, Errique included. There was no emotion in it, no hatred, just a cold unfeeling gaze. She might just as well have been confirming the tariff on a tedious inventory. The ledger wasn't closed; the balance hadn't yet been settled.

Her attitude would've stung a more sentient person, but Errique had no feelings. "That's most uncharitable of you," he chided. "I've worked very hard to reconcile myself to the defeat you dealt me. Mind you, that's not an easy admission for me. I'm not in the habit of acknowledging anyone as my superior." He paused to glare at her, then more humbly noted, "But, in this instance, I can think of no way to deny it." Offering a slight tilt of his head, he allowed, "To you alone, I bow to my superior."

Catlyn appeared passive and disinterested. I absolutely marveled at her self-control. She wasn't the least bit taken in by Errique's patronizing tactics. I'd have been dancing a jig at this, if it weren't for her face. There should've been *some* evidence of response in her expression. A hint of gloating victory maybe. Even disgust or loathing would've been normal. Something of that nature should have surfaced, but there was nothing, not the flaring of a nostril, no alteration in her breathing, not even the blinking of an eye.

Errique must've come to that same conclusion because he suddenly became plaintive, like someone fishing for sympathy. "It's taken more effort than you might imagine, Miss Stacey. It's cost me many sleepless nights." He paused an instant, pondering his plight, then said, "But I've put all of that behind me, and I've come to be at peace with myself."

He squinted as though there was something not quite right. Then it seemed to come to him. "It's an inward peace, right enough, but for people like us, like you and me, that's not enough, is it? People like us are never satisfied with anything less than complete, absolute achievement. So you can see my problem. Without your forgiveness, my peace is incomplete. That's why I'm compelled to reach out to you. Nothing less than your personal forgiveness will make my penitence real and my peace complete."

His appeal was impassioned, I'll give him that much credit, and it might have succeeded, except for the fact that it had none of the backbone of sincerity required to make it so. The growing sharpness in Errique's voice made his real intent clear enough to me, and I admit, he was succeeding. He was growing stronger, shifting from plea to harangue, and the transition was absolutely flawless. Right in front of me, he was becoming a bully, browbeating a timid child, or trying to. And he relished it. I think that truly annoyed me. I would've been less disturbed if I'd been sitting calmly in my office. But here, on his turf, so to speak, I was incensed, and I'm afraid I allowed it to show. "And your punishment," I asked him, "do you accept that, too, as fair and just?"

An irritating fly might have had more effect on Errique; he brushed the question aside with a wave of his hand. "Punishment is never pleasant." He added considerately, "But I count myself more fortunate than many."

Another self-effacing ploy. Another plea for sympathy. I was beginning to understand why Catlyn talked about having a safety net. Debating Errique was like conducting a fencing match on a high-wire tight rope. I fell back and tried to deflect his thrust with a stock-in-trade question. "In what way fortunate, Mr. Errique?"

Knotting his brow in thoughtful pose, Errique said, "I suppose I'm thinking of my former associates, Maggor and Rimwell. They'll spend the rest of their days in prison, which is just as well for them. Kidnapping and murder, I just can't abide either of those things, really I can't. I tried to guide them, mind you, I did try, but they simply were not redeemable." He paused to look sternly at Catlyn. "They just wouldn't listen to me." His tone had the sound of a pointed warning. "Had they done what I asked of them, they'd have been spared their present unpleasantness." He stared at Catlyn another second, allowing the thought to steep into a pungent bitterness.

"Is it your belief, then," I intervened again, "that you have such strong influence over other people's lives?"

He shrugged with such insolence I could feel my own patience being strained. "I have no influence over anyone, certainly not here. I merely observe" – and here he again turned a stern face to Catlyn – "that those who have defied me have suffered unpleasant consequences."

That wasn't mere insolence. That was a threat. I started to say we were done here, but Errique cut me off. How stunning it was to watch him work. Before I could open my mouth, he anticipated my intention, and just that quickly he was overflowing with concern. "Miss Stacey," he worried, "you seem quite unwell. If it's anything I've said, I beg your pardon."

I admit I was enthralled with his finesse. Any well-schooled normal person will tell you, it's impolite to be insensitive to someone who's expressing concern for you, and that's exactly how I responded to him. I hesitated, compelled not to be rude. I swear it was just a second's hesitation, but it was all he needed to launch another verbal attack.

"But, of course, I know you've been unwell for some time now. I suspect that as long as there is discord between myself and yourself, you will continue to feel unwell." And there he was again, reaching into Catlyn's mind to plant another suggestion, another prophesy for her to fulfill with endless moments of anxious thoughts.

I could see the tension rising in Catlyn's face. Errique was baiting her, trolling for the easy catch. I was sure she understood that, but Catlyn's strength ultimately rests on the rationality of her mind, and a rational mind is conditioned to refute an illogical claim, not to ignore it. That's the hook. You can't ignore it, and once hooked, the triggered emotional response elicited from your rational mind may be unstoppable.

Which made me all the more desperate to stop him. So I attacked, and before you ask, no, I'm not ashamed that I lost my cool. It's what the situation called for.

"Penance, Errique? Aren't you really thinking of parole? That's why you need an expression of forgiveness, isn't it? It's just not going to look good for you if the parole board thinks you're still a threat to Miss Stacey. Admit it; that's the real gist of this pathetic little ploy of yours."

Errique closed his eyes; he was the picture of a wounded soul, staggered by injustice. It was just insufferable how he could turn my snide remark into his personal injury.

"I know how it must look to a person like you."

I.e., like the inferior person that you are, he was telling me.

"It's your job to judge me, to pretend to understand me, to call me self-serving. That's what you're paid to do, so I accuse you of nothing. I simply tell you truly, I've given no thought to myself in any of this." He canted his head slightly towards Catlyn. "Truly, Miss Stacey, I think only of you."

Catlyn mimicked the tilt of his head. "You misunderstand me, Mr. Errique." The flat, emotionless voice had disappeared. Catlyn's tone was bitter and sharply etched with a highly acidic wash of disdain.

And it left me astonished. Astonished and distraught and distracted. I forgot about Errique and focused solely on her. The appearance of this new aspect of her personality was evidence of the very thing I warned her against, becoming more like Errique. In that moment, she was ruthless, and she was dishing back as callously as Errique had dealt to her.

"Your peace of mind is of no concern to me. I'm not even touched by your tale of woe." She shook her head in disappointment. "I must say, Errique, prison has dulled your wit. I expected better of you. This pathetic charade of decency? Really, Errique, how am I supposed to feel any sympathy for that?"

She looked scornful in a way I would never have believed possible, if I hadn't been there to see it myself.

Her expression changed to a smile as disingenuous as any Errique could conceive. Her voice was a taunting vibrato.

"But, as you know Errique, I am a considerate person. You've reached out to me, and I am moved to offer you this piece of advice."

The smile faded. Her tone hardened.

"Go back to your cell. Sit. Contemplate what has become of your Saint Sanaa. He was your invention to torment me. Let him now counsel you."

Catlyn stood to leave. We joined her.

Errique jumped up. To our backs as we walked away, he called out, "You are mistaken, Stacey." Harsh in tone, he blistered, "I sit in my cell, right enough. I sit, but I think of nothing but you. I think only of you."

It wasn't intended as a pleasant thought.

Chapter 13: Tilly

I just wanted to die. Why didn't she trust me?

It hurt, and I wanted to hurt her back.

And then I just wanted to die.

I couldn't understand why Miss Stacey would do that. She went to see that man in prison. She took Rose, but not me. She didn't even *tell* me.

I felt so awful I ran out from the house and out to the meadow. Rose came after me, but I didn't stop. I wanted to be alone. Biscuit, though, thought we were out for fun, and her barking gave me away. Rose found me by the creek.

I'd stopped crying by then, but I was still mad. I turned away and wouldn't look at her. I didn't even say hello.

That didn't stop Rose. She came along side and just stood next to me and started talking. I don't remember what she said at first. I was trying to ignore her. But then she asked, "Do you really suppose Catlyn doesn't trust you? Don't you think, just maybe, she did what she did to protect you?"

Rose can be like that, you know. Just when you've worked up a good snit, she goes and spoils it. I couldn't decide. I wanted one answer so I could be mad at everyone, and I wanted the other answer so I wouldn't be. Then she asked, "Do *you* trust *her*?" Rose is good at that too, making you be honest with yourself.

I didn't answer her, but she understood. "So do I," she said.

She let that stew in my mind for a few seconds, and then she told me, "There's so much on her plate right now, she really needs us. I think she knows we all want to protect her, and she needs us to do that. But I think she's afraid to ask us for help because she sees herself as the problem. *She wants to protect all of us from what's happening to her.*"

She, us, her. That made sense to me. I mean, it's exactly like Miss Stacey to want to protect us, and her needing us was exactly what I really wanted to believe.

Rose gave me one those like-it-or-not looks. "We can't let her do things that way. It's up to us to insist on helping her."

"But how, if she won't let us?"

"We don't take 'no' for an answer. It's just a matter of finding ways that don't make her feel like she's helpless and that don't make us look like we're acting out of pity."

"You know I'd do anything at all," I pleaded.

"I know," she said. "You and me both."

We stood there quietly for at bit. I was racking my brain for inspiration and getting nothing. Then Rose remarked, "You're her anchor to what's normal. That's something you should know. She told me that herself. More than anything else right now, she needs you to be her anchor. And another thing, she needs someone to accept whatever she does without question."

"Without question," she repeated like she was thinking about it. She put her arm around my shoulder. "I know it's a hard thing to ask of you, and it's probably not even fair. But you're the only one of us who can really do that for her, the only one. It has to be you. Without question."

Chapter 14: Whinehardt

The most basic, fundamental duty of a domestic is to serve the master of the house, or the mistress, as the case may be. Do that, and all else will follow as needed. In this day and age, the position of a domestic, indeed the very idea of such obedience, is soundly thrashed by much of the civilized world. Yet, I remind you that a long-standing tradition honors it. I myself have felt privileged to be part of that tradition for some three decades. In all my years of service to Southjoy Mission, I can say in all humility, I've never been accused of wavering in my duties. Always I've believed myself faithful and dependable.

Irregardless, I failed Miss Stacey, even if there is none but me who will say it. Oh, I know; to my face, people say, "It's not your fault." But, behind my back? That's different. I try to tell myself there wasn't any way I could know what Gaston was up to. But do I believe it? No, and neither to they. Listen to them, and you'll hear it in every word they don't say; they might just as well be pointing their fingers at me.

I can't say that I blame them any. They can't help it. Whether they want to or not, they judge me. They all do. Everybody except Miss Stacey. And how I wish she would. How I wish she would curse me with her disappointment.

Did I say "disappointment?" She should've been furious.

I felt so superior to her foreign ways when she first came to us. She was a fish out of water. It didn't matter that she was a Stacey. She didn't belong here.

That was only the first time I failed her. It was my place to serve her, and I didn't. It was my place to be tolerant of her foreign ways, and I wasn't. To the shame of myself and my position, it was she who was tolerant of me.

As much as I didn't want to discover the Stacey spirit in her, I couldn't help myself. She was alive with it. Can you imagine it? A real Stacey *and* an American. Now that's a spirited combination. And let me tell you, that spirited woman, so young in her years, somehow reminded us Brits of our own British pride. She saw a pride in our service that I think we ourselves had forgotten over the years. The only excuse that I can offer is that it just wore away with familiarity. Old Mr. Stacey said, do such and so, and we did it. It was the natural order of master and domestic. But not so with Miss Stacey. She didn't buy into that for a moment, and we resented her for it. She had an obligation to be superior, and we felt she wasn't. It seemed so obvious to us; she was flouting her American ways and belittling the station she inherited. But we soon learned that wasn't the case at all. She wasn't belittling herself; she was raising us up.

Thinking back, in many ways, she reminds me of a young captain I had in the war. He had no battle experience when he was given command over us. So of course, we were piteous in the crude and vulgar jibes we made behind his back. But, by god, in that first fire fight, he was steel against flint, a veritable barrage of flaming courage, and we owed him our lives. After that, we'd have followed him through the gates of hell, every man jack of us. That's how we came to feel about Miss Stacey.

And then I failed her again.

The staff is my responsibility, mine, and I should have noticed the irregularities in Gaston's behavior. He'd lost his wife; that seemed to me to excuse his conduct. I didn't press him, and I should have done. I should have questioned him. I should have demanded that he keep no secret from me.

When Gaston betrayed Miss Stacey, he betrayed me too. I'm sorry to make it so personal, but there it is. It's how I feel every time I see a worried look on Miss Stacey's face.

Like when she went to see that man in prison. There was much to see on her face after that. I've seen her worried before, and that wasn't worry. Something was eating away at her from inside.

Everyone talked about how brave she was. Even her doctor said so. He gave us a big pep talk about how she came away unscathed. But I don't think she did. There was no joy in her face. Something wasn't right.

That's why I told the staff I'd tolerate no problem in their tasks. Absolutely no one was to do anything that would trouble Miss Stacey in any way. I just wouldn't have it.

I suppose that's why I took particular umbrage with the workman who came to service our phone system. I hadn't ordered anything of the sort, and no one else would have done so without telling me first.

"What can I tell ya," he jabbered away at me. "It's what it says on the work order, check phone system."

"Check it for what, might I inquire?"

"It don't say, which it should. I don't mind, if ya know what I mean. It don't make no never mind ta me 'cuz I get paid the same no matter. Customer complains, I gotta check it out, ya know? So I just give it a once over, see what's what."

"I can well imagine. But let me save you the trouble. There's no what's what to be found here. Our line is quite satisfactory. So, I'm afraid you've made your journey here for nothing."

"Oh, it ain't for nothin'. I get paid, and you get billed. That's how it works. You got a problem with that, call the main office. They'll straighten it out."

Paid or not, I was miffed with the man's attitude and didn't apologize when I sent him packing. I wasn't tactful with the staff either. They all knew my order. I had warned them as clearly as I know how. So now, somebody would have to answer for this.

Missus Sweetgrove was as much mystified as I was. On her suggestion, I next checked with Rose. Miss Stacey gives her a free hand, more or less, about the estate, so it was possible that she could have ordered a repair of some kind without telling me, but that too proved not to be the case.

Maybe we were getting worked up over nothing, but it was a mystery, and we didn't like it. It definitely worried Rose. "Did he actually touch anything? I mean, did he do anything to the phones?"

I was glad I could tell her, "No, nothing at all. I sent him away, and he left without an argument."

"Did the work order say who asked for the work? Did he leave a copy?"

He had, but there was nothing useful on it. I suppose all they needed was a phone number and an address.

That prompted Rose to say she'd show it to DI Malbec. "There are two things Ned doesn't like, coincidences and things left unexplained. There's been too much of that here."

Chapter 15: Tilly

I was swept up by the idea that I was the only person who could make Miss Stacey feel good in spite of everything. I knew Rose was only consoling me for being "left out" when they went to see Rupert Errique in prison. But I also knew that what she was saying made a lot of sense. Everyone was trying to help Miss Stacey, which, in a sense, meant everyone was telling her what was wrong with her. No one was just accepting her, telling her what was right with her. So, that was going to be me.

Still, I wanted to actually *do* something.

I found my chance in the coming holidays. It was going to be Miss Stacey's first Christmas at Southjoy Mission, and she seemed excited about it. Maybe "excited" wasn't exactly the right word. She wasn't all bubbly about it, but if you looked hard, you could see a hopefulness underneath all her worries. I could see it anyways, and that was enough for me.

I'd never myself actually thought of Christmas as exciting. There were always a few decorations in the staff quarters, of course, and a few in the grand foyer, but nothing extravagant. Maybe it was out of respect for Mr. Stacey who was sick for such a long time. But sick or not, he always made a point of passing out gifts for the house staff on Christmas Eve. Following that, we always had a special meal that Cook prepared for us. It could've been catered so Cook could have the day off too, but it seems Cook wouldn't stand for it. "The very idea," she huffed and steamed and grumbled until Mr. Stacey gave her leave to take charge of the whole thing.

Mr. Stacey's gifts to us were really more like Christmas

bonuses than gifts; they just weren't personal. Except for the first gift Mr. Stacey gave me. Cook said it was the only time he ever did something like that.

I still remember it because now it's a memory filled with mixed emotions. I was happy, then sad, then happy again. You see, it wasn't what it seemed to be at the time, but it turned out to be even better, which I've only just now discovered.

It was after he first took sick and while I was still more mascot than staff. He called me forward by name, right there in front of everyone. Nobody had warned me he was going to do that, and it frightened me because he'd never even spoken to me before. I was frightened, and I didn't know what to expect. I hadn't been running or making lots of noise, and I hadn't spilled anything. So what did he want?

While I was trying to stop shaking, he told me, "There are too many forgotten people." That's all he said. He just stood there looking very sad and very old, and then he handed me a gift wrapped in beautiful paper and tied with curly ribbon, which I still have. I almost spoiled the paper because I started crying. He patted me on the head and said, "We should always remember our real families. Of all the lessons there are in life, that's the most important one. I pray always for mine, wherever they might be. Wherever."

At the time, I didn't really know what a family was supposed to be. I just knew I didn't have one, and I guess I wanted to believe this was his way of saying I could be part of his. "Of course it is," Cook told me. I wanted to believe that, but it was very strange. He didn't even know who I was. He had to ask somebody to point me out to him. Still, I wanted it, and it made me feel that I really belonged here. So, true or not, I insisted on remembering the experience the way I wanted it to be. To me, it proved I belonged here.

It was only after Miss Stacey was kidnapped that I finally learned the truth. He wasn't thinking about me at all. He was actually thinking about his granddaughter, Miss Stacey, who never knew he cared. I can't ever know that for sure, of course, but I keep remembering little things, like how sad he was every time another letter came from the States and how angry he pretended to be when he'd tell Whinehardt to take it away without opening it. It wasn't until we learned how he was protecting her that any of it made any sense.

It turned out Mr. Stacey was working "under cover" to help Scotland Yard capture some bigtime art thieves. He didn't want them to know he had a granddaughter because they might have done something to her. As you know, after he died and Miss Stacey inherited the estate, that's exactly what they did; it's what Rupert Errique did anyway. But Mr. Stacey wasn't to know that Errique wouldn't be captured or that he'd be so bizarre and twisted and so hateful.

So, all things considered, I know Mr. Stacey cared about his granddaughter, and that's what I'm going to tell Miss Stacey at Christmas. That's going to be my gift to her. And it is a gift, because I have to give up the only piece of "home" I ever had in order for it to be real.

Anyway, while Christmas Eve at the estate was filled with festivities, Christmas Day itself was quiet. Those staff with family or friends nearby usually went visiting, and often they took longer vacations at that time. I had no place to go, so I just stayed here. I wasn't lonely or anything like that because there was a lot to do to get ready for what came next.

It was the tradition of the estate that everyone be reunited on Little Christmas, which is the day of Epiphany.

We celebrated that day with a big feast that was always held in the great banquet room. We all got to invite our friends and relatives, and Mr. Stacey always invited the estate's tenants because, he said, they were as much a part of the estate as we were.

Little Christmas was a new idea for Miss Stacey. She was fascinated by it, but I don't think it was the feasting that intrigued her. It was the thought of having everybody together, like remembering your real family. Leave it to Dr. Ulma to spoil it by saying he hoped this wasn't just another desperate attempt to avoid her grief instead of confronting it. Someday *I am* going to kick him in the shins.

Nevertheless, for quite a while, it seemed like we talked about Little Christmas over breakfast almost every day. After Miss Stacey's rescue, Rose and I had started taking breakfast with her every morning in the tea room. It wasn't anything anyone ever discussed. It just sort of became our daily routine. I think we both felt that Miss Stacey didn't like being alone. That was something else we didn't discuss, and we didn't say anything about it to Dr. Ulma either, or about how she always wanted to be near a window.

We did talk about the holidays, though, and that's what led to today's agenda. Miss Stacey was taking me shopping.

We'd done serious shopping together only once before. That was to find Miss Stacey a dress for her dinner with Lord Silverworth before, well, you know, before all that other stuff happened.

This shopping spree was to be different. We weren't looking for anything special; we were just going to do a lot of browsing, some window shopping, and maybe a bit of wish-listing. It was too soon for the Bath Christmas Market, which would begin at the end of November, but there were plenty of shops and windows to keep us busy in

Milsom Place where, as it turned out, we spent the whole morning and most of the afternoon. Miss Stacey said the one thing she wanted to do for sure today was go shopping on Pulteney Bridge, so that was our one fixed destination. But something happened.

We were standing outside on a sidewalk in Milsom Place looking at a window display when suddenly Miss Stacey caught her breath, you know, the way you do when you're startled by something that's frightened you. Her eyes were drawn tight, and she was staring at the window. I followed her eyes into the display, but I couldn't see anything that should've bothered her. I looked back at her to ask, "Is something wrong?" That's when she very carefully put her hand on my shoulder, you know, like she was trying not to make any sudden moves. Then, very calmly, she asked, "Do you see the two men in the window here, watching us from across the street?" She meant the reflections in the window, and yes, I could see them and said so. They were standing at the curb, and they definitely seemed to be watching us. She said, "I've seen them before. They're the ones I saw outside Dr. Ulma's office." I didn't understand what she meant, but before I could ask her about it, she whirled around to look straight at them. They jumped back like they were surprised, and then they were quick away, almost running.

Miss Stacey stared at them until they disappeared around a corner. Even then, she kept staring like maybe they'd be coming back.

She was upset and angry, and it was scaring me. "What's going on?" I asked her. "What was that about?" She didn't answer right away, and that scared me even more because the longer she stared, the angrier she was getting. I pulled at her sleeve to get her attention and tried asking, "Miss Stacey?"

Finally, she took a deep breath and turned her head to look at me. She tried to pretend it wasn't anything, telling me, "Nothing I hope. Just an overactive imagination. Nothing to worry about." But it wasn't so, and I knew it.

I knew it wasn't just her imagination because very quietly she said, "Let's go home," but we didn't turn to go until she'd looked back again across the street.

All the way home, Miss Stacey kept gripping her arms like she was cold, and she kept casting sharp glances at Jason. Then she'd look hard out the window, first one side then the other, and then back to Jason. She was "preoccupied," and we didn't talk much. Nothing more was said about Pulteney Bridge.

Chapter 16: Appeal

The watchword for the day was "ominous."

Having been alerted to the situation by Tilly, Amelia decided to be on-site early so she could join Catlyn for a quick cup of coffee before setting off for her day's project. It seemed like a good idea at the time, but when she announced that she'd be spending the day at the cave, Catlyn's face flashed in several hues of apprehension.

"Alone?"

The surprise in Catlyn's voice was vividly reflected in the worry on her face. It was foolish of her; you could see she knew that. But the shopping incident with Tilly had put her on-edge, and now this? She was trying not to yield to her anxiety, but her startled expression was too quick to suppress. She did stop short of arguing against Amelia going to the cave; that much she could still manage, even though she was *inclined* to argue.

Most often these days, Catlyn's biggest arguments were with herself. It had never been easy for her to be restrained in the heat of an anxious moment, but she was becoming more accustomed to it. She really had no choice in the matter. Still, it's hard to be restrained when you're afraid. Compound that fear with a flare of anxiety, and it's reason enough to ignite a blaze of doubt and worry.

Fortunately, Amelia understood Catlyn's dilemma all too well. Their relationship had progressed beyond that first bond formed between them when desperation gave them no other option. True enough, captivity imposed that bond by the sheer necessity of it. But now, there was more; there was a mutual dependence derived from the fear of letting go. They were afraid to meet the world alone and move forward on the strength of their own courage. Inevitably fear pulled them closer together. So fundamentally, it was still the lingering terror of captivity that impelled their closeness.

One of the goals Dr. Ulma had set for himself was to separate the memory of the event from the emotion of the event. It's possible, he contended, to remember a bad dream in detail and not be as frightened by it as you were when you were dreaming it. While the memory might never be erased, the theory was that the fear of it could be extinguished.

For both Catlyn and Amelia, the terror of captivity had deeply stained their lives, and that stain was yet imbedded in their memories. They both wanted and needed to get past the emotion of it, as Dr. Ulma insisted, and past the irrational sense of shame it made them feel. The crux of the matter was that the desperation they'd felt in captivity had never truly relented. Getting to that point had become a quest they shared. They were grasping for a lifeline, and there wasn't yet one to be found. There was, however, a sense of security in the knowledge that they were reaching for it together. Perhaps it was like that old adage about friendship – a worry shared is a worry halved.

Security and friendship. It seemed so little to ask for. Why then, they would sometimes despair, why did it seem to be so far beyond hope? They tried. Of course they tried. And they were nearly halfway there. They nearly had the assurance of true friendship. Nearly.

The biggest issue, of course, was trust. Between them, there'd always be a trace of tension in that regard, probably. Nothing in nature required it, but they both seemed to understand that's how it was always going to be. But it wasn't anything they couldn't handle. They'd just always have to be careful to suppress their suffering so it wouldn't intrude on them.

For Amelia, there was no question about it. She wasn't ever going to relinquish her obligation to Catlyn. Privately, she was adamant about that. Talking heart-to-heart with her grandfather, she told him, "Catlyn's anxiety is my fault, and I don't think I can ever stop being ashamed of it. I know I was duped, but that just makes it worse." In her own self-recriminating estimation, she'd been absolutely pathetic in the way she was so readily manipulated by Wythiry and Errique. And, of course, the history of that affair weighed heavily on the issue of trust. But they worried for each other, and that was good. Worry is just one of the avenues you have to travel on the route to trust.

Like going to the scene of your captivity; that was cause for worry.

"I know what you're thinking," said Amelia, "and yes, I'm going alone. Unless," she added hopefully, "you'd like to come with me?"

Catlyn stiffened. "I... I don't think I could do that just yet."

"You wouldn't have to stay long. It's not a terrible place."

"I know. One day..." She shuddered. "Just not yet."

"Okay," allowed Amelia. "It's okay."

She peered at Catlyn for a second, at the desolate look that seemed to descend over her. "You know," she began, "you're my hero; my personal hero. You know that, don't you? You had the courage to face Rupert Errique. Surely, if you can do that, I can face an empty cave."

She took a sip of coffee, watching Catlyn's reaction. "In a sense," she encouraged, "the cave was a victim too. We shouldn't be afraid of it. Whether it's you or me, or the cave, or even Southjoy Mission, victims shouldn't be punished for being abused. That's what the cave is, another abused part of the estate. It needs our care and attention."

Firm and confident. Spot on rational. It was nearly too much. Catlyn felt herself drenched in anxiety, felt herself drowning in the dismay of it, sinking into the angst of surrender. Her expression, visibly disturbed, exuded her private torment. She forced herself to say, "Ariana couldn't have said it better." The thought of it caused her to swallow softly. She pushed, "If you keep up that attitude, you just might become the new champion for Southjoy Mission."

She'd said it honestly, but wished it wasn't true, wished she could still see herself as carrying Ariana's banner, wished that she didn't feel like she'd stumbled and fallen. It was a struggle not to look away, not to feel like she'd failed in the one quest she firmly believed had been entrusted to her by her greatly great grandmother, Ariana. Her Ariana.

"That's the plan," Amelia answered with a self-conscious smile. She wanted it to be true, knew that maybe it was already true, and she felt guilty that it was. She submitted, "But you'll always be Ariana's champion. No one's as close to her as you are, and no one ever will be. You're her champion."

That was perhaps a step too far distant for Catlyn to go at this moment, and abruptly she did look away. Her eyes searched into the distance as though something was fleeing from her; her own life, perhaps, her purpose and her reason for being. She had to find them and bring them back.

She fought off a sudden urge to cry. *Grit your teeth*, she scolded herself. *Stop being such a wimp. Take a deep breath and hold it; hold onto it until you're good and ready to fight again. You can do that. Hold it. And fight.*

She cringed. She hated this, the feeling of being weak and helpless. And they were wrong, all of them. She wasn't a fighter. She wasn't. She didn't want to fight anymore.

Urgently she changed the subject. "Any news from Rip?"

The sigh from Amelia was a mixture of longing and frustration. "Nothing," she lamented. "He called about a week ago to tell me he was going on a job tour to interview with five labs in three states. I was hoping he'd call me along the way with updates, but it's difficult, you know, with time differences and airport schedules and, well, you know him. He's probably spending every waking moment cramming his mind full of facts and figures before each interview. That makes it hard to coordinate our schedules. Still, I wish he'd at least leave me a voice message or text me or something."

The day continued in that out-of-kilter mode when Whinehardt interrupted them to announce that a Mr. Taunton had rung up to speak to Miss Stacey. "He says he's a solicitor." There was something not quite neutral in Whinehardt's expression.

"Says?" asked Catlyn. She was puzzled. "He's not from Mr. Galler's office?"

"He made no mention of Mr. Galler. Shall I inquire further?"

Amelia swung around to face Whinehardt. "Yes, you should!" She seemed indignant that there was any question about it. She turned back to Catlyn who was frowning at her. "It's a simple precaution," she insisted. On-site meant on-guard, as far as Amelia was concerned. She justified, "You can't be too careful these days with all the scams and shams out there calling every random number they can generate." It was unlikely, though, that scams and shams were anywhere near the focus of her thoughts at that moment.

Nodding, but distracted, Catlyn was trying to remember, "Taunton. That name sounds vaguely familiar." She tried to recall the many solicitors who had talked to her when she first learned of her inheritance, but no one by that name came to mind. "Patch him through to me," she directed. Glancing at Amelia, she allowed, "I can always hang up if I don't like what he has to say." Amelia's glare suggested she didn't quite agree. "It'll be fine," Catlyn assured her. "Besides, you need to get going. Your cave's waiting."

"It can wait a few minutes more," Amelia suggested.

Catlyn countered, "Procrastination is asap's evil twin, you know."

Amelia canted her head. "Grannie Effie?"

"Un-huh." Catlyn lifted her chin in a defiant challenge.

"Did she have a saying for every situation?"

"Pretty much, and if she didn't, she made one up."

"Made it up? Why do I get the impression there's a grannie kid following the footsteps of Grannie Effie?"

"What? You think I'd make up a thing like that myself?"

Amelia considered that. "I don't know. Maybe, if..."

"If what?"

Amelia was quiet a moment. She didn't want to say.

Catlyn demanded, "If what?"

Amelia sighed. It needed to be said. "Sometimes you make me wonder if you use Grannie Effie as a shield."

Catlyn swallowed. The shock of truth is hard to refute. "And if I do, don't you think I need a shield sometimes, all the time?"

"Not all the time. Not if I'm here too. Or Rose. Or Tilly."

Stress lines around Catlyn's eyes pulled tighter. Amelia soothed, "Okay, I'm going to the cave. But promise me. You'll hang up if it's anything to do with Rupert Errique."

"Of course I will," Catlyn snapped. Horrified, she relented. "I'm sorry. I'm..." A sigh finished her thought. "You're right. I'm sorry. I'll hang up. I will. I promise."

"Okay," Amelia allowed softly.

"Okay," Catlyn replied. Eased, she said, "Okay, then. So, your cave?" Amelia conceded with a nod and stood to leave.

Shooing her out the door, Catlyn sighed. Holding fast against the rising clamor of fatigue, she took the call.

§§§

The voice of the caller was a deep, silky baritone; smooth, some would say; confident and ingratiating. The kind of voice that ensnares your acquiescence. The kind that croons in your ear – "Miss Stacey, my name is Anton Taunton. My firm represents Mr. Rupert Errique." Screeches, shrieks, and squawks. A note sung off key. Such as these would make a more pleasant sound than the name of Rupert Errique.

Catlyn fumed, "Then you've got the wrong number."

"Forgive me, Miss Stacey," the voice soothed urgently. "That was indelicate of me. I only meant it by way of introduction. This is not a legal matter, I assure you."

"Nothing about Mr. Errique is ever legal, as far as I've ever heard."

"It's an unfortunate reputation; you're quite right about that. But, if I may say so, in all the years I've known Mr. Errique, that view of him is more hearsay than fact."

His voice sang his words, purred them softly, and floated them into a soothing melody. Or it could have done, were it not for the refrain of "Rupert Errique." How inordinately offensive was that sound. It was all too easy to imagine this Mr. Taunton sitting in a sleazy rented office space drenched in the stale odors of mildew and burnt tobacco.

He claimed to know Errique and wasn't repulsed by

him? That didn't seem likely. Not unless he was of the same species as Errique. You know, birds of a feather and all that.

"Miss Stacey," said Taunton, coming straight to the point. "I've been petitioned by Mr. Errique to contact you about a personal matter."

"Personal?! Mr. Taunton, let me save you a lot of wasted time. There's nothing personal between me and anyone remotely connected with Errique."

"If you would allow me to explain..."

"Explain?" Her voice was rising. "If there was anything to explain, you'd be talking to my solicitor, Mr. Galler, not to me." Suspiciously she added, "If you were a real solicitor, you'd know that."

"Under normal circumstances, I would agree with you entirely, but Mr. Errique assures me this is a delicate matter."

"Mr. Taunton, you clearly don't know Errique at all. Delicacy is inconceivable in anything involving him."

"Mr. Errique anticipated your reluctance and instructed me to convey to you a very simple message. It doesn't mean anything to me, but he insists you'll understand it."

Foul play, that, appealing to the vanity of the intellect. Every fiber of her being was telling her, *hang up, hang up now*, but the vanity of understanding something other's don't? The mind can't help itself. It wants to know.

"What do you mean?"

"Just this, and I'm instructed to say it to you verbatim: *Your forgiveness, and then no more of thee and me.*"

Catlyn was stunned into silence. How did... There's no way he... unless... She felt herself reeling. She reached. Tried to steady herself. Blood drained from her head. The room turned. Her lungs rebelled against the air. Her mind descended into darkness.

§§§

Dr. Ulma had administered a mild tranquilizer to calm her, and she was resting, eyes closed, retreating into a sheltering sleep. After the incident of paranoia at his office, Dr. Ulma had taken the precaution of insisting that everyone close to Catlyn should have an emergency contact number speed dialed straight to him. It was an unusual precaution for a patient who seemed to have no imminent risk of harm or danger to herself, but the present incident seemed to justify the doctor's instinct.

It was Sweetgrove who summoned him. Hearing the crash when Catlyn fell, Sweetgrove had rushed to her side. She found Catlyn semi-conscious and writhing with agitation. Grabbing onto Sweetgrove, her fingers digging hard into Sweetgrove's arms, Catlyn began gasping hysterically, "Make him stop. *Make him stop!*" Whinehardt arrived, and together they moved Catlyn to the sitting room where she remained erratic in thought and inconsolable until Dr. Ulma arrived.

"She received a call from a Mr. Taunton," Whinehardt volunteered when Catlyn had been mercifully sedated. "After that, I don't know."

"The phone was on the floor," acknowledged Sweetgrove, "but I didn't know there was a call." She looked at Dr. Ulma. "I just called you and put it back on its stand."

They turned to see Amelia rushing in. Heinrich had been dispatched to alert her to Catlyn's collapse. As she hurried to join them, she heard Rose asking, "So who's Taunton?"

"He claimed to be a solicitor," Amelia answered.

Whinehardt's confirmation left Rose unsettled and

shaking her head. A quick call to Ned turned up the name of Anton Taunton, a solicitor in the same firm that represented Rupert Errique. Incensed, Rose rang up Taunton's office, demanding to speak to him immediately. A polite receptionist said she was sorry, but Mr. Taunton was away for the day, and no, there was no call placed to Miss Stacey.

§§§

Awake, calm, yet under the influence of the tranquilizer, Catlyn opened her eyes to see Dr. Ulma's encouraging smile hovering over her. She was lying prone on the large sofa in the sitting room. Tilly was on the floor crouching on her knees beside Catlyn, while across the room, Amelia was standing next to Rose. They all seemed to be engaged in a chorus of furrowed brows, intent stares, and taut postures.

Confused and disoriented, her vision blurry, Catlyn closed her eyes again trying to come to grips with what happened. She remembered a phone call and Amelia heading out to her day at the cave. Suddenly she sat bolt up. "How did he know?" she demanded. Looking fiercely at Dr. Ulma, she demanded again, "How did he know?"

Tilly twisted around to Dr. Ulma. "Know what?" Seeing the perplexed look on his face, she swung back to Catlyn. "Know what?" She reached up to take Miss Stacey's hand.

Catlyn clasped both of her hands around Tilly's fingers; her breathing was labored. Staring at Tilly, she took a second to calm herself, then she nodded. "Of course." Another second lapsed, another breath taken, then she forced herself to say, "My nightmares." Her eyes snapped into a glare at Dr. Ulma. "You're the only one who knew, the only one who knows what Sebastian says to me." Her plaintive tone turned to bitterness. "How did he know?"

"I'm at a loss..." he started to say, but hesitated with a look at Tilly. "Tilly, I think it'd be a good idea to let me talk to Miss Stacey alone."

"No! I'm not leaving." She appealed to Catlyn. "Don't make me leave."

"None of us are leaving," Amelia challenged. She took a threatening step towards Dr. Ulma.

Catlyn sided with Tilly. "I've disturbed Tilly's sleep enough with my nightmares. She deserves to know what we're fighting against. They all do."

Restraining his frustration, Dr. Ulma acquiesced. "Alright then, tell me, first, what did Mr. Taunton say?"

Still clinging to Tilly's hand, Catlyn adjusted her position on the sofa. She motioned for Tilly to sit next to her. The distraction gave her time to settle her thoughts.

"Mr. Taunton claimed he had a message from Rupert Errique. He said he didn't understand the message himself, but Errique assured him I would." She hesitated. A dread pummeled her thoughts; her ears filled with its deafening drone causing her to shudder, to look down, to close her eyes. Her grip tightened around Tilly's fingers. She forced her eyes open to look at Dr. Ulma. A deep breath allowed her to say, "Your forgiveness, *and then no more of thee and me.*"

Dr. Ulma looked stricken. He seemed disoriented. "That's not possible," he muttered. Confused, thoughts plunging in disarray, he absently found the armchair by the sofa. Slowly he lowered himself onto it. A frown overshadowed his face.

"I don't understand," said Tilly. "What's it mean?"

Catlyn closed her eyes and took another deep breath to calm the agitation churning her thoughts into a tangle of anger and fear. Retreating deeper into the privacy of her mind, she sought the comfort of her last sheltering refuge. Sebastian was there, still watching and protecting her, still smitten, still saying, "...*and her light was like unto a stone most precious.*" That was a real memory. They'd just met. Courtney had introduced them. Catlyn smiled to him now. He gazed on her. Encouraged her. Gave her strength to tell them what they needed to hear.

She opened her eyes and drew another deep breath. Staring then at the floor, struggling to speak, she tried to say, "*And then no more of thee and me*; in my nightmares..." She choked. Struggled. Began again. "In my nightmares, those are the last words Sebastian says to me." Tears seeped uninhibited from her eyes. "He loved me. He never wanted an end to us. And yet, it's always the same. *And then no more of thee and me.*" She glared through her tears to demand again, "How did he know that?" She implored him; she begged and pleaded, "How did he know?"

Stricken still, Dr. Ulma was shaking his head. "I'm at a loss." He tried to think. He suggested, "It's conceivable that it's just a coincidence." He didn't sound convinced.

Tilly wasn't buying it. "How?" she challenged.

Leaning forward, he supported his elbows against the armrests of his chair. Stress showed in the way his right hand clasped over left fist. The clenching grip suggested desperation. There had to be an explanation. "Those words are from the Rubáiyát of Omar Khayyam. It's conceivable..."

"No it isn't," Catlyn refuted him. Her tone was harsh and accusing. "It's not just the words. He said he *knew* I would understand it. There's only one way he could know it means something to me."

She stared at Dr. Ulma. A cold anguish was gripping at her heart. She denounced him. "You told him."

The accusation stung. Vigorously, fervently, he protested, "No! I've told no one. I'd never do that, certainly not to you. *Never* could I do that to you. I've not discussed your case with anyone. I'd never do *anything* to hurt you. I'd *never...*"

Their eyes met. She wanted desperately to believe him. Anger had stifled the flow of tears, but not the suspicion that went with it. That still gnawed at her thoughts, and it bristled in her tone. "What else could it be then?"

Desolate, assaulted by futility, he pleaded, "I don't know. Unless somebody's broken into my records, then..."

Tilly's eyes flared. "Where do you keep them, your records; on your computer?"

"Yes, of course, but it's a secure system, if that's what you're thinking. You can't access it without a password."

"Cloud storage or on your hard drive?"

"I'm not sure. It's a shared system. It's run by the hospital for their medical records. We all use it, but as I said, you need a password."

Tilly was shaking her head with disgust. "Any half-decent nerd can hack that system. There's always a back door."

Amelia was nodding as she looked at Catlyn. It made sense. "A flaw in computer security." It was common enough these days, even likely. "That explains the how. But what's the why? What are you supposed to understand by it?"

Thoughts were churning in Catlyn's mind. A double meaning? Both threat and promise? *I can taunt you*, he was saying, *but I'll leave you alone if you do what I ask?*

Catlyn studied her hands, her fingers, the way they were interlaced over Tilly's hand. Her expression darkened. "Errique, Wythiry, and Ormy," she declared. "It's back to them again. They're up to something. Don't ask me how I know. I just know it."

Then, an understanding.

"Somehow, they need me for whatever they're planning. But they can't approach me directly, so..." Her eyes flared. She stiffened. "He's luring me." Her face radiated disgust.

But it was intriguing, too, the way Rupert Errique was reaching into her mind again. Luring her.

She fumed, "That has to be what it is. He wants *me* to go to *him*, to meet with him again."

"I forbid it," Dr. Ulma declared in vehement rejection. "I absolutely forbid it."

Catlyn looked into the distance. Her face had turned pale, like a mask of prophesied death. "Of course," she nodded without regard to anyone, her voice a whisper breathing into the silence of a foul-fated scene. Her expression was pensive and quiet. Vacant and isolated. Ominous.

Chapter 17: Ethan

There's something very soothing about a mundane chore, don't you think? Maybe the monotony of it dulls the senses. A tranquillizer does that too, of course, but pills take your mind out of the picture. A task, even a mundane one, can give you a sense of accomplishment.

That's what came to mind when I listened to Amelia's account of Catlyn's episode with the phone call. Nobody wants to say it out loud, but the truth is, Catlyn's problems are, in fact, all in her mind. This latest episode just made it that much clearer how much Catlyn's mind needed a diversion, specifically something to pull her thoughts away from Rupert Errique. As Dr. Ulma put it, a wound can't heal if it's continuously irritated, and Errique was most certainly an irritant to Catlyn's mind. It seemed to me, the misery in Catlyn's life, thanks to Rupert Errique, had gone beyond mere irritation. It was festering like an infection.

That made me think of Gerald. It's not a great exaggeration to say Gerald's life was also infected with misery. According to Lady Stacey's diary, Prunella was the remarkable antiseptic that cured his particular infection. I intended she'd do the same for Catlyn.

I rang up Willy and asked him to email Catlyn the next Prunella letter, asap. I didn't care if it was fully vetted or not; just get it to her. Then I rang up Catlyn to say I'd be at the estate later that day so we could talk about it.

I would have preferred to get out there sooner, but I was committed to giving one of my little lectures that morning for the hospital auxiliary. It seems that all the attention in the news stemming from Catlyn's abduction and rescue has made me something of a local celebrity. It's nothing more than fame by association, but it's made me "in demand" as a speaker. Mrs. Ock, who heads the program committee, has been quite persistent. She's a widow, nearly a year older than me, but acts ten years my junior. She calls me her "wise old fool." Lately, I've started to believe she's got me pegged spot on. I'm wise in matters of history, and downright foolish when it comes to the present day. Sometimes I think my mind has gone blind to what's happening right around me.

I took great pleasure in telling Mrs. Ock about working with Catlyn on the history of Southjoy Mission. "How thrilling it must be for you," was her first thought. And she was right. Early on, it was all about being focused, being alive, so much so that I rather neglected my attention to Amelia. I was lax too in noting how Catlyn's personal issues were mounting. I didn't see the trouble brewing, and I completely missed the hand of Lady Wythiry in it all.

A wise old fool, that certainly was me. I suppose I should be grateful to Rupert Errique for the wakeup call. Well, not grateful, but I've certainly learned my lesson. "Study the past," Mrs. Ock admonished me. "Don't live in it." She was right, of course, as she often is.

When I went out to the estate with Prunella's letter, though, I didn't need any wakeup call to see the darkness in Catlyn's eyes. At first, I was inclined to think it was just a result of sleepless nights, but that wasn't it. It wasn't just the puffy eyes with the dark rings about them. Every feature of her face had been ratcheted to a severe tautness. I would've been less disturbed if she were merely brooding or even wallowing in her misery. But this seemed to be much darker than that, like she was contemplating doing something she'd regret, knew she'd regret it, and was going to do it anyways.

I know, I know. I'm interpreting without all the facts,

but even an old fool can be worried sick for someone he cares about.

I had hoped that the anticipation of reading the Prunella letter would at least encourage a fleeting smile when I arrived, but there was nothing like it. She was all business.

Even reminding her of the voyage Prunella was making with her new husband, Gerald, didn't raise any interest. I was sure that mentioning Gerald's name would encourage her to talk about Gerald's namesake, her own ancestor, Gerald Aloysius Stacey, who was Lady Stacey's youngest son. That used to be something Catlyn loved to talk about. But, no. She merely nodded and pickup up her tablet to begin reading.

> *I have endeavored to cultivate an acquaintance with other passengers, but that has proven difficult. One of the officers, Mr. Joshua, has paid particular attention to me, and that has aligned most of the women passengers against me. They say I am a flirt, and one matronly woman said I was a shameful hussy. But, dear Ariana, I am not! I think them jealous of me. I am pretty and fresher than they, and that is the whole of it. I would not mind their unkind gossip, but I fear Gerald is beginning to side with them. I cannot be sure, of course, but there was an instance of unpleasantness between Gerald and Mr. Joshua after Mr. Joshua tipped his cap to me. I do not believe there was anything improper about it, but Gerald said something very harsh to Mr. Joshua. I have never seen Gerald upset in such manner, and I am chilled to think of what might have transpired were it not for my own presence.*

Catlyn paused to "humph." She said, "She shouldn't

have been upset. He was protecting her."

I was surprised by the way Catlyn said that. You could almost say it was bemused, and the small, tired frown resting briefly on her face gave that impression as well. "Good people are like that." She spoke like she was musing aloud. "They don't let the gossips or the Durke Ormys of the world abuse the people they care about." She didn't even look at me for comment. She just continued reading.

> *Later, there was another confrontation involving also Mr. Jackson, the gentleman lodged in steerage. Mr. Jackson speaks with much refinement, but I judge him to be of devious nature, and Mrs. Mimms reports he is coarse with his fellow lodgers in steerage. Gerald and Mr. Jackson were speaking, I know not what of, as I was some distance from them, when Mr. Joshua came forth to interrupt them. It seemed to me, Mr. Joshua was very rude to Mr. Jackson. Gerald stepped between them and offered reply, which appeared to give cause for Mr. Joshua to be upset to the point of anger. Fortunately, Captain James was at hand to insist that there be no disturbance. Gerald has since declined to explain the situation to me, and I am fraught with suspicions.*
> *– Prunella, Letter No. A2, 1810*

"Yes. Now that she should be disturbed about."

That she said with some disgust, and she definitely looked miffed about something. I wasn't looking to start an argument, but Catlyn was breaking the rules, and I think she knew it. She was veering into the forbidden realm of personal judgment, and she was completely lacking the requisite support of academic evidence. I had to object. "That seems a rather damning assertion to make when there's so little evidence of any wrongdoing."

"Maybe, but it's a sensible view," she countered at once. "Look at the dynamics of the three men. They're not acting like jealous men. You've read all the things Ariana wrote in her diary about Prunella and Gerald. After what they went through together? The way they clung together in crisis? Nothing's going to come between them. And Gerald knows that. Uh-uh, I just don't believe it. He's not concerned about Prunella. There's something else going on with those three."

She was jumping to conclusions that I couldn't see, but I didn't want to argue about it. I thought it best at that point to change our focus to the context of the letter; that is, where were they at this point in their journey and what conditions might they be experiencing? We developed an action plan and dispatched Tilly with the bulk of the assignment, which principally was a matter of searching the internet for information.

That still left me with my concern about Catlyn. She was reading things into our observations in a way that seemed very aggressive, and it wasn't productive. It was like she was deliberately trying to pick a fight, with us or them or both. She *wanted* something bad to be happening on that ship.

I was worried enough to ask Dr. Ulma about it, because I didn't want to be guilty of doing the same thing myself, jumping to conclusions without sufficient evidence.

"It's quite possible she's projecting her own dilemma onto Prunella in a way we didn't intend," he told me. "Instead of merely identifying with Prunella's problems, she's *giving* Prunella the very issues Catlyn herself is struggling with."

"So you think she's mixing her own circumstances with those of Prunella?"

"I know that sounds peculiar, but it could explain why you see her jumping to conclusions while she sees it as logical deduction. When she combines the two sets of circumstances, she's looking at data that you can't see."

I didn't much like the murky implications behind that explanation, and I told him so. He allowed that there were other possibilities. People whose minds have been put on extreme alert, he explained, may well be sensitized to details the rest of us miss. If that's the case, Catlyn might be latching onto little nuances in the words and expressions that Prunella used in her letters.

That sounded more plausible, but not entirely convincing. The more I thought about it, the less I liked it. I mean, doesn't a mind on-edge start to imagine things? In my experience, nuances aren't objective. You've got to read something into them. Isn't that like seeing things that aren't there? An active mind can play tricks on you. You've been warned to watch out for something, and suddenly you start seeing it. Or you want other people to have problems because you've got problems, like wanting something to be wrong on Prunella's ship. That's the same as witnessing something that didn't happen, isn't it?

Still, Dr. Ulma wouldn't miss something like that.

Chapter 18: Amelia

Jumping to conclusions? How about jumping off a cliff?!

Grandfather wasn't a happy camper when we talked last night. He'd been fretting all evening, and that's always a good clue he's got something on his mind. It was an easy guess it had something to do with Catlyn. I could see he was aching to get it off his chest, so I decided to indulge him. I tempted him with a glass of sherry, which we took in the gentlemen's leisure room. That's just what the room's called; it's not for gentlemen only; long ago maybe; but now it's just more masculine in décor; leather furniture, paintings depicting hunting and fishing scenes, and things like that. I like it because some artefacts I recovered from the cave are displayed there. The skeleton I'd found early on dated from 1430 to 1570 AD, which was the right time period for Edmund Plagyts (d. 1503 AD). So the artifacts found nearby could've belonged to him, which made the find exciting (to me) and relevant (to Southjoy Mission).

Grandfather's displeasure, it seems, was incurred because Catlyn had been "wildly jumping to conclusions" about the Prunella letters when she knew very well her speculations couldn't be proven. That's a cardinal sin in academia, and the little quirks he gets when he's riled up were popping out in abundance. Catlyn's attitude worried him greatly, but he wasn't really angry with her, just worried to distraction.

I reminded him, "Distracting her, wasn't that the idea?"

It was, but that was last night. What Catlyn had just told me tonight was way beyond jumping to conclusions. Pardon the reference, but it was insane.

Visit Rupert Errique again in prison? Warning bells were clanging in my head. "If you wanted proof that you're out of your mind," I told her, "this is it. What in the world would possess you to go there again?"

Catlyn had drawn me aside after dinner. She wanted to speak to me "privately." That alone should have had the claxons clanging from ear to ear. I could see my grandfather following me with his eyes, and even Tilly paused in her chatter to squint at us. In the 20/20 of hindsight, I should have said, whoa, stop right there, let's not start having secrets. But I'm sorry, I just wasn't thinking in that mode. She singled me out for a confidential matter, and yes, I admit it, I was flattered. That's how much I wanted her trust.

But, visit Errique? No, no, no, no, no; a thousand times, no. That's what I should have said.

She basically pooh-poohed my objection, even when I reminded her that she'd fainted dead away on hearing a mere message from Errique. "Besides, Dr. Ulma has absolutely forbidden you to meet Errique ever again."

"Yes, I know," she said so very reasonably. "That's why I can't ask him to go with me now. He'd be all protective and pulling strings to keep me out of there, and I'd never find out what I need to know."

"Which is?" My brain was absolute mush. I should've been shouting "*Help!*" at the top of my lungs. But this was Catlyn. If it'd been anyone else...

"I need to know what Errique meant."

"You know what he meant. You said it yourself, he was luring you so he could manipulate you the way he manipulates everyone else."

"He is, you're right; there's no doubt about it. He's luring me, and he's using one heck of a lure to do it. But that's the point, don't you see? He was deliberately obvious about it. He meant to lure me, not to frighten me away. Why? There's got to be something else behind it."

"Aren't you afraid of him?"

"Terrified."

"Then why go? You're here, and he's stuffed away there."

"Is he? Physically, yes, he's there in prison, but still he knew a very specific detail from my nightmares. He's here, Amelia, maybe not in person, but he's here."

I had no comeback to that, or perhaps there were too many comebacks, none of them reassuring. I was racking my brain for ways to dissuade her, but no matter what I said, she out-maneuvered me. I don't know which peeved me more, that she was quicker than me or that she wasn't listening to my advice. But neither of those things could overcome the fact that she'd singled me out for her confidence, and that was a big deal to me. In the end, what could I do but yield?

"If I can't change your mind, how can I help?"

"Just come with me. Help me to sort this out."

"What do you mean exactly, sort this out?"

"Let's suppose Errique is just amusing himself, bullying me because he wants to see me break."

"But is that likely? I mean, he's tried that once, and failed. You were a helpless captive then. He had you at his mercy. You're not helpless anymore. Surely he sees that."

"I'm sure he does, but don't you think that's got to be eating at him? He gloated over me when he thought he was in control, but when I went there with Dr. Ulma, Errique told me I'd beaten him at his own game. But people who gloat when they're ahead don't make good losers. Maybe he felt threatened when I told him it wasn't a game, and it wasn't over. This could be his way of telling me the same thing. It's not over, and he's in it to win."

"And if he is, then what?"

"We stop him cold in his tracks. We show him we're not afraid of him. He's got no hold over us."

"What if that's not what he had in mind? What if he's luring you for some other reason?"

"Then we find out what it is."

§§§

I'd never been to a prison before, and I wasn't at all reassured by the armed guards watching us. Prisoners, convicted of who knows what crimes, were sitting at tables without shackles. As we entered the room, I felt my insides tightening up. I grabbed Catlyn's arm. "I'm going to puke," I told her. "No, you're not," she instructed me. I tried to look her in the face to tell her, yes I am, but what I saw on her face left me speechless; or maybe it was what I didn't see. No wrinkle, no worry line, not even a furrowed brow. I swear she looked absolutely settled. Not serene, but untroubled. I was dumbfounded. She'd done it. She'd mastered her fears and had taken control of her emotions. I almost pitied Errique.

Errique was surprised too. His eyebrows shot up an inch when he saw me walking along side Catlyn.

"Miss Stacey, I must say, it's a great pleasure to see you again, and you've brought our dear Amy with you."

"It's Miss Endbrook to you, if you don't mind, Mr. Errique. I merely thought she deserved a chance to see you in your natural habitat."

She wasted no time hurling the gauntlet straight at him. He didn't even flinch. But I did. You know how you feel a chill in the air when somebody snubs you? This was no snub, and the shiver it sent through me made me want to heave right then and there. *They're only words,* I tried to remind myself as I swallowed against the bile rising up in my throat. My mind pleaded, *This wasn't a good idea. We should go. Please, let's just go.* But my mind couldn't find my voice.

Incredibly, Errique decided to play the coquet. "I knew you'd come," he simpered.

Catlyn was smooth as silk. She replied in kind. "When you were so, what shall we call it, poetic? Who'd have guessed it? Such a poetic message, how could I not be intrigued?"

Errique shrugged. "I'll have to defer to you when it comes to poetry, Miss Stacey. I'm rather ignorant on that subject. I find too much of today's poetry is merely bad prose straining to be misunderstood. I simply cannot fathom it. As to my note, I merely meant to suggest that we hadn't really reached a proper closure to our engagement. And look, here you are; so it seems you must agree."

I'd given up trying to read Errique's expression, but what he said was clear enough. He denied knowing anything about poetry? So, that poetic line in his message was, what? Errique is no Omar Khayyam, so what it was, was Errique taunting Catlyn. He was saying, "See, I can reach right into your mind, and there's nothing you can do to stop me."

My insides were doing acrobatics now, and I wasn't sure how long I could hold out. But Catlyn was ice.

"You're quite mistaken, Mr. Errique. Seeing you enclosed here is closure enough for me."

"Now, Miss Stacey," he chided, "that's not very sociable of you. Even here in this horrid place, good manners are still expected of fine young ladies."

"Oh, I don't know, Mr. Errique. It doesn't seem like such a horrid place, for someone like you. Food and lodging and adoring inmates. Surely, this is way more than you deserve."

"Miss Stacey, I can't believe you could be so unkind as that, and at this time of the year? I'm so disappointed in you. I'd've thought you'd be more charitable."

I think he was trying to look disappointed in Catlyn, but then, maybe he was just mocking her. Then suddenly, he was acting like we were his best friends.

"Do you know what I miss most at this time of year, Miss Stacey? Holiday shopping."

Shopping? Like he was reminiscing? That just threw me for a loop, and the aghast look on my face must've betrayed my surprise. He exploited it to confide directly to me, "It's true. All the hustle and the bustle, the window shopping."

He did a slow turn of his head to look again at Catlyn. He peered at her for a second. Then he spoke very slowly as though he wanted to be sure she understood every one of his words. "People stopping to greet one another, to chit chat before running off. Don't you just wonder what they were talking about, what made them hurry away so quick? Doesn't it just make you want to dash away yourself?"

I knew exactly what he was describing, and so did Catlyn. The ice in her manner was starting to crack, but beneath the ice was a layer of stone. The confident sheen was gone, but the expression on her face was hard as granite.

Suddenly he asked with too much gaiety, "Have you done your Christmas shopping yet?" He paused like he really thought Catlyn was going to answer him, but then he continued on in a perfectly normal voice. "But of course you have. By now, you've been out gadding about with that little urchin you're so fond of."

"That's something you'll never know," Catlyn snapped at him. He'd stung her, and she knew it. So did he. Her breathing was strained and turning rapid.

"Of course I won't. I mean, it's not like you ever call me. If I were more sensitive about such things, I'd have to wonder if your phones were even in proper working order. They are, aren't they? Have you had them checked out lately?"

Catlyn was rigid in her chair. Nightmares, men on the street, disrupted shopping, unscheduled phone service – He knew it all, and he was using it to lash her into submission.

He tweaked the little smirk on his face. "Have you no charity for me, Miss Stacey? None at all?"

Feigning a weary patience, he said, "You know, Miss Stacey, you really should be more receptive of my attentions. We're two of a kind, really, deep down. We see the world differently than others do. That's why I think we should be working together, helping each other. Indeed, I believe we could work wonders together, you and I."

This perplexed me beyond anything I could've imagined. After his bare knuckle sparring routine, he was luring her again. I'm pretty sure he winked at her.

"That's how society is supposed to work, isn't it? People pooling their resources, connecting thinkers and backers."

I hadn't a clue what he was suggesting, and when Catlyn didn't respond, he added, "What I'm trying to say, Miss Stacey, is that opportunity and influence should go hand in hand. It shouldn't be left to chance, and it doesn't have to be. Now you take us, for example. I'm a thinker. I have influence, but lack opportunity. You have opportunity, and you're much in need of influence to support what you've been thinking."

"Forgive me, Mr. Errique," Catlyn interrupted, "but you don't seem to be in a position to know my thoughts or to influence anyone, least of all me. I'm doing just fine."

Errique sat back confidently. He nodded, studied his hands. He made a steeple out of his fingers, then pressed them against his chin. "Tilly," he said without looking up. He allowed the word to hang suspended in the air. "That is her name, I believe, the child you wish to adopt?"

Fury and fear clashed vividly in Catlyn's eyes.

He nodded again. "No doubt you're wondering, how did he know about that? Well, Miss Stacey, it's just what I've been talking about, influence. And how does one gain influence in prison? Knowledge, Miss Stacey, knowledge is influence. You can't imprison knowledge. In your own mind, you know I'm right. Indeed, I dare say I've demonstrated that to you quite clearly, don't you think?"

Catlyn was taking short, quick breaths, but she steeled her nerve. "Influence, Mr. Errique? All you've demonstrated is an amusing degree of resourcefulness. An eye here, an ear there, and you have a few incidental facts gathered for you. Knowledge that can't be used has no influence."

Errique had that insipid smile on his face again. "Ah, Miss Stacey, from the very beginning, I knew you and I were a match. You are constantly in synch with me. We step like exquisitely paired dancers. Listen, follow me for one more step. What can be gathered can also be disseminated. I think you know that. Rumor, innuendo, suspicion, it can all be quite effective. Mix in a little truth, and it becomes persuasive information useful in so many ways."

"Such as?" She was trying too hard to be indifferent. Because she was afraid. But she had to know.

"Suppose – just hypothetically, you understand – suppose there is an application for adoption by a person of questionable emotional stability. That kind of information could be devastating. Seen in the worst light, I could well imagine a dedicated social worker being alarmed at leaving a child even merely exposed to such a person. They might feel obligated to take her away for her own protection. And yet, seen in the right light, that same fact could demonstrate a strong moral fiber much to the person's credit."

He suddenly made one of those hand gestures so expressive of bewilderment. "But listen to me, all this talk of unsavory possibilities is positively morose. You must forgive me, Miss Stacey. It's this place. I invited you here to give you an opportunity to demonstrate your moral fiber by means of an act of charity, by which I mean, of course, your forgiveness of me. Just that, and nothing more."

He studied her face. "Opportunity and influence," he said. "Charity and self-interest. There's hardly any difference, so long as it's what you Americans call a win-win deal."

Catlyn returned his stare. "My Grannie Effie used to say, ain't no winnin' when the devil's dealin'."

§§§

We left with Errique staring at our backs, and I couldn't leave fast enough. Catlyn insisted on a slow, unhurried pace, but I couldn't help it. I ran. My insides were coming unglued, and I had to find a restroom, asap.

In the car, I unglued even more. I was unwinding like a tight spring. My mouth was spewing a nonstop barrage of chatter, and I couldn't sit still. I would've bounced off my seat, but suddenly I realized how quiet Catlyn was. That doused my frenzy cold. "You did great," I tried to cheer her.

She looked over at me. Tremors were shaking her head,

her shoulders, her body. Her face was vivid with desperation. She nearly shouted, "Don't you *ever* let me do that *again*!"

Wait. I was the incredibly stupid one? I found myself pushing back against my seat. I mean, yes, I was incredibly stupid, but it wasn't my idea. Then my brain kicked in. I'd thought she was ice, rock solid, hard as steel. But she was none of that. She was trembling. It never occurred to me what tremendous restraint had been holding her together.

Call me twisted, but I suddenly felt there was a kind of whimsical caprice to the way her frustration was letting go.

So I teased her.

"*Whatever* was I thinking?"

She stared at me for about a second, then she kind of gasped for air, and a second later, she started to giggle. It was one of those choppy, out-of-my-freaking-mind kind of giggles, and it was infectious. Once started, it wouldn't stop.

She gasped again, caught her breath, and then, with wide-eyed innocence, she gushed, "But it was some kind of awesome, wasn't it?" Then we both lost it, laughing in uncontrollable hysterical gasps, chortles, and trills.

It was awesome. It was crazy. It may even have been out-of-my-freaking-mind stupid. But all things considered, it was just crazy awesome.

Chapter 19: Dr. Ulma

I was angry with Catlyn to the point of being furious. I'm sorry to say, I was not at my professional best.

"Are you out of your mind? Have you completely lost your senses? How am I supposed to prove to the world that you're sane when you pull a stunt like this?"

Professional that wasn't. There was no maybe about it. I felt betrayed. And it hurt. Professionally and personally, it hurt, and I was furious.

"I explicitly forbid it!"

I glared at her with every intention of shaming her.

She was unresponsive, but I could see her stewing.

"Have you any idea what you've done?"

"I'm not a child," she snapped back at me. "It's my life, and I did what had to do."

"What you *had* to do was stay away from him. What you *had* to do was prove that you've dissociated your life from his, that his existence is inconsequential to you. What you *did* was demonstrate quite the opposite."

"No! I proved I had the courage to face him. I proved that he couldn't control me ever again."

"He summoned you."

"He lured me."

"And you went to him."

That brought her up short. She glared at me, squared her shoulders, then stopped. Something flashed into her mind, and it wasn't about the cave. She looked away from me. In profile, I could see the rapid flicking movements of her eyes. Thoughts were racing through her brain. She was questioning herself, probing, and doubting. I couldn't have been more delighted, and yes, I know, that was a personal reaction, not a professional one. But, as it happened, doubt at this moment was good for her, very, very good.

But that wasn't enough. She needed to step back from her emotions. She had to see how Errique was manipulating her. I was reasonably confident she could do that. I knew I could guide her to do exactly that if she'd let me, but that was a very big "if." Catlyn had been drawn into Rupert Errique's lair. There was no denying that. Going there was rash, but no "I told you so" was going to make her understand that.

Even in the best of circumstances, it's difficult to admit that a careful plan has gone awry, but it's way worse when the plan wasn't as careful as it should have been. And then, if it was rash, and your mind is thoroughly riled? Good luck to you then. But that's where Catlyn was at that moment.

Her concession, when she'd come to grips with it, came in words low in grudging timbre, subdued and brooding.

"He summoned me."

In that instant, I could feel the tension rising; mine, not hers. Catlyn wasn't one to be subdued. Her admission was hard-wrought, and as with everything gained through struggle, there would be consequences. When they came, they surged over Catlyn in a rage of trembling driven by the duplicity of her fear and shame. The full force of her frustration burst in a fierce condemnation of herself, her vanity, and every evil thing fate had thrust upon her.

"Damn him," she unleashed in a fervent shriek of protest. "Damn him," she railed again in castigation of his evil.

Abruptly she stood. Then she was turning and twisting and shouting, her arms flailing in wild gestures fighting off all the villainous phantoms that came now to mock her, rising from the rancid refuse of her nightmares. Willfully, she clamped her hands behind her head trying to gain control of herself against her invisible attackers. Abruptly she sat again, holding herself rigidly upright. Then from deep within, she exploded into a further aggressive tirade, her hand slapping against the chair.

A moment of fury. An outburst of anger and frustration.

A final acceptance of frailty and imperfection.

Depleted then, expended and exhausted, the outburst subsided, dying to a wail, waning to a whispered lament, a hollow surrender. "He summoned me."

Came then the silence. Private, staring, doleful silence. Until silence grew into shame; head down, face-buried-in-her-hands shame.

A quickening resurgence of anger thrust her to her feet, standing and pacing. Then she was sitting again. Distraught, she struck another blow against the chair.

I'd never seen Catlyn erupt in such disturbed and violent manner. In another setting, she'd probably have been restrained, strapped down on a table, or confined in some manner so she wouldn't hurt herself or anyone else.

But as frightening as it was to see, I was relieved to see it. She'd been pushed to an extreme, and her mind had handled it. She'd activated one of the emergency release valves protecting her mind from imminent devastation. The profusion of tears that quickly followed in angry, choking sobs was wonderfully, beautifully normal. I could have kissed her, I was so relieved and happy and proud and fascinated.

I watched and waited. Because this was one of those situations where time actually was the best healer. I waited for the spike in her anxiety to relent. When she could mop her eyes and clear her head, I offered, "Yes, he summoned you, and now it's time for you to summon yourself."

She paused long enough to squint at me. I freely admit I

was spouting nonsense, but not without reason. It was one of those rousing remarks filled with motivation and lacking in meaning, a pep talk you give your team when you're trailing at half-time. She seemed to take it that way and nodded like she was agreeing to it. That was another good sign. She was pulling herself together, taking deep breaths, recouping her strength. I was rather expecting her to ask, what next? Instead, her face was sober and covered with desolation.

"He threatened Tilly."

Her eyes trained on me in a pleading lament, inviting me to blame her for this new evil. I sat back in my chair and took a few seconds to regroup. Victims often do that. In their shattered self-esteem, they see themselves deserving whatever ills have befallen them, and they want others to confirm their blame, to condemn them without pity.

This was cause for panic. Could Errique have gotten that far into her mind? I didn't want to believe it. A mind like Catlyn's has the capacity to be objective in a crisis. It just doesn't succumb to irrational thoughts. But if you believe you're the cause of injury to someone you care about, it's hard to be rational.

I urgently needed to know, was the threat perceived by Catlyn's mind real or imagined? Or was it a new avenue into some darker persuasion of her mind?

It couldn't be denied that Errique had successfully played on the fragile state of Catlyn's emotions. She was drained by it, physically and emotionally. My biggest worry now, or so I thought, was that her reserve might be so depleted she would shy away from talking about it at all. It turned out another concern was going to trump them all, but I didn't discover that until later.

Slowly and methodically, Catlyn gave me a fairly

thorough accounting of her confrontation with Errique. She was unrelenting in her description, punishing herself in every detail of their interaction. This too was alarming. It was too succinct, too one-sided, too judgmental. She was skewing the details against herself. She was building a case slanted against herself so the hostile world around her would see how guilty she was for everything that was happening. I couldn't allow Catlyn to do that.

So, step back. Go slow. Engage her thoughts. Be patient.

"Errique manipulates people. It's what we expect of him."

We, not you. Be a team.

"He depends on that. When he threatens to use his influence against us, we tend to believe him. But let's not give him that satisfaction. Let's ask if that's even possible. Did he say what or how he might do something to Tilly?"

Catlyn took a deep, calming breath. "Hypothetically, yes."

That seemed deliberate, like her thoughts were focusing.

"He suggested that rumors could be used to discredit me. He could make me appear to be so unstable that I'd be seen as a danger to Tilly. Then a social worker would have to remove Tilly from the estate to protect her, from me."

"Taking Tilly away from you. That's a powerful threat. But in the end, all he's doing is pushing an emotional button, nothing more. I'm sure you see it that way yourself."

Encourage her. Reinforce her confidence.

"He couldn't do any of that from inside the prison. He'd have to get help from somebody outside."

"He's got it, lots of it." A fact, stated calmly but firmly. "Somebody hacked into your computer system. Somebody's watched my every movement. He knew about the shopping incident. And the business with the phone system at the estate. I can't prove that he caused any of that, but I believe he did." She looked squarely at me. "That's probably what's important for you to know, that I believe he did it."

There was renewed confidence in that. Catlyn's inner strength was once again emerging and asserting itself. Her self-assessment revealed much – fact, belief, significance, and the capacity to distinguish them, and she rolled it all up into one concise statement.

In this tangle of thrusts and feints and suppositions, I was so engrossed with my admiration for Catlyn, I almost failed to see how flagrant Errique's scheme had become. Errique was practicing a psychological form of action-at-a-distance, priming her for self-fulfilling delusions propelled by fear. Disgust for Errique filled the words that came out of my mouth. I didn't even bother with any cautious preamble.

"He's stalking you."

"In prison?"

"It doesn't matter whether he's watching you in person or by means of one of his henchmen. He's using the act of watching you to impinge on your life. I'm no lawyer, but psychologically, that's stalking."

Chapter 20: Rose

This time she went too far. It wasn't fair, and it wasn't honest. That's how we saw it, and it's what we told her. It wasn't like she didn't have a choice. It wasn't a necessity, and she didn't have to be secretive about it.

All this time, we believed Catlyn was being upfront with us, and here she went behind our backs. Angry doesn't begin to describe how we felt.

Tilly was probably the only one who accepted Catlyn's conduct, and that really miffed me because, of course, I was the one who told Tilly that's exactly what she needed to do.

But what of the rest of us? How else could we see it but that she hadn't trusted *any* of us? That's what we demanded to know when we tracked them down, Catlyn and Amelia, in the "Lady Sylvia" drawing room where they'd taken refuge.

"It wasn't my finest hour, okay?"

It wasn't okay.

"You could've confided in us, all of us; you know that. We'd've supported you a hundred percent."

"That's just the thing, don't you see? I had to know if I could do this on my own. If I had to lean on you, I wouldn't have known where I stood. I wouldn't have known if I could function independently as a normal stable individual. Your support is always important to me, and I'm always going to need it. I know that, and I wouldn't have it any other way."

She looked away. She was groping to bring her thoughts into focus.

"A person who exists solely on life support isn't alive. As

long as Sebastian had a spark of life inside, he was alive. When that spark went out, he was dead."

She looked hard at me. "I have to stay alive inside, or there won't be any purpose to your support outside."

I was torn. I wanted to refute her argument; maybe I even wanted her to feel the hurt she'd caused us. She was talking about basic tenets of life, things that I believe in even if others don't. And one of the things I believe is that God always has a plan. Living and dying is part of that plan, including that spark of life, and God always has a say in how it works. We might not like the choices he makes, but there's always a purpose to it, and God uses us to carry out his purposes. So there's always a purpose to trying. That's what I believe, and that's why I didn't want to accept her argument. But I suppose I did understand it.

We all did, in the end. We all listened to her; we heard what she said. But we weren't any less hurt by it. Nobody budged to console her or to sympathize with her. Her concession just wasn't enough. There was no apology to it, and we demanded more.

She tried to explain, "It was a private war between me and Errique. And I wasn't alone. Amelia had a stake in it, too. That's why I asked her to come with me."

Ethan pounced on that. "Yes, wasn't that considerate of you." It wasn't a question. "You exploited her. You knew Amelia couldn't say no to you. You forced her to break her trust with me. She's my granddaughter, and you had no right to come between us."

Amelia defended. "She didn't. It was my choice." She moved to stand next to Catlyn facing the rest of us. "I didn't tell you because Catlyn was right. It was a private war, and I was part of it, and in case anyone has any doubt, let me tell you right now. I'll stand in battle with Catlyn anytime, anywhere, side-by-side, back-to-back, whatever it takes."

She was pumped. Her eyes were glaring, and her face was flushed to a dark crimson, but I couldn't tell if she was furious or going to cry. We were all staring at them in a dead silent standoff, but there wasn't one of us who was going to challenge her. In the heat of that moment, Catlyn whirled around to Amelia, grasping her in an arm-wrapping embrace clinging like their lives depended on it, and I don't know, maybe they did. That's exactly how they were holding on to one another, like their lives depended on it. In this clasp of life, their emotions suddenly drained into a stream of tears.

There was no denying the contrition in them or us. Whatever discord we felt a moment before, dissolved into the oblivion of forgiveness. Tilly hurled herself forward to throw herself into the mix with Biscuit prancing and turning circles at their feet. The rest of us followed suit, closing the distance between "them and us," dispersing the reprimands and hurt feelings. We were a family, whole and united.

When we'd all had sufficient time to mop our eyes and regroup, I suggested that we reconvene in the atrium sitting room. That's just one of the things we seem to do here, you know, change the scenery and give yourself a fresh start, and I think it's the room Catlyn likes best. It's sheltered from prying eyes, yet it looks into the open space of the garden which always has something peaceful to look at, like the arbor and the Greek and Roman statuettes, and of course the miniature trees and shrubs are there, and the flowers when they're blooming. Anyway, everyone liked the idea, mostly because it gave us all a chance to refocus our thoughts.

When we reconvened, Amelia sat next to Catlyn on the small couch, while Tilly sat on the floor with Biscuit. Catlyn had asked Whinehardt and Sweetgrove to join us, and they chose to stand together off to one side. That left Ethan and me to sit on the larger couch facing Catlyn. Evidently, Catlyn was tacitly agreeing to involve all of us in her affairs, and we were all leaning slightly forward so as not to miss a single word of what she was going to say.

"It's about family. I get that. And it's important to me. So." She hesitated; inhaled slowly, exhorting that one last surge of resolve to push past her anxieties. Facing her, I could see in her expression how hard this was for her. It requires great courage to drop your guard, especially when the intent is to reach deep within yourself to expose your most vulnerable emotions to the proclivities of fate, and to haul them all out into the open where everyone can see how imperfect you are.

Even so, I was expecting her to be defiant. But she wasn't, and that worried me in a different way. Despite her courage, it seemed like she was surrendering, as in giving up the fight. I wanted her to keep fighting, just not with us.

"If we're really going to function as a family," she began, "everyone needs to know what we're up against."

Analytical and to the point. We were in a crisis, and there was Catlyn, once again pulling herself together. So, she wasn't surrendering, but then, why couldn't I shake the feeling that something was different?

It seemed to me, this wasn't *just* about pulling herself together. A moment ago, I was ready to cry for her. Now I was feeling disturbed. There was a distinct shift in her attitude, and it was making me uneasy. Sometimes you see things in people's expressions, like the way the eyes look or the head tilts; things like that. I suppose I was looking for the determined spirit I so admired in Catlyn, and I wasn't seeing it. That spark of life she likes to talk about wasn't behind the look on her face. This wasn't about life; it was about anger and fear and surviving. Even as she talked to us, I felt her drawing away. She wasn't reaching out to us. She was entrenching herself. I could see a growing darkness in her face like a battle was coming, and there were going to be casualties, and she just wasn't going to think about them. That was it exactly. She was just hard and analytical and dispassionate. She was totally disconnected from the crisis, from us, from everything, and I was afraid for her.

I watched and listened to her as she reminded us of all those peculiar events that we more or less knew about already. Then she wove them together, and there was no mistaking Errique's intention. He was taunting Catlyn cruelly, and his intention was to damage her. I was ashamed of myself. I'd been peevish with Catlyn because I'd been hurt, but I clearly didn't know what hurt was.

"You were right to confront him," I conceded.

Ethan looked at me like he was reading my thoughts. "I agree. I see it now. His objective, to put it bluntly, is to destroy the person who destroyed him."

That startled Tilly enough to clutch Biscuit's fur in her hand. The yelp from Biscuit startled us, but Catlyn merely glanced down at them. As Biscuit settled again, Catlyn nodded to Ethan. "I believe that's exactly what he's after."

"And when he's finished with you," said Ethan, looking then with dread at his granddaughter, "he'll go after Amelia just for his own amusement."

"Not if we don't let him get that far," Amelia challenged.

"And he won't." There was no backing down in Catlyn's voice, nor in her attitude. "So far, there's been no physical threat, no hit man to wreak revenge on me. I don't think that's what he wants. Dr. Ulma thinks he's trying to destroy me emotionally. He wants me to suffer."

She hesitated to look directly at Tilly. "He's threatened

Tilly."

That brought a wail of protests from all of us, except Tilly. She was frozen in a stare with Catlyn. Then Catlyn said quietly, "But we're not going to let that happen either."

Tilly was awash with confusion and fear and trying to be as brave as Catlyn. You could see the struggle in her face, but she didn't for a second take her eyes off Catlyn.

"Whatever you need of us, Miss Stacey." That was Whinehardt, ever practical, ever steadfast, and like the rest of us, ever ready to stand guard. He got straight to the point. "Where do we begin?"

It was the very question we needed answered, and yes, Catlyn was right, we needed it answered in hard, dispassionate, analytical terms.

"Let's assume the threat isn't physical. We can ensure that somewhat if Tilly is never alone when she's outside the house."

We all agreed to that, and Tilly promised she'd be careful.

Sweetgrove asked, "If we keep her safe, what else is there?"

Catlyn took another deep breath. This was the real issue. "In the worst case scenario, social services would deem it necessary to remove Tilly from the estate for her own protection." She looked at Tilly. "Protection from me."

That truly incensed Sweetgrove. "I won't stand for it, and neither will Cook."

"And they'd have to go through me first," declared Whinehardt, taking a step further into the room.

"Errique will be vicious in his campaign against me," said Catlyn, and her next words seemed stern and calculated. "My only defense will be all of you. They won't take my word for anything, so it'll be up to you to prove

Tilly's safe here."

I knew she was being spot on rational. I knew she was doing the right thing, but her lack of emotion still worried me deeply. She was changing, and I didn't know if that was good or bad. Either way, it didn't matter. I wanted the real Catlyn back, and I wanted her back right now.

She instructed us, "You need to document facts and figures. That goes for you, too, Tilly. Things like the number of hours spent in study and reading; the kinds of books you read; how much time you spend watching television; how you're involved with the house; and what kinds of things we do together and how you feel about them."

I knew that enumerating all these details was probably important, but it made me wonder if she was skirting some other issue. "I understand why we need to do those things," I said, "but what's to be done beyond all that?"

"Being normal. Dr. Ulma has made that very clear. It will be up to me alone to demonstrate that I'm well-adjusted and have no behavioral quirks that would put anyone at risk of harm. The public will judge me, and so will Dr. Ulma."

She paused to pan the room, making eye contact with each of us. "I need all of you to help me. If I'm unhinged in any way, you've got to tell me." She meant that for all of us, but she was looking straight at me when she said "you've got to tell me." I nodded like I understood, like she meant me specifically, like we were "going to the mats," and I was to be her designated counselor. We probably all felt that way, but she was looking at me.

"No concessions. No being polite. If something in my behavior bothers you, tell me. Even if I get angry, keep telling me. Someday I'll remember to thank you."

Tilly asked, "What about Dr. Ulma?"

"He'll be privy to everything I do, as well as what I think."

Something in that thought surprised her and caused her to pause. Her mouth flexed into the hint of a smile, and her countenance momentarily rose to a faintly pink glow. I remember it distinctly because it was so unexpected, and so *not* dispassionate.

In this suddenly pensive mood, she said, "You know, he's seen me at my absolute worst, and never once has he said I'm a terrible person. He's not blamed me for anything. He's always working so hard for me. All the time. He's always there for me. Sometimes I think..."

Suddenly she looked down so we couldn't see her face, but I was pretty sure that faint glow had flamed into a vibrant blush. It made me think... Well it made me think, and let's leave it at that.

Then she seemed to recall what she wanted to say, and she was all business again. "If he asks you anything, I want you to tell him honestly what you know. I promise to do the same, and I mean with all of you, not just with him. Above all else, day-to-day, we must appear perfectly normal." She hesitated; looked at each of us again. "Please. I need you to do that for me. Even if you have to pretend."

Chapter 21: Ethan

It's hard to stay mad at someone who's trying so hard to do what's right. All you can really do is say, "okay, enough is enough; let's all try harder," and get on with it.

So that's what we all were doing, following Catlyn's instructions to get our lives back to normal so she could do the same. The idea was to surround her with so much normality that some kind of social osmosis would kick in, and it'd all be absorbed into her life. It'd be like spreading one of those intensive creams over your hands to heal the little cracks you get when the dry cold turns them rough.

I knew exactly what I was going to do. I started with Willy Hartsdell at the Somerset Lesser Archives. I wanted to make sure he wasn't neglecting the Prunella letters. We'd need them anyways, and if I could get a two-for-one deal out of them, that wouldn't be bad either. I wanted to use them to test Catlyn's resolve. Now, before you start chiding me for having doubts about Catlyn's determination, let me point out that she knows my philosophy. In any research, it's essential to observe and pose questions. In true discovery, we suppress nothing. We let the facts speak for themselves. That's what I intended to do with Catlyn.

Willy sent me the digital copy of the latest letter via email, but only to me. I had expressly instructed Willy not to copy it to Catlyn. That wasn't how this process was going to work. Willy's a good friend; we go back a long ways. Come to think of it, he's my only living friend from the old days. He's Catlyn's friend too, and he was more than eager to team up with me on what we now called "the Catlyn issue."

The only immediate problem was that a persistent cold drizzle was making driving conditions hazardous. As you probably know, I don't drive in bad weather. I had to appeal to Catlyn to have Jason fetch me in the limo. That could've been awkward. Why not just send her an email and meet with her when the weather cleared up? But Catlyn let it pass. It wasn't that she was negligent of my thinking or disinterested in it. She grasped the issue well enough and simply declined to complain about it. If I was to be part of the observing public, I had to be in a position to observe, and that was all there was to it. Call it a "pop quiz" on her new resolve. I gave her a passing grade, at least on that.

Actually, when I arrived at the estate, Catlyn seemed to be in fairly good spirit. I said something to that effect, and she confided, "I am. Dr. Ulma's forgiven me, the household is back to routine operation, and now that you're here, the day seems complete. So, all's right under the heavens."

That seemed a little flippant for Catlyn, but sometimes good news is just good news, and I chose to take it that way. And it was good to see Catlyn being so determined, even if she was trying too hard to look normal. I've forgotten now the occasion, but she once said, sometimes the effort counts more than the end result. I hoped it'd work that way here.

Tea had already been laid on for us, so we migrated from the grand foyer to the tearoom which stands at the front of the mansion. While the tea was being served, Tilly took my flash drive to load the new letter onto their e-tablets, and Catlyn and I settled into our seats at the largest of the three tables that now occupied the room along with an antique sideboard for serving.

Outside, the drizzle was continuing its pitter-patter rhythm against the windows, coating them in seductive little streamlets. Catlyn seemed to be entranced by them. She used her finger to trace the path of one sizeable drop as it caromed in hesitant, erratic slips and skids down the window. When the droplet reached the bottom of the window pane, she left her finger poised there for a minute while she drifted away in an indistinct meditation. Her daze was broken by a soft, forlorn sigh that prompted her to flash me a quick smile to let me know everything was okay. It wasn't genuine. I knew that, but I accepted it and smiled back. It's the polite thing to do.

When Tilly returned with Catlyn's tablet, she took the side seat at the table facing the window and set up the tablet in front of herself so there'd be no glare on the screen. Catlyn and I scooted our chairs around the table to either side of Tilly so we could all examine the letter together. Tilly was beaming. She had a new bluetooth keyboard, and she was going to use it to append our notes as we discussed the letter.

In retrospect, I was amused to realize we were adapting technology to bridge a gap not only between Catlyn's moods and emotions, but also between social eras. Much of today's technology seems to minimize face-to-face interactions. In the "old days," bringing people together around the fireplace helped to create a coherent family. We were doing exactly that with an e-tablet! The more things change...

Prunella's letter was to her friend, Elly. We presumed that was Elly Howshim of Wolverhampton.

I have made a friend! Gerald and I were taking a turn on deck as is lately become our custom. We chanced upon a family of three, and soon to be four, a mother and father and their small son. The mother, Katherine, is again with child. Her husband, Mr. Frank Bowermun, has made this voyage before, for he has property in the Carolina region. He returned to England some months back to fetch Katherine and son to live there, but I fear Katherine may have a difficult time of it. She is frail and retiring, and her constitution seems poorly suited to hardship.

"If she was so frail," Tilly wondered, "why would she go?"

"I don't think it was a matter of her being frail in a sickly sense," I speculated. "Given that her husband was a landowner, it's likely she came from a well to do family and was bred to society. Remember, America was still a fledgling wilderness. She'd be considered frail for a place like that because she had neither a useful skill nor physical strength."

The objection formed quickly enough to furrow Catlyn's brow. "What makes you say she had no skill?"

"Prunella herself," I explained, "was bred to be pampered, but according to the diary, she was very assertive. She would've been at the center of attention in social gatherings, and that made her socially influential. That was, and still is, considered to be a very important womanly skill."

That invited a different objection. "Womanly skill, Ethan? It seems to me, working a crowd is a highly valued skill, and it doesn't matter if the crowd's being worked by a man or a woman. Just ask any manly lobbyist or politician."

"Point well taken. In Katherine's case, however, Prunella describes her as being retiring, so she probably wasn't very resourceful in a social gathering."

"So it was just a sex thing," Tilly observed in her straightforward bludgeoning of an old man.

"Tilly..." Catlyn tried to exclaim without laughing. It was worth the bludgeoning to see her smile.

"They told us at school we shouldn't be embarrassed to talk about sex," Tilly defended.

"And quite right they were," I said as I recovered my bearings. "So long as it's talking only." While Tilly's jaw dropped with feigned shock, I said, "But, to answer your question, no, it wasn't a sex thing. He wanted the son."

Catlyn challenged, "So, not sex, but certainly sexist."

I wasn't going to get into *that* argument and suggested instead that we keep our focus on Prunella.

> *Mr. Joshua has made light of Katherine's destination and has teased her quite meanly that when we land, we shall all be regarded as immigrants! I was much put out by this declaration. Gerald has explained that it is not meant to demean us. To be an immigrant, he insists, is to seek a new beginning. We are bringing our good selves to a new land and offering ourselves to be a part of it. I am persuaded they shall receive us as happily as we receive them. If they do not, then we shall simply have to convince them they are wrong. I have never before been a foreigner or an immigrant, but I know I shall be ever so good at it.*
> *– Prunella, Letter No. E2, 1810*

I expressed surprise at how naïve Prunella was in this letter. "Not so," Catlyn was quick to react – and my heart quickened its beat. That was the spirited Catlyn of yore speaking. "Prunella knew very well he was demeaning them." She frowned, paused, and she was gone. "It's what they all do. Bullying, humiliating, shaming people into submission."

My heart went still, and Tilly stared. She wasn't talking about Mr. Joshua, unless he'd been reincarnated as Rupert Errique. How tenuous was the equanimity of Catlyn's mind. How she yet teetered on the edge of a precipice, so close to falling, so close to plunging into a deep abyss.

I think she sensed the tension in the air, because she asked, "Am I waxing philosophic again?"

Tilly nodded. "Yes, you are."

"Sorry. It's just that, foreigner or immigrant, it doesn't stop there." Anger flared. "It's like there's a denigration gene ingrained in our DNA. We seem to go out of our way to compartmentalize, not only our countries and our communities, but also the lives of the people in them."

Suddenly she "humphed" like she was surprised about something. Sitting back, a grin you might call sheepish formed on her lips. "Sebastian and I had a long discussion about that once. I was trying to berate the aristocracy, and he rather scornfully chastised me for all the classes of people we're so quick to identify in the US, even if they're not formal or legal entities. I think we both had it partly right, but of course, neither of us wanted to admit it to the other."

Her gaze drifted again into the distance, but this time it focused on a pleasant memory, a moment with Sebastian.

It was the first time in a long time that Catlyn had mentioned Sebastian by name and hadn't shed tears.

Tilly smiled. I contented myself with a sip of tea.

Chapter 22: Amelia

My grandfather and I had another long discussion last night. About Catlyn, of course. He'd been moody, good moody, but still moody. On the upbeat side, he told me, "Catlyn talked about Sebastian and didn't cry. She actually felt good about it." Then he sighed, which he rarely does. "She's still such an enigma to me," he said. "One minute I'm mad as blazes with her; the next, I'm proud of her."

"That's because you care about her," I told him.

He nodded his head gently. After a second, he asked, "You and Catlyn, you're as close as sisters, aren't you?"

"We are."

"And you meant what you said, that you'll stand beside her in any fight that needs to be fought?"

"I meant it. Every word of it."

He admitted quietly, "I do too." He smiled at me. "I'm proud of you, you know that don't you? You've done so much for her. She's engaging life again, trying so hard. We all are. You know, I've studied every era of history in every part of the world. If there's one constant in all that history, it's that you always find disparate people coming together to make a civilized world. It seems to me, that's exactly what we're doing, you and me and Catlyn, with Tilly and Dr. Ulma and Rose. We're melding together, actually melding together and forming a cohesive unit. We're a principle of history in action. It's breathtaking. And to see it at my age!"

Grandfather's always been inspiring in my eyes, and this little passionate speech gave me a great idea.

Today, at my insistence, Catlyn and I were making an excursion away from the estate. Nothing adventurous or profound, just a stepping away from seclusion. "You can't hide out here forever," I scolded her. She was reluctant and tried to make excuses, but I argued, teased, and prodded her until she understood, "no" was not in the vocabulary today. In the end, she agreed, but only as a favor to me.

I drove my old Mini Cooper. It's well on its way to becoming a vintage antique, but it's dependable and I think Catlyn rather liked the idea. It lent an air of anonymity to our outing, something the limo would never be able to do. I didn't tell her where we were going, and she kept casting suspicious glances at me as we traveled south from Bath on A36, then east on A366. As we got close to our destination, I slowed and pointed to the remains of an ancient castle atop a rise. "There. That's our destination, the Farleigh Hungerford Castle." The expression on her face was priceless; surprised, restrained, and slightly aghast. "Isn't it beautiful?" I asked.

She gave me one of those are-you-for-real looks. "Ruins? You brought me out here to see ruins?" But she did smile.

"Not just to see ruins, no." I told her, "This is going to be an exercise in applied history." I, too, can be enigmatic. "This is actually a special place for me. Grandfather brought me here when I was very young. It was just a fun outing. He was regaling me with tales about the ruins when, all at once, I swear, absolute truth, I heard what he said like it was the ruins speaking. They spoke to me, like Ariana speaks to you. After that, I just had to know all there was about archeology."

I was trying to keep it light, but this really was an anxious moment for me. I was reaching out to share a small but cherished memory of my life. It was personal, a memory I valued, a small one, admittedly, but one that easily could be ridiculed. I was allowing myself to be vulnerable. It's what we were asking Catlyn to do, so I wanted to show her I trusted her in the same way I was asking her to trust me.

I watched as she swept her eyes over the view. After a second, she decided, "It reminds me of one of those castles in an old Tyrone Power movie. You know, with all the clashing swords and the catapults tossing fireballs at the castle." That seemed to delight her, and she asked, "Is that what happened here? Did clashing warlords destroy the castle?"

I had to laugh. Like most people, she assumed the history of a people is about the wars they fought. "Not exactly," I explained. "This wasn't much of a stronghold. It's too remote to be of strategic value. The thinking is, the fortifications were mostly for basic security. The only battles that came out this far were the Wars of the Roses. The House of Lancaster battled the House of York. The Hungerfords backed the Lancasters, so they were attacked by the Yorkists. They lost the castle, but when the Lancasters finally won, Henry VII, now king, gave the castle back to Sir Walter Hungerford II as a reward for his support. But the castle was still standing at that time. The destruction came about 200 years later, early 1700s. The Hungerfords had run into financial problems, so they sold the castle, but that wasn't a go either, and eventually one of the owners tried to cut his losses by harvesting the building materials. I guess you can't really blame them for doing that. They had a lot of issues, and preserving legacies was a luxury they just couldn't' afford."

Catlyn frowned. "Is that what I'm doing with Southjoy Mission, entertaining a luxury I can't afford? Because the price is too high; because it's cost too many lives?"

I was startled. I hadn't seen that coming at all. "No, and don't you ever think such a thing. Ariana's vision inspired you. That's no luxury. People need to be inspired. They need to know good things can survive even when they're abused, and even if they're reduced to ruins. Life needs inspiration."

Catlyn glanced at me. She didn't say anything, but she offered me a small weary smile, and she nodded her head like she understood. Which I knew she did, better than me.

I found a good spot to park, and I insisted on paying our admission fee. By that point I was getting excited because there was more to this excursion than sightseeing, and I practically herded Catlyn to the gatehouse. We were approaching my exercise in "applied history."

"It was begun in the late 1300s by Sir Thomas Hungerford."

"1300s?" I could see her doing the math.

"Yes, in the medieval era. Sir Thomas was building his castle more than a century before Columbus knew anything about the New World; actually, before there even was a Columbus. Sir Thomas's son expanded the castle while it was occupied by the Hungerfords, but the castle changed hands a few times over the next 150 years or so, during which it was allowed to decline into disrepair. Sound familiar?"

"Like what happened to Southjoy Mission."

"A lot like it. Eventually, the Hungerfords recovered the castle, and their dynasty went on to be very influential for a while. But they had their share of intrigue and executions and hangings, and even a murder or two. But that's not why we're here. We've come to see the chapel. There's a very special tomb in the chapel that dates back to the mid-to-late 1600s. That's what I want you to see."

Our steps ground to a halt. I'd alarmed her yet again, and I knew she must be thinking, tomb equals death. I planted my hands on my hips to stare her down. "Trust me?"

It took a second. I'd promised her a special day, and I think she knew I wouldn't be thoughtless about it. At least I hoped she'd give me that much credit, and in the end, she did say "Okay," but she was leery about it.

Once inside the chapel, though, her restraint vanished as she became entranced by the beauty of the stained glass windows. Those windows infused the chamber with a warm and gentle ambiance that seemed to invite your attention to the murals on the walls. As I led Catlyn into the side chapel, she was about to say something about the painting of St. George when she turned and caught sight of the raised tomb. She stopped dead still, stunned, I think, by the two polished stone figures lying prone on top of the tomb.

I motioned for her to come all the way into the room. "Allow me to present Sir Edward Hungerford III and Lady Margaret, his wife."

You might think there should be darkness looming around a tomb like that, but not here, not when you have the illumination of beautiful windows and the inner warmth of a romantic soul. The chapel provided the windows; Catlyn provided the rest.

She took a deep breath, like she was inhaling a rare and precious aura given off by the figures. A smile flashed, and I knew she'd forgiven my audacity in bringing her here.

"I hadn't imagined it could be so romantic," she said. "Buried side by side, like Cedric and Ariana." She stepped all the way forward then, laying her hand on Sir Edward's shoulder. "Right here, side by side, now and forever." Her eyes were examining the figures, but I suspected her mind was back at Southjoy Mission thinking of her own ancestors.

When she turned to look at me, I nearly cried. Gratitude

and trust were beaming from her face. So much had I sought that between us. Now, it came so unexpectedly. It gave me a joy that I'd cherish forever in my memory, right next to the incomparable elation I felt when Rip told me he loved me.

It was also memorable as one of the rare moments when Miss Catlyn Stacey of Southjoy Mission had difficulty finding the words to express her own feelings. She settled on, "Thank you," and we both just stood there for a second or two or three, or longer I suppose, more like a few minutes. We were just quietly appreciating the moment, allowing our thoughts to flow without inhibition.

I like to think that Catlyn, for that brief time, had dispensed with all the emotional encumbrances that had bogged her down these many months. For those few minutes, her spirit was free to embrace life. She had no need to be detached from it.

I took her through the rest of the site, the castle towers, the priest's house, and the gardens, but I don't think she really saw any of it. She was too preoccupied with other memories. Ariana, Southjoy Mission, Sebastian, and Tilly; I'm sure they all came to mind. That was the influence of the castle. There it stood, proving that dignity can persist even in the abandoned ruins that others had thought to destroy. It's like preserving a memory to honor the future. Reason enough, even, to *want* a future.

Chapter 23: Rose

With Catlyn away for the day with Amelia, Tilly joined me to help with the seasonal photo record I was creating for the estate. I thought we both could use some stress-free time, and it gave Biscuit a good chance to roam around a bit too, which appealed to Tilly. The focus today was the fall vegetation along the eastern shoreline of the creek.

I love this time of year with all its cold air and warm colors. Already yellow maple leaves were carpeting the approach to the stream. Their brilliant colors formed a blazing backdrop for the deep reds of the Bloodgood Japanese maples which were sheltering the banks of the stream. And right along the edge of the creek, there were scatterings of yellow-green mahonia shrubs, randomly mixed in with rusty red nandina and vibrant yellow-orange juneberry trees, all forming a very pleasing border.

Today, there was an intriguing sense of innocence to the bright sunlight. It washed the sky to a vivid blue that was shaded only intermittently by great islands of rolling clouds.

There's enough openness to the vegetation at this time of year that the light has a very natural, affable diffusion straight through it. That's not a technical term; it's just how I think of it. The light just seems to spread with extra efficiency as it scatters and reflects through the gaps beneath the denser brush. The net effect is that you get some really spectacular terrain level photos.

Biscuit seemed to be enjoying the cold air too. She had her own form of dizzying delight, scampering and charging about without particular aim, but, of course, never very far from Tilly. The pair of them made quite the picture of carefree delight churning through the leaves.

I had equipped Tilly with a wide-angle digital camera with autofocusing and a small zoom ability. She very quickly mastered the basics, so when not chasing Biscuit, she was applying her new camera skills to taking photos of the fall foliage or capturing candid shots of Biscuit. They were a picturesque duo themselves, so I took a few surreptitious shots of the two of them together to show Catlyn later.

The day progressed with perfect lighting. The highlights in the foliage were quite superb, and you had to love the dramatic shadows that were shifting and changing as the sun moved across the sky. It didn't matter where you looked, every view captured some aspect of the wonder and excitement of nature in transition. I immersed myself in them all. I was in no rush to be anywhere but here.

About the time we were running out of steam, Catlyn called to say she and Amelia were on their way back to the estate. It was decided that we'd all meet at the house, which would put us there just in time for afternoon tea. We'd all worked up an appetite by then, and Catlyn said she'd call ahead to ask for cookies or something chocolate for us. "Why not make it chocolate chip cookies?" I suggested, and Catlyn laughed. How wonderful it was to hear that laugh, the wonder and excitement of Catlyn in transition.

A few minutes later, Catlyn called again to say everything was arranged, and tea was "a go." There was something gleefully indulgent in the good nature of her voice. I could almost imagine her glowing with contentment. It was just that kind of day.

§§§

Coming up the path on foot, we could see Amelia guiding her Mini Cooper to the garage. We waved to her and then spotted Catlyn who was waiting for us at the front of the mansion. She seemed quite gregarious in the way she waved back to us. I couldn't help noticing how Tilly smiled at that. It did seem a rather long time ago that we last saw Catlyn in such high spirit.

Whinehardt, of course, was waiting at the door and ushered us into the foyer. Our hubbub was boisterous enough that I think our gaiety was bouncing every which way off the walls. Poor Whinehardt was so taken aback by it that he didn't know which way to turn. Catlyn rescued him by announcing, "We're doing everything a little different today, just to be different. So, I've decided we should have tea in the small sitting room next to the study."

Whinehardt nearly smiled. A good moment for Catlyn was a good moment for all. He acknowledged, "So Missus Sweetgrove has informed me. I believe everything is ready for you."

This *esprit de corps* continued the several paces needed to cross from the foyer to the small sitting room.

It stopped there.

Everything was off. The room was in shambles. Chairs that should have formed a congenial setting were turned on their sides or back-to-back around the perimeter of the room. The small couch had been tipped over, and all the tables were skewed at odd angles. Everything had been pushed back leaving a clearing in the middle of the room. Isolated right in the center, was a stool standing by itself.

I was trailing the group at the time, but I could see the flash of panic on Catlyn's face. Her eyes locked briefly on the stool, but she couldn't stop them from sweeping down the height of the stool to the floor where a small length of cord was laying at its foot. She seemed to freeze on seeing it.

An instant later, Amelia was grabbing Catlyn's arm, forcibly turning her away from the scene, pushing her. Amelia was commanding, "Everyone out! Out!" She didn't wait for anyone to respond or even to understand what she wanted. She just pushed Catlyn right past us.

Out in the foyer, Sweetgrove was hurrying towards us when Amelia suddenly whirled around to confront her. Amelia was shouting at her, "What have you done here?!" I've never seen her face flaring with such angry hues. This was way worse than when she accosted Lady Wythiry. She was screaming, "What have you done?!"

I freely admit I was scared. Catlyn looked to be in shock, and she was mumbling something that sounded like, "This can't be happening." Meanwhile, Sweetgrove was making awkward gestures, reeling in confusion, and backing away from Amelia who kept demanding, "How could you do this?"

Stumbling backwards, Sweetgrove looked desperately to Catlyn. In spite of her own state of shock, Catlyn managed to insist, "Amelia! She's one of us. Give her a chance to speak."

"Speak about what?" pleaded Sweetgrove, looking rapidly back and forth between Amelia and Catlyn. But Catlyn had already lapsed into other thoughts, and Amelia was pressing hard. It seemed to me, fear for her own safety was gripping Sweetgrove like nothing she'd ever experienced before.

I didn't yet fully understand what was going on, but it wasn't looking pretty. Taking my cue from Catlyn, I inserted myself bodily between Amelia and Sweetgrove. I tried to get Amelia to calm down. "At least let her see the room before you accuse her of anything."

Amelia glared wildly at me. Even her eyes were screaming. Her expression was so harsh it made me think the blistering anger in her mind was turning indiscriminate, and she'd be lashing out at me next. I braced myself and stood ready to grab her if she thought about hitting me. I really don't think Amelia's ever hit anybody in her life, but in a raging temper, who knows.

Come to think of it, there was that tempest in the cave when she and Catlyn took down Maggor. Thankfully, I'd forgotten about that. As I recall now, she had a vicious kick.

In the present conflict, I think my own aggressive stance caused Amelia to hesitate. It seemed to startle her. I think she could see I was as much protecting Catlyn as Sweetgrove. Whether that was the case or not, she stepped back and opened a pathway to the sitting room door.

Sweetgrove, though, was so petrified with fear and confusion she couldn't move. "Miss Stacey," she stammered, "if I've done anything to offend you, please, tell me."

Amelia didn't wait for Catlyn to respond. She motioned impatiently for Sweetgrove to move to the door.

I turned around to Sweetgrove to guide her past Amelia. At this point, Amelia's fury seemed to be contained, but Sweetgrove was still much in need of moral support.

Even though she was hesitant and shaking her head and muttering that she didn't understand, Sweetgrove did as directed. When we reached the door, she took scarcely a glance into the room. She caught her breath, pressed her hand over her mouth, and then her eyes absolutely flared with disbelief. "What is this?" she demanded.

Her fear was overridden by her own surge of

indignation. Whirling around, she charged straight at Amelia. Face to face, their confrontation erupted into a clamor of mutual glares and shouts and protests filled with the ire of shocked accusations.

As their voices rose in pitch, Catlyn seemed to glance past them into the corridor leading into the servants' wing. She was squinting and tilting her head like she was trying to hear something behind all the noise. I looked, but didn't see anything. By this point, Amelia and Sweetgrove were panting and more glowering than shouting, so I raised my own voice to get everyone to calm down and step back.

§§§

It took some minutes to get Amelia to stop ranting. Someone was responsible, and if it wasn't Sweetgrove, then she was going to lash out indiscriminately until she hit the right target.

I couldn't tell if Catlyn had gone into shock or was just deep in thought. Either way, she'd withdrawn and was holding herself apart from the chaos. After several repetitions of "How could you let this happen?" and "It was right and proper as I left it," Catlyn recovered enough to say, "Amelia. Please. They don't know what it's about. Tell them. They need to know."

Amelia stopped. She looked intently at Catlyn. She stepped over to stand close to her. "Are you sure...?" She placed her hand on Catlyn's arm. "Would you like to go...?"

"No." Catlyn was firm. "I need to think. But they need to know; I need them to know. Please. Tell them." But then she hesitated. Another worry creased her brow.

In some chamber of her mind, concern for Amelia took precedence over the need to think. Amelia had her own demons, her own haunting memories. Perhaps it was too much to ask of her. "No, wait," Catlyn corrected. "I'm sorry. That was thoughtless of me. It's my burden. I should tell them myself."

Amelia gripped Catlyn's arm tighter. "No. It's our burden. It's ours together. Let me tell them. I can still do that much."

Together. Side by side. Back to back. Whatever it takes.

§§§

The stool. Its isolation. The length of cord. Put together, they formed another unmistakable message from Rupert Errique. That was the long and short of it.

I called DI Malbec. It couldn't wait. We needed his help.

"This isn't some mischief intended as a joke, Ned, and it's not a coincidence. It's just like it was in the cave. The stool was right in the middle away from everything else. It's a different stool of course, but it was set apart just like it was when Catlyn was interrogated by Rupert Errique. Amelia said the cord was exactly like the one used to bind Catlyn's hands; exactly like it."

Ned detoured long enough to collect Dr. Ulma. Somebody clearly had breached the security of Southjoy Mission, and there'd be consequences. Dr. Ulma needed to be here. There was no point pretending otherwise.

I met them in the driveway and ushered them to the scene. "We haven't touched anything. We've left everything exactly as it was."

We were quickly joined by Amelia, and I'm embarrassed to say, Amelia and I launched into a competition, plunging headlong into a race to describe everything we'd discovered.

Ned is a patient man, but this was too much. "Ladies!" he commanded us, raising his hands to get our attention. We were startled enough to stare at him like we hadn't a clue what his problem was.

Seeing that he had our attention, he thanked us quietly and asked with some deliberation, "Can you think of any reason someone on the staff might want to do this?"

"None."

It was Catlyn who replied, and it caused everyone to turn around to look at her. She was frowning, deep in thought, ignoring how startled we all were.

"And I don't understand why somebody would laugh about it."

That puzzled all of us. Ned asked, "Excuse me?"

"I heard someone laugh. After Missus Sweetgrove looked into the room, someone laughed."

"I heard it too," Tilly insisted.

Dr. Ulma shot her an angry look. "That doesn't help, Tilly."

There was a presumption of lying in his glare.

"I know you're sticking up for her, but that doesn't help. It's important for her to distinguish what's real from what she's imagined, and she's got to do that on her own."

"I didn't imagine it." Catlyn was incensed. She pointed aggressively past the foyer. "It came from there."

Ned looked where she pointed. "Did anyone else hear it?"

What a picture we were. Averted eyes. Shifted weights. Discomfited grimaces. We did anything but look at Catlyn. I remembered seeing Catlyn looking in that direction and said so, but I had to admit I didn't know what she was looking at. "I think we were all too distracted at that moment."

Catlyn stared hard at Dr. Ulma. He didn't believe her.

You didn't have to be a psychiatrist to see how much that hurt. She struggled to speak through this new misery. "You don't have any right not to believe me."

At that point, Ned appealed for everyone to remain calm. "First things first," he directed. "Is anything missing?"

Catlyn took a calming breath; forced herself to turn her eyes away from Dr. Ulma. "I don't know," she acknowledged. She looked at Sweetgrove. "Would you..." she tried to ask. "Of course," said Sweetgrove as though she couldn't say it fast enough. Relief swept over her face. But as she jumped to the task, she stopped after only two steps. She looked back at Catlyn. Her expression was solemn. "And thank you," she said. Then she whirled around to march on the room, fortified that Miss Stacey still had confidence in her.

When Sweetgrove reported back, it was to say, "Nothing's missing that I could see. Everything's just topsy-turvy, and of course that stool doesn't belong in there at all. And there's a small piece of rope laying on the floor. I've no idea where that came from."

Ned was forced to say, "I'm afraid that doesn't leave us with much to work with. The room's a mess, but other than that, there's nothing pointing to a crime here. On the surface, this just looks like some domestic shenanigans."

"No physical crime," Amelia erupted again, "but it's obvious Rupert Errique had some hand in this, and it's just as obvious his intent was to harass Catlyn. Surely there's some crime in that."

"I don't dispute the strong coincidence, but it's a long way between coincidence and conviction."

"You said you don't believe in coincidence," I reminded him as gently as I could.

"I don't," he admitted, "and I don't want to in this case.

But I'm constrained to work with the facts, and as perverse as they seem, the facts are still circumstantial."

Catlyn was looking at him like she was trying to probe his thoughts. "Grannie Effie used to say, the wake of a snake is a weave of waves; read the weave to find the snake."

Tilly blanched. Whinehardt's mouth gaped. Sweetgrove pressed her hand over her heart, her eyes flaring in alarm. All of us seemed frozen in a fixed stare at Catlyn. Except Tilly. Every feature of Tilly's ghost white face was etched with panic. She looked sharply at Dr. Ulma, her whole face shrieking, *Stop them! Make them stop! It's too much!*

I don't know about the others, but I agreed. They were pushing Catlyn too far. "Denial" didn't begin to explain Catlyn's retreat into some fantasy world. I could see Tilly's body knotting with fear, and I wasn't faring much better. I turned urgently to look at Dr. Ulma. I was scowling at him, looking for any sign of scorn, any hint of righteous, condescending I-told-you-so gloating.

But there was none of that; not even surprise. He actually seemed pleased, as though Catlyn had said something miraculous. Or maybe the miracle was that she'd said anything at all, even if it was about snakes.

Ned startled me even more. "That's much to my thinking, as well, Miss Stacey, and if we're going to read this weave, as you put it, I'll need you to walk me through it, step by step."

Tilly and I looked at each other. Had they all gone crazy?

"Wait," I asked. "Are you saying you'll treat this as a crime anyway?"

"I'm saying I'll investigate it as a suspicious circumstance, until the facts say otherwise. Personally, I agree with you. Somewhere behind this, there's a crime, or a crime in the making. And it's got Rupert Errique written all over it."

We were yet standing outside the small sitting room. Ned suggested, "Perhaps we could all go sit down somewhere and try to form a collective picture of what happened."

"The atrium sitting room," Catlyn offered without hesitation. This had become almost an automatic response for her lately, like a default option; because of the large windows giving an open view into the garden, I suppose. "We'll all be more comfortable there."

The suggestion itself was very practical, like you'd expect from a normal, sane person. It caused Dr. Ulma to exchange another look with Tilly. His expression seemed almost contrite, like an apology.

§§§

Thoughts were racing as we reconvened. It took a few minutes for everyone to settle into a new re-grouping of allies and foes, of accusers and defenders. Dr. Ulma touched Catlyn's arm very lightly on the way into the room. She hesitated before looking up at him. He said something, I couldn't hear what, but I hoped it was "I'm sorry." She didn't reply except to nod her head the way you do when you mean, "It's okay. I understand."

From where I stood, though, all I could see was how much she was hurting. We who loved her thought we were protecting her, but all we were doing was smothering her defiance in the name of sanity. It seemed wrong. It just seemed so wrong. The situation *was* insane, and *we* were the ones who weren't prepared to see it.

They continued into the room, and Dr. Ulma took the

armchair that allowed him to study Catlyn. I know that's his job and he's supposed to do that, but it gets under your skin after a while. Catlyn didn't look at him. I'm sure she knew he was watching her, and I suppose she understood that's just how it had to be.

Amelia came alongside Sweetgrove and paused beside her. Neither looked at the other. "I'm sorry," said Amelia. "I know," Sweetgrove acknowledged; "it's forgotten." Amelia tried to explain. "No, it's not forgotten. It's just, I see something like this, the pain it causes Catlyn, and I know it's my fault, and I just want to make it all go away. If I could just do something, I don't know, throw myself off a cliff, anything to make her pain go away, I'd do it." Sweetgrove gently reached a hand across to Amelia; she patted her arm the way a mother consoles a child. "It will," she promised. "It'll all go away. For all of us."

Ned took a moment to look quietly about the room. I knew he was looking at our faces. It's just something he does when he wants to make sure people are ready for the hard stuff. Basically he was going to ask us to look at a good day and find something wrong with it. It made for an interesting dynamic. Stay low key but unmask the heresy; be deliberate, but do it as quickly as possible.

"Start at the very beginning," he told us. "Take me through the whole day. Don't leave out anything, and don't try to pick and choose what you think's important. Let me and Dr. Ulma do that."

That was Ned at his best, calm and methodical; it's what I first loved about him.

§§§

We did our best, but the day had just been a good day.

There were no unusual comings and goings, nothing unexpected, nothing amiss until that moment when we arrived at the small sitting room.

So, it came down to two critical questions. Who had access to the room, and how was he, she, or they connected to Rupert Errique? The "who" was relatively easy; it had to be someone on the staff; there wasn't anyone else. The connection to Errique was a presumption, but a sensible one. No connection made no sense. There was no mystery to it, but it was a puzzle.

Whinehardt volunteered, "There are the two footmen, of course. You may recall that fiasco here with the wine cellar after Miss Stacey's abduction. They'd gotten mixed up with that scoundrel Rimwell who was thick as thieves with Rupert Errique."

There wasn't anything about that case that Ned couldn't recall. As you know, he was the one who put all the pieces of that puzzle together. "I do remember them, yes. Rimwell had them searching the mansion for a hidden passage. They hoped it would lead them to a stash of stolen artwork. That was part of the sting Scotland Yard had set up with Mr. Stacey. They're still here?"

"They are, yes. I believed their story about being tricked by Rimwell, and Miss Stacey was inclined to be forgiving of their folly. But, if I may say so, Inspector, neither of them has wit enough to pull a stunt like this."

"I suspect you're right about that," Ned allowed as he recalled his interviews with them. "Let's accept that for the moment. Does anybody else come to mind?"

Whinehardt frowned. "There's some gossip," and he looked sympathetically at Sweetgrove. She sighed with evident frustration. Nodding her head, she confirmed Whinehardt's thought.

"I couldn't say if it's reliable," Whinehardt explained,

"but it seems one of the housemaids is quite upset with Missus Sweetgrove. The talk is, she's bragged about someday 'evening the score.' I believe that's how it was put."

"That would be Lucy," Sweetgrove acknowledged. "She helped set up the tea; I suppose she could've returned after I left the room. There was plenty of time."

Sweetgrove shook her head with disappointment. "I've tried everything with that girl. I've talked and scolded and disciplined her, but nothing takes. Still," she defended, "she's basically a good girl. She spends nearly every weekend with her ailing mother. Surely, that speaks well of her."

No one seemed inclined to encourage that view. Resigned to the inevitable, Sweetgrove asked, "Should I fetch her?"

Ned had that thoughtful Detective Inspector look again. "Supposing Lucy's the culprit, what would we gain from a confrontation with her?" It was a rhetorical question, so we waited while he considered his own answer. "She might admit the whole thing, but then what? Admit the deed, and lose the link to Rupert Errique? That wouldn't be good."

He seemed to be thinking out loud, and no one wanted to disturb him. Even Tilly was sitting perfectly still.

"The housemaid and the footmen are in the right place, generally speaking," he allowed. "The footmen have a past connection to Errique by way of Rimwell, but he's doing life in prison, so that link is probably broken. It's a known connection, so I'll question them. It would seem strange if we didn't. We've got to keep that in mind," he emphasized with a quick glance over all of us. "Errique is getting information from somebody, and that somebody must be close to the estate. We can take that as a fact, and whoever it is will report back to Errique on all of this. So, it's important that we be seen doing what's expected of us."

"What about Lucy, the housemaid?" I asked. "Shouldn't you question her as well?"

"She certainly had the most direct opportunity." He wondered, "Is she friendly with the footmen?"

"Not at all," Sweetgrove disparaged. "In fact, I'd have to say the staff is less tolerant of Lucy than I am."

Whinehardt agreed with her and added that there were minor complaints from the footmen; they claimed that Lucy had been rude to them on more than one occasion.

That seemed to satisfy Ned. He said, "Okay, the housemaid had the necessary opportunity, but if it's not through the footmen, where's the connection to Errique?"

"Could it all be an act?" I wondered, "Could Lucy and the footmen be working together? They could be pretending."

Whinehardt didn't think so. "The footmen have never shown any talent at deception, in my experience with them."

"I'll bear down on the footmen," Ned decided. "Let's see if they have any ties yet to Rimwell, even indirectly." He paused, arranging pieces of the puzzle. "If it's *not* the footmen, then most likely the housemaid's acting alone."

He considered that. "The housemaid's a bit of stretch, but if she's involved with Errique in some way, we'll have to tread very carefully around her so as not to tip our hand. I'll have to question her, of course. As unlikely as it is, we need to know if she saw anyone loitering around the room after the tea was set up. Beyond that, we need to keep her off guard. She mustn't even think she could be a suspect. That means all of you have to keep your suspicions to yourselves."

Tilly sat forward. "Do you want us to spy on her?"

"That's basically the idea."

"I'll do it," said Tilly. "I'll stick to her like glue."

"Not quite that close, and probably not here. Unless Lucy is making visits to Errique in prison, I think it's safe to assume, somewhere between here and there, there's at least one other person who makes the connection complete, and that's the person we need to find."

"Reading the weave," remarked Catlyn. She glanced at Dr. Ulma. He was smiling.

Chapter 24: DC Peters

I first worked with DI Malbec and DS Koogan just after the first Stacey case. That was old man Stacey, not the current Stacey. Old man Stacey was Catlyn Stacey's grandfather.

I was a TDC at that time, a Trainee Detective Constable. I'd already completed the National Investigators Exam, but I still needed to build my professional experience portfolio. I was assigned to work cases with DI Malbec, and most of what I've learned I learned from him. That's where I got my first real taste of murder cases, working with Malbec and Koogan on the kidnapping of Catlyn Stacey. There were three homicides connected with that case. I completed my training with them and was finally approved as a full-fledged Detective Constable. Now with this new investigation centered on Miss Stacey, I counted myself lucky to get to work with them again.

Being on the bottom of the totem pole, though, meant I still got most of the scum-butt jobs, like the surveillance on Lucy Dyson. This was old school surveillance, old school like DI Malbec. He's not much for high tech. You've got to feel the crime, he tells me. You've got to get inside the criminal's mind if you want to know what makes him tick. You only learn that first hand, like by keeping an eye on somebody from a distance and trying not to seem too obvious about it. That was his way of telling me a rookie DC won't look too good if he's reported as a stalker or a pervert by the person he's supposed to be tailing.

Surveillance on Lucy Dyson proved to be not such a bad deal. Lucy caught a ride into town with Heinrich, the gamekeeper at Southjoy Mission. This was a fairly regular thing, it turns out. Lucy made a point of keeping Heinrich up to date on her mother's illness, which was interesting because Heinrich, I've heard, isn't the most sociable person on the estate. It seems, though, according to Rose Honeywhiel, he's not the hard headed cuss you might think. She says he's really a big softie who's just not sociable.

That got me to thinking. Soft hearted and not sociable? Even a rookie like me can connect those dots. It's about as sweet a deal as you can find, if you want to hitch a ride on the QT. Who'd be the wiser? Unsociable Heinrich wouldn't likely be talking to anyone about it.

To my way of thinking, Lucy knew all that and used it to her advantage, which was fortunate for us because we caught a break by it. Heinrich wasn't sociable, but he did respect the chain of command. That meant whenever he left the estate, he informed Rose, and on this occasion, she informed me.

Heinrich told Rose he'd be dropping Lucy off at the bus depot. This, he said, was their usual routine. So, that's where I planted myself to see what Lucy did next. You know what? It wasn't to catch a bus. Some bloke in a little pickup pulled right up to her, she hopped in, and off they went.

It turns out Lucy's sick mother must live in a cowboy joint called the Lariat Saloon, because that's where she went, and that's where she stayed. I was going to slip in behind her to check it out, but I discovered real fast I couldn't do that and remain inconspicuous. This was cowboy all the way. Imagine that; cowboy in Bath!

I'd never been much of a fan of American cowboys. I mean, if you want to watch a bunch of guys ganging up on somebody, taking shots at each other, and piling on in a good brawl, then I say, give me a good soccer match any day. Anyway, so I had some homework to do, which meant watching a passel of John Wayne and Clint Eastwood movies, along with *The Electric Horseman* and *Rodeo Girl*. And just to be well rounded, I added in *The Good, The Bad, and the Ugly*. After all that, I was ready to mosey on over to the Lariat Saloon to take a gander at all them varmints hiddin' out "in them thar hills."

Turns out, Lucy's sick mother is a bloke named Ramon. He runs the Lariat, and I had the impression that he and Lucy were an item. They didn't try to hide the fact, and pretty much everybody I spoke to thought Ramon was shagging Lucy.

"Think they'll get hitched?"

"Ramon? No way. He don't hitch his wagon up to no filly."

Fling or relationship, it seemed pretty regular to me. If it wasn't anything deep, they was sure play acting the parts nonetheless. They had a gig, every Friday night to Sunday night, as near as I could reckon, and then it was back to their day jobs.

So why'd she lie about it? DS Koogan didn't see anything strange about it. "Would you go blabbin' something like that to your uptight house matron?"

I supposed he was right. There could've been any number of reasons to keep her trap shut. It was her private life and maybe she wanted to keep it that way. Maybe she was afraid of what Missus Sweetgrove would say about it. All things considered, as far as I could see, she wasn't doing sod all that you'd call incriminating.

I wasn't keen on reporting back empty handed, but that's all I had. Malbec, though, wasn't peeved at all. "Not bad for a start," he said, and then he reminded me, "We're not looking to nail a housemaid for being untidy. We're looking for a link to Errique, and if the saloon's all we got, then let's see what we can find out about it."

§§§

The Lariat Saloon was a local watering hole patterned after an American Wild West bar from the golden age of cowboys and rough-riding outlaws. The owner, Ramon Lorenzana, known affectionately as Spur, had rocketed through a very brief career as a professional bronco rider in the American southwest, having been thrown from every bronco he'd ever mounted in every rodeo event he could talk, buy, or scam his way into. After a broken arm, two cracked ribs, three broken teeth, and a femoral stress fracture that left him with a permanent limp and chronic pain, he retired.

Restless as a tumbleweed, he drifted home to Wyoming, where the winters made his joints ache, then back down to Kansas, where hard work was expected of the help, and thence cross-country to New York, which was inhospitable to an out-of-work cowboy who sometimes drank too much.

From there, he conned a ride on a container ship to Barcelona. Finding the subtropical climate not to his liking, he bummed his way farther north through France and up to the UK. There, he took refuge in London where he was surprised to discover that Londoners had developed a certain appreciation for Argentinian cuisine and especially everything gaucho.

A little upscale for his taste and far out of the range of his budget, it was, nonetheless, inspirational. He knew nothing about being a gaucho, except that it's kind of like a South American cowboy, but cowboys he did know about. It seemed to him that if the upscale crowd liked gauchos, maybe some salt-of-the-earth types would be eager to spend their hard earned shillings for a cowboy experience.

But London was already seething with ethnic diversity. He wouldn't be truly unique there. What he needed was a location where strange costumes would get you noticed but wouldn't make you an outcast. The local ambiance in Bath, with its mingling of Roman togas, medieval buildings, and regency gowns, seemed like just the sort of eclectic culture that might take a shine to a cowboy from Wyoming.

It did, and he did, and in no time, an investor with equally eclectic tastes agreed to finance the grubstake needed to give birth to the Lariat Saloon.

Therein settled and living his dream vicariously in a bar decorated with rodeo memorabilia, Ramon rapidly became an iconic curiosity attracting the attention of many curious people. It helped enormously that he was disposed to being an agile facilitator of illicit affairs and any other manner of lucrative enterprise that required nothing more of him than to look the other way.

He was otherwise congenial and engaging and entertaining. While he could never ride a bronco, he did know how to work a lariat, and did so from time to time to the delight of his patrons. He'd form a loop, start it to twirling at his side, bring it up over his head, then let it descend down around his feet, all the while keeping it twirling at a steady rate. Then, to whoops and hollers, he'd skip in and out of the loop until his back got to achin', at which point he'd float the loop up overhead and send it hurling through the air to lasso Lucy Dyson.

Cheap talk to the contrary, Lucy was sweet on Ramon. One of the housemaids at Southjoy Mission, she was often teased for her quirky tastes and was always at odds with the footmen. She had few friends and little prospect of ever being called charming, except by Ramon, which could account for her frequent visits to the Lariat. To hear her tell it, there wasn't much in her life that could surpass an evening when she could dress up like a cowgirl, chow down a plate of beans and bacon, and sidle up to the bar to exchange a bit of gab with the barkeep.

Lucy adored beyond words Ramon's triumphant exploits on the rodeo circuit and fully believed he was robbed of his championship crown when a gateman released an ill-mannered roughstock bull from its chute before Ramon had given his nod. The bull couldn't be headed off by the pickup men, and the resulting injury ended his career. Granted, it wasn't much of a career and there wasn't any bull except the story he was telling, but it was mighty entertaining.

Lucy's clinging attention was as close to hero worship as a has-been, never-was rodeo champion was ever likely to get. She was no Mae West, but then, he was no Hoot Gibson either. Truth be told, neither one had more'n a half ration o' looks, but there being no other suitors, it was only natural they'd sashay up the back stairs to his room over the saloon and spend every weekend pleasurin' one another.

Like many underachievers, Lucy was most particular to lament her dismal lot in life. It wasn't that she'd tried and failed or that she'd even fantasized about trying or achieving. Neither assertive nor ambitious, she was content to complain, which she did often and at length to Ramon. Not about him, of course. Mostly about her coworkers, and most especially about Missus Sweetgrove. Sweetgrove was bossy, always going on about this mess or that mess that Lucy had left behind, always scolding her for being untidy, never satisfied with the "level of performance" exhibited by Lucy. It was a frequent litany, and it got Ramon to cogitatin', which led to a rather revealing exchange that several patrons at the Lariat

Saloon remembered with great clarity and endless amusement.

"I do declare Miss Lucy, somethin's eatin' attcha powerful hard. But don'cha fret none, ya hear? I aims t'hep ya. Y'all'll be sittin' plumb square in yer saddle quicker'n a leapin' lizard kin lick a sow bug."

As anyone at the Lariat could tell you, Lucy loved it when Ramon talked cowboy.

"Meanin' no disrespect, ma'am, but this here Sweetgrove ain't no lady and she ain't treatin' ya kindly. Seems ta me, there's a score t'settle."

The regulars whistled, stomped their feet, and slapped their knees like it was a right good show, but for us, it was the link we were looking for. It wasn't an admission of the fact, but the notion and the fact went hand in hand. Lucy had a score to settle, and we were certain sure Ramon helped her do it. That would mean the script came from Ramon, and no doubt Lucy thought it was perfect. Why wouldn't she? Give Sweetgrove a taste of her own medicine? How sweet would that be? But Ramon wouldn't know about the cave, so where did he get his script? That was the critical question, and the answer, we knew, would lead to Errique.

R. G. Munro

Chapter 25: Ethan

When Amelia rang up to tell me about the latest disruption at Southjoy Mission, I was appalled. Who could be so sick as to torment Catlyn by recreating the scene of her kidnapping?

An event like this makes everyone's blood boil, and needless to say, it was a long conversation with Amelia. She alternated between steaming in anger at whoever did this thing and venting her frustration with herself. It was disturbing on multiple fronts, and as Amelia said, it was designed to be. It was the kind of thing that made you think, if God is watching us right now, he must be so ashamed of how little humanity has learned about humanity. I shuddered to imagine the effect it was having on Catlyn.

I was due at the estate the following day to review the next letter in the Prunella collection, but I thought perhaps I should cancel. I rang up Catlyn and suggested, "Maybe it'd be better to take a break before we push on."

"Push," Catlyn told me. "There's no point in trying to hide, and as Dr. Ulma would say, there's no getting ahead by running away. It's my life, and I don't have an off button."

If this event was supposed to have shattered her psyche, somebody seriously miscalculated. You could hear the anger in her voice. And it riled her to a state fit for battle.

"Rose thinks this stupid incident proves I'm in danger even here in my own home. She's tried to convince me to go away for a while for my own safety. But this is my home, and I can't call it that if I'm not willing to protect it."

And that was the end of any debate on that subject.

Sometimes it's difficult to tell the difference between being strong in one's resolve and just being stubborn. I was reminded of that when I kept my appointment with Catlyn the following day. Out of defiance or perversity or just some innate rebelliousness in the American DNA, Catlyn informed me, "We'll be in the small sitting room today."

The look on my face must have been rather telling of my discomfort with that idea, but she assured me, "I know what you're thinking, but it's okay. DI Malbec had his team in here photographing everything, dusting for fingerprints, and whatever it is they do. After they left, Rose and Tilly went in and took their own photos of every little thing in there."

She shrugged at my puzzled look. "I know. It was a pointless exercise, but it made them feel like they were taking charge of the situation. If it makes them feel better, I'm all for it. Anyway, this morning, Sweetgrove got the room back in good order, and now I'm reclaiming it. Okay?"

It wasn't really a question, but I said "Okay" anyway.

Something in the way Catlyn was handling this latest crisis reminded me of a passage in Caesar's Commentaries about the Gallic Wars. Caesar wrote, "Gallia est omnis divisa in partes tres." All Gaul is divided into three parts. He meant regionally as determined by three rivers. The Garonne separated the people known as the Gauls from the Aquitani. The Marne and the Seine rivers further separated those two from the Belgae. Much later, Victor Hugo would write about a different kind of partitioning, again all divided into three parts. The rulers, backed by the military. The church, backed by God. And the peasantry, backed against a wall. I thought that rather seemed to describe Catlyn's current state of mind. It too was divided into three parts similar to Hugo's partitions. Fierce, pious, and desperate. Whereas Hugo had talked about the vox populi, Catlyn had had enough of voices. She was more like Caesar. She was intent on conquering it all.

Tilly was standing guard over the room. She already had Catlyn's tablet set up for us, so we got straight down to business. Tilly claimed her own part by reading the letter out loud. It was another letter to Ariana.

We had more unpleasantness today, and it caused such calamity you would have thought someone had been murdered. It seems Mr. Joshua has discovered contraband hidden in the hammocks of two sailors. He has seized the two sailors and placed them under arrest. But, there was such a ruckus made on deck that everyone demanded to know the particulars. The sailors were shouting their innocence, and that's when Gerald decided to intervene. Gerald told Captain James that the goods in question belong to him and that the sailors were merely helping him with storage. Mr. Joshua was furious, but he stopped short of calling Gerald a liar. As you may recall, Mr. Joshua is the officer who argued with Gerald on a previous occasion. Mr. Joshua has demanded an inquiry because he says the goods should have been examined by the Customs Agent before leaving dock, which was not done. The captain has agreed, but he "belayed" the order for now. He gave no reason for his decision. Gerald has given me no reason for his interference, except that he has not denied what I know to be true, that the goods are not his. I begin to worry.
– Prunella, Letter No. A3, 1810

"I'll bet they were smugglers," Tilly decided.

I had to admit she was probably right. "This was one of

those transitional periods in the operation of packet boats. You see, up until then, a little business on the side was okay. It was actually a long-standing and expected practice among the sailors. It wasn't at all unusual for sailors to supplement their wages this way, and they very often did it on commission from respectable merchants back in England."

"But was it legal?" That caused me to smile cautiously to myself. This was the incisive Catlyn we'd all adored, slicing through the blur of details to get to the heart of the matter. How I had missed that gift of hers. Focusing under composed circumstances isn't so unusual; lots of people can do that. But doing so when harried with strife and distraction requires a special capacity. Somebody was trying very hard to hassle Catlyn with psychological warfare. But this gift of hers hadn't yet been taken prisoner.

"Not exactly," I replied. "It had become prohibited by law, but it was a law that no one was enforcing as a general rule."

"So it was there to be enforced if it served their purpose."

"Possibly, but it was probably more than that. Right around that time, enforcement was being stepped up in an effort to remove what the government considered to be the blemishes of a corrupt system. But, to overcome a popular practice, it would've required some zealous enforcers, and Mr. Joshua might have been one of them. That said, however, that vigorous enforcement effort was putting a big crimp in a sailor's income. Later in that same year, matters came to a head. The more zealous the enforcement became, the more the packetmen resented it. Finally, in Falmouth, they retaliated with what was basically a mutiny; they banded together and refused to man the ships. Without them, the packet ships couldn't sail, and the official mail service was disrupted."

Catlyn wasn't convinced. "This seems more selective than that. I think Mr. Joshua was using it to his own advantage."

"The captain, though, agreed with him."

"He agreed, yes, but then he belayed the order. Why?"

"Because," said Tilly, our rising conspiracy theorist, "he was in on it."

"That's not a bad guess," Catlyn allowed. "The captain's decision left a lot of room for suspicion. Gerald, on the other hand, was a bigger puzzle. What was he up to?"

"I couldn't even begin to speculate on that," I admonished them looking straight at Tilly, "and neither should you. The more we speculate when we know so little, the fuzzier what we do know tends to become."

We all sat there a few minutes more reviewing the letter, re-thinking how it might be interpreted differently, but finding nothing more to add to our conclusions, or at least nothing useful, we retreated into the quiet of our own thoughts.

As our silence deepened, Catlyn got our attention with a big sigh. "I used to think that their era was so much simpler than what we have today, but Prunella's letters are showing me an entirely different picture. It's not as pretty as I wanted it to be. Sebastian was right; we're too quick with our labels. Dark Ages, Age of Enlightenment; they're nothing but different faces of the same culture. It's always been the Age of Conspiracy."

That too I found disturbing on multiple levels. She spoke of Sebastian without the slightest hint of sorrow. I chose to believe that was a good thing and that it wasn't camouflage for some new defeatist attitude coming out, as might be suggested by the way she was deferring to him or by the way she seemed to be quitting the fight. And that negative view of people? That wasn't Catlyn at all. It sounded a lot more like an encroachment of depression, and it was growing stronger, and it was my fault because I dragged her into this project.

I had just about convinced myself that I'd blundered in a big way when out of the blue she said, "It's not about contraband. There's something else going on." She nodded, confirming her own assessment. "We need more information. Tell Willy to get cracking on those letters."

And there she was again, slicing through the blur. I wanted to think the best of that, but realistically, I could see she was at a balance point, ready to teeter either way. That in itself was highly encouraging, because it meant all she needed now was a little surcease from harassment, and she'd be sailing on an even keel.

Chapter 26: Lady Wythiry

I must say, a positive word in the press can be quite stimulating, even if it's from someone as repulsive as Durke Ormy, and even if he did reserve his best words for Rupert Errique.

Encouraged by Lady Cecelia Wythiry, convicted extortionist Rupert Errique is making a valiant effort to rehabilitate himself.

Errique, a mere extortionist? I suppose "mastermind" would have been too lacking in sympathy, and "thief" would be too demeaning. I suppose anything else would have left everyone indifferent to the whole story. But, still, him being valiant and all by himself? Really, now. And me, merely encouraging? Well, I intended to correct that misperception.

I still had friends, people who respected my breeding and position in society. They know who I am and what I'm capable of; indeed, they do. They depend on me in many ways, and of course they know enough to appreciate my financial support when it's needed. As to their stations in society, one hand washes the other, as they well know, and they certainly understand how much they're owing to me in favors. Even with my diminished public esteem, they owe me, and they know it. And they know I'm not above reminding them, in public.

So, I was cashing in my chits.

That's why I felt confident I'd have no difficulty pushing forward to the next step in my campaign to re-establish my public image, which ultimately required elevating Rupert

Errique into a better grade of society than he'd ever enjoyed in his past. Certainly, he could never hope to belong to a superior class, but I had no doubt he could do better than thief. That's what I intended for him, but even that modest advancement could be accomplished only if the general public could be persuaded to admire him in some small way, and I don't mean with respect to his villainy.

In this objective, I was determined not to be denied. It was a matter of principle after all. And I don't mean all that honor and dignity claptrap. Anyone can do that. I'm referring, of course, to a principle of station. Something few people truly comprehend. For the most part, the more vulgar elements of society interpret a necessity of station as mere class exploitation. They only see the greener grass on the other side of the fence; the ingrates envy it yet fail to observe how my green grass enhances the very air they breathe.

A case in point is the repatriation of a lost soul who's wandered down the more unseemly paths of society. Decidedly, there can be no greater service to a community than to guide such a person back to decency. Superior classes, of course, do not wander in such manner, but it may be necessary for them to venture boldly into those illicit realms to retrieve someone who *has* had the misfortune to wander into them.

Such is the basis for my Rupert Errique project. By the time I finish, everyone will be calling me Rupert Errique's guiding light. Mark my word on it, I'll be esteemed above all society, high and low. Perhaps then I may dream again of a baronage, quite possibly in my own right. Baroness. Not an unworthy aspiration, I should think, as a matter of station.

However, it'd be most foolish not to remember who

you're dealing with. A man with Mr. Errique's past, misunderstood though he may be, had to be approached cautiously. But, the greater the risk, the greater the glory, what?

Specifically, I wanted to be absolutely sure Errique wasn't double dealing me. He followed my instructions well enough earlier in meeting with Catlyn Stacey, but I'd since heard that all was not well between them. I'm sure it was all just hearsay, but that kind of rumor needs to be nipped in the bud before it becomes a raving scandal. A sympathetic view of Errique was vital to my plans.

It was essential, therefore, that I be certain Errique wasn't contriving another one of his illicit schemes. That necessitated a return visit to the prison. Face to face; that's how you deal with men like Errique.

I was quite brutal about it. "If you're burning the candle from both ends of the stick," I told him, "you're going to get doubly burned."

That set him on his heels, so to speak, and left him no doubt about my resolve. I meant business.

"As you can see, Mr. Errique, there are no cameras today, no reporters, no fanfare. Just you and me, and I want straight answers from you."

Well, I think he got the message clear enough. If he had any hope of getting out of prison sooner rather than later, he'd best understand. The exit door would open to him only if I, and I alone, opened it for him.

He seemed most contrite after that. Indeed, he begged my pardon most touchingly. "Your Ladyship," he exclaimed, "I've been maligned so many times in my life that sometimes I find myself believing it could all be true. Indeed, I do! I believe it could all be true."

He took a deep breath and looked at me most admirably. "But your kindness, Your Ladyship, your kindness overcomes it all. You understand what it is to be abused by the press. You know how unfair people can be."

He did seem to be quite impassioned about it.

"That's why I've so ardently embraced you as my guide. Your word to my ear is an inspiration."

He carried on in such fashion until it was simply too embarrassing to allow him to continue, and I told him so. I accepted his sincerity and, because of it, I believed him ready to take the next bold step in our program. For some reason, that made him apprehensive.

"Please, Your Ladyship, instruct me. What have you in mind?"

Sincere he may have been, but it made him no less suspicious of me. Given his history, I couldn't really fault him for that.

"Mr. Errique, people mistrust you because you are a stranger to them. If you are to be accepted into society, you must be *of* the society; you must be seen to fit in."

I could see at once he was intrigued.

"Your Ladyship, I can think of nothing that would suit me better, but you see how it is in this place. I think you must agree, there are certain obstacles to fitting in from here."

"Not here, Mr. Errique."

I relished this moment when he would look at me so filled with bewilderment.

"With suitable endorsements and assurances, Mr. Errique, your prison officials would be eager to place you into a work release program."

The surprise, the elation, the hope; it was all too gratifying.

"Your Grace..." He actually called me Your Grace. I didn't have the heart to correct him; besides, I rather liked it. "...tell me what I must do, and I shall do it."

"For starters," I instructed, "we mustn't begin with anything too extravagant. It must be a simple task, something that could be completed with only a brief excursion outside these walls, and it must be humble in appearance. Most importantly, it must be some form of community service."

He looked at me rather slyly; he is, after all, an intelligent individual. "I presume you've something in mind already."

"Indeed I do," I confessed. "As you know, I have a significant relationship with our hospital's affairs. There are many small tasks, menial in nature for a man of your abilities, but quite suitable to our purpose. A word from me, and it is a done deal."

"And they'd just let me walk out of here on your say so?"

"Alas, no. A person of your reputation, you understand. They simply cannot permit you that much liberty, given the particulars of your case. The protocol I've arranged for you is this..."

"You've arranged it? Already?" He was quite taken by surprise. I was delighted.

"Of course, Mr. Errique. I leave nothing to chance – ever." I think that bit of comeuppance lifted his appraisal of me several notches. He sat back and crossed his arms, and then he tilted his head as though he was trying to fathom what great depth there might be in my thoughts. The man can be a true delight.

I got straight to the point. "This is how it's going to work. First, in the care of armed guards, you'll be escorted to the hospital. There, your custody will be transferred to our armed security personnel, and you will change out of your prison garb into proper civilian clothing. We must maintain the appearances of the hospital, you understand. We wouldn't want other patrons alarmed by the presence of a prisoner. The cost for all this, of course, will be covered by a grant from me to the hospital. Then, under the watchful care of our security service, you'll perform whatever task has been set aside for you, after which the sequence reverses, and you return to your cell."

The latter remark was a bit unkind, but I felt it was essential that we keep this matter in its proper perspective.

I do think he appreciated how I had arranged it all. Indeed, other than the formalities, there was very little for him to do beyond signing a few pieces of paper. When interviewed by the prison officials, he eagerly accepted my proposal. I do believe his superlative praise for Her Majesty's correctional wisdom helped enormously to seal the deal, and of course, he was unstinting with his praise of myself.

In short, it was a triumph. Durke Ormy said so.

Chapter 27: Dr. Ulma

It was incredible. Absolutely incredible. It defied reason. Yet, there it was in the Daily Reveler.

Rupert Errique To Be At Large.
Work Release Program Approved.

The news was full of the story. Somehow Errique, a known sociopath, had scammed his way into a release program. Notables of every ilk were rushing to be interviewed. Reporters, pens frantically scribbling, newscasters with microphones in hand, and political commentators of every leaning, all scrambled to get quotes from everyone who cared to offer an opinion.

Except from me, that is.

I left messages for the Director of Prison Affairs and for the magistrate who could override the release order. Neither would take my call, and neither was available for comment. Both opted to reply via PR specialists who assured me that Rupert Errique was a model prisoner.

"We take our responsibility to the public very seriously, Dr. Ulma. There is no danger whatsoever to any member of the public. Mr. Errique will be under the watchful care of armed guards the entire time." Furthermore, they lectured me, "All due diligence has been exercised in this matter, and we have the personal assurance of Lady Cecelia Wythiry that she'll be taking full responsibility for Mr. Errique."

Do you suppose they ever listen to themselves? What does that even mean, she'll take full responsibility? Is she going to blush if somebody's life is ruined?

They just didn't care. This was a front page photo-op, and nobody wanted to be left out.

In the end, they dismissed me in their usual supercilious manner. "We appreciate your concern, but there's really no threat to Miss Stacey." In afterthought, they allowed, "Please feel free to convey that assurance to Miss Stacey."

I had no better luck with the hospital administration. Lady Wythiry is a formidable patron of the hospital, and it seems there's a potential here for a new, fully equipped rehab center. They expect the publicity from this affair to be exceedingly helpful in generating the necessary funds for it. Never mind the fact that Errique's alleged rehabilitation had nothing to do with physical rehab.

After forbidding me to speak to Lady Wythiry herself, or to intervene in any other way, they did remember to say, "Please convey our assurances to Miss Stacey."

There seemed to be a fire sale on assurances this week.

There was no way I was going to face Catlyn and tell her that everything was going to be okay. Against my better judgment, though, I did try to say we could find a way to make sense out of it. Honestly, I did try. But I didn't believe it any more than she did.

Catlyn sat rigidly in her chair. Her posture radiated suppressed anger and frustration. There was no eye contact.

"We could talk about it, if you'd like," I suggested.

"Why?"

"Because, if we bring our thoughts and emotions out in the open, we can understand them better."

"No, not that. Why is Lady Wythiry doing this?"

"You don't believe what they're saying?"

She made eye contact on that. "Not for a minute. And neither do you."

There was no point trying to deny it. I agreed with

Catlyn one hundred percent regarding the pretense of Lady Wythiry's intentions, but I wasn't so sure we were on the same page yet. "What do *you* think Lady Wythiry is up to?"

She was silent a few seconds, studying my face like she was reading my thoughts. This was something new in her behavior. Usually it's the analyst who tries to read the patient. The patient is more likely to focus on evasion and concealment. This new behavior was more *in*vasion than *e*vasion. It was a fascinating change in attitude, but it was an unwelcome kink in her complexity at this juncture.

There was certainly a lot for her to distrust in the present circumstances, and that's what I was seeing in her eyes and in her posture right now; distrust. It was good that she was being alert, and maybe it was even sensible. But I had to wonder, who was she distrusting? She had every right to believe "the system" had betrayed her, but I truly hoped she wasn't including me in that category.

As it was, I had my own issues with "the system" at the moment because there was a bigger concern. What would happen if this new development triggered a new trauma in Catlyn's mind? To put it colorfully, a new source of anger coupled so closely to her existing anxieties could send her deeper into the darkness of her persistent nightmares.

"What Lady Wythiry wants isn't the issue," Catlyn corrected me. "The real question is, what is Errique up to? Wythiry's just a cog in Errique's machinery. Once we know what Errique is up to, we'll know how she fits in."

Catlyn lapsed into further thought; she seemed to be re-thinking something. "Errique was behind the staging of that scene in the small sitting room." She held up her hand to stave off my objection. "Yes, I know, we don't have any physical proof of that, but when you eliminate all other possibilities, that's the only conclusion left."

I reminded her, "There was a lot of news coverage about

the kidnapping and how you were held in a cave. All the news reports..."

"...reported the general layout at the cave, I know, but not the specific detail of the cord that was used to tie my hands. The only thing ever reported was that my hands were bound; not how."

I was astounded. She said it as a statement of fact; no grimace; no flinching. Just an ordinary fact, like it all happened to somebody else, not her.

"The only person at the estate who knew that specific detail was Amelia."

And Amelia was above reproach in Catlyn's estimation.

I said, "You place a lot of trust in Amelia."

My tone might have been a little more abrasive than I intended. No, let's be honest about it. I did intend it. I suppose I was envious of Amelia for being so close to Catlyn. I made a note to think about that later.

"I do," she acknowledged comfortably. "She risked her life to help me. She didn't have to do that. She could've played along with Errique to save her own life. But she didn't."

That I could understand. Combat units, line-of-fire police officers, first responders of every sort, all have the same experience in the field; you learn who's got your back. Catlyn and Amelia had that kind of trust. End of discussion.

"Okay. Let's take that as a fact, then. Rupert Errique staged the scene at the estate. What does that get us? How does that relate to Lady Wythiry?"

"I don't know yet," she said with remarkable ease, "but we'll get there." She asserted, "What I need right now is a reliable eyewitness."

"Witness? To what?"

"I'd do it myself, but it wouldn't be wise for me to be

there when Errique's there. But you could go. The hospital's your domain. Nobody would question why you're there."

"You want me to go to the hospital for Lady Wythiry's gala unveiling of Rupert Errique?" I was just catching up to her train of thought.

"Yes. Go there. Observe them. See how they interact, what their body language says, that kind of thing." She paused to look at me rather cunningly. "You're very good at that." She was actually smiling. At least I think it was a smile.

I, on the other hand, must have been staring. She asked, "What?"

I was perplexed, that's what. I was supposed to be helping her through a crisis, and here she was, giving me an assignment and expecting me to report back to her.

"I don't think that's how this is supposed to work, Catlyn. I'm supposed to ask you questions, and you tell me about your feelings and perceptions."

"We don't have time for that. Errique is on the move, and we've got to stop him."

I latched onto that. A perception of threat was something I could sink my teeth into. Except for one detail. Where was the flight response?

Suddenly, I didn't like where this was going. This had all the earmarks of an obsession in the making. I wanted Catlyn to be strong, to fight hard, but this? This wasn't being resolved. This was seeing Errique as evil incarnate. This was seeing Errique as a monster, a dragon that Catlyn intended to slay, and in her present state of mind, it was beginning to look like a very real possibility.

Slay Errique.

I wanted to think this was just an idle fantasy, but there wasn't anything idle about her thought process. It was deliberate and devoid of emotion, aka, cold premeditation.

Eliminating the root cause of her fears was something we'd talked about in a different context. But eliminating it physically? As tempting as that might seem, a rational mind should understand; that only replaces one nightmare with another. It won't erase the agonies already embedded in her mind. More likely, it would only amplify them.

Still, a desperate mind might risk it.

Slay Errique.

And she wanted my help to do it.

Chapter 28: Tilly

The more things got riled up with Rupert Errique, the more I looked forward to quiet time with Miss Stacey. By that, I don't mean our portico time when we'd stand in the cold waiting for the sun to rise. That was certainly quiet, but it was a different kind of togetherness, and it wasn't much good for talking. At most, she'd say to me, "You don't have to do this with me." I wanted to say, "Let's neither of us do it," but I knew she'd just smile and look back to the sun. "I want to," is what I did say to her, "because I want you to know I'll always be with you. Promise me you'll remember that. Whatever happens, I'll always be with you." She turned sharply to me, and there was a flicker of fear in her eyes. "Don't you ever doubt it," she commanded. Then she took a quick breath and smiled, because she knew I never would.

You can see how that'd make for a pretty quiet time. What I had in mind was different, a together time when we'd talk and at least pretend that life was normal. Breakfast was supposed to be one of those times. It was "us" time. Miss Stacey, Rose, and me, in the tea room. "Reconnecting time" Miss Stacey had called it. But lately, "quiet" was more like "mute," and nothing was connecting to anything else.

If Miss Stacey talked at all, it was about Rupert Errique or Lady Wythiry. She'd be steamed or grumpy, and then she'd clam up tight. She'd sit there sulking and grinding her teeth and flexing her jaw, even though her mouth was closed, and it had nothing to do with chewing, unless she was chewing on Errique and trying to think of some way to spit him out.

She didn't respond much to anything we said, except for a nod or maybe an "em-m." Rose tried to tell me Miss Stacey was so preoccupied that she needed to use our quiet time for thinking. But I didn't see much evidence of thinking. I won't say she was brooding, but if I acted like that, that's what everybody would say I was doing, brooding.

It almost seemed like we weren't allowed to talk about everyday things anymore, not even the holidays. That bothered me the most because I was in charge of our holidays. That was my contribution to Miss Stacey's life right now. If she didn't have time for the holidays, maybe she didn't have time for me either. How could I not worry about that? And, yes, before you say anything, I know I was being selfish about that. But being selfish didn't make it wrong.

Little Christmas had been one of the few things that Miss Stacey had been excited about. For a while, we were making and changing plans almost every day. But now, making plans wasn't even on the agenda.

So naturally, I decided to do something about that.

First, I talked to Rose. She agreed. She told me Miss Stacey was operating in "reactive mode." All of us, she said, were doing the same thing, just reacting to our circumstances. How so, I wanted to know, and she basically explained, if you bump your head, you react because it hurt; you say "ouch." So, reacting to our circumstances meant reacting to things that hurt us and watching our backs for trouble.

I didn't like the sound of that at all. If you're watching your back, you can't see where you're going, which means you'll lose sight of your quest, which puts trouble up ahead of you, not behind you. Maybe I just didn't get it.

Anyway, for some time now, I'd been thinking of asking

Miss Stacey if we could go shopping again, but I knew she wanted to wait for the Bath Christmas Market, so I hadn't said anything. Besides, I didn't want her to say "no" or even "not yet." Dr. Ulma said we had to "think positive," and that's what I was trying to do. I was now on a mission to find something she'd say "yes" to without an argument.

Breakfast this morning was pancakes with strawberries and whipped cream. Cook came in to ask, "Them cakes and berries like what your mom made? Not too dry?" Miss Stacey surprised us by jumping up and giving Cook a big hug. "You remembered," she said to Cook, and hugged her again. "They're just perfect."

That was no nod or "em-m," and we wanted to know what was up. Miss Stacey sat down looking very pleased. Then she told us how her mom used to make this for her before she got sick and how it was still one of her favorite meals. Leave it to Cook to know that. She does know her kitchen.

I said, "I thought all Americans ate corn flakes for breakfast and hamburgers for everything else."

And that's when I got inspired.

"Except for Thanksgiving!" I was beside myself with delight. "Miss Stacey," I begged her, "could we celebrate the American Thanksgiving Day? I've never had a Thanksgiving Day dinner, but it's always sounded so wonderful in the movies. We could have everybody together, right here."

"Oh, I don't know, Tilly. It's a lot of work to do it right. I haven't done a Thanksgiving Dinner since my father died, and here..."

"But we could do it. You're American. Dr. Ulma's American. And we're all thankful for something. You're thankful you're here, aren't you?"

I could have slapped myself. The words came out of my

mouth before I knew what I was saying. I cringed at the sadness that came over Miss Stacey. She peered at me, then looked away; she looked away from me, and I wanted to cry.

I watched her tilt her head like it was all some doubtful proposition. I couldn't see her face, but I'm sure she must've been frowning. She usually thinks of her father or Grannie Effie at such times. Maybe she was remembering what they would've said about it all. Then, like a miracle, she looked back at me, and I could breathe again, because there was no frown. Very softly, she said, "I am thankful." There might've been some sadness in her voice, but when she added, "very thankful," I was sure she was smiling inside.

I decided that was as close to "yes" as I was going to get, and I took it. "You won't have to do anything," I promised, "except tell me what to do. I'll help Cook with the food."

I looked at Cook and asked, "Would that be okay?" She got a big smile on her face. "Oh, my, yes," she said, and I think she was every bit as pleased as me. "Miss Stacey," she declared, "it's a grand idea."

Now I was really beside myself.

"And Rose will help me with the decorations. You will, won't you Rose?"

"Of course," Rose joined in. "We'll decorate the big dining room for the main course, and maybe we could use the sitting rooms for hors d'oeuvres. We could use all of them, and people could circulate and talk or sit or whatever. It'll be fantastic."

We were off and running, and I think Miss Stacey got swept up in the excitement. "Now wait a minute," she said, "I'm in on this too, you know."

Suddenly we were all laughing and talking, and best of all, we were making plans. At least for a few minutes,

Rupert Errique was forgotten; harassment was banished; and there were no troubled thoughts to bother our lives.

§§§

We didn't have much time to prepare. I hit the internet after breakfast to gather what I could about decorations and recipes. We were going to have to improvise on some things, but Miss Stacey said that decorating for Thanksgiving is always a matter of improvising and that was part of the fun. The main focus was supposed to be on the blessings of a good harvest; small gourds like pumpkins and squash were favorites, along with fruits like apples and pears, even ones made of wood or plastic. Bind it all together with colorful fall leaves, and you've got yourself a Thanksgiving décor.

When I was ready with my list, I pestered Rose until she couldn't take it anymore. She revved up her car and off we went, heading into Bath. Miss Stacey had given me a budget, with strict instructions to Rose not to add to it. Rose would advise me as needed, but otherwise, the choices were mine to make.

I was really glad Rose was willing to drive me around, but I suggested that if she wanted to go visit Ned while we were in town, that'd be okay with me. "It's tempting," she told me, "but when he's working, he's on call, so to speak, and has to go when and where his cases need him. That doesn't leave much room for being social. We'd just be in his way."

"Are you going to marry him?"

She didn't even mind the question. She kept her eyes on the road ahead of us, but she was smiling. "As soon as he asks." That sounded kind of dreamy to me, and I couldn't help noticing she looked a little dreamy too, like in her mind she was picturing Ned asking her, "Will you marry me?"

Right then, she got self-conscious and laughed like it'd all been said in good humor. "As soon as he asks," she repeated, but this time she said it like, yeah, right, like that's ever going to happen. But to us, it seemed like a done-deal. We knew it was going to happen, and we were just waiting for the announcement.

I told her, "Miss Stacey's happy that things have worked out so well for you. And for Amelia, too. She told me that herself. I just wish..."

I wanted to wish, but I couldn't finish my thought. My mind was flooding to overflowing with things I was wishing. If only her nightmares could stop. If only she could be allowed a little happiness, a few moments of peace, just an end to her sadness. But all my wishing was like what Edgar Allan Poe wrote in *The Raven*, "...vainly I had sought to borrow, From my books surcease of sorrow." That's what we were all doing every day now, vainly trying to get a little surcease of sorrow for Miss Stacey.

But even if we had, that wouldn't have been exactly right. That wouldn't purge the evil, the personal agony, the torment. All of that was still there. I could still sense it when I looked at her. I wouldn't say so aloud, but I could sense it. I sensed it, but I couldn't say it. I wouldn't say it.

I think Rose understood. After a second, she said, "I know. I wish for her too. For all of it."

Chapter 29: DC Peters

I couldn't believe my eyes.

Chrisy Olivar, Errique's once upon a time girlfriend and all-around gal Friday from the On'A Go Café, was out of jail, and she'd just sauntered into the Lariat Saloon. She wasn't looking my way, but I tilted my wide-brim imitation Stetson hat to hide my face anyways, just in case she might recognize me as one of the cops who arrested her. She went straight as an arrow to Ramon.

In exchange for immunity to kidnapping charges, Chrisy had testified for the prosecution. Though never part of the inner circle of conspirators in Errique's ring of thieves, she'd been well placed as a liaison between them. The On'A Go Café had been like a clearing house of information, Errique to Chrisy to Rimwell, and vice versa. Add in Gaston, who was Errique's eyes and ears at Southjoy Mission, and Durke Ormy, who was both recipient and source of scandalous stories, and you had a well-informed operation.

Chrisy's testimony was highly skewed against Rimwell, who was described as Errique's hit man and gofer, and against Victor Maggor, an engineer who was Errique's technical advisor and second in command, though both Errique and Maggor disputed the latter role. Errique, you know, wasn't fond of sharing control with anyone. If they'd intended to discredit Chrisy as a witness by disputing that part of her testimony, it didn't work. Rimwell was doing life for two murders, and Maggor might just as well have been with twenty-five years for kidnapping, accessory to murder, one count of manslaughter for the death of Lord Silverworth, plus extortion and assault with a deadly weapon. All that, and he only got twenty-five years. But what do I know? I'm just a cop.

Chrisy understandably painted a kinder, more generous picture of Errique. He was merely trying to help his friends who'd made some mistakes. It was Maggor and Rimwell who kidnapped Stacey; they were the ones keen to dispose of witnesses. Errique was only trying to rein them in, trying to "extricate everyone from a bad situation." Nobody even asked who fed her that line.

Neither Maggor nor Rimwell disputed Chrisy's account. To do so would have crossed Errique, and no one ever crossed Rupert Errique. Largely owing to Chrisy's testimony, Errique was only convicted on the extortion and assault charges. Because of her cooperation, charges against Chrisy were reduced to accessory to extortion for which she received a sentence of eighteen months with probation after only three.

And here was Chrisy, chummy with Ramon Lorenzana who was advisor to Lucy Dyson who worked at Southjoy Mission. *Game on!*

When it comes to surveillance, this was as good as it gets. The lasso around Errique just got cinched a whole lot tighter.

Still, I kept a low profile. This contact was after the fact. What we needed to know was, was there contact before the events at Southjoy Mission? With Malbec's approval, I became a regular at the Lariat Saloon. People soon began to open up to me because I was a familiar face. I got to know the inside jokes, who talked too much, and who was touchy. I made it known to the touchy ones that I didn't much like the townies and didn't much like how "they was always lookin' down on good folks like us."

Down a pint or two with your new mates, and they start sharing their own likes and dislikes, which I did my best to encourage. "Workin' stiffs like us ain't got hardly nowheres to go, 'ceptin' the Lariat." Lots of sympathy on that one and good advice. "Try the On'A Go Café," one of me new mates said, and another one added, "Yeah, that's a good'n. Ramon hisself chows there now 'n ag'in."

Spot on.

I added Chrisy to my watch list, and when not hanging out at the Lariat, I was keeping tabs on her. Like Malbec said, you've got to keep your eye on the objective.

Chrisy returned to the Lariat at least twice that I saw, and probably more because folks there seemed to take her in stride. Strangers draw looks and stares from regulars, and nobody paid much mind to Chrisy.

Patience paid off. She came in a few days later, head down, charging straight for Ramon like she was going to gore the livin' daylights out of him with a pair of sharpened horns.

She launched into a real barn burner, a dead serious whisper-in-the-ear, heated discussion with Ramon who kept trying to edge away from her. Suddenly, Chrisy went all red-faced angry, and Ramon backed off big time. A second later, he kind of shrugged his shoulders and gestured with his hand as much to say, okay, okay, whatever. At that, she pulled an envelope from her purse and handed it to Ramon. He took it without comment, placed it under the counter, and drew her a half-pint from draft. She took one sip, set her glass down, nodded once, and left. She looked worried and nervous; she walked straight out without so much as a "howdy" to anybody. Ramon looked like she'd never been there.

Chrisy was lookin' a whole lot like a wildcat stalkin' a wounded doe. It was time t'stay in m'saddle. The next time she moseyed into the Lariat, I was tailin' her. I don't rightly know what happened inside 'cuz she was in and out quicker'n a cricket leaps a thicket. I never even made it out of my car. In and out like that, I could'a see'd it acomin'. She went in empty handed and came out carrying a small package that looked a whole lot like a pistol wrapped in an old t-shirt. After that, Chrisy went to ground.

Chapter 30: Ethan

I still had hopes that life would turn a kinder face to Catlyn. Just one ray of kindness, that's all she needed. But my hopes were being crushed under the onus of Rupert Errique's vile campaign. The man had no shame, no conscience, and no redeeming value. I disliked what I saw of him when he was on trial, and now I disliked him intensely.

Because of recent events, I'd also begun to understand why Catlyn saw so much that was sinister in the Prunella letters. It was everywhere around her; why not there too? I didn't approve, but I did understand she had her reasons.

Even so, sometimes she tried my patience. Just little things, like, for example, Prunella clung to Lady Stacey's friendship. At first, Catlyn was keen on that. Now, she avoided even talking about it. My suspicion was, the thought of Prunella sailing away was too personal. Prunella would be unlikely ever to see Lady Stacey again. Dwell on that, and you're halfway to homesick. So Catlyn found it preferable to interpret the letters by reading into their words all sorts of unsavory possibilities. To put it bluntly, she was using the letters to reinforce her own misery. If misery loves company, Catlyn was finding it, or inventing it, in Prunella's letters. That just seemed wrong to me, academically and personally.

I was upset, too, with Dr. Ulma. How he couldn't be concerned about this change in her attitude was beyond me. He actually defended her, as if that were even possible. He stubbornly maintained that it's therapeutic for Catlyn to transfer her fears, be they real or imagined, onto Prunella. It makes them somebody else's problems, so it's easier to think about them. They're not a threat to you personally.

I wasn't entirely convinced that he'd made his case or that it really made sense or that it was the right thing to do, but he's her doctor. He's supposed to know what's best. So, I decided to stay the course for now.

Resolved or not, I was a bit out of sorts when I got to the estate. I was gruff even with Whinehardt, and I knew better than that. Those who stand in service in any capacity are always easy targets for abuse, and it's just reprehensible to yield to the temptation to dump on them, no matter how out of sorts you are. Thankfully, Whinehardt is the consummate domestic. While I fumed impatiently, he did nothing more caustic than look at me somewhat askance.

Given my mood, I was expecting Catlyn to meet with me again in the small sitting room, the Debacle Room I'd come to think of it. I was sure she'd do that just to aggravate me.

So when Whinehardt said, "in the library," I was surprised and I showed it. I'm fairly sure Whinehardt was grinning at my reaction, and from the way he said "Indeed" so meaningfully, I was certain of it. I do believe it was the most upbeat moment of the day.

The library is across the corridor from the small sitting room and adjacent to one side of the atrium garden. Its seating was less comfortable than in the small sitting room, but its ambiance was decidedly less controversial. Light seeping in from the atrium provided a pleasantly soft illumination. I've always rather liked the way the shadows spread away from the windows and reach into the far corners of the room. Shelves extending into the room from the wall opposite the windows created cozy nooks if you were looking for a more secluded sitting area.

Tilly had set up her tablet on one of the two tables

flanking the atrium entrance where we'd have plenty of natural light. I chose the seat where the lighting would give me a good view of Catlyn who chose to sit looking into the openness of the garden. I myself was more intent on reading her expressions than on reading the letter, which anyways I'd already read. It was another letter addressed to Lady Stacey, and the nature of this particular letter would make a good proof-test of Dr. Ulma's theory.

> *Please forgive me if I unburden myself to you, but I believe I shall burst if I do not. I cannot sleep, so agitated have my thoughts become.*

Tilly, who was reading the letter aloud, hesitated almost at once. She looked over to Catlyn, who merely returned a quizzical look to Tilly. I had expected Catlyn to be tense or uncomfortable with those opening lines, or annoyed at least. Her lack of reaction left me undecided and unsettled. Tilly must have felt pretty much the same way. Subdued by Catlyn's steady gaze, Tilly said, "Sorry," and continued.

> *I overheard a conversation between Mr. Jackson and one of the sailors accused of contraband. I heard Mr. Jackson say in a very loud voice, "He don't bother me none. I knew a bloke like him in Westminster. Making trouble, he was. So I did him what for." I had the impression they were speaking about Mr. Joshua who seems put out with everyone since the captain "belayed" his inquiry. At that moment, Katherine said she was growing tired and would like to return to her cabin to rest, which we did. I believe Mr. Jackson was "in his cups," as Gerald put it, and that could account for his less refined language. From the beginning, I thought him less*

*the gentleman than he professed to be, and I now believe
this slip into ungentlemanly discourse confirms my first
view. He much reminds me of Mr. McCloguns, the
scoundrel who caused so much trouble for Cedric and
Gerald, a history you know only too well. I told Gerald of
my fear, and he said I was not to worry. He would take
care of the situation.*
    – Prunella, Letter No. A4, 1810

Catlyn's brow was knotted in preoccupied thought. Tilly
looked my way, and seeing how I was peering silently at
Catlyn, she turned and did the same. Whether we had the
same thought or not, we waited until Catlyn elected to
share her deep contemplation with us.

"Mr. Jackson is trouble," she declared. "I don't trust
him."

I'm afraid that rekindled my irritation, and I just
couldn't hold my tongue. "Catlyn," I interrupted her, "you
can't condemn people so summarily when you know so
little about them. That's just wanton and irresponsible."

The expression she cast my way sent a chill right
through me. It held such a cutting glare that I felt not only
like a heel, but that it was I, in the end, who'd lost his
mind. I was relieved to see her expression soften. "We
know a great deal about Mr. Jackson," she explained
patiently, "if we are prepared to accept Prunella's
observations of him."

Catlyn can be so disconcerting. Especially when she's
right. I try not to think of how many years I spent teaching
my students, "Don't make it personal." It's a basic tenet of
research. And there I was, allowing my observations to be
clouded and distorted by personal issues. Granted, my
issues concerned the well-being of Catlyn, but that didn't

excuse the rudeness of my conduct, nor the negligence of my analysis. I was embarrassed, and I told her so and apologized for my thoughtless outburst.

She reached over and patted my arm. "There's no need for apology, Ethan. I've accepted the fact that you and Tilly are distracted by me. I know you care. I know you want to help me. But sheltering me from everything doesn't make me stronger. That's what I need you to do for me. Make me be stronger." She started to pat my arm again, but her hand came to rest. She hesitated and looked away. A weary sigh escaped. "Please, I need to be stronger. Much stronger."

For a moment, we all sat there in silence, the three of us, Catlyn and Tilly peering out into the garden, and me peering at them. I couldn't imagine what Catlyn was thinking, or even if she was thinking. She might have been blocking out all distraction of thought. If you could have seen her face...

The sound of a sudden deep breath followed by a heavy sigh broke through our silence, and Catlyn was all business again. "So, about Mr. Jackson. What do we know?"

That brought us all back to attention with a little start. Fortunately, Tilly's mind is quick. She decided, "He was pretending to be a gentleman, but he wasn't really."

I was a little slower to recover, but I agreed as quickly as I could. "On the basis of what Prunella said, which is the only basis we have," I humbly acknowledged to Catlyn, "that would seem to be correct."

"And he was lodged in steerage," Catlyn recalled. "Why was that?"

I smiled inwardly. Once again she was taking charge of her unruly circumstances, leading us who thought to lead her. Maybe she'd been paying more attention to Dr. Ulma than we realized. He has a flair for leading questions too.

Catlyn seemed to be getting in sync with him.

"I can think of one or two reasonable possibilities," I said. "He could've been leaving England because of a failed business, in which case he probably couldn't afford the price of better accommodations."

"Or, maybe there just weren't any left," suggested Tilly.

I noticed how Catlyn's eyes were resting on Tilly. She was pleased with Tilly, and it showed. Tilly's thought was indeed the most logical explanation. "Especially," I added, "if he booked his passage late."

Catlyn was nodding in that thoughtful way of hers again. "Westminster," she noted. She pointed to a line in Prunella's letter. *So I did him what for*, she read. She turned a smile to me. "Any archives on Westminster in 1810?"

Incisive and alert. Once again, she surprised me. "Bloody marvelous," I said in a way that sent Tilly into a paroxysm of laughter. I know it wasn't my most academic appraisal, but in my many decades, I've learned what marvelous looks like, and all things considered, this was it. It cost her dearly, but she was forcing herself past all the unkindness dealt to her, and it was just plain bloody marvelous to see her do it.

Chapter 31: Lady Wythiry

What a grand day it's been. My heart's been palpitating double quick since I rose up ready and eager for this day of days. Mr. Errique has been completely won over to my way of thinking, and I say so without reservation. Nothing could have elated me more than the way he's embraced my project, and with such admirable dedication.

I had my husband's personal tailor create one of his signature single-breasted, double-button executive wool suits to Mr. Errique's exacting specifications, and I must admit, he was quite the handsome figure in it. All the ladies quite agreed. He beamed a smile at them that made every last one of them swoon when he glanced in their direction.

I, of course, was showered with accolades for making it so. Every important person in the region shook my hand, while galleries of people cheered.

The only slightly disagreeable blemish on the day was the presence of Dr. Ulma. He was there spying on us for Miss Stacey no doubt. I'd been warned that he'd made a fuss with the hospital board of directors. They rejected his claims and told him not to interfere. To his credit, he stayed far away on the upper level overlook and wisely made no attempt to spoil my moment.

The hospital entrance had been decorated with balloons and flags and streamers, and even though it was cold outside, some thirty or fifty people had gathered to join in the celebration. That's indeed what it was, a celebration. You could see the eager anticipation in each and every face.

We had prearranged Mr. Errique's official arrival to be a few minutes after the announced time to pique the crowd's excitement. He'd actually arrived earlier, very discretely, so he could change into his new civilian clothes. I wanted his well-wishers to see him at his best.

On my signal, the prison van approached the entrance, the guards took up their positions, the van door slid open, and Mr. Errique stepped out. A breathless hush gripped everyone. Then Mr. Errique, surrounded by his prison guards, one in front, one behind, and two at his sides, began a regal procession to the entrance.

The crowd parted as Mr. Errique approached, like the Red Sea parting for Moses. To everyone's delight, there was a formal "changing of the guard" at the entrance. Mr. Errique stayed facing the entrance until the prison guards had returned to their van and I stepped out to greet him. At that point, Mr. Errique turned around. He raised his arms high in the air, and the crowd just went absolutely wild.

A podium had been set up on the front promenade for me to say a few words of welcome, which I deliberately kept to a minimum. I didn't want to diffuse the energy of this crowd. However, not to miss out on such a propitious opportunity, I had arranged for the auxiliary to give tours of the hospital and, of course, to accept the cash donations that these generous patrons would be very much inclined to bestow upon the hospital on such a memorable occasion.

Throughout the brief ceremony, I was the envy of everyone in attendance. To be this near to the notorious Rupert Errique simply made their hearts flutter with excitement. Just as we were about to go into the hospital, Mr. Errique suddenly stepped forward towards the crowd and offered an enthusiastic wave to all his well-wishers. Well, you cannot imagine the thunderous cheer that went up from that whole body of assembled people. They adored this brave man who was described by Durke Ormy as being the "quintessential model of reformed humanity," and, of course, they adored me for giving them their very own celebrity.

In the exuberance of the crowd, a young woman suddenly ran forward to hand Mr. Errique a single flower, a chrysanthemum. It was such a charming moment. The woman held the little flower out at arm's length, and I do believe she was trembling when she said, "A chrisy- anth-a-mum for you." Well, it was so endearing that not a sole laughed at her mispronunciation, and Mr. Errique himself was just absolutely gallant. He smiled with delight and said, "My favorite" and immediately displayed the flower on his lapel. The poor girl instantly dashed back to disappear into the crowd, a shy admirer.

We proceeded at once into the lobby where volunteers were standing by to manage the large number of visitors. The doors were momentarily closed behind us to give me time to usher Mr. Errique to our reception room. Then the crowd was allowed to enter and be entertained by our volunteers. They handed out souvenir brochures about both the hospital and Mr. Errique, served refreshments, and conducted brief tours of the hospital. All of which was done, of course, to accommodate the many people who simply longed for another chance to spot Mr. Errique.

I must say, through it all, Mr. Errique proved to be not only congenial, but also an exemplary guest. We had no task for him to perform for this special day except to enjoy a grand tour of the hospital and the special luncheon prepared for him in the cafeteria, which was also attended by honorary guests who paid a handsome fee for the privilege. Officially, the tour was so Mr. Errique would be familiar with the layout of the facility. So technically, the tour counted as his task for the day. He was most gracious about it, expressing a keen interest to see every department, including heating and cooling systems, water supplies, and everything to do with building maintenance, right down to the broom closets. He was so attentive, we gave him one of our more detailed brochures which included a guide map intended to help you find your way through the maze of corridors.

Before leaving, he declared, "Your Ladyship, I'm overwhelmed with gratitude for you and this hospital. I fear a meager thank you under these circumstances would seem trifling and paltry." With that, he put his hands on his hips and looked around the lobby like he was ready to roll up his sleeves and get to work right then. He looked into every corner, then turned back to me to say, "I can never match your generosity, but I do love a challenge. With your kind permission, I'm going to use every moment I spend here searching, probing, and examining every detail of this hospital until I can discover some suitable expression of my very deep appreciation."

If that isn't the attitude of a reformed man, I don't know what is.

Chapter 32: DC Peters

What a bunch'a hooey. Her Ladyship struttin' around like she'd just been made queen bee. Rupert Errique puffed up like a big shot. All them so-called good citizens salivatin' for any bone Errique might toss at 'em. And don't you believe it. Nobody in that crowd was there to see the reformed Rupert Errique. "Right there!" they'd be telling their mates in the pub. "I was this close to the mastermind of crime himself."

You know what I think? I think people *don't* want Errique reformed. Errique gives them a rush. In person or in the news, they put themselves in these little fantasies like they're right smack dab in the middle of all the action, "stickin' it to the man," whatever that means. They think to themselves, "He makes'em sit up an' take notice, makes'em squirm like they do us." And they tell themselves, "He didn't do me no wrong," like that makes it alright.

Well, let me tell ya, it ain't. They're victims, too. Every time Errique gets away with something, everybody ends up paying for it. But people are just blind enough to see him as the anti-hero thumbin' his nose at authority, and it doesn't matter to them how many lives he's ruined or how many he's injured, just so long's it's not them.

And ya know why they do it? Here's what I think. It's 'cuz they're bored. What else've they got? Sod all, that's what. Squat. Humdrum. How'd that old brainy nerd put it, lives of quiet desperation? Right. So here's Errique putin'm on edge, vexin' their tootsies with a bit of fret just so's they can feel alive.

But whatta ya gonna do? It's their funeral. They makes their choices; they pays their dues. Ya know, I don't think it'd make any difference to 'em if they even knew how much they was gonna pay in the end.

So, okay, that's just my rant for today.

That's not why I was at the hospital. I was there because I had a job to do. I'm a cop, and to me, Rupert Errique ain't nothin' but a hardcore crook. He's scum as dirty as they come, and I don't care what anybody says, blokes like him don't ever change. That's why I was there, to see what he was up to.

And *ka-ching*, I got me an answer, and it was a good'n.

Just as they were about to go into the building, some gal broke away from the crowd and ran straight up to Errique to give him a flower. Don't'cha just know it was Lucy Dyson. Another piece of the puzzle, or, as DI Malbec would say, the dots were connecting.

And that's just what he did say.

"Chrisy-anth-a-mum?" Malbec asked me when I reported back to him. "Chrisy-anth-a-mum?" Even stone-faced, he had to shake his head at that. "Now that's just too much." It was time to corral that little filly and have a right good chat with her.

§§§

Lucy was fit to be tied when we brought her in. She was carryin' on something awful, and she kept whinin', "I don't know nothin'!"

I tell ya, she was squirmin' in her seat and makin' nasty faces at us. For certain sure she was lookin' rode hard and put away wet.

And then Malbec got started.

"So what were you doing at the hospital?"

"Same as everybody else."

"You were there to see Rupert Errique?"

"Yeah."

"Why?"

"It was in all the papers. Mobster goes straight. I jus' wanted t'see, that's all."

"You brought him a flower."

"So?"

"A chrisy-an-the-mum?"

"Yeah."

"Why'd you choose a chrisy-anth-a-mum?"

"It was pretty."

"Where'd you get it?"

"Some ol' gal had'em in the Lariat Saloon."

"So Ramon bought one for you."

"Yeah."

"And you gave it to Errique."

She hesitated; looked embarrassed. "Well, yeah."

"He didn't get mad at you?"

"Ramon? Nah. He ain't like that."

"How'd he know Errique?"

She stiffened a bit on that one, and it seemed to me she was looking worried. "How should I know? I tell ya, I don't know nothin'."

"Okay, let's leave that for now. How long've you known Chrisy Olivar?"

She was fidgeting now, getting antsy. The trail up yonder was lookin' a mite rocky.

"I don't know nobody named Chrisy."

"Sure you do; at the Lariat Saloon."

"Oh, that Chrisy. She ain't nobody."

"So how long have you known her?"

"Not long. Ain't no crime knowin' somebody, is there?"

"She's done time, you know."

Lucy was clutching her hands together in a ball. She

pulled them back against her chest like she was getting ready to bolt, and the way she was working her lips and agitating her jaw, she looked like she was going to snap at us any second now, which she did.

"What's it ta me?"

"Chrisy used to hang out with Rupert Errique."

"So?"

"And now you're hanging out with Errique."

She froze, head down and mouth shut, very still except for her eyes. She was straining to see us out of the corner of her eye. The look on her face was as hopeless as it was telling. The posse was closin' in on her, and she'd just rode straight into a boxed canyon with no way out.

"You don't much like Missus Sweetgrove."

That startled her. She looked up. Her eyes darted about the room. She was frettin' somethin' powerful.

"Do you?" Malbec goaded her.

"No, I don't. So what? I should'a known she was behind this. She's always on my case, blamin' me for everything."

"But you taught her a lesson, didn't you?"

She sneered. "You bet I did. I..." She stopped. She was frowning, confused, and frightened.

"How'd you come up with the idea?"

She shrugged. "I don't know."

"Ramon must have helped you with it. He likes you."

"He loves me," she snapped. "And, yeah, he helped me. Why wouldn't he?"

"No reason. But such a strange trick to play. Where'd he get such a weird idea?"

"How should I know?"

"It was after he talked to Chrisy Olivar, wasn't it?"

She sat up. Jealousy was flaring. "Her? He planned it with her?"

She was furious, and Malbec added fuel to the fire. "It

was Chrisy who brought the flower in. Didn't that tell you something?"

"No. No, it wasn't like that."

Lucy was trying hard to believe it herself, but she sure seemed torn between protesting to Malbec and wanting to scream at Ramon. If we'd a'let her loose, she'd a'been buckin' and a'kickin'.

"There ain't nothin' goin' on between them. Nothin'. It was just a message. A chrisy-an-the-mum to show Errique that Chrisy was waitin' for'im. That's all it was. Ain't nothin' between Ramon and that woman."

R. G. Munro

Chapter 33: Dr. Ulma

The Daily Reveler was bursting with pictures and articles about Lady Wythiry and her new protégé, Rupert Errique. Anecdotes of their past exploits filled the columns. Quotes from adoring fans were boxed in bold type. And according to the Durke Ormy opinion piece, a bright future was awaiting them both. You'd have thought they were a celebrity couple, minus the rings and vows and anything holy. But I suppose that's redundant.

From what I observed at the hospital, Her Ladyship didn't have a clue what she was getting into. Turning a sociopath loose in her hospital? Not the most rational thing to do. Except to another sociopath, perhaps. But I wasn't about to go traipsing down that road.

My attention had to stay sharply focused on Catlyn. I was seriously concerned that all the sympathetic attention to Errique would accentuate her anxiety. You always worry about that one straw too many, and Errique was a whole bale.

I'd been at the hospital at Catlyn's request. I was her eyewitness, watching from the overlook. If I hadn't gone, she would have, and that would've been a disaster.

She wanted me to observe Rupert Errique first hand while he was at liberty and roaming in the wild, so to speak. We agreed to meet in my office today to talk about it.

I picked up two papers with similar headlines and spread them out on the big coffee table to give us a starting point for discussion. I made sure the meditation waterfall was trickling with soothing splashing sounds, and I positioned myself next to the aquarium. I use a collection of neon tetra and honey gourami fish that school nicely together. Their schooling provides a subliminal message of unity, while their fluid motion suggests tranquility. As it happens, they're also remarkably sensitive fish. I haven't a clue how they do it, but they seem to sense mood changes near them. You see it in their movement as they translate the change in ambient mood into a sudden motion of the school.

I was counting on the aquarium's calming influence to help ease us into what was going to be an intense session.

It didn't help.

She didn't even look my way.

"It made me so mad," she declared as she plopped herself down in her usual chair. I don't think she even noticed the newspapers, and she didn't wait for the question.

After enough of these sessions, I suppose you get used to being asked, how did that make you feel? Being mad was certainly one normal reaction, but beyond that, Catlyn's thoughts were riled and unsettled.

"How can people be so stupid? Why can't they see how he's just manipulating them, sucking them in? He's playing them, and they're going to lose." She shook her head. "Ain't no winnin'," she scolded. She took a deep breath and ran her fingers through her hair, giving her head a little frustrated shake as her fingers emerged at the end of their sweep.

Her mind was awash in undisciplined thought. She was venting without focus, and I thought it best to take her diatribe down a notch.

"It's what you were expecting, though, wasn't it? It's what Errique does. And maybe Lady Wythiry isn't so innocent in all that either. Be that as it may, a good many people still respect Lady Wythiry. Maybe Errique's using that; maybe not; I don't know. They've made a big deal out of the way she's trying to be a pillar of the community. People *can* change. It's been known to happen; all they need is sufficient motivation. The question is, can Rupert Errique change?"

"No."

"You don't believe he's reforming under her guidance?"

"No I don't, and you don't either. Nobody guides Rupert Errique."

"I don't dispute that, but Lady Wythiry probably would, don't you think?"

"Lady Wythiry has too much vanity. Whatever Errique is up to, Her Ladyship is nothing but a means to an end. Just look at this picture." She tapped one of the front page articles setting on the table. "Look at this. Errique is already in charge. He's stepped away from her. He's left her in the background. And where are the guards?"

I'd looked at those pictures several times, and I'd never noticed the absence of the guards. But of course Catlyn would pick up on that detail. Even in a picture she can sense the threat.

"He's already in control," she accused.

"You sound angry and bitter."

"Of course I am," she scoffed. But then she turned a look of alarm at me. Her brow was furrowed with sudden concern. "With them I am, yes," she emphasized. "Not with you. Never with you. Please don't ever think that."

She was genuinely worried. "I know you're my doctor," she added quickly, "but you're more than that." She hesitated and her tone softened. "We're friends, too, aren't we? I mean..."

The concern on her face seemed to penetrate right into my thoughts. It isn't very often that what you feel, personally, and what's best for your patient, professionally, are the same thing. Professionally, I should say, "No, I'm not your friend. I'm your doctor." But if I said that, it wouldn't be true, she'd know it, and that wouldn't be good for her.

There's a certain level of personal trust that I believed was absolutely essential for the care she needed to receive from me. It was my judgment that I couldn't reach a comparable level of trust in a strictly dispassionate, objective, professional capacity. Trusting me, and trusting me to do my job, weren't the same thing. So, despite all the good advice I'd ever given or received about getting too close to patients, I allowed myself to want a closer relationship with her, for her care, you understand.

Yes, I know. I was rationalizing big time. If I hadn't been, maybe I'd've paid more attention to the sage pundits, you know, the ones who talk about giving an ant an inch and it takes a yard. Caring can be like that too. I cared for Catlyn, and it was personal. And truth be told, I just didn't want it to be anything less.

However, I did tell her as forcefully as I could, "I hope you'll always think of me as an exceptionally good friend. But as your friend and your doctor both, sometimes I need to talk to you about things you'd rather not think about. But no matter what, whether you see me as a friend or as your doctor, you can be sure of this. Whatever unpleasantness you have to face, I'll be there to face it with you."

She smiled. "That sounds to me like a pretty good definition of a friend."

She smiled, and my pulse beat faster. I tried not to dwell on it, but undeniably, the personal side of our relationship had just taken a big leap, and I couldn't deny wanting it, because I did want it. It wasn't even an awkward moment.

We talked a bit more about what friends are for, nothing deep, just reassuring. And then, just as natural as could be, she sighed and was right back on track.

"You said you had an update from DI Malbec."

"I do," I said as I swept up the newspapers and tossed them onto my desk. I replaced the papers with the coffee service I had at the ready, and poured her a cup. "He called me this morning. They've solved the sitting room mystery."

I watched her reaction as I poured a cup for myself. She was alert and anxious, but more importantly, the clarity and focus in her eyes was good, and her attention was sharp without being fearful. I tried to remove my own emotions from my speech pattern so as not to disturb any of that.

"Apparently, your housemaid, Lucy Dyson, had it out for Missus Sweetgrove."

"Lucy?" Her voice was toned in disappointment; yet another betrayal. "Lucy," she repeated. A hint of resignation in that? Perhaps. "It's what Whinehardt suspected then."

"Yes. According to Lucy, Missus Sweetgrove is always on her case. She wanted to get even with her."

"But, how..."

"Lucy has a boyfriend named Ramon Lorenzana. He runs a bar called the Lariat Saloon. It was Ramon who told her what to do."

"I still don't see..."

"Patience. We're reading the weave here."

A quick smile brushed her face on that, and I almost couldn't breathe. But I did, but only because it was necessary.

"DI Malbec had the bar under surveillance. That's where Lucy went every weekend. It turns out Ramon knows Chrisy Olivar."

Catlyn's eyes flared. "Errique." She spit the name out like a curse, and there was a world of complex emotion in her tone. "So she's been to see him in prison?"

"Malbec says not, but Chrisy Olivar is represented by Anton Taunton."

"He's the one who called me at the estate."

"Yes, the very same. So, the weave reads, Lucy to Ramon to Chrisy to Tauton to Errique. Effectively, that gives Errique unobstructed access to both Olivar and Southjoy Mission."

Catlyn nodded without emotion. She took a sip of hot coffee while coldly distancing herself from the fact. Fact became mere artifact, something to appraise in her mind.

"Lucy was there yesterday, at the hospital," I told her.

That brought Catlyn's eyes back to me.

"I saw her myself, but at the time, I didn't know who she was. Apparently DC Peters was there too, and he identified her. As the shindig was ending, Lucy dashed up to Errique and gave him a flower, a chrysanthemum, except she pronounced it, chrisy-anth-a-mum."

Catlyn's expression became grave. "Lucy admitted this?"

"Yes. She tried not to, but Malbec caught her off-guard with one of his questions. Before she realized what she was saying, she had admitted everything. The flower was a signal of some kind."

Catlyn acknowledged that with a simple nod of her head. She sat back. "Then she's in danger."

No question. No alarm in her expression. Just one more routine fact. Lovely day, rain tomorrow, Lucy's in danger.

She advised, "You've got to tell Malbec. Errique doesn't leave witnesses." Another fact.

A second later, a long, yielding sigh escaped from Catlyn, like the encroachment of fatigue after a long day.

"So, the sitting room mystery is solved."

She leaned forward, planting her elbow on the armrest of her chair, and propped her head against the fingers of her hand. Eyes closed, she seemed to be collecting her thoughts. Decisively, then, she sat back and crossed her arms. "We knew Errique was behind it, and now we know how. But the question still remains. Why? What's he after?"

"You," I said without thinking.

"I know, but to what end?" Uncrossing her arms, she braced her hand against the table. She grimaced. "To kill me?" She tilted her head in thought. Doubtful, she observed, "Malbec says Errique thrives on bizarre crimes." She peered into her half-empty cup of coffee. "Does he have some perverse notion of revenge? Is he really trying to drive me insane?" She sat back. "Or is it what Chrisy thought? Chrisy was jealous of me. Was she right to be?"

"All good questions," I admitted. "The thing never to forget about Errique is that he's a sociopath. Take that as a given, no matter what. He's not capable of attachment."

I held her eyes in a steady gaze. Not capable of attachment. That was the key to solving the riddle of Rupert Errique. And I suddenly understood what it was.

Catlyn turned her head very slightly, as though to hear more clearly what I was about to say.

"Dominance." I said it like a foregone conclusion.

Her attention was fixed on me. A mixture of thought and suspicion shadowed her face with a pensive, probing frown.

"It's all about dominance," I told her. "That's what you saw in that newspaper photo, Errique in a position of dominance over Lady Wythiry."

She nodded. Strain was tightening around her neck and shoulders. She raised one hand to massage the back of her neck. "So it's not revenge?"

I shook my head. "No. Remember, Errique getting caught was nothing more than an inconvenience to him. He has no feeling about that whatsoever."

She considered that while pulling against her head to further ease the accumulating strain. She hunched her shoulders forward in isometric tension before sitting back again. Her hand lay relaxed now at the side of her neck, supported at her elbow by her other hand which lay across her abdomen. Behind us, the splashing babble of the waterfall suddenly loomed around us like waves crashing against a craggy shore. The look on her face was stern and sober. Her thoughts seemed to be racing as her eyes locked unto mine. Across the room, the school of fish turned sharply and darted to the far corner of the tank.

Neither of us could look away. She, because she was determined to fight for her life. Me, because I was determined to defend it.

The conflict ahead of us was obvious, but I said it anyway. "It's you he wants. You eluded him. You've become an obsession to him. And it's not just that he *wants* to dominate you; wants can be deterred. This is different. He feels *compelled* to dominate you. There's no deterrent to that. He won't stop. It's all or nothing."

Chapter 34: Ethan

There's a code of honor among staff, and Lucy Dyson had violated it. I'd been rather intensely briefed by Amelia about that affair and its connection to Rupert Errique. She was angry with Errique, angry with Lucy, and distraught that Errique had managed to infiltrate the estate. The way the man played with people's minds, the way he perverted simple folk to carry out his cruelty was just vile. No. It was more than vile. It was evil. At least Errique's psychological sabotage against Catlyn had been decisively thwarted.

Nonetheless, Amelia made it sound like gang warfare. The incident in the Debacle Room, she said, was like a drive-by shooting. She'd so thoroughly indoctrinated me that I arrived at Southjoy Mission stricken with paranoia almost as much as she was. And yes, she *was* being paranoid. I'd been remiss in not taking note of that before, but I was taking note of it now, and I'd act on that as soon as I could. At the moment, though, I happened to agree with her.

In that frame of mind, it was easy to spot how the affair had riled the staff. Enter a room, and their eyes darted suspiciously at you. As trained as they were to be servile in appearance, every one of them was clearly aligned with Sweetgrove and her decision to dismiss Lucy.

I plunged into this charged atmosphere angry and determined. More than ever, Catlyn needed a reprieve from all the discord, and my basic premise still held true. A mind always occupies itself with the most pressing problems or the most disturbing issues. It followed that the only way Catlyn would ever get any respite from Errique was by engaging her mind with other thoughts, giving her

Fortunately, Willy had completed two more of the Prunella letters, and his timing was particularly good. Catlyn had been neglecting her attention to the history of Southjoy Mission, pushing it off to a distant back burner. That was understandable, but our project still presented the best opportunity to divert Catlyn's attention, and she had more than a mundane interest in it.

Dr. Ulma still insisted that any keen interest activating the mind and exercising its rational capacity was worth pursuing. I didn't always like the way Catlyn's mind had been working in these exercises, but at least it didn't involve Rupert Errique.

These two letters were written about events that occurred on the same day, but the first one was to Prunella's friend, Elly Howshim, while the second was to Ariana. That made some sense because the first letter was about children. Ariana's first child wasn't born until the following year, 1811, while Elly Howshim of Wolverhampton already had children before Prunella left England.

I was taking a turn on deck with Katherine and Mrs. Mimms. Katherine was so great with child our pace was slow. As we walked, she confided in me that her term was drawing near, and she was worried about her son. She asked if I would look after him when her time to deliver arrived. I promised at once. I have never before attended to a child, but I know I shall be ever so good at it.

As we rounded the deck, there was a sound of a terrible commotion. There was shouting, and I could hear Mr. Jackson hollering "bugger off" to someone. Just

R. G. Munro

Fortunately, Willy had completed two more of the Prunella letters, and his timing was particularly good. Catlyn had been neglecting her attention to the history of Southjoy Mission, pushing it off to a distant back burner. That was understandable, but our project still presented the best opportunity to divert Catlyn's attention, and she had more than a mundane interest in it.

Dr. Ulma still insisted that any keen interest activating the mind and exercising its rational capacity was worth pursuing. I didn't always like the way Catlyn's mind had been working in these exercises, but at least it didn't involve Rupert Errique.

These two letters were written about events that occurred on the same day, but the first one was to Prunella's friend, Elly Howshim, while the second was to Ariana. That made some sense because the first letter was about children. Ariana's first child wasn't born until the following year, 1811, while Elly Howshim of Wolverhampton already had children before Prunella left England.

I was taking a turn on deck with Katherine and Mrs. Mimms. Katherine was so great with child our pace was slow. As we walked, she confided in me that her term was drawing near, and she was worried about her son. She asked if I would look after him when her time to deliver arrived. I promised at once. I have never before attended to a child, but I know I shall be ever so good at it.

As we rounded the deck, there was a sound of a terrible commotion. There was shouting, and I could hear Mr. Jackson hollering "bugger off" to someone. Just then, I saw Gerald hurrying towards the noise, but exactly then, Katherine let loose a little scream of her own. I called for Gerald to help, and together we took Katherine to the ship's doctor. I dispatched Mrs. Mimms to fetch Mr. Bowermun. Katherine was giving birth, and the doctor commanded us to assist.

It was not, however, a quick birthing, and matters were made dire by a terrible storm that very suddenly swept over us. Captain James called it a squall.

It was terrifying. Elly, the ship was rolling and pitching, and it was crashing against the waves with such great thuds they jarred my innards. Gerald did his best to secure the bucket of water, while I tried to keep Katherine from sliding off the cot, all the while Katherine was squeezing my hand and arm so hard I fear I shall be wearing bruises for some weeks.

The storm "abated" and the baby, a daughter, arrived just as the ship's watch sounded seven bells. In honor of that moment, Katherine and Mr. Bowermun named their baby girl "Belle."

– Prunella, Letter No. E3, 1810

"I've never witnessed an actual childbirth," Catlyn remarked. "One of the secretaries at the school where I taught was pregnant with her first child, and she was at work when her water broke. It wasn't the embarrassing gusher you see in the movies, but it was unexpected. She wasn't due for another few weeks, and she began to panic. So, one of the teachers called the paramedics. Meanwhile the school nurse came and tried to keep her calm. Even though she wasn't having contractions, the poor girl was terrified. She was convinced something must be wrong. This just wasn't supposed to be happening yet."

Catlyn paused. Her head was tilted down, and her eyes seemed vacuous, peering at the table. "The fear that comes from not knowing what's happening can be terrifying." Her voice was distant, pensive. "It doesn't really matter what the circumstances are. Maybe she should've been better prepared, but even so, when you don't know what's happening, you can't help it. Not knowing is terrifying."

Tilly was entranced by Catlyn's expression. She started to ask, "When you were kidnapped..." She stopped. She pressed one hand over her mouth. She looked horrified. "I'm sorry," she tried to say. "I shouldn't've..."

I was so shocked I couldn't speak. I knew Tilly hadn't meant to be thoughtless, but she was clearly both thoughtless and insensitive. Catlyn, though, merely glanced her way with hardly any expression at all. Her face had gone blank, and her mind had gone somewhere beyond us. It was as though Tilly wasn't even there.

Catlyn's eyes flickered a little, like she'd heard a noise and was searching for what might have caused it. Then she blinked and turned to me to ask, "Was the second letter about the same event?"

"The second...? I... Let me see."

I was completely unsettled. First Tilly's blunder – that's the kindest thing I can say about it – and now Catlyn being totally oblivious to it. For what little I know of such things, Catlyn had just dissociated herself not only from Errique and her own dilemmas, but from us as well!

Maybe that was a good thing. I don't know. Maybe it was the only way she could handle it. Maybe it was even a brave effort. I wasn't sure. I just know I was unsettled by it, and I was having trouble speaking. I cleared my throat and managed to mumble something about the second letter being to Ariana.

Tilly – a hundred times a blessing, Catlyn had once said

of her. Tilly took that as her cue and started reading aloud. Her voice was a little shaky in the beginning, and then the letter itself had its own astounding aspects. But that was just what we needed to get us all resettled and back on track.

Mr. Joshua has disappeared from the ship! There is speculation that he is gone overboard, and worse, that it was done by foul deed. My mind is a tempest – Gerald is suspected! Mr. Jackson reported, "A squall was churning up and I was looking for shelter. That's when I observed Mr. Treavor arguing with Mr. Joshua. I presumed it was about the illegal contraband. I thought it best not to intrude, so I ducked off right quick. I was some steps away when I heard a shout, or so it sounded. I retraced my steps, but there was nobody there. So I went straightway to the mess. You can ask the lad there. He'll tell you. I had to wait for him to finish counting off the bells before he'd fetch me my rum."

Gerald has denied it, but no one has disputed the account of Mr. Jackson. However, the lad in the mess reported that Mr. Jackson had consumed a large quantity of rum earlier, and if any soul was swept overboard in the squall, it should have been Mr. Jackson.

Captain James has made no charges as yet. He said there was room for doubt on the matter because of the squall. But, he has told Gerald that he is to be confined to quarters until a decision is concluded.

They are wrong, Ariana. They are wrong. I know it in my heart. Gerald would not do such a thing, not without cause.

– Prunella, Letter No. A5, 1810

Tilly looked at me for a cue to what's next. I looked at Catlyn. She had a small, distracted smile on her face, like she hadn't even been paying attention to us.

"It's a pretty name, don't you think? Belle."

I wasn't sure how to respond. I wanted her to be distracted from her own anxieties, but that much? I was beginning to panic about the way she was distancing herself from us. We'd just read about a terrible situation for Prunella, a man missing overboard, Gerald essentially accused of murdering him, and all she heard was "Belle."

Catlyn smiled at me. I hadn't even thought to conceal my consternation, and my face must have been livid with it. She said, "Gerald didn't do it."

I didn't know what to think, except, *where did that come from?* While I was scrambling to put two and two together, Tilly asked quite sensibly, "How do you know that?"

Catlyn's smile turned to delight. She was actually enjoying this moment. While it was the effect I wanted, I was utterly befuddled at this point.

"Because of Belle," she said. "Belle's all the proof he needs."

"Catlyn," I appealed, "be kind to an old man. Tell me. What am I missing?"

"Didn't you hear the bells? There were seven of them, twice."

I think I might have blushed. I started to think, *Maybe I'm getting too old for this*, but then, no, that wasn't it. I just cared too much. I was so focused on Catlyn that I just wasn't paying attention to the letters.

"Of course," I agreed with evident relief. "Mr. Jackson couldn't have seen Gerald during the squall, which was just ending at seven bells, because, at seven bells, Gerald was assisting in the birth of baby Belle."

It was right about then that Catlyn did one of those agile mental twists that her multitasking brain was so good at. "Lucy to Ramon to Chrisy to Errique." She looked squarely at me. "Links. Like Inspector Malbec says, we need the links. Keep digging. If we're going to make sense of this, we absolutely need to know what happened in Westminster."

I think Tilly and I were now both flustered by Catlyn's mental gymnastics. We kind of looked at each other trying to understand what just happened, and then I stammered something to the effect of "Of course, yes, Westminster. I'll get right on it."

I think I was starting to stand up like I might be leaving, when Tilly objected, "Wait! Not right now!"

Tilly, it seems, was focused on more immediate priorities. "You promised! My research on Thanksgiving? You said you'd check it over for me; make sure I didn't miss anything."

Catlyn looked back and forth between the two of us like we'd been conspiring. "Humph," she declared, and I think there was some genuine amusement in that. "Well, then," she said, "I guess I should leave you to it. Is there anything I could do for you?"

Catlyn may have been fishing for an invitation to join us, which Tilly considered for about a second, and then said, "Some tea would be nice."

I think I blinked at that. Whatever spirit resides in Catlyn, I do believe it's taking up residence in Tilly as well. Just to be clear in the present circumstances, as Rose would say, I mean that in a good way.

"Tea. I see," quipped Catlyn, and the delight in her eyes was worth a treasure. "I shall attend to it at once, m'lady."

They were so natural and confident together, I had to marvel at them. A moment such as this had become a rarity at Southjoy Mission, and if I might be indulged a brief aside, I felt very privileged to be part of it. In a way, it was déjà vu all over again. When Amelia was about Tilly's age, my son and Amelia were visiting me. Amelia had asked me to help her create a special card for her father who'd soon be shipping out to the Persian Gulf and might not be home for Christmas. In much the same way as Tilly had done just now with Catlyn, Amelia dismissed my son so she and I could work privately. It was a memory I will always cherish, and the quirk of its recollection, here, at a time when Catlyn was engaged in a personal war with no certainty of its future, became a defining moment in my thinking. I could see it with absolute clarity. Tilly and Catlyn were a family, right then, regardless of what anyone else might say.

But history was repeating the worry as well as the fond sentiment. We all wondered, would Catlyn be home for Christmas? Here, I mean. Would she be here, wholly here in person and in spirit? Stable and sane?

Tilly was right. We needed to be thankful first.

Chapter 35: Tilly

Thanksgiving Day had never been celebrated at Southjoy Mission. It was an American holiday, so I suppose there was no reason to celebrate it here. Cook said they used to do Michaelmas and Harvest Festival long ago, long before I came here, but as far as anyone could remember, neither of those days had been celebrated on the estate in at least a couple of decades.

Miss Stacey had said okay to the idea, but she added one condition. She said it wouldn't be right to celebrate Thanksgiving if I didn't really know what the point of it was. There was more to it than what was in the movies, so I had to do a report on it. She allowed Professor Endbrook to help me do it right, but I had to do the actual research myself.

I was surprised that it all started back in the 1600s. According to Professor Endbrook, "In many ways, it was a brutal time of political and religious unrest throughout England and Europe. If you didn't believe the right things, politically or religiously, you'd be tortured until you did or you died."

"You mean like Edmund Plagyts being tortured and killed for heresy right here."

"Exactly like that."

"Why were they so cruel? People can't change what they believe, can they? If you can change it, it isn't really a belief."

"They didn't see it as being cruel. They thought, 'might makes right.' Some people still think that. It was ignorant and intolerant, but in the 1600s, a statement like the one you just made could get you burned at the stake for heresy."

"And that's why the Pilgrims left England?"

"More or less. They weren't actually called Pilgrims at that time. They were Puritans. Their more radical members had renounced the Church of England, so technically they were breaking the law. They could either stay and be punished for their crime, or flee and stay true to what they believed."

I'd never thought about how far people would go for what they believed to be right. The Pilgrims/Puritans left England for religious freedom. Prunella went looking for a new start. Miss Stacey's father went to America to make his own life. And they all made sacrifices to do it.

Nearly half of the Pilgrims who went to America in 1620 died during their first winter. They'd been trying to get to Jamestown in Virginia which was already settled, but they got lost. Where they landed, winter was much worse than they'd expected, and they weren't prepared for it. If it hadn't been for the Indians who taught them about growing crops and what game to hunt, the Pilgrims wouldn't have survived. So their Thanksgiving was all about gratitude.

When I reported all this to Miss Stacey, she seemed very pleased with me. "These days, she said, "Thanksgiving has become a day of remembering to be thankful for all kinds of things. New jobs, good health, friends, fond memories, pretty much anything that can be counted as a blessing or just dumb luck, it doesn't matter. It all counts. So for the most part it's still all about gratitude."

"If the Indians hadn't shared, or the colonists hadn't said 'thanks,' would anybody have remembered that time?"

"Not in the same way. What made it especially memorable was that people were reaching out to help one another, sharing what they had, and not just for a single day. That often gets lost in modern festivities, but it's still remembered on a smaller scale, usually by community shelters and church groups. They make special efforts to provide food for people who've fallen on hard times, which is more in keeping with the history than the modern tradition. Their main focus is usually on homeless people. In a sense, that's what the Pilgrims were too, homeless in winter, with no place to go."

"Could we do that too? I mean, do something to help the homeless?"

For a second, Miss Stacey went wide-eyed weepy. Then she reached over and hugged me hard. She didn't say anything, but something about the thought of homeless people touched her so deep she couldn't speak. I wondered if it was because it's been hard for her to feel like she belongs here. If you feel like you don't belong, you feel homeless. The feeling's the same, even if the circumstances aren't.

When she sat back, she was already deep in thought. "The full experience," she said, "historical and modern; that's what the first Thanksgiving at Southjoy Mission should be."

Her face started to light up. "Could I... Would it be okay with you, if I do the historical part, you know, the part about remembering people less fortunate?"

"You'd do that? I mean, and really want to?"

"I would. And together, we'll do the whole thing up right."

Now I was excited. "We'd be like a team!"

She put her arm around my shoulders. "We would, a team of two, heeding what we're supposed to be heeding."

§§§

Heeding and begetting a simple deed, a simple deed begetting a great glory. That was our pact and Grannie Effie's wisdom combined. For this little while, Miss Stacey was a whole and spirited person. She was animated and charged full of energy. Rose said she was focused. Amelia said she was alive. Myself, I think she'd just found a piece of the quest she'd lost for a while, a small piece, I know, but it was still a piece of it. And I helped her find it.

Miss Stacey put everything else aside to do her part. She called a church who put her in touch with a coordinator for local homeless shelters. Through them, she arranged to provide a meal at A Share of Life Shelter.

"It's only a token gesture, I know," she said. "It's only a small patch to a gaping wound. Someday, someone will find a more lasting solution. Our little effort will barely make a dent in what's needed, but it'll help. It keeps the hope alive, and if you reach out, somebody else will too. Help when help is needed. That's what makes good people good."

That last part struck close to home. I think we all understood it in a way that maybe Miss Stacey hadn't intended. I know for myself, I wanted to believe it was her subconscious trying to tell us she still needed our help. Anyway, when she volunteered "we girls" to help with the serving, "we" being Miss Stacey, Amelia, Rose, and me, we all pitched in. Nobody wanted to be left out.

§§§

The shelter provided both a good meal and a safe place to sleep. Homeless and jobless people, families whose savings had been depleted, people wanting a chance to escape rough sleeping, and anyone who had nowhere to go could find a temporary place to stay, a hot meal, showers, and a safe place to sleep at A Share of Life.

The shelter occupied the central portion of an old shops building. On one side of it was a thrift store; on the other was a food pantry that provided canned foods and other items.

Two rooms were used for sleeping quarters, one for men and one for women. They were equipped with a dozen cots each. On each cot was a pad, one warm blanket, and a pillow. Each room had the luxury of an attached water closet and a bathing room, and all guests were given a personal hygiene package with soap and shampoo, toothpaste and brush, and other items. Every room had at least one person attending them day and night for everyone's safety and security.

The kitchen was arranged like a cafeteria. Food preparation was done on one side of a dispensing aisle, which was also where we stood to serve the food on ecofriendly plates and plastic trays. Four large tables that could seat eight people each sat in the dining area, along with two tables just large enough for one person each. The latter tables were kept apart from the others. Those were for the occasional guests who suffered from social challenges, which meant they didn't get along well with other people.

On the night we were serving, one of the isolated tables was being used by a man who seemed very old. Mrs. Brasile, who was in charge of the shelter that night, told us not to go near him. He had a very bad temper and became unruly whenever anyone got too close to him. Something about him caught Miss Stacey's attention. She glanced at him several times and finally just stared at him.

He sat hunched forward, head down, and eyes fixed on

his plate. I had the impression, though, that he was seeing everything around him. He ate with minimal movement. He held a spoon in his hand and swiveled it about his wrist to scoop the food. Spoon to mouth to eat. Spoon back to plate. Chew. Repeat. Never once did he look up or take any interest in anything around him. He just looked mean and old.

"Not old," Miss Stacey said. "I've seen that look. I've stared at it in the mirror. He's not old. He's beaten."

Amelia went livid. "Don't you dare say that. Don't you dare say you've seen it in the mirror. I won't have it. You hear me? You're not beaten; you're not broken, and you won't ever be."

Miss Stacey continued to watch the man. "I'm not beaten, I know that; and I won't ever be; I know that too. But I *have* seen that look. Maybe it's only the face of my doppelganger, but she's there, watching me, inviting me to give up."

Rose was incensed by such talk. "Enough! Another word like that, and I'll make you leave. I'll slap you silly and make you leave." And we all knew she meant it, and she'd do it.

Miss Stacey nodded, but she couldn't stop looking at the man. Her voice was low in key. "You're right, of course. I was just feeling sorry for myself." She shuddered at the thought and looked at us. "I'm sorry," she said, and she did look embarrassed. "That was small of me. Their problems are real and tangible. Except for his; there's more to his, I think."

She smiled apologetically, and we all went back to work. I watched her out of the corner of my eye, though, and I saw her glancing his way several times. When the dish she was working was empty, she stepped away from the line and pulled off her serving gloves. She turned away from us, but I could see she'd put her hands over her mouth and was taking deep breaths. After about a minute, she shook her head, you know, like she'd decided something. Then, to my horror, she calmly walked over to the man sitting apart from everyone.

She quietly borrowed an empty chair from the closest table and carefully placed it only a step away from the man. She sat down, slowly, leaned forward, forearms on her knees, hands overlapping, and stared at the floor. The man kept eating but turned his head to glare at her. At that angle, his gaunt face and sunken cheeks made him look even meaner, and very threatening. Mrs. Brasile started to hurry over to them, but Rose stopped her and urged her to wait.

Miss Stacey continued to stare at the floor, gazing into a lost world. Another minute went by. Then, without looking up, she said, "It doesn't stop." Her voice sounded hollow and distant. The man paused. I could see his jaw moving, and I couldn't tell if he was chewing his food or getting ready to scream at her. Then, surprisingly, he dropped his eyes back to his plate. "It don't stop," he said in exactly the same tone.

We watched, breathless and fearful, even Mrs. Brasile. A minute passed, then Miss Stacey slowly raised her head, and the man did too. They stared eye to eye. "Ain't no tomorrow," he strained, "if they snuff the fire dead. Ain't strong n'more."

I could see a tear on his cheek, and a matching one on Miss Stacey's face. A brief, fleeting connection hovered between them. Miss Stacey reached out to lay her hand on his arm. "One day," she said. He looked down; slowly covered her hand with his. "So," he nodded. "So."

I couldn't breathe. Even we who watched could feel the tenderness in the touch of their hands. Mrs. Brasile was shaking her head and saying, "Mysterious wonders" like she was in awe. We all were, I think. And it was mysterious and wondrous. Like an unquenchable glory.

§§§

She wouldn't talk about it. The man had retreated into his silent shelter, and all the way home, Miss Stacey was silent too. A smile would flicker on her face, and then she'd look out the window. If I asked her anything, she'd just look over at me and pat my hand. I was trying to ask, was she okay, and what'd the man mean about snuffing the fire? She just didn't want to talk about it.

But Rose and I did. We talked about it a lot because we both agreed, there was a change in Miss Stacey. Rose described it this way. She said, when Miss Stacey first came here, she was passionate and spirited and always looking for the good in people. And she was right. I remembered how Miss Stacey got upset with me when I said rude things about Alister Knipsyk before we even knew anything about him. And I remembered how she tried to be friends with Lady Wythiry. Rose said when all the horrible things happened, the compassionate part of Miss Stacey's spirit went into hiding, like it was hibernating. If that's true, then Miss Stacey's "token gesture" was the nudge she needed to awaken her compassion and bring it out of hibernation.

Rose also made a big deal about another thing. She said, being at the shelter was a soul searching experience. If we could link that experience to something joyous, the combination might propel Miss Stacey's spirit completely past all the anxieties weighing her down. By "something joyous," she meant my plans for a Thanksgiving Day feast.

I knew Miss Stacey was totally in sync with that idea, although in her mind, I'm sure she thought she was doing it for us. She was certainly determined that all of us would be part of it. Without any encouragement, she became intent on convincing her "core family" to join us for the celebration. I don't think any of us really needed much coaxing.

Professor Endbrook, of course, didn't take any persuasion at all because he doted on Miss Stacey almost as much as on Amelia, and Amelia was happy because it meant Rip, who's American, would make a point of being here too. Miss Stacey insisted that Willy Hartsdell come, and she asked Professor Endbrook to invite Mrs. Ock, his friend with the hospital auxiliary. Rose made sure Ned came, and Dr. Ulma, another American, rounded out our group to make a party of ten, counting Miss Stacey and me. Miss Stacey asked Whinehardt if maybe he, Sweetgrove, and Cook would consider joining us for this occasion, but he nixed that idea at once. He said he was honored to be asked, but for them, gratitude was best expressed in the honor of their service to Miss Stacey. Pride of service. Who could argue with that?

The celebration at Southjoy Mission was to be "modern traditional," meaning it would be observed like in the movies, with good company and good food. Lots of good food. I saw to that.

Rose and I spent the whole day before Thanksgiving decorating. The new housemaid, Sophie, who replaced Lucy, helped a lot too. I like her, by the way. She's fun and easy to work with. Rose calls her a free spirit because she's always eager to try new things. So the three of us gathered all the decorations Rose and I bought when we went Thanksgiving shopping, and we started improvising.

We began with a table runner that depicted fall leaves in

various shades of reds and yellows. Then, we used a large cornucopia basket made of wicker to create a centerpiece for the dining table. We laid out every last one of the colorful gourds and fruits we'd purchased, and positioned them to make it look like they were spilling out of the basket to form a winding path down the table.

The sitting rooms were actually harder to do because the decorations had to be scattered around in all the rooms, and we wanted each one to look different. In the end, we decided to use figurines as much like Pilgrims and Indians as we could find, and then we composed a different scene on each of the smaller tables. Sophie helped a lot with that, and she made sure there were plenty of decorated paper napkins stationed on those same tables. The napkins were actually meant for Harvest Festival, but Miss Stacey said they'd be perfect because it was really the same idea. As she put it, thankfulness doesn't have any borders.

I think I got goose bumps every time I saw how upbeat Miss Stacey was becoming. She seemed so energetic, the way she went from room to room, the way she stopped to talk to everyone. I'd ask her, "Is this okay?" and she'd ask back, "Do you like it?" and I'd say, "I do," and she'd say, "Then I think it's perfect." That's exactly how mellow she was.

On the big day itself, we got everyone warmed up with hors d'oeuvres: baked brie with raspberry preserves, bite-sized quiche with spinach and bacon bits, little Italian meat balls, healthy dishes of celery pieces and broccoli and sliced carrots, along with a variety of crackers and sliced cheese pieces; and for that authentic touch, we added bowls of candy corn. Okay, call that modern authentic – That got a laugh from Miss Stacey. Her eyes were bright and sparkly, and more than once I heard her declare, "I love it!"

In case that wasn't sumptuous enough, dinner in the main dining room began with a southern American favorite, peanut soup made like they do in Colonial Williamsburg in Miss Stacey's home state of Virginia. That was followed by roast turkey with a savory herb stuffing that used pecans, dried apricots, apples, and golden raisins. Then you could fill up your plate with sweet potatoes dressed with cinnamon and butter, cranberry chutney, cheddar chive biscuits, and Sally Lunn buns which Miss Stacey requested in memory of her friend, Courtney Haversmith. Even though Miss Stacey understands that Courtney's murder wasn't her fault, the thought of it still caused a few tears to escape her control. But, she assured us, they were a good kind of tears and they were certainly allowed. Even Dr. Ulma agreed with that.

For beverages, we had sparkling cider for me and Mrs. Ock, and wine for everyone else. A red wine was served, a Châteauneuf du Pape, in memory of Lord Sebastian Silverworth, along with a deluge of good tears that Miss Stacey had some difficulty stopping. However, when the wine had been poured and Miss Stacey had mastered her tears, she stood up to get everyone's attention.

"I was going to make a speech," she told us, "but there's so much I wanted to say to all of you, I was having some difficulty putting it all together. I decided to look in Ariana's diary for inspiration, and I found that she'd already said all that needs saying, as she usually does. So, as my speech and my toast, I'm just going to read what Ariana wrote. It actually had to do with her birthday, but it seemed perfect for today."

On the completion of my sixth decade in this world, my

children asked me, what were the most important words of wisdom I could share with them? I was unprepared to be wise, and this was all I could think to say: Be ever thankful for those you love. Make a feast of your gratitude, for in that way, you will nourish the harmony of your life.
  – Ariana's Diary, 1850

Miss Stacey sighed in a way that seemed very contented. "I hope you will all join me, wise or not, and make that your thought for today."

We did. How could we not when Miss Stacey was so radiant? To me, she was exactly what harmony should be. I really thought, for this one day, we'd created a dream world for her that was the extreme opposite of every nightmare she'd ever had. It was warm and caring and pleasant and filled throughout with good spirit. Before sitting down again, she lifted her glass of wine and offered, "To Thanksgiving." We all raised our glasses and saluted her toast, but actually, to a person, we were all saluting her.

After dinner, while we indulged ourselves with apple pie, pumpkin tarts, mini chocolate swirl cheese cake, crème brûlée, and a selection of Belgian chocolate truffles, our conversations were the only part of the day that could be called light and easy.

At some point, I mentioned the Bath Christmas Market. Miss Stacey seemed very excited that I'd remembered it and wondered, wouldn't it be a wonderful idea to make tomorrow our own official Christmas Market day, you know, as a way to extend our Thanksgiving celebration. Dr. Ulma was very much in favor of it and said it was a lovely idea. He commented that he'd always thought the Market had a certain romantic allure to it, especially in the evening when the lights from the booths filled the area with a kind of golden glow. That's when Miss Stacey linked arms with us, one with Dr. Ulma and one with me, and said just as natural as could be, "Then let's do it." I was so excited by her idea that I almost missed the fact that she really did mean the three of us, her and me and Dr. Ulma.

He looked at her and said, "That's a wonderful idea."

She looked at him and said, "You *will* come, won't you?"

"Better than that," he said. "Let's make a full evening of it. We'll have dinner first, just something casual in town, and then we can walk to the Market, and you can stroll to your heart's content."

He meant me too, of course.

§§§

Later, as the evening was coming to an end, Miss Stacey was in the foyer saying goodnight to Dr. Ulma. I was waiting near the door with Whinehardt who was holding Dr. Ulma's coat. Miss Stacey and Dr. Ulma were standing very close, and Miss Stacey was speaking softly, like she was still drifting pleasantly in that dream world we'd created for her. I was convinced she was whispering so as not to break its spell.

"I can't keep calling you Dr. Ulma. Do you have a first name?"

He smiled modestly. "It's Wyatt."

"Wyatt? You mean like..."

"Yes, like him. My parents wanted their son to be the hero at the OK Corral, you know, saving the town from all the bad guys."

"Then they must be very proud of you, because that's

what you do every day. You just do it one person at a time, and without the violence."

"I'm not sure they'd see it quite that way."

"Then I hope one day I can tell them."

The way "Wyatt" was peering into Miss Stacey's eyes made me want to swoon. Someday I hope somebody'll look at me that way, and maybe I could be lost in his gaze the way Miss Stacey was transfixed by Wyatt's.

She placed one hand lightly against his chest, and I could see the tension in her body as she leaned towards him, touching his elbow with her other hand. She was lifting her lips to him, her eyes slowly closing. Then suddenly, Dr. Ulma abruptly pulled away. He grabbed her firmly by the shoulders and urgently propped her up like she was about to fall over. "Catlyn," he cried out, "What's wrong? You look faint."

That startled Miss Stacey. She looked confused and embarrassed.

He looked worried and perplexed.

I was disgusted.

I kicked him in the shins.

§§§

I hadn't hurt him, except maybe his pride.

I stood there with my hands on my hips, scowling at him until he suddenly seemed to understand. Then we all laughed, and it was like the world began anew.

Miss Stacey pointedly said "Goodnight, Tilly" before ushering "Wyatt" outside. She raised her eyebrows at Whinehardt who seemed to understand what she meant. "Very good, Miss Stacey," he said and gently closed the door as they left.

For the rest of the evening, Miss Stacey was "incommunicado," so naturally, the next morning, I pestered her with a thousand questions about what happened outside.

"That was private," she told me, but by then, everyone else wanted to know too, and another thousand questions later, she relented.

She started to say something, but then changed her mind. "Wait here," she instructed us and left the room. When she returned a few minutes later, she said, "Here, read this."

It was a page in her personal diary. That was one of the positive things she started doing after she was rescued from her kidnapping. She wanted to be more like Ariana, so she kept a diary like Ariana had. Dr. Ulma much approved of the idea because it gave her a very personal and private way to bring out her inner thoughts. By writing them, she could observe them without feeling threatened. Sometimes she takes her diary to the cemetery where she reads it to Ariana. Dr. Ulma said he had no problem with her doing that. It gives her one more way to meditate on whatever's troubling her, and still be calm and balanced in her thoughts. I don't know about the meditation, but I can well imagine her holding a one-sided conversation with Ariana. And it's true, when she comes back, she's always calmer.

Thoughts in a diary, though, are supposed to be private, but for this one time, Miss Stacey decided to allow us a brief glimpse into a small part of those thoughts.

Before handing me her diary, she said to all of us, "I've been learning – maybe I should say, I've been forced to learn – that we rarely can choose what memories our minds preserve for us. Sometimes we want that choice, like when a moment is precious because of how you felt in that moment. The details of the moment might not be unique or profound or even exceptional, but the emotion that you felt is all of that. Last night, I discovered a moment like that for me, and I never want to forget it. So, I wrote something in my diary to help me remember what I felt. I promised I wouldn't hide anything from you, at least not anything important, and this memory is important to me. So, I'll let you read it for yourselves. All I ask is that you not make too much of it. Just accept it for what it is, just me, trying to remember and understand that moment. It's a poem, sort of."

She entrusted her diary to me, then went out to stroll through the atrium garden, probably remembering every word she wrote.

§§§

We paused beneath the amber moon
And shared upon our lips a kiss.
But, no, not only this.
Say more, as fire from an ember flames,
Love into a heart exclaims.
An ambered moon. An embered kiss.
If God should grant my fondest wish,
Then in my soul forevermore shall live
The ember of that amber kiss.

Chapter 36: Ethan

I had stayed over after the Thanksgiving dinner with the intention of spending more time with Catlyn. She really seemed to be coming to grips with the reality of an imperfect world. The security of the estate was fully re-established. There'd been no further incidents. And Rupert Errique was absorbed with his work release program and otherwise seemed to pose no additional intrigue against Catlyn. I'd even begun to think we all might have misjudged Lady Wythiry. As difficult as it was to admit, she may well have been due more credit than any of us thought possible. Something to be thankful for indeed.

As were the signs of normal life that were reappearing in growing abundance at Southjoy Mission. Amelia and Rip had plans for the day, and Catlyn and Tilly would be out with Dr. Ulma in the evening. I myself would be meeting Willy later for dinner because we didn't get to talk much last night. It seems we took turns chatting with Mrs. Ock. At any rate, that all meshed well with Catlyn's plans, so we agreed to take a look at the last Prunella letter before lunch.

It was a mark of Catlyn's growing self-confidence that we decided to convene again in the small sitting room. In some ways, it's the coziest room in the whole mansion, and quite simply, that's how Catlyn was choosing to think of it. This was no longer about being obstinate. She told me, "There's a sense of comfort here. I want Southjoy Mission to know I understand that." She gave me one of those chagrined looks she's so good at. "That's just me being romantic, not crazy."

And it was romantic. She chose to remember the fond

sentiment rather than the nightmarish disruption. I think that counts as romantic, and in a well-adjusted way.

It was also a fitting choice because we were on the verge of shedding some light on the controversy plaguing Prunella's voyage to America. You already know, of course, that crossing the ocean by packet ship in 1810 was a perilous adventure in the best of circumstances, scarcely any different than when the Puritans set sail to the New World. But, make that same crossing on a ship fraught with intrigue, and it becomes downright harrowing.

As we settled in, I reported, "We may have found an important clue regarding Mr. Jackson."

"In Prunella's final letter?"

"Not in the letter, no. Willy and I decided to explore all the online library archives we could find for Westminster. We were looking for anything out of the ordinary. But to make sure we didn't go too far afield, we confined ourselves to the months just before Prunella's ship departed from Falmouth. We found this in the London Gazette."

> *WHEREAS a great Number of disorderly Persons have, during the Four last Days, assembled themselves together, in a riotous and tumultuous Manner, and have been guilty of many Acts of Outrage, having attacked the Houses of many of Our loyal Subjects in several Parts of Our City of Westminster, and having fired at and wounded several of our Subjects employed by the Civil Magistrates, in keeping Our Peace, and in preventing such unlawful Proceedings; We, therefore, taking the same into Our most serious Consideration...*
>
> *By the King, A Proclamation, London Gazette, Tuesday April 10, to Saturday April 14, 1810.*

"It goes on from there with more whereas's, but Willy and I agree, this rioting in Westminster constitutes the smoking gun we were looking for. People were attacked, shots were fired, and numerous people were wounded, including people employed by the civil magistrates to keep the peace."

"Was anyone killed?"

"There's nothing mentioned about fatalities, but that's not what Jackson said. Let's go back to that earlier letter."

Tilly quickly found it on her tablet. I pointed, "Here, this part. According to Prunella, Jackson said,"

I knew a bloke like him in Westminster. Making trouble, he was. So I did him what for.

"If I were to go out on a limb, that bloke who was 'like' Mr. Joshua could very well have been one of the peace keepers or even a magistrate."

"And if Jackson wounded him," Tilly said, "it'd be spot on to say he'd done him what for."

"That all fits together," noted Catlyn, "but would that have been enough to make him flee England?"

"Maybe. As you can see here in the conclusion of the proclamation, His Majesty was so displeased with the rioters that he was offering a reward for their capture."

We are graciously pleased to promise, that if any Person shall discover any Person or Persons who, directly or indirectly, was or were concerned in firing at and wounding any of Our Subjects... such Discoverer shall have and receive, as a Reward, upon Conviction of such Offender or Offenders, the Sum of FIVE HUNDRED

POUNDS...

"Five hundred pounds was a lot of money in 1810. For most wage earners, that would've been a full year's income."

Catlyn was cautious. "Mr. Jackson doesn't strike me as the type to get involved with rioting."

"But he could certainly have used it for his own purposes."

"Of course," said Catlyn. "The rioting would've covered a wealth of sins." She seemed suddenly distracted. "Misdirection would do that too."

"Pardon?" I didn't understand, and I didn't like it when Catlyn went off on her sudden tangents, especially now when she's been doing so well. It's like she's drifting away from us on a receding tide. I fear for her when she does that. It'd only take one strong undertow to carry her away forever.

Catlyn seemed to be thinking out loud. "Errique wants to dominate me. That's Dr. Ulma's assessment. He says Errique has no sense of fairness, and he doesn't play by any rules. Anything that gets him what he wants is..." She looked sharply at me. "Ethan, you need to be careful now, too. I should have seen that before. He might very well see you as a means to get at me or Amelia. He's capable of anything. Like Mr. Jackson. You see that he killed Mr. Joshua, don't you? And then tried to blame Gerald for it. Errique will stop at nothing, and I don't want you to be the next Mr. Joshua. I couldn't live with that." She reached over and gently touched my arm and said very softly, "I just couldn't."

That kind of took the wind out of my sail for a minute. I don't know if multitasking is conducive to adaptive learning, but if so, Catlyn was excelling at it. At least, I wanted to believe that's what it was. That was, after all, all I had to go on at that moment, the belief that Catlyn was still being rational.

My options were otherwise limited. I really didn't want to encourage her to see Errique hiding in every shadow, which it seemed to me she was doing, and I certainly didn't want to get into an argument. So my thought was just to let her remarks go unchallenged and move on.

I knew this letter would help. I'd read it earlier and realized it provided a certain measure of closure to Prunella's discord. I was hoping it'd have that same effect on Catlyn.

Tilly was of a similar mind, I think, and when I nodded to her, she began reading at once.

We have made port in Halifax. Gerald was released from his confinement some days ago, and we ended our sea voyage here in relative freedom. Mrs. Mimms said her goodbyes to us this morning, and I have wished her well in all things. I shall miss her, but you need not feel sorry that I shall now have no domestic. I have faced worse moments, and I find I am more than ever I imagined, and I have Gerald. I think that I shall never need for more.

Regarding Mr. Joshua, Captain James recorded the episode in the ship's log saying, "Mr. Joshua washed overboard. Good man lost." Captain James went so far in his consideration of us as to allow us to use our ship quarters for another two days. On the first day, we explored the area to see what our prospects might be. As we were going ashore, I observed the very same two sailors also going ashore and with the very same goods Mr. Joshua had declared contraband. We were on board again when they returned some hours later, absent their goods. They reported at once to the captain. A very short while later, the three of them came out on deck, and they were all of good humor and smiles. Nothing more was said about contraband, and Gerald was never questioned.

The same cannot be said about the tiff between Gerald and Mr. Joshua. People talked about Mr. Joshua disappearing before the inquiry on contraband could be conducted. It seems they are determined to convict Gerald by their scorn if not by evidence. I fear we are condemned to shame once again and will find no comfort here. So we shall travel now by land in hopes of making a new start somewhere else. Katherine and Mr. Bowermun have entreated us to continue on with them to the Carolinas, but Gerald and I are agreed, we shall be no more at sea.

– Prunella, Letter No. E4, 1810

In the momentary hush that followed, Catlyn was once again someplace else in her thoughts. "It's always the same, isn't it? Why are people so quick to accept baseless opinions as fact? Is it jealousy? Surely it can't all be ignorance. They proclaim Lady Wythiry a paragon of the community. Why? Do they really think she'll rehabilitate Rupert Errique? They don't know what Errique's up to or what he's capable of doing. And not a word about Mr. Jackson. If they'd been paying attention, they'd all know what we know."

At that point, I surrendered. I wasn't sure who was supposed to know what, but if it made sense to Catlyn, I was convinced it had to be right.

Chapter 37: Incident

Witnesses said it was over in a matter of seconds. Rupert Errique was standing in the lobby with his two hospital security guards. That was their routine. Lady Wythiry was to arrive soon.

Three men carrying cameras came into the lobby through the main hospital entrance. They appeared to be reporters. They approached Errique asking if he'd like to share a few words of encouragement for other prisoners who might see him as a role model.

"How about a quick picture," one of them asked.

The camera men immediately fanned out, one directly in front of Errique, and the other two on either side of him. All three took a group picture of Errique and his two guards who puffed up their chests for this proud moment.

"Maybe we could get one of you alone, Mr. Errique?"

The man in front motioned the two guards to step away, which they did with smiles all around. As the man's camera flashed in front of them, shots rang out from the other two. The guards were dead instantly, a double tap each, chest and forehead, signature professional hits.

Mr. Errique didn't seem to be surprised or disturbed. He nodded to the gunmen and turned to leave. That's when the door of the lift opened and Lady Wythiry stepped into the lobby. Witnesses on the upper level overlook said she either screamed or gasped or shrieked. The gunman closest to her advanced on her while she stared in shock. He hit her hard with a backhand blow that sent her crashing to the floor.

Mr. Errique glanced back at her for scarcely a second. He seemed amused about something. Then he calmly walked over to her crumpled body. He used his foot to nudge her. She was limp. He frowned at her, then stooped to rummage through her small "demi jour" handbag. He found what he was looking for, which witnesses thought might possibly have been a wallet. He put his plunder into his pocket, stood, adjusted his coat, and then calmly made his exit out the front door.

Chapter 38: Market

Dr. Ulma arrived at the estate in his BMW. He had insisted on calling for them rather than meeting them in town. After the message Tilly delivered to him by way of his shins, he had to admit, it was personal. Catlyn's goodnight kiss left no doubt of that.

He couldn't say exactly when he'd left off being her doctor and had transformed into her suitor. He had never said, you're cured; go live your life. The file on Catlyn Stacey was still open, and yet, he couldn't imagine how anyone could improve on who she'd become. What he could easily imagine doing, though, was spending the rest of his life trying to understand her.

Catlyn raced ahead of Whinehardt to open the door. "I've got it," she said to Whinehardt.

"Of course, Miss Stacey."

She paused. "Whinehardt; you're smiling."

"I beg your pardon, Miss Stacey. It's most unseemly of me. However, as it is entirely your fault, I believe I may be excused for it."

"How is it my fault?"

"Seeing you like this. It overcomes me. There's no help for it. I'm compelled to smile. Lord forgive me if I err, and I do beg your indulgence for it, but I pray that it shall never be otherwise."

"Consider yourself indulged, Whinehardt. Besides, it's not entirely my fault," she defended as she opened the door. "Wyatt has to take some of the responsibility for it."

Wyatt's eyebrows rose. Between this snippet of conversation and the twin beacons of smiles cast upon him, he felt himself hijacked by an assault of goodwill. He rather liked the effect. Being otherwise derelict for words, he lifted his chin and conceded, "Absolutely. If it's anything to do with you, count me in."

Catlyn responded by throwing her arms around him as Tilly came to join them. Seeing Wyatt eyeing her over Catlyn's head, Tilly teased, "Not to worry; I'm wearing soft soled sneakers today."

It was an auspicious beginning to a magical evening, and if an elevated mood feeds anticipation, theirs, indeed, thrived on it.

§§§

With the opening of the Bath Christmas Market, a determined gaiety seemed to be throbbing to and fro along the streets and walkways surrounding the Abbey. Truly special occasions are always like that, don't you think? Call it an ethereal gaiety exuding from the crowd. That's what you get when the good cheer runs deeper than mere superficial frivolity. In the present case, had there been any doubt of it, all you had to do was listen to the running commentary provided by Tilly. Catlyn, as the newbie, was a showcase of smiles with suitable exclamations of her delight. Wyatt, beside her, was content to gaze upon Catlyn, her face, her gestures, the way she tilted her head or flared her eyes with amazement; the way she laughed. It was an easy, comfortable laugh, natural and uninhibited.

Tilly repeated the question. "Are we eating now or later?"

"Um?" Wyatt took a second to get his bearings. "Ah, yes, now. Eat now, shop later."

They had parked at the Podium Shopping Centre and were now strolling down High Street. "We go just there to

Northumberland Passage and then up a ways to the Coeur de Lion. It's famous for being the smallest pub in Bath. It'll be crowded already, but I thought it'd give us a perfect start, and then it'll be just a short walk from there."

"You see the Abbey over there?" Tilly pointed to the spired tower. "That's the main staging area for the Market, between the Abbey and the Roman baths. It's an easy walk from here, but don't eat too much right now. There'll be food and stuff at the Market besides as all the neat things to buy."

"Spot on," laughed Catlyn as she tried to say it like a Brit. Her goodwill was swiftly ascending. "I want the full experience. So, as you say, just enough now to be fortified, but not enough to slow us down from the serious shopping."

That surplus of goodwill was much in demand as they wedged themselves into a table amidst the crush of all the other people trying to do the same. Following yesterday's elegant feast, what was called for now was some good, honest, down to earth charm, and the baguette sandwiches with chips and salad were exactly that. It was a feast of a different nature, presenting just the right degree of rustic ambiance and all the homespun flavor you could ever want.

"Take note," Wyatt informed Catlyn. "The history of the pub is required reading, especially for Americans."

"I can see why," Catlyn remarked. "Here's yet another enterprise founded before the American Revolution. History and pride of history; it's everywhere you go here. I find it almost incomprehensible. No wonder Lady Wythiry resents anyone who's joined the world scene only so recently as America." By "anyone" she really meant "me," as in herself. Everyone knew Catlyn was the most resented person on the planet as far as Lady Wythiry was concerned.

Catlyn was quiet a second, probably contemplating that very fact. A second, but only a second, and then she sat up sharp. "But Christmas is for everyone." And she was determined to have her part in it. And so was most of Bath.

Meal finished, they worked their way back out to High Street, swinging up to Cheap Street and thence around to the front of the Abbey, where well over a hundred booths awaited them. They decided their best strategy was going to be to cruise the booths beginning right along the Abbey and then circulating from there. As they stopped at the first booth, a young boy just walking away in the opposite direction waved to Tilly; she waved back. "One of the kids from school," said Tilly. "We sort of hang out together. Everyone says he's a nerdy geek, so he's not very popular. But I like him. He's just smart."

A few minutes later, Tilly's mobile vibed and binged. "He sent me a text message," said Tilly. Popular or not, there was genuine delight in Tilly's voice.

Wyatt had to smile as Tilly's thumbs tapped out a reply. "Thirty feet apart, and they're sending text messages."

"We *are* in the brave new world, you know," Catlyn mused. "A century or two ago, she'd've been using fans and gloves to do exactly the same thing."

The density of bodies in the walkways was already reaching the saturation point. It was beginning to be like one of those chicklet slide puzzles having only one vacant square; you have to move one chicklet into the open slot, leaving a new a vacancy behind it to be filled by the next piece you move, which in turn...you see how it goes, until everything is reordered the way you want it. The object in the present game was to move bodies to the front of a booth so you could browse, touch, and sometimes buy something from the vendor. Progress was delightfully slow, and it didn't seem to matter to anyone. Nobody wanted to rush, least of all Catlyn and Wyatt.

Tilly's mobile vibed again; it had probably binged as well, but the noise level was now too loud to hear anything as innocuous as a bing. Another text message. She stopped to check it out. She frowned. It wasn't from her friend. Incredibly, it was from Lady Cecelia Wythiry.

> *Pardon my intrusion. Christmas is a time to forgive. Meet me privately? I beg you, help me make amends with Miss Stacey.*

Tilly stared at the text message. Lady Wythiry? In Tilly's mind, Lady Wythiry was the Last Adversary, a paragon of aristocratic villainy. Repelled by the notion of Lady Wythiry corrupting her phone, Tilly nearly hit "delete." But she hesitated. It *was* kind of fascinating. She read the message again. There was no mistaking what it said. Lady Wythiry was waving the white flag; she wanted to surrender; and she wanted Tilly to be the closer in the deal.

It was true that Miss Stacey never wanted to make an enemy of Her Ladyship. Miss Stacey had even invited her to the estate one time. If Miss Stacey could make an effort like that, even though it hadn't turned out so well, she'd probably welcome another chance.

Tilly could feel her excitement spiking at the prospect of being the one person who could reconcile Her Ladyship and Miss Stacey. And to do it at Christmas time! Decided, she replied,

> *Where?*

A few seconds later came,

By the booths just opposite the Roman Baths near York Street.

Tilly's excitement was surging. That placed Her Ladyship on the opposite side of the square from where Tilly was standing. A quick glance showed that Miss Stacey and Dr. Ulma were deeply engrossed with a jewelry booth. The aisles between the booths were teaming with so many people, it'd be easy to slip away for a few minutes. It'd be a wonderful surprise.

"I going just over here," Tilly called out. "Okay, but don't go far," Catlyn permitted as she held up a skillfully crafted bracelet for Wyatt to see. "For Amelia, maybe?"

Adrenaline coursing, Tilly disappeared into the crowd. She worked her way as best she could in fits and starts. The throng ambling along the front of the Abbey drifted in slow lurches that restrained her progress to a crawl. Approaching the Roman Baths, she turned left and headed towards York Street.

She strained to spot Lady Wythiry. The early cold front had everyone bundled snugly into warm winter coats with scarfs and caps. It was hard to distinguish who was beneath them. She tried to imagine what Lady Wythiry would be wearing, but at close range, she didn't see anything Her Ladyship would be caught dead in. She thought to call out her name, but between the music and the loud chatter, it was hard to hear what anyone was saying.

As she neared York Street, though, a hand touched her shoulder. She turned eagerly, but the wide smile forming on her face was suddenly smothered by a large damp cloth placed sharply over her face. Startled and instantly blinded, her scream was muffled; her struggle brief; then she went limp. "Poor child," someone said. "Let's get you home."

§§§

Catlyn hadn't reached the panic stage yet, but when she couldn't spot Tilly immediately, her mind progressed quickly from wondering, *where'd she go*, to the concern of *where is she?* At first, Catlyn thought Tilly must be buying a gift privately and didn't want Miss Stacey to see it. Wyatt said he'd go look. Catlyn allowed a reasonable amount of time, but when neither she nor Wyatt could locate Tilly in the crowd, Catlyn powered up her mobile to call her. She knew Tilly's mobile was turned on; she'd been texting just moments ago. No answer. She tried again to no avail. Panic began to quicken.

Rose. Maybe Rose would know what Tilly's up to.

"Thank God, you've called," declared Rose on answering. "I was so worried. You weren't answering your phone. You've heard about the shooting at the hospital? Errique escaped."

"Rose!" Shock tore the words out of her throat. "Tilly's missing!"

"Missing? How could she be missing?"

Catlyn quickly explained. She entreated, "Call Ned, please. We're searching, but we can't wait. If Errique's got her, Rose, if he's got her..." She choked. Sucked a gasp of air. "Oh God," she cried as panic ripped through her. "God help me, I can't take this anymore!" Savagely she vowed, "I won't do this again. Not again! So help me, I'm going to put an end to it. I have to, don't you see? He's evil, Rose, he's *evil*, and he won't ever stop. There's no other way.

285

Rose, *I have to kill him! I...*"

"Catlyn, stop that. Get a grip. I'm calling Ned now. You've got to stay calm."

"I can't," she cried. "You know I can't."

§§§

Randomly pushing and pulling, Catlyn plunged through the crowd with Wyatt in tow. She grabbed the arm of a constable. He tried to calm her. Radio in hand, he alerted the security detail. One more missing girl. Keep an eye out. Not to worry, he assured. Already, kids lost, kids found. More every half tick or so. "They always show up, mouths stuffed, hands full of candy, no idea why the fuss."

Unable to stand still, Catlyn tore into the crowd. Wyatt stopped her. "Over there," he pointed, "a first aid station."

"A young girl, tall, about five foot, dark hair; she's wearing a bright yellow down jacket with brown trim; blue jeans and sneakers. Have you seen her?"

"We've treated nobody like that here." A patient smile. A little shrug. The same harried look he'd given to all the other worried parents. If they hadn't been so careless... No point in that. Just explain. "Mostly we get bloody noses and minor scrapes and cuts." More keep-them-calm smiling. His buddy said, "There was that one report of a young girl fainting just up the lane here, by York Street."

"Was she wearing a yellow jacket?"

"Couldn't say. We responded, but they were gone when we got there."

"They? Who're they?"

"Sorry, don't know." Another patient smile. Commiserate. Step back. Ease away. "They were gone. That's all I know. There wasn't anything we could do, so we came back here."

"Okay, thank you," Wyatt took the time to acknowledge. "Catlyn, we... Catlyn?" He turned in time to see her disappearing into the crowd.

Rudely pushing and shoving, Catlyn made her way to York Street. A woman in the refreshment booth said, "They was right here. The poor girl fainted right into her father's arms. He picked her up, and they was quick off to home he said."

"Which way?"

"Just through there, towards Abbey Green."

The crowd was thinner up the side street. Catlyn broke into a run. The booths on Abbey Green were arrayed in an oval. Beyond them, an archway opened onto Abbey Gate Street, and if they'd gotten past that point... they'd be gone, *Dear God, they'd be gone.*

Her shoulder caught somebody's arm, sending a bag of toys spewing over the walk. The man cursed her, while another man held up his hands to slow her down. She pushed him out of her way, rushing onwards in an unstoppable churning of her legs, pumping in ever more forceful strides. People turned, pointed, scowled. Angry blurs in a thick fog.

Then – *There!* Bright yellow jacket. Rupert Errique framed in the arch. In his arms – *Tilly!* One arm dangled loose. Then Errique, beckoning to a woman. She, head shaking, *No!* Errique, a gesture, *Here!* She, marching; stiff and angry; at him; menacing steps.

Behind Errique, a shriek. He craned to see. Driving towards him, a savage beast in the form of Catlyn Stacey, a hurtling rage, screaming and running, churning into a wild wounded boar charging through the underbrush, a sightless fury plowing into Errique at full stride. Tilly rolling to Errique's side. Ferocity unleashing, propelling the wild beast to gore and rip at Errique. Kicks. Shouting. Screaming. Pummeling. Punish him! His head! Grab his head! Thrust it back...

A sudden gasp. *Dear God, the pain!* Such excruciating, crushing pain! Errique's elbow viciously buried deep into her chest. A fierce paralyzing pain seizing her body, suspending her senses. Lungs dysfunctional. Body frozen. A breathless, motionless heap.

A second blow sent her body spewing off Errique, tumbling like a formless, raggedy doll, limbs agape, the world in violent spin.

A sucking sound. A gasp of air. A glimpse. Errique. Blood spurting from his nose; his face, a horrid bloody sneer.

He staggered to his feet. Steadied his balance; faltered; then lurched towards Catlyn who lay crumpled on her side.

"Ruppie!" A sharp, piercing, virulent hiss.

He whirled. "Chrisy. What're you... Put that gun down."

A shrill squeal answered, *"No more!"*

Disgust and contempt knotted Errique's face; foul and fetid with disdain. "You" he scorned. He started towards her.

Then a loud detonation. Errique staggered. A bullet ripped through his shoulder. Confused and stunned, he attempted another step. A second round caught him in the chest as Chrisy advanced on him. "Why, Ruppie, why?"

Dropping to his knees, Errique waved his hand dismissively. Standing over him, condemning him, fury erupting, Chrisy swung the gun, hitting Errique at the back of his shoulder, knocking him to his side. "Why?" she raged.

Horrified, she dropped to him, wrapping her arms around him. "Why, Ruppie, why?" she pleaded. "Why couldn't it be just you and me? Just us. We could go away, just you and me. Why'd you have to have her? Why her?"

A sudden seething wrath filled her eyes. She whirled. Sighted Catlyn. "It's you," she hurled in deep smothered judgment. "It's you. It's you," she screamed. Delirious in rage, the gun rising in her hand, the wavering barrel pointing towards Catlyn.

Errique's arm flung out from beneath Chrisy. It caught her below the elbow slamming her arm against her chest. The discharge snapped Chrisy's head back, the bullet slicing upwards through her chin. A snarl of disgust escaped Errique. He pushed her lifeless body aside. On hands and knees, he crawled to the gun; picked it up; studied it; looked at Catlyn; studied her. She'd propped herself up by her arms.

He lamented, "It didn't have to end this way."

"She loved you."

He shrugged. "I suppose. I guess you'd say she died for me." A humorless laugh. He shrugged again. "Would you do that? Would you die for me?"

Catlyn was shaking her head. "You don't have to do this."

He ignored her. "Like Romeo and Juliet," he decided. "First you; then me. Star-crossed forever."

Slowly he pointed the gun at Catlyn. His sight blurred. He squinted; brushed his eyes with the back of his hand.

The blur morphed into the outline of a man. Commotion guiding him, Wyatt had broken through the last ranks of the gawkers. His reaction was spontaneous. No deliberation of a rational mind. He simply acted, thrusting himself between them, Errique before him, Catlyn behind him.

Hovering there, he appealed, "It's over Errique; you know it's over. Just put the gun down. We can talk about this."

"Ah, the good doctor." Errique was choking on his own blood. "Too late. It's too late." He swayed. Righted himself. "Save yourself, doctor. Step aside."

"No."

"No?" Errique grunted, choked again. His strength waning, he raised the gun. "No matter." His arm was wavering under the weight of the gun. He tried to steady his aim.

"Rupert?" It was Catlyn. Struggling past the fierce pain in her ribs and shoulder, she willed herself to stand, to step out from behind Wyatt. "Rupert," she said calmly. "Don't spoil this moment with him. It's just us, just you and me, alone."

Errique started. He teetered; rocked back; extended one hand to support his weight. "Rup... You called me Rupert."

His elbow yielded. He slumped. The daze of weakness descended over him. Wyatt rushed forward; he seized Errique's arm, claiming the gun. Errique caved, too weak to resist, too consumed with Catlyn to care. His eyes trained fixedly on Catlyn. "You called me Rupert."

Up the block, a van was screeching away, while DI Malbec, lights flashing, was bringing his car to a skidding stop. Two constables rushing forward from the crowd converged on Errique. They took charge of him, and relieved Wyatt of the gun, which he held dangling at his side.

Catlyn rushed to Tilly who was yet lying unattended on the walkway. Her plea of "Tilly" was answered by a small movement in one of Tilly's legs. "Help her," Catlyn was shouting. "She needs help."

"We need an ambulance," Dr. Ulma called out. A constable snapped his radio, made the call.

"She's coming to," Dr. Ulma noted for Catlyn's benefit. "I don't think she's injured. Give us room here," he commanded the onlookers who were gathering about them.

Breathless from running, DI Malbec took in the scene in one quick glance. He focused on Errique who was struggling to reach his hand out toward Catlyn. Errique slumped once and fell still. Malbec stooped, felt for a pulse. He shook his head at the constable who was supporting Errique's body. The constable released the body, allowing it to sink to the pavement.

Malbec looked to Dr. Ulma, questioning him with a slight tilt of his head indicating Tilly. "She's going to be okay," Dr. Ulma reported. Malbec nodded; he understood; that would do for now. His attention was needed elsewhere. Prioritize. Assess the scene. Control the crowd.

Already a mob mentality was stirring. This was now their crisis. They owned it, and they were heaving themselves into a frenzy, inciting themselves with the horror strewn in front of them. The throb was growing, that ancient pagan pulse of hunt and kill, their eyes fixed on the scene, the pooling blood, the slumping bodies. The uninvolved, you see...

And they were encroaching too much. Malbec ordered them to back off. On the ground, he spotted a folded cloth lying next to Errique. A quick sniff. "Chloroform," he guessed. A constable stood ready to bag it.

"Check his pockets?"

"Just this; a mobile, fancy cover, monogram *W*. No ID."

"Name's Rupert Errique."

"This is Rupert Errique?" Impressed.

"Was," said Malbec. Unimpressed. He turned to look at the crowd. The glaze was already fading from their faces. Some were leaving. Things to do.

Not so for Catlyn. The shock was yet to come.

But now, Tilly was regaining consciousness. Clutching

her, holding her, rocking her, Catlyn was sobbing as Tilly's eyes fluttered open.

Tilly was still dazed and disoriented, but her eyes found Catlyn. Their eyes locked, Catlyn onto Tilly, Tilly onto Catlyn. And they saw as with one vision. Like a revelation of understanding. A rising of thought from a single mind. A comprehension of one spirit caring beyond one's mere self.

And they rejoiced.

Together in this moment, in the sobbing cry of deliverance, in the deep, deep elation of survival, they rejoiced. They had survived. That was all that mattered.

There would be a tomorrow, and they would be part of it. Tomorrow, a point in the future. What great glories may yet be, if there is yet one more tomorrow.

Chapter 39: Rose

They were safe. Ned brought them home. Catlyn, Tilly, and Wyatt. Ned called ahead to let us know, and we were all there to welcome them. Even Heinrich was standing in the driveway in front of the house. Heinrich, the gamekeeper who shunned civilization, who was fearful only of people. He stood in stoic pose watching the road. He'd accept no assurance of Miss Stacey's well-being except what his own eyes could see. I came out to wait with him as Ned's car came into view. There were tears seeping from his weathered eyes. I wanted to touch him and tell him he was a brave man and it's okay to care. But he already knew that. As Catlyn stepped out of the car, he swallowed once, nodded to her; she smiled to him; he tapped the brim of his hat with one finger, and returned to his forest.

The rest of us, though, had neither his modesty nor his restraint. We converged on the car like it was bringing relief supplies to a starving village. Whinehardt had the front door open and stood two paces outside with Sweetgrove, while Amelia ran past them and past me to throw her arms around Catlyn who winced at the pain in her ribs and shoulder, though she clung to Amelia just as hard. Their tears gushed in great torrents.

Rip stopped short of us, still hesitant to be too demonstrative of his feelings; he probably always would be. Once upon a time, he toyed with the idea that he loved Catlyn, but there was no toying now in his feelings for Amelia. He knew he loved Amelia without reservation. He just wasn't sure, wasn't confident enough, that other people would see it that way, if he should hug Catlyn, if he should cry in happiness for her.

There was no such reserve for us swarming at the car. We formed an ensemble of intertwined arms and hugs that wouldn't quit. As we set our conglomeration into motion, we stumbled and rolled towards the house, collecting Rip along the way, Amelia hooking his arm and pulling him close. As we approached the door, Sweetgrove could restrain herself no longer; she launched down the walkway to wrap her arms around Tilly and Catlyn like they were her long lost beloved children. And, I suppose, in a way, they were.

We plowed through the door in a raucous, delirious dance of victorious warriors. It was a time for rejoicing, a time to celebrate the endurance of humanity.

As we reached the center of the foyer, though, Catlyn stopped. She closed her eyes and took a slow, deep breath while tilting her head back until she was facing upwards. Then she exhaled and opened her eyes to peer at the portrait of Ariana. I don't know what thoughts ran through Catlyn's mind just then, but her countenance seemed to be bathed in a luminous aura, an acclaim of benevolence bestowed uniquely on her by her greatly great grandmother.

The spell of the moment was broken by a sudden eruption of applause and cheers. The rest of the household staff had waited with as much restraint and respect as they could manage, but they too were overcome by the exhilaration of the moment. It was a time for cheering.

Errique was dead, and we were glad of it.

I was glad of it.

I know I'll have to say many prayers for his soul and for mine, and for my lack of charity towards him, and for rejoicing at his death. I tell myself, I'll grieve that his life was wasted, but I'll not grieve for the end of his wasted life.

I can only speak for myself, of course, but I think we all felt more or less the same way.

§§§

The following day, Ethan came and brought with him news of Lady Wythiry. She was resting in the hospital where she was being treated for a concussion. It didn't seem to be life threatening, but her head did hit the marble tile rather hard when she fell. She also suffered facial bruises, and one tooth was knocked loose when the assailant struck her, but she was otherwise fine. The doctor, though, felt it was best to keep her under observation for a day or two. Her Ladyship may have exerted some influence on that decision because it seemed she was reluctant to be seen in public where she would now be subjected to the vindictive ridicule of the disenchanted members of that public. For some people, to be made a fool by the biggest fool is unforgivable.

Catlyn heard this news without emotion. She did ask, though, if anyone had been to see her. To the extent that Ethan had heard, no one had. We later learned that no one from the greater Bath vicinity, not even her husband, would journey to the hospital to visit Her Ladyship, except for Catlyn. Catlyn went to the hospital that very afternoon where she learned that Sir Nigel Wythiry had called the hospital to say he had important business affairs to attend to, but that he granted them whatever permission they might need in treating Her Ladyship. Before disconnecting, he asked to be kept informed as to her progress should she take a turn for the worse.

The same was not true for Catlyn. On that morning, we all fluttered around her in a constant barrage of attention that scarcely left her with two seconds to herself. At one point, our babble was so intense she suddenly stood in our midst, clapped her hands to silence us while decreeing, "Everyone! Everyone listen up! Tilly and I are taking Biscuit for a walk. Stand down. Take five. Catch your breath. As you were. Thank you all very much. We'll reconvene at lunch."

She looked over at Wyatt. She smiled. He smiled. She held out her hand; he took it in his; and together, Catlyn, Wyatt, Tilly, and Biscuit took their leave of the madding crowd.

When they'd gone, I asked Ned for more details of what happened. We were lounging in the atrium sitting room, sipping tea. It seemed to me, we were all struggling to find a closure to all the horridness wrought by Rupert Errique, and I hoped more details would help. That, after all, was Ned's gift, putting the pieces together and making sense of them.

"Sociologists long ago were predicting a violent death for Errique," he said, "and it seems they were right to think so."

"You mean, living and dying by the sword?"

"Not exactly. Errique was always clever enough not to wield the sword himself. That he left to his henchmen. No, I think his case had more to do with being an outcast. His whole life was framed by the rejection of who he was."

He was quiet a moment, sorting through his links, I suppose. He took a sip of tea, then set his cup down. He turned towards the garden and let his eyes peer aimlessly out the window. I suspect he was struggling to follow his links to a definitive conclusion on Errique. So he could move on too.

For a police officer, Ned's unusually compassionate. He says, to understand the criminal mind, you have to get inside it, see what's there. I suspect while he's in there, he's looking for what went wrong, what turned the person bad. He's told me, "You can't excuse the criminal mind, but it's important to understand it, because there'll be other criminals to track down, others to stop before they inflict their evil on the world." He'd say, "Learn the criminal mind. Use it against them." He was trying to take his own advice with Errique.

"Early on, I think Errique's mind was poisoned by a world that rejected him. Dr. Ulma said Errique had no sense of guilt for what he did. I've wondered if that's because no one felt guilt for what they did to him. What I can't believe is that he had no feelings. Maybe they never surfaced, but rejection leaves such a bitter taste. As I see it, Errique was a very bitter man. Everything he did was tainted with bitterness. He dispensed it like retribution for being rejected."

"You're saying, he was obsessed with Catlyn because she was the ultimate rejection? So in his mind, she deserved the ultimate retribution? Wouldn't that make retribution against Catlyn his grand finale? Then what? He wanted to die?"

"I'll leave that question to the experts. Deep down, would it be so strange? Wanting to end his own misery?"

Amelia was scowling at him. "You can't really believe that." Anger framed her words, along with contempt for Errique.

Ned grimaced. "No, I don't suppose I could accept that any more than you. Whatever was driving Errique, however he got to this point in his life, there's no doubt he was hellbent on dominating Catlyn, even if he had to destroy her and himself to do it."

"What about Chrisy?" I asked. "Are you saying he never had feelings for her?"

"Not according to Dr. Ulma. Errique used people. That seemed to be the front and back of any thought he ever had for anyone else, until his obsession with Catlyn."

"So Chrisy was just another twist to his bizarre crimes."

"I think so. His crimes and his whole life were just twisted contests to him. He pushed people to see who would break."

"But not in this case."

"No, not in this case. In a way, it's almost sad. Such a waste of his abilities."

Amelia flushed with anger. "Don't you dare pity him." She steamed, "It was never a game. He hurt people."

She was suddenly standing and shaking with anger. "You say he didn't feel anything, but he did. I saw it. He taunted Catlyn and he reveled in it. In the cave. Hands tied. Unable to defend herself. *I saw it.*"

Tears broke in rolling waves over her lids. I reached to comfort her. "No," she declared, pushing me away. "I will say this!" She clenched her fists and railed, "He hurt people. He ruined lives." She inhaled sharply, a deep, fortifying breath, clinging to it, steeping it in the vehemence of her wrath until she could decry in fiercest rage, "I'm glad he's dead."

§§§

Errique was dead.

Dead. Gone. Perished from this earth.

Yet for some of us, the finality of it was illusive, and closure, true and whole, would be slow to come.

Chapter 40: Lady Wythiry

I've never minded being disliked, not really. For the most part, I've put it down to envy. My privilege and position, you see, irks people of a lesser rank who fail to recognize the responsibility that comes with the privilege. I have many acquaintances, of course, people who depend on my patronage, and many who are anxious to attend any soiree or gala that I might sponsor. Even though I've been accused on more than one occasion of using and manipulating them for my own ends, the truth is, I've always accepted all of that as my duty. Yes, I say it again, it is my duty to use and manipulate lesser people for their own good. It's called being a responsible member of society. My station in society imposes on me an obligation to the community, and I fulfill it by maintaining a certain social balance among those who associate with me. Although they would never acknowledge it, I do believe they are grateful to me in that respect. Yet, I am mature enough to understand that any expectation of fidelity from such acquaintances is a forlorn hope.

If I had not known that before, my current situation would have been a painful lesson confirming it. Word of my injury was instantly disseminated to one and all, and yet I lay in my hospital bed without the well wishes of even my closest associates. No flowers. No cards. No messages of any nature. Nothing to suggest that I get well soon, or ever.

I do not bemoan that fact. Why should they come? Why should they expend their pithy wishes on me? They are not my equals. Let them come and mourn me when I have passed away; that is their sole obligation to me.

In short, the threshold to my room was uncrossed by any visitor, save one, the one person in all the world who had every right to despise me.

She tapped lightly on my door and waited politely for my attention. I was more unwell in spirit than in body, and her tapping struck me like angry pounding; some part of me wishes it had been. It was not. But if it had been, I would have been less distraught than by the tapping of her gentle hand on my door.

"Catlyn!" I blurted her name as though I were horrified, as though her presence outraged the most sacred of the sacred acts of decorum. You would've thought Matron had caught me doing something excessively naughty. Can you imagine it? Me, being startled by the intrusion of an unexpected visitor? I should be above such things.

The peculiar look on my face must have betrayed my distress. Catlyn had naturally begun to enter the room – such is how privacy is so little regarded in a hospital – but she stopped in mid-step. In retrospect, I attribute her hesitation to her lack of breeding and refinement. Because I was startled, she undoubtedly thought she was interrupting me in the midst of some indelicate moment, as are common enough in hospitals. But as I recovered my composure, she smiled and continued into the room, without so much as a by your leave to do so. She's American, you know.

I was a frightful sight, what with my head bandaged and myself being draped in common hospital attire, and of course there was a total lack of beauty products to hide the many blemishes of my age or even those of my injury. But straightway she came to my side and placed her hand over mine. "I came as soon as I could," she comforted me.

There she was, feeling sorry for me. It was hard to fathom, but I could sense it clearly in the way her hand rested on mine. There was forgiveness in her touch. I don't know why, but suddenly I wanted to pull away from her. I wanted to turn away and hide. But I couldn't. I couldn't even move. I suppose I felt embarrassed and awkward and ashamed, and I didn't know how to express any of that. So I was what I've always been, arrogant and dismissive.

"The doctors are making a fuss over nothing. They're good at that, you know."

It was disingenuous and untrue, and Catlyn wasn't the least bit distracted by it. I suppose, after all, some part of me appreciated the sympathy she offered me. Maybe the truth of it was, I knew that I wasn't worthy of either the good treatment of the doctors or the kindness of Catlyn. I was hurting inside, and I wanted others to hurt with me. But, lying in that bed, deserted by my friends, and having that brave woman touch my hand, I wanted – no, not just wanted. I *needed* to make amends. Something inside me was demanding it. All those horrid deeds. I was utterly deserving of the pain and the hurt and the guilt that plagued me.

I looked straight at Catlyn and tried for the first time in my life to be sincere; I mean, not just polite, but sincere in the plain and unrefined way that Catlyn is.

"That was a lie, what I said. The doctors have been exceptional. Thanks to their good sense, my physical pain is well managed. But there is," and I groped for how to say it, "there's a different kind of pain inside me. It's not a physical pain. The doctors can't take it away with their pills and their IVs. It's what's in my mind, the knowledge of what I've done. I can't stop thinking about it. I've caused you grief, and it haunts me. In my mind's eye, I see what I've done to you, and I shudder at it. That's what pains me. I have a fear, a very great fear that I shall be condemned for what I've done."

For a second, I lost my courage and looked away from her. I was suddenly tired, so very tired of every effort. I felt myself depleted. I had no strength, and I knew, when the pity and the scorn came, I would be unable to refute it. The guards had died instantly. Why couldn't they have killed me too?

But they had not killed me. I had not died. This was my punishment, to live and face the scorn.

I forced myself to look back at Catlyn. I searched her face to accept from her the first scorn to be cast upon me. I was nearly breathless to find there was none, no hint of deprecation. Nothing but understanding could I find. I nearly couldn't bear it. How could she be so accepting of me?

I wanted to be punished, chastised, condemned. Yet I felt drawn to her. I have since come to believe that what I felt in that moment was compassion; a plain, plebeian compassion reaching out from Catlyn. It made me want to talk to her. My inner voice argued, *She'll truly hear what you say. Speak to her. She'll truly listen.*

And I did talk to her. Words I could never have imagined saying spoke from my own mouth. "I'm not good at being ashamed," I began, "but I'm learning. Honestly and truly, I'm learning what it is to be ashamed. At this moment, the shame I feel overcomes me like grief. I don't know how else to express it. One day, perhaps I will. I know that I will. When I have more courage."

I closed my eyes, so harsh was the judgment I was feeling from within myself. I looked anxiously back to Catlyn, fearful that she might leave if I didn't speak honestly.

"When that day comes, I'll tell you how truly sorry I am for all the ways I've been cruel to you, and all the ways I've wronged you. I'm too afraid to imagine it right now."

I'm sure you know what she told me. "There's no need, not now, not later." She squeezed my hand to assure me that it was so. "My father used to say, the grief of shame speaks a language all its own. It talks to each of us in its own way, in its own time. It seldom needs to speak aloud. Yet, you hear what it says to you. And in the end, you always know how to answer it." Her kindness was like a smile. "That's where you are right now. You've begun that dialog. You're hearing the voice of that grief, and you're trying to answer it. It's what we all must do."

With one hand, I clung to her courage; with the other, I covered my eyes. I wept as never I had wept before. I was a weak, whimpering old woman, and yet, in her presence, I felt unburdened and restored. She, who suffered so much misery because of me, was helping me shed mine.

Suddenly, I was angry. I had scarred her life. She had no right to be kind to me. I let my anger demand, "How can you be so forgiving? My position in society? My station? I should be judged, and harshly." I regretted my anger at once. I pleaded, "What makes you so strong?" I begged her to tell me, "How did you become so extraordinary?"

She denied it, of course. "I'm not," she told me. "I'm just an ordinary person. Society judges us in its own peculiar ways, you're right about that. It judges our importance by what we have, our wealth, our degrees, our stations in life, as you say. But society is wrong. Who we are has little to do with our possessions or any citation of fame; what we do, yes, but not who we are. The artificial stations we occupy in society don't define who we are inside, nor do our privileges. I'm not extraordinary. The circumstances have been extraordinary. That's all."

She stayed with me some little while, and we chatted wonderfully about totally inconsequential things. She does have a very good bedside manner. I suppose she has acquired a familiarity with it, more like that of a weathered and worn old woman who has seen too many lives perish unfairly.

Before taking her leave of me, she offered me a word of encouragement. She didn't say, but I knew, it came from her own experience.

"Your dismay does you credit, Cecelia. You might not think so right now, but I suspect it's because you're a stronger woman than you've ever imagined. You'll endure and survive this indignity. I'm certain of it. And when you have, perhaps you'll agree to have tea with me again one day."

She took her leave of me, and I was left to myself to think.

I'm sure you've heard it said, there's greatness in humility, said most often by people who've never experienced what it means to be humble. There was a time when I was disdainful of all the insufferable weaklings who had ever spouted such drivel. But, for a few moments in the solitude of my room, I witnessed the truth of it. The absolute truth.

Chapter 41: Dr. Ulma

I talked at great length to both Catlyn and Tilly after the incident at the Christmas Market. Professionally, I was satisfied Tilly's trauma would need no counseling beyond the attention she'd be getting from Catlyn. She's remarkably resilient as kids often are. In some respects, I think it's quite possible that the unsettled nature of her early childhood, learning to cope with different people and different environments, may have given her a thicker and tougher emotional hide than she might have had otherwise. There's no doubt her resilience was strengthened by her bond to Catlyn, which seemed now of immeasurable capacity.

Ironically, the most important factor for Tilly may have been that she'd been chloroformed. Errique wanted to prevent her from any resistance. In consequence, she was neither resistant to nor aware of the struggle between Catlyn and Errique. As for the shootings, she hadn't witnessed them at all. So other than the initial surprise, the impact of the incident was largely blunted. A blessing overall, I think.

Catlyn was a different matter. Her emotional balance before the incident was tenuous at best. She'd been growing stronger, and given sufficient time, a full restitution of her emotional stability was all but certain. But the shock of this new terror, the threat to Tilly, to herself, and to me, was another potential disaster waiting to explode within her mind. If you start thinking, what if Errique hadn't waited, what if Errique had shot us, what if he'd freaked out, what if... Your mind can only take so much, and then it yields to an insatiable panic. I couldn't let that happen, and I knew it had to be addressed urgently. But there was another issue.

I'd become too personally involved with Catlyn. It would've been both unwise and unethical to continue a doctor-patient relationship with her.

Catlyn professed confidence in my judgment, but I couldn't allow it. My judgment, for both of our sakes, was to have a colleague, Dr. Willus, provide an independent assessment of the possible issues for her.

I reviewed my notes and knowledge of Catlyn with Dr. Willus, and then made an appointment for Catlyn to meet with him. At her request, I was present at the appointment. Dr. Willus allowed it, and I sat in a chair beside Catlyn, but otherwise took a vow of silence.

Dr. Willus was a senior member of the staff and had a well-honed dispassionate objectivity that I was now lacking with respect to Catlyn. That was evident in my reaction to his first question, a mere stock-in-trade device.

"How do you feel about Mr. Errique's death?"

Catlyn looked away from him for a few seconds. That loss of eye contact knotted my stomach tighter than it already was. Her eyes, unsettled and darting, suggested she was being evasive, or wanted to be. Dr. Willus seemed to think so too; he was jotting something on his notepad. My mind was quick to form rebuttals; subjective, personal, and unhelpful rebuttals, which thankfully I kept to myself.

Catlyn, though, didn't need my counsel. She spoke for herself in a response that was both rational and useful. "Part of me is relieved, but another part of me is still afraid that it isn't really true."

"Witnesses said you attacked Errique while he was holding Tilly."

"While those same witnesses stood by and did nothing," I interrupted heatedly.

"A point you and I can discuss at another time, Dr. Ulma."

It was a well-deserved scolding, and I apologized at once. I knew full well I shouldn't have said anything. I was present on the promise that I'd be silent. But I'd never promised I wouldn't be angry about the situation. Another reason to recuse myself. As was his next question, which I don't think I could have asked.

"Were you going to kill him?"

Catlyn held her gaze steady. She took two shallow breaths. Frowned. Swallowed. She looked away, but not to avoid him; it seemed like a thoughtful pose. She was struggling with how to answer him, and two psychiatrists watching her wasn't helping her concentration. After a bit, she tilted her head as though a thought had come to her.

"My father was a reconnaissance analyst in the service. He told me he always thought of his work as saving lives. He and others like him weren't directly engaged in the battles, but they all understood; what they did to save lives made attacks and escapes more effective, often at the cost of enemy lives. So it was ambiguous. It was just better to think of it as saving lives, because what you don't save, the enemy takes."

Her eyes turned back to Dr. Willus. "I was saving Tilly."

I could see Dr. Willus debating the validity of her answer. He mulled it over a second or two, then seemed to accept it.

"You were helpless and lying on the ground when Errique pointed his gun at you. What went through your mind when you knew he was going to kill you?"

Anger flashed across her face. It was fleeting, but it was clearly perceptible. But anger for whom? Errique? For Dr. Willus who dared to ask the question? For me, who permitted it? Regardless of its intent, her fingers flexed into a fist, and I could see her trying to decipher and interpret her thoughts. I wanted to tell her, don't interpret, but Catlyn was Dr. Willus's patient now, and he chose to let her think.

She thought, then chose not to dwell on it. "I'm honestly not sure. That moment was such a blur."

Dr. Willus made no comment. He just continued to study her. Catlyn cast her eyes downward. Downward, but thoughtfully; that was good; she was trying to recall the moment. That seemed to be what Dr. Willus wanted.

She looked back at him. "I'm sorry. I can't say for sure. I might have been pleading with him not to do it, but I don't really remember. All I can recall is Wyatt throwing himself in front of me."

"He was protecting you."

"Yes."

"When Errique threatened to kill Dr. Ulma as well as you, you stepped out from his protection. Why? Why didn't you run away and save yourself?"

"I'd never do that." The insinuation of desertion was offensive, and the anger of it flared hard without hesitation. Dr. Willus noted it too.

"So you stepped out where Errique could kill you. Why?"

"I couldn't let him kill Wyatt."

"Why?"

She looked at me. She was struggling with her emotions, and even I wanted to shout at Willus. But she took a sudden breath and said, "Because I love him."

"I see, and you loved Sebastian, too." No judgment; just impartial observation. And irritating.

Her eyes snapped back to him. "You know that I did." Aggressive. That tilt of her head, wary and suspicious.

"Would you have died for him?"

"What kind..." Indignation seethed in her face.

So calmly he regarded her.

She looked away; her eyes darted about the room; they turned to me; she was pleading for my help.

"Don't look at Wyatt," he lashed out at her. "Look at me. Answer my question. Would you have died for Sebastian?"

She stared at Dr. Willus, helpless with unspeakable anxiety. "How could I know that? It's not fair to ask that. No one can know that, not really, not until you must."

She fell quiet. Dr. Willus waited.

He allowed her the time necessary to look inward. He wanted her to wrestle with the knotted tangle of emotion and obligation that kept her encumbered with fear. He wanted her to internalize the question. To consider it in different scenarios. To let her thoughts churn until the churning scraped and peeled away the layers of fear.

"I loved Sebastian, yes, and I do love Wyatt. But it was different with Sebastian."

She was frowning, and I wanted to tell her, *Don't stop there! Those last layers of fear must be peeled away. Do it now! Tear and shear and strip them! Let the simple truths known already to your heart be revealed even to your mind.*

Her eyes suddenly flared, and she sat straight up. Such truth as there was came upon her like a wind of passion.

"I wanted to love Sebastian. I felt I should love him. Then he died, and I felt, I believed..." She faltered and gasped. She cringed as a cresting tide of emotions tore from her, "I believed with all my heart I had to love him and must have loved him and ought to have loved him and needed to love him." Shattered emotions buried her face into her hands.

But that wind of passion was strong, and it was propelling her onward, hurling her beyond the candor of her passionate confession. She inhaled sharply; caught her breath; waited for the turbulent emotion heaving through her body to desist from its fury. Finally, she could look up. Calmly, firmly, she could say, "But none of that matters now, not did I or could I or should I have loved him, because I have a true and honest and lasting love for him now."

She retreated into silence. She took another slow, deep breath, untethering, I think, the last of her emotional restraints. At last she could recall, "While my father was alive, he tried to teach me that there was no such thing as degrees of love, no loving more or loving less. He said, in matters of love, there's no 'should have' or 'could have.' Love is singular, unique. It simply is."

She looked then at me. "That's how I feel about Wyatt. No thoughts of 'could have' or 'should have.' My love for him simply is. It's plain and it's honest. I don't pretend it to be otherwise. I don't need to. And yes, I would've died for him. It was never a question in my mind."

"Because you love him." He said it like it was a proposition to be examined and confirmed or refuted.

"Is that the only reason?"

In the objective part of my mind, I knew why he asked that question, even as I dreaded it. Victims sometimes want to die. When nightmare and daymare merge to consume the whole of their existence, they just want it to stop, to be fully and finally ended. That possibility had to be eliminated. Nonetheless, I was stunned to hear the question asked.

So was Catlyn. Her head turned ever so slowly back to him, an agonizing, assessing, accusing turn. I could see the swelling of outrage in her eyes, in her shallow rapid breaths; in her posture projecting menace. Her torso was tensing, and in her battle weary mind, she was readying an attack.

Yet, fear was surging, too. I could see the trembling about her head and shoulders, not the quiver of anger, but the tremor of dread. Suddenly her eyes were dressed in desperation, eyes that bore into Dr. Willus with a wild rage. Reluctant syllables slipped through her gritted teeth.

"I couldn't let another person die because of me."

Dr. Willus merely nodded. "You mean, the way Courtney died, and Sebastian, and Lenny Distal."

She didn't respond. Her breathing turned into a labor of restraint. He was goading her, and it was deliberate, a controversial psychological stress test that could go spectacularly wrong. Catlyn's muscles were taut with anger, and I felt certain her mind must be reeling in a torrent of outrage.

I hunched forward frantically to demand that he stop, when suddenly something unbidden seized Catlyn's thoughts. Something clearly arrested her attention. The face of Tilly, perhaps, or a memory of Sebastian. I couldn't say what, but something unambiguously touched her thoughts and lay them still and calm. A quiet courage flowed through her, and she held together. This time she would refuse to yield. Neither would she succumb to the urge to lash out at him. Neither would she run away. She refocused and peered back at him.

Dr. Willus observed, noted, waited, then remarked, "So you thought, if he killed you, he wouldn't kill Dr. Ulma."

"Yes. No. I don't know what I thought."

"Why the confusion?"

She met the question with a rational answer. "He said, first me, then him. I suppose I thought that would be the end of it. But now, I mean this very minute, not then, I remember how he was when he was holding me prisoner. He bragged how he leaves no witnesses. So, I don't know.

At this moment, I can't be sure. Maybe I was wrong. Maybe he would've killed Wyatt and Tilly, too. Probably would have killed them."

Dr. Willus nodded again. Made another note. He asked, "Tell me again how you feel about Mr. Errique's death."

She turned to look at me. In that moment, a serenity I'd thought never to see now encompassed her face. She reached out to me, poised and confident, and I took her hand. Her eyes spoke not of death, but of life, and I could see the dawning of many tomorrows in her gaze.

She turned back to Dr. Willus. Because she could answer now. Because she had no doubt.

"I feel awakened from a bad dream. I feel renewed. I feel..." She closed her eyes and inhaled deeply. She smiled, and upon her countenance there came *a light like onto a stone most precious.*

Finally she could say, "I feel unburdened and vibrant and teaming with life. I feel wildly impatient for tomorrow."

She looked boldly at Dr. Willus. "I feel relieved, irretrievably relieved."

Chapter 42: Tilly

My head's still reeling. From the parlor where I was waiting with Biscuit, I could see Miss Stacey running towards the house. I launched into a hard run myself with Biscuit barking at my heels all the way to the foyer. Rose and Amelia came rushing in behind me from the sitting room where they'd been pacing and fretting. Miss Stacey flew past Whinehardt who was holding the door open for her. She just burst through the entrance like a runner at the end of a hard-run race, and Biscuit and I were there cheering her on. Then in one final drive, she crossed the finish line, arms reaching out in victory and shouting, "Tilly! Tilly! I'm okay. He said I'm okay."

She flung her arms around me and hugged me so hard she lifted me right off my feet. The whole foyer was ringing and echoing with our voices. Miss Stacey kept saying, "I'm okay! He said I'm okay!" and we kept hugging and squealing and cheering, and then Amelia and Rose were hugging us and squealing and cheering, and it was like we were a crowd gone wild on winning the world championship against all the contrary odds that ever were or ever could be.

Dr. Ulma came home with her and said it was true, the crisis was over. Miss Stacey's new doctor, Dr. Willus, had declared her as sane and stable as you or me. Saner. It would take much more time, of course, to be fully and truly healed, but for now, that was just detail.

It was a crazy happy scene. Sweetgrove was standing back by the corridor. She was crying and say over and over, "Oh, Miss Stacey, Miss Stacey." She was too choked up to say anything else, so she just kept repeating that. When

Miss Stacey saw her, she rushed over to her and hugged her good and hard too. Then she went to Whinehardt. Big, stoic Whinehardt, the imperturbable, immoveable Whinehardt was weeping like the rest of us. Small as she is, Miss Stacey hugged him hard enough to take his breath away – if you want to believe that. I think he was holding his breath so he wouldn't be seen crying, because it was "unseemly" of him.

We carried on for some minutes. Then, right as we all thought we were reaching the point of exhaustion, Miss Stacey walked to the middle of the foyer and looked up at the portrait of Ariana, her greatly great grandmother. She took a deep breath and tried to smile. But suddenly she halted like she'd been shaken. She gasped and choked like she couldn't breathe. Then months of strain and agony and torment caught hard against her lungs and tore loose into a surge of choking gasps that doubled her over into a fit of bawling and shaking and choking and gasping and she couldn't stop trembling and wailing and sobbing and her reaching for Dr. Ulma and him rushing over to her and wrapping his arms around her and she burying her face into his chest and crying and choking and clutching him and he holding her and rocking her and saying "It's okay. It's okay. It's over. It's over." Over and over and over.

§§§

It really was; it was over. The torment, the fear, the terrible anxiety. It was all over. At last, Miss Stacey could move on with her life. We could all move on.

And we did. We moved on. Days became weeks. Life took on a natural rhythm, planning and talking and thinking, all the things that make a life normal. Then, there were no more reasons to stop us. Miss Stacey said it was time to adopt me.

Dr. Ulma agreed. The last barrier, an impediment Dr. Ulma called it, had been removed. There remained just one more hurdle, convincing the adoption panel that our lives, from here on, would be normal and healthy and happy.

Our panel had three members, of which Mrs. Jonson would serve as the presiding chairperson. Dr. Ulma said it was really more than that. She's the one to watch because, "as goes Mrs. Jonson, so goes the panel."

The panel sat behind a large wooden table at the head of the room. A much smaller table with a heavy wooden chair was positioned directly in front of the panel's table; that would be for any person giving testimony. A pace or two farther back of that were two other small tables, one on either side of the "witness" table. Miss Stacey sat at one of those, and I sat at the other. Dr. Ulma sat with me. That was Mrs. Jonson's doing. Rose and Amelia stood beside Miss Stacey until Mrs. Jonson made them take seats in the "gallery." That was behind the two small tables, three rows of folding chairs with an open aisle in the middle which had been set up for anyone who might be attending the panel meeting, which was nearly everyone from the estate. Rose and Amelia sat in the first row behind Miss Stacey, and Professor Endbrook joined them. Cook and Sweetgrove sat right behind me, like sentries guarding me for safekeeping.

"The agenda here is very simple," began Mrs. Jonson. "We've previewed all the pertinent facts and figures, and we believe that information to be complete; we'll examine it in detail later. We've spoken to Tilly in closed session, and we are satisfied that her interest has been clearly expressed."

She paused to look at her notes. She seemed to be

debating something with herself which, to my way of thinking, meant she was putting on a show to set us all on edge. *Just get on with it,* I kept thinking. Suddenly she did, turning abruptly to look at Miss Stacey. "There is one point, Miss Stacey. Tilly seems to be unusually shy. That sometimes happens with older children whose early lives were unsettled and who've been passed from home to home. I'm wondering, Miss Stacey, if you've noticed that behavior as well."

That made me angry, and I started to stand up to say it wasn't true, but Dr. Ulma put his hand on my arm to keep me seated. He motioned with his hand and nodded like he was saying it was going to be okay.

"I've heard that said about Tilly, that she's shy, but I've never seen it myself. Quite the opposite, really." She glanced over at me with a quick smile. "Actually, when she gets excited, there's no getting a word in edgewise." It was like she was teasing me, and I smiled back at her.

"I think maybe in the past, she might have had good cause to be withdrawn. I can't speak to that time in her life. But I can say it doesn't seem to be the case anymore."

Mrs. Jonson seemed to be satisfied with that. "In speaking with Tilly, she seemed to be very pleased with a number of things you've done to keep her occupied. Let's see," she referred to her notes again, "you got a dog for her, her own mobile, and even one of those tablet computers. How's that working out? Is that actually a good way to keep her occupied?"

I could see a small smile pulling at Miss Stacey's lips, although I think she was trying not to show it. "Tilly needs no assistance staying occupied. She's endlessly inquisitive. Her mobile and tablet are actually very practical. They keep us in touch wherever we are, and she's working with me and Professor Endbrook on some historical documents which are not only valuable to me, but educational for her."

"And I suppose the tablet must have a number of games that she can play when she's by herself. Does she spend much time on those?"

"I doubt it very much. Tilly and I share at least one common trait; we like to be connected with the people around us. It seems to me, a child who's abandoned to computer games is no less deserted psychologically than is a child who's physically abandoned on a street corner."

I was cheering silently for Miss Stacey. That answer seemed to miff Mrs. Jonson like she'd just been reprimanded by a schoolteacher for misbehaving. The smile on my face probably said as much.

"And the dog, Miss Stacey? Does Tilly attend to the dog, or do you just have a servant take care of it?"

"Biscuit is not just a dog or an 'it.' We think of her as part of the family. And she is. Biscuit is all about belonging and caring. She has her own personality and her own quirks and her own way of communicating with us. She's as unique and special as any person. Most sheltie lovers will tell you, shelties are as close to innocence as you'll find in this life, and you can learn a lot about trust and loyalty and caring from them, as Tilly does. So, if you want to know what the purpose of Biscuit is, her purpose is life, as it is for all of us."

If Mrs. Jonson had intended to rattle Miss Stacey, she must have been sorely disappointed. I noticed Dr. Ulma was beaming an adoring smile right at Miss Stacey, and he didn't care who saw it.

Mrs. Jonson paused to study her notes for a few seconds like she was distracted by something. Then she said, "That seems satisfactory, Miss Stacey," like it was hardly worth the bother. She leaned over to her co-inquisitors, whispered something to them, and they whispered back. It all seemed a bit rude to me. Then Mrs. Jonson turned back to us and said, "It seems we are agreed. There is sufficient basis to proceed with the application. That said, there's really only one issue that concerns us today. Is Catlyn Stacey suitable to the task?"

I disliked Mrs. Jonson instantly. She obviously didn't know Miss Stacey at all. What good are facts and figures if you're convinced before you start that she's not up to the task? It wasn't fair; it just wasn't fair, not after all we've been through.

Mrs. Jonson declared, "There's no need to beat around the bush. We're all aware of the recent events, the violence, the murders, the kidnapping. We are satisfied that Miss Stacey was not responsible for any of that."

Now I was really mad. She wasn't just being rude, she was being mean and snide and talking like Miss Stacey wasn't even there. I tried to scowl a mean face at her, but Dr. Ulma patted my arm lightly and whispered, "It's going to be okay."

It seemed to me Mrs. Jonson had a different idea. She continued, "However it must be said, Miss Stacey was clearly targeted, and while the threat has been removed, we are concerned that there may be persistent effects that might be a detriment to the well-being of the child."

So I was now just "the child" and what she wanted to know was, is Miss Stacey crazy. I wanted to shout in her face, *You're the one who's crazy!* I didn't, but I wanted to. Miss Stacey was sitting across the room from me, held apart like she was on trial. But she was calm, more or less. I saw her swallow like she was nervous, but she still seemed confident.

What Mrs. Jonson was getting at was that she wanted to hear what Dr. Ulma had to say on the subject. She asked him to "address the mental health of the applicant." I swear, I could've punched her in the nose. She was just being mean. I pitied any "child" who had her as a mother.

Dr. Ulma had worn a suit and tie and looked more like a business executive than a doctor. He moved to the witness chair, and before addressing the panel, he put his notes on the table in front of him. As it turned out, he never once looked at them. He told me later that it was a little trick he'd learned. The portfolio just made him look more important and official. "Bureaucracy always loves that," he said.

He squinted like he was trying to remember something before saying, "My first exposure to Miss Stacey was not as her doctor. I was on standby to assess the cognitive condition of Lord Sebastian Silverworth who had suffered a gunshot wound to the head."

"For the record, Dr. Ulma," Mrs. Jonson wanted to know, "that injury was sustained during the rescue of Miss Stacey from her abductors?"

"Yes. His Lordship was shot during a struggle with one of the kidnappers. His bravery ultimately was responsible for saving her life."

"They were in love?"

"Yes. I believe she loved him very much."

I had to admire how he said that. He didn't seem to be upset or jealous of the fact at all, and his voice was very professional, as much as I could judge such a thing. Miss Stacey told me afterwards that he was "a study in objective neutrality." I wasn't so sure about the neutrality.

He continued his review, how at first he only talked to her informally and how his concern evolved into treating her as a patient. He was open and honest with all of that. If anything, he was too honest because he went on to say how his concern for her as a patient changed to caring about her as a person. Mrs. Jonson seemed to take a lot more interest in that than in what he was doing to help Miss Stacey. She kept picking at his words, trying to trip him up, suggesting he was biased by his own "personal involvement with the applicant."

In truth, I didn't hear much of what they said. I was absorbed with Miss Stacey. It didn't seem right that they were making her sit right there on public display, forcing her to relive so many painful memories. Her eyes were glistening while they were talking about Lord Silverworth, and I really admired how she kept herself together. Her chin was up, and her eyes were fixed on Mrs. Jonson. I saw her quickly wipe away a tear when Mrs. Jonson glanced down at her notes. But Miss Stacey never took her eyes off Mrs. Jonson.

Dr. Ulma concluded his testimony by saying Miss Stacey was "a remarkable woman. She's healthy, sane, resilient, determined, and most of all, loving and committed and unswerving in her devotion."

"And you've no doubt about any of that? Your judgment isn't swayed by your affection for Miss Stacey?"

"If anything, I'd say my affection is swayed by my judgment, as it should be."

"There are no lingering issues?"

"None, and I might add, my colleague, Dr. Willus, has concurred. He was unable to attend today because of an emergency at the hospital. In lieu of that, he's offered this affidavit, which I'm presenting to you now. He is, of course, willing to come in person at a later time if that should be necessary."

She started into a slow nod of her head, then suddenly looked sharply at Miss Stacey. "Do you agree with that assessment, Miss Stacey? Do you believe you're in a state of perfect mental balance?"

Dr. Ulma was shocked by the question. He started to stand up, but Mrs. Jonson ordered, "Please remain seated, Dr. Ulma." He hesitated, then looked over at Miss Stacey. She offered him a reassuring smile. Her eyes said, "It's okay," so he settled into his seat. But he watched her intently.

"Miss Stacey?"

"Am I perfect? Probably not. But my father used to say, few things in life have to be perfect; they just need to work. For most people in the world, I think that's actually what passes for normal."

Mrs. Jonson didn't comment on that. She gave a little shrug to her shoulders, you know, like saying 'whatever' when you know you're wrong and you've been found out.

At that point, Dr. Ulma was excused, and Mrs. Jonson sat back to turn the questioning over to the other two panel members, Mr. Keith and Mrs. Gibson. The woman would probably be called middle age; I'm not a very good judge of that; and the man looked older than Dr. Ulma, but not old, if that helps.

Mr. Keith seemed a bit nervous as he picked up from Mrs. Jonson. He shuffled some papers in a small panic like he'd misplaced his list of questions. "Pardon me; so sorry," he said as he reached into a folder. "Ah," he exclaimed as he lifted out a piece of folded paper.

It turned out it wasn't a list. It was a letter from Lady Wythiry. This was totally unexpected, and it put us all on edge because Lady Wythiry had never really approved of me or Miss Stacey or any part of the whole idea, besides which, she wasn't even there. Her absence, it was explained, was because Her Ladyship didn't want to "distract the panel from its due consideration" of Miss Stacey. I thought the real reason was that she just didn't have the nerve to show her face. But it turns out I was wrong about that.

Lady Wythiry declared, "I know of no more exemplary individual than Catlyn Stacey. I wholly endorse her without reservation." All of us must have been holding our breaths because we all sort of exhaled at the same time which made for one very big, very loud sigh, loud enough to cause the panel to turn their heads in our direction.

But the panel seemed to be just as much surprised by Lady Wythiry's endorsement as we were. Mrs. Jonson's eyebrows rose up over her glasses and she said, "Well, well." Then she kind of "humphed" like Her Ladyship had just spoiled Mrs. Jonson's game plan and she was annoyed about it, which seemed rather to please Mr. Keith. He lifted his chin up and said "Well, then, with Her Ladyship's good wishes, I think by all means we should proceed to hear from those interested parties who are, indeed, present here today."

He started with Professor Endbrook who was asked about his experience with Miss Stacey. Professor Endbrook, as you know, loves to lecture to an audience. He gave them a seminar on how it had all begun for him as a matter of history, but how, as they got to know one another, the two of them had grown to have a "mutual regard and respect." He said, "Whether you're young or old, respect is critical to your contentment with life. If there is one thing I can say with absolute certainty, it's that Miss Stacey has repeatedly demonstrated her respect for me and for herself and for Tilly." I think they liked that way more than his comments about her "remarkable intellect."

Mrs. Gibson perked up to say she totally agreed with the importance of respect. "What you say is quite admirable. But I find myself wondering if that applies also to the staff who are required to do Miss Stacey's bidding."

To answer that, she turned then to Cook, who was my legal guardian, and had been for more than half a decade, which incidentally seemed like a very long time to me. I flinched at the way they said it, though. They made it sound like no one wanted me, and I knew that wasn't true. I wasn't some freak; they all cared about me. Maybe old Mr. Stacey didn't care about me personally as much as I once thought and wished for, but everybody else cared about me.

For the most part, Mrs. Gibson's questions were routine. How long have you been Tilly's guardian? What changes have you observed in Tilly since Miss Stacey arrived? How do you think Miss Stacey would do as Tilly's mother? If they were looking for something burning in the kitchen, they weren't going to get it from Cook. She'd been running the kitchen for a good many years and didn't take any guff from anybody. She knew when a recipe was right.

"The gist of it is, Miss Stacey's got fiber. Whether things is hot or cold, she'll hold together in the heat, and she won't crumble in the cold."

I think they were amused by her answer because they sat back, and from the way they were smiling, you could see they liked what she said.

At that point, they looked at each other, nodded, tilted their heads, frowned and squinted until, suddenly, it seemed like it was over.

I had forgotten about Mrs. Jonson.

When the other two sat back, she leaned forward. She held her hands folded and resting on the table in front of her. She was vaguely smiling, you know, the way someone does when they're about to say "okay, let's cut to the chase."

She said, "I think I speak for us all when I say how sincerely happy we are, Miss Stacey, for your full and sound recovery from the emotional trauma you suffered. I would say, quite frankly, I have nothing but admiration for the way you conducted yourself during that recent terrible business at the Christmas Market. One doesn't need any more evidence than that to see how brave you are in a crisis. Beyond that, in your application materials, you speak of how Tilly has helped to define the direction of your life. The way you talk about it reminds me of how, in some religious circles, we are told that a child shall lead us. Is that what you had in mind, Miss Stacey? Do you see it that way as well?"

Next to me, Dr. Ulma tensed. He tilted his head, and his eyes were peering at Mrs. Jonson in a suspicious way, like he was saying, "What are you up to?" Suddenly, I understood. It was a trick question. I didn't know how, but I realized, no matter what Miss Stacey said, Mrs. Jonson was going to twist it around until it came out wrong.

Miss Stacey didn't answer immediately. She looked over at me, and I could feel the warmth of her smile all the way across the room. She looked back at Mrs. Jonson and spoke very quietly. Her words were assured and confident. A mother's love must sound like that. If it doesn't, it should.

"I have to admit, I didn't have that thought in mind, and perhaps I should have. It has a wonder and a beauty to it that we all need sometimes. But I guess what I'd have to say is, if it's true that we look to a child to lead us, think how enormously blessed is the one who leads the child."

A hush settled over the room. Miss Stacey seemed like the most radiant being I'd ever seen. I thought Dr. Ulma was about to cry; I know I was, and I think Cook and Sweetgrove sitting behind me must have been. Whinehardt and most of the staff from the estate seemed ready to leap up and cheer. Even Mr. Keith and Mrs. Gibson were nodding and looking like they were going to start applauding any second now.

And Mrs. Jonson? Her smile was true. "Well said, Miss Stacey," she acknowledged, and I knew she meant it. "Well said."

§§§

The panel had a protocol to follow which, in this case, meant they'd take all the testimony, facts, and figures away with them to review, just to be sure nothing had been overlooked. Then, they'd reconvene in closed session to review jointly, to debate if necessary, and finally to make a decision. We would be "duly informed in due course" as to their decision.

We left them to their protocol, but in our minds, there was no doubt of the outcome. The proof of that came the next morning.

I was sitting in the drawing room across from Miss Stacey's suite. The sun was up, the coffee was cold, and Miss Stacey was asleep. When finally she emerged from her room, she promptly stopped in the corridor, startled, I think, by my smiling face.

"It is indeed," I said.

She canted her head to one side, and I could see from the confusion on her face that she didn't know if I meant "It's a good morning" or "It's late." Then, just as suddenly, she straightened and flashed that broad, bright, glorious smile that none of us had seen in some very long while.

No nightmare. No restless tossing and turning. No crying out into the darkness. The sun had risen without Miss Stacey's assistance, and she was content to let it be so. And not just content with herself or me or that we'd reached this point in our lives. Her countenance exuded a deep contentment with life, with being alive, with being part of a tumultuous humanity, even one that had cast her so far down into the deepest depths of anxiety.

I know I'm prejudiced on this matter. I know the world for me lived and breathed in the very existence of Miss Stacey. I know I could see no world that included me and didn't include her or the spirit she gave to life. But that aside, I just knew. I'd always known. Her destiny was mine.

True, the formalities had yet to play out, but from that moment, it no longer seemed to matter. Let them play out however they would, they were no longer relevant. Life for us had become personal, sublimely personal.

Chapter 43: Dr. Ulma

A light snow had fallen overnight, but by late morning, brilliant white clouds were drifting like magnificent tall ships on a quiescent blue sea. Sunlight glinted off the softly mounded layers of snow while dazzling reflections imparted a sparkling glow across the entire atrium garden.

Catlyn was sitting near the lighted fireplace with her bare feet tucked under her, her arms wrapped around her curled up legs, and her chin resting on her knees. Her face seemed nearly angelic in that moment, an oval in figure rounding gently at the chin and extending gracefully back along the fluid sweep of her neck, all wondrously invoking the peaceful allure of a William-Adolphe Bouguereau painting.

She was peering at Tilly who was sitting on the floor away from the fire. Biscuit, nestled up beside her, was panting in appreciation of Tilly's attention. From time to time, should Tilly leave off stroking her, Biscuit would raise up her head to nuzzle Tilly until Tilly redoubled her attention.

It was Christmas, and watching them, I couldn't help thinking how wonderful it would be to relive this scene year after year. It was, of course, too soon to be having such thoughts. A deep wound heals slowly, and emotional trauma, the psychological wounding of the mind, is deeper still. Catlyn had need of time, caring attention, and all the contentment life would permit her.

I intended to do my part for her, but not as her friend or her doctor. Our relationship had deepened beyond friendship, and in all the mercy of a sane world, it would deepen daily for all the days and years it may be our privilege to witness. I wanted every one of them.

Catlyn's life was now on track, and the good Dr. Willus would help her keep it that way. He'd handle any follow-up visits Catlyn might want, and I had encouraged her to want them. I told her, you don't stop a course of antibiotics just because you start to feel better; you complete the course so nothing lingers behind to flare up later.

Tilly was already doing her part to brighten their lives. If ever there'd been a shy, sedate Tilly, she was no more. Today Tilly was expressing herself. She'd chosen for this Christmas Day the most amazing multicolored trousers I'd ever seen, which she topped off with a maroon sweater embroidered with stars, baubles, bells, and tinsel, all in glistening threads of many hues. In case anyone had missed it, Tilly was announcing to all the world, it's a new day.

Catlyn seemed unequivocally serene that Christmas morning, relaxing before her guests arrived. When she turned her eyes in my direction, I was nearly overcome by the absolute power of her presence. In Catlyn's romantic way of thinking, I could feel that presence reaching out to me, anointing me with a flourish of incomparable grace, every drop of it pouring out from a chalice uniquely fashioned by her unquenchable spirit.

Was that me in love? Yes, undeniably.

"I wish I could stop this moment in time," said Catlyn. "Our lives should be exactly this forever and ever."

"They will," said Tilly. "I know they will, because," she hinted, "there are things to come we've always wanted, but didn't know we had."

She'd been teasing us for days now with this little riddle. She allowed only that it concerned a special gift for Miss Stacey, but what it was, she divulged to no one.

I too had a special gift for the two of them, a letter

entrusted to me by Mrs. Jonson. In very un-holiday language, the letter detailed the conditional approval of Catlyn's application. In view of the recent extraordinary circumstances, a formal trial period would be observed during which "either party would be permitted to terminate the application."

I put the letter in a holiday envelope that bore a picture of a horse-drawn sleigh approaching a big country home across a field of deep snow. Above the scene in glittering letters were the words "Peace on Earth." I couldn't decide whether the words in this case were meant as a promise or an appeal, but in my heart, I advocated for both. On the front of the envelope, I added, "Catlyn and Tilly," and on the back I wrote "May there always be joy in your heart."

§§§

It was a casual gathering. Catlyn had declared the day a holiday for the staff, and had forewarned everyone that today would be a self-served day. Catlyn herself had laid out some finger food and beverages, although Cook insisted on preparing the tea and coffee, which left Catlyn to handle the water and sparkling cider.

I waited until everyone had arrived before presenting Catlyn and Tilly with the letter from Mrs. Jonson. I got everyone's attention and then, standing next to Catlyn and Tilly, I said, "This isn't exactly a Christmas gift, but it bears all the glad tidings anyone could wish for on Christmas."

Catlyn looked at me suspiciously, then she caught her breath as her mind seized on the only possibility that made sense. Her hands started to tremble, and she asked Tilly to open it. "Careful," she said more out of nerves than necessity, as I hadn't sealed the envelope.

As the letter came out of its sleeve, they stared, they squealed, they hugged, they cried, hugged some more, then Catlyn whirled about, peered at me, and in one breathtaking moment, we melted together into a warm, wonderful kiss, which I would add to those memories to be cherished forever.

Tilly took a turn hugging me too. She paused to tap my shin lightly with her foot, then hugged me again, even harder than before.

Clinging together in that moment, Catlyn, Tilly, and me, we were a living ensemble of the Christmas spirit. Peace reigned on our earth, and in our hearts there was joy.

And it wasn't over yet. Tilly's special gift for Miss Stacey awaited, and we all wanted to know what it could be. She bided her time until we all grew quiet again. Then, she said, "Over here."

We followed her over to the Christmas tree in the foyer where she lifted from one of the branches a scroll tied with a curly ribbon that made it look like a decoration. Tilly said, "Your grandfather wanted you to have this. He gave it to me because he couldn't give it to you himself."

I don't know how much thought Tilly had given to what she'd say at this moment, but nothing would have been more riveting. You could hear the trepidation in Catlyn's voice.

"And you kept it all this time?"

"Uh-huh. It was a Christmas gift for you. The words and the ribbon are from your grandfather; the scroll was my idea. I put the words together from the words he spoke to me, and I made the scroll from the wrapping paper he used that year."

Catlyn held the scroll in her hand, but she was peering at Tilly. She was studying the intensity in Tilly's gaze, most especially the tears welling up in her eyes. These were not the tears of joy flowing just minutes ago; there was an aspect of sadness to them, a letting go of something you've clung to for a very long time.

Catlyn put her arm around Tilly. "Let's sit down over there. It seems to me, there's a lot more to this story than what you've said."

She paused to glance at me. "There are no shortcuts to understanding what's in the mind, *or* the heart." I smiled at this private memory that had been such a cornerstone to understanding Catlyn's mind itself.

She looked back at Tilly. "I want to know all there is about this, and your part in it."

Tilly held back nothing. She was too excited to even think of holding back anything. She wanted to share every last bit of the memory she'd so carefully preserved. Describing the tradition, she told how she was called forward to receive that first gift, how wonderful she felt at the time, and how she had only later realized that all the while Mr. Stacey was speaking to her, he was thinking of his granddaughter.

"When I finally understood that, it made me really sad. It made me feel unwanted again. But then," and suddenly she wasn't sad at all, "but then, I felt he'd given me something more than ever I could wish. He'd made me your surrogate. Isn't that a wonderful word, surrogate?"

Decidedly excited now, she exclaimed, "I was you! For a little while, I was you. And then you came, and I understood how special that was. But then, you were sad, because you didn't know any of that. And that's why I'm giving him to you now, so you'll know, he always wanted you, and you won't be sad about that anymore."

Hugs and tears seemed to be the order of the day. Catlyn said, "Open it with me. It surely was meant for both of us."

Surely it was meant for the both of them, but as Catlyn

read aloud, I think every one of us could feel the ineffable touch of glory filling our lives, and it was unquenchable.

> *My Dearest Granddaughter,*
> *Of all the lessons we learn in life,*
> *Nothing is more important than this,*
> *That we should always remember our real families,*
> *Whoever they prove to be.*
> *I could not know you in this life,*
> *But I have remembered you in my prayers.*
> *I give you now my love.*
> *If you would remember me,*
> *I am your Grandfather,*
> *Who knows you now always.*

Tilly had said it so clearly. "Things to come we've always wanted, but didn't know we had." If there's a glory greater than such love, I cannot imagine it.

§§§

Between Christmas and New Year's Day, I took Catlyn to a small community theatre to see a live show. Being out in public was part of the healing process. Not incidentally, it also gave us some private time together. It's remarkable how private a theater full of people can be.

It was a lightly romantic play with nothing controversial and a happy ending that everyone knew was coming and which everyone was glad to have. As the play drew to a close, the hero gracefully took the hand of the heroine, kissed it lightly, and spoke his closing lines, "I must be away until the rose shall bloom again. Only 'til then, and then, no more."

It had been a good performance, and as the curtain came down, the audience applauded their approval. Catlyn, though, didn't join them. She was motionless, except for the tear I could see brimming and slowly descending over her cheek. The actor had said "and then, no more," but in her mind, it was another voice she heard speaking. It said to her, and to her alone, "and then no more of thee and me."

It was still a trigger. But it was no longer something fearful. In her mind, it had become a sweet memory of Sebastian, even if it was tinged yet with sorrow. I knew it was a memory she'd always have. That, after all, is what minds do; they remember. That's their job, and what they remember isn't arbitrary. How they remember, though, can change. In time, Catlyn's memory of Sebastian's last words, spoken only in her dreams, would evolve into a mature recollection, just as it had evolved from nightmare to bittersweet remembrance.

I reached over to take her hand. She squeezed it and turned comfortably to look at me. Her eyes were shaded in a quiet melancholy, but there was a delicate smile stirring on her face as well. Gently and shyly, that smile was clearly emerging from the ruins of her beleaguered inner peace, venturing to rejoin the vibrant world around her. That boldly venturesome, incipient smile was like the renaissance of a warm and radiant aspect of Catlyn's spirit that had been too long suppressed. At last, it was daring to come forward where it could embrace and comfort and enlighten her troubled life.

She was well in mind and body and spirit, of that I was certain. Strong enough to look squarely at life. Secure enough to engage it. She was going to be okay.

We were going to be okay.

R. G. Munro

Epilogue: Tilly

They were married in the fall. It was a simple ceremony held in the grand foyer, which has always been mom's favorite place in all of Southjoy Mission. Besides, it was the one place where Ariana, looking down from her portrait, could watch the ceremony and give them her blessing.

It's also where she goes to meditate, and I've found her praying there, too. She prays a lot now, since Rupert Errique was killed trying to kill all of us. I don't know if she prayed before then; I suppose she did because she was desperate for courage to get through those days. Because they were horrid days, and the torment they heaped on her was choking and smothering her life. At times, the anguish of it was so deep in her spirit, not even Ariana could've rescued her anymore.

Not long ago, I found her sitting on the bottom step of the grand staircase. Her eyes were closed, and she was gripping her hands like she was praying, but harder. I could see the muscles in her arms pulling tight like she was holding something with all her strength, like she feared it was going to get away from her and she didn't want to let it go. Her elbows were resting on her knees, and her forehead was pressed against her hands. After a bit, she sighed and shook her head like she was clearing her thoughts. Then she wiped away a tear just starting down her cheek.

When she opened her eyes, she saw me watching her. "Sorry," I said, "I didn't mean to... You were praying?"

"Uh-huh." We just kind of looked at each other, and then she said, "And you want to know what I was praying for."

"Uh-huh." I nodded, "If it's okay." Because I was afraid

of why. I think she understood.

She motioned for me to sit beside her on the stairs. "I was praying for guidance and forgiveness," she said. "Guidance for what I need to do. Forgiveness for what I haven't done but should have. It's not complicated. Those things give me strength and hope. I need those. Strength and hope so I can stop being destructive of myself." She sighed, "Beyond that, I'm trying to remember to be thankful. I'm so richly blessed, and I don't know why. I believe there's a reason, and I want to be worthy of it. I've gone from nothing to everything. I had no family, no friends, no one to love. Now, I have you and Wyatt, a whole family of friends, and so much to love."

"Is that why you were crying?"

She smiled at me with her eyes. "It was, yes," she said very softly, "because sometimes I'm just overwhelmed by it all. It's like I'm suffering from an agony of happiness, and I just want to cry." A smile seemed to dance lightly on her face. "That's not crazy. That's just me being romantic. And it is, because now... Now I have the courage to remember it all. That's what life's all about in the end, you know. When all is past, we have only memories. Then, one day, we become memories ourselves. I'm blessed with past memories, and I'm trying hard to cherish all the new memories being made this very instant, so they'll be part of me always. And somewhere in all that, I suppose I'm praying that I'll be remembered too."

The day before her wedding was a case in point. Mom went to Lord Silverworth's grave, alone. I didn't think that was such a good idea and offered to go with her. She just smiled and told me it wasn't necessary and I wasn't to worry, which of course I did. It was a private moment, and that's how she wanted to leave it. Later, after I'd darted many concerned glances at her, she confided, "He gave me my life. I had to thank him for his love."

The following spring, we started a new tradition. On the anniversary of Lady Stacey's death, we all went to the cemetery together – mom, dad, and me – as a true family, whole in life and whole in spirit.

The early spring azaleas were blooming and adding their soft texture to the landscape which was framed by evergreens and highlighted in between by sprays of multicolored wildflowers.

When we arrived at Lady Stacey's gravesite, which she shares with Sir Cedric and their aunt, Lady Sylvia, mom pointed to an open grassy area opposite their gravestone. "There, right there. That's where I want to be buried, right there facing Ariana."

"Mom!" I objected.

She smiled. "I'm not planning on joining her anytime soon. I just know that when my time does come, I want to be here, facing Ariana. She and I will have a lot to discuss. It'll probably take us centuries just to talk about you."

She put one arm around me and hooked her other arm around dad's arm and said, "Let's introduce ourselves properly to the founders of our home, shall we? I think they just might want to see what's become of their lives."

It's always such a marvel to me to see how comfortable mom is talking to Ariana. It's like we're all just in different stages of one existence, and mom refuses to recognize the boundaries between them. On this occasion, there was an added note of pleasure in her tone as she talked about us as a family. I think it was the warmth of mom's words that made it sound that way. As mom spoke, we listened, and what we heard was a dialogue between Ariana's simple virtues and mom's plain sincerity. They just spoke with the same voice.

After that, mom did what she would do every year from

then on; she read the poem that Ariana had written in 1825 in remembrance of Lady Silvia, *A Song of Fallen Leaves and Rising Hopes*. It was the poem mom had read on the day she was abducted. Ironically, it was for her, then and now, an inspiration, a reason to hope, a commitment to a future.

She cried all the way through, but she wouldn't stop and she wouldn't let anyone else read it for her. When she'd finished and had mopped all her tears away, when she'd taken a deep breath and had calmed her multitude of emotions, she said to Ariana, "I know you wrote that for Lady Sylvia, but you left it for me. The task you posed is mine now. I accept it, as you knew I would. It's all still true, you know, the journey, the quest, the need for harmony, because the world is still plagued with bitterness and discord. So, yes, there's still many a step to tread. I didn't know where my path was until you showed it to me, and I don't know yet where it's leading. I simply trust it'll go where it must, because it's not really about the endpoint, is it? It's about how we get there, the path we follow, the quest we make of our lives. And now I have Tilly and Wyatt to travel with me. Together, we'll travel all the steps allotted to us, firmly and faithfully. And we'll make a feast of our gratitude in every step of it. That's a solemn promise, from me to you, as you knew it would be."

Portrait of Catlyn Stacey

R. G. Munro

Glossary of Unfamiliar Terms

Greatly great grandmother – an abbreviation adopted in the novel, *Lingering Missives*, for great-great-great-great-great-grandmother.
Ariana was Catlyn's greatly great grandmother.

Lollard – a practitioner of Lollardy, a religious movement that was a forerunner of Protestantism. Lollardy began in the early 1380s and is attributed to the teachings of John Wycliffe who was a theologian, biblical scholar, philosopher, and Oxford University professor. He is credited with publishing the first English translation of the Bible.

Missus – The proper address used for a female housekeeper of the estate; it's independent of whether the individual is otherwise Ms, Miss, or Mrs.

Packet boat – a boat or ship originally used to carry official mail, called "mail packets," between British embassies, colonies, and various outposts. Eventually, these ships had regular schedules and carried cargo and passengers as well as mail.

Made in the USA
Las Vegas, NV
16 October 2021